THE
FRON
PART 2: ROGUE CASTES
EPISODE 3

RESURRECTION
RYK BROWN

CHAPTER ONE

The gleaming, red-trimmed, glossy, black shuttle came to rest on the landing pad atop the Hall of Nobles in the Takaran capital city of Answari. Within seconds of touchdown, its boarding ramp lowered from the stern, and a plethora of well-armored guards marched out confidently, forming a line on either side.

Takaran guards on either side of the elevator entrance exchanged worried glances at the sight of the well-armed, strictly disciplined contingent of troops. Their instinct was to defend their position, but their orders, which they wisely chose to follow, dictated otherwise. No resistance was to be offered...

...Not yet.

The enemy guards, twenty-four in all, stood facing outward with weapons held at the ready, as several officers made their way down the ramp. At the bottom, the officers scanned the ground, checking that the area was secure. One of the officers raised his right hand and signaled to those still inside the black and red shuttle.

Next, one man dressed in a form-fitting black uniform came down the ramp. He was tall, with a foreboding presence that instantly struck fear in the hearts of all who laid eyes on him. He was square-jawed and muscular, with well-weathered features that matched the graying hair at his temples and on his perfectly groomed goatee. But what struck the Takaran guards most was the deadly confidence in the man's eyes as he headed toward them, without hesitation or concern for his own safety.

The lines of enemy guards flanked their leader with

practiced precision, maintaining a wall of firepower that all but surrounded him. No one walked in front of this man...ever.

The two Takaran guards kept their weapons slung, moving aside as ordered. The door opened, and the leader and several of his guards and officers stepped inside the elevator, turning around to face the door as it closed.

Once the door had closed, the remaining officer barked a command, and the rest of the guards spread out to secure the rooftop landing pad. Once satisfied that his men had properly repositioned themselves, the officer turned back to the two Takaran guards standing nervously astride the elevator doors. He looked them both up and down, eyeing both their weapons slung on their shoulders, as well as those holstered on their hips. A small smile crept across his face as he noted their failure to conceal their fear. "Place your rifles on the ground in front of you, and remove your waist arms," the officer ordered, in surprisingly perfect Takaran.

The two guards shared shocked looks with one another.

"I shall not ask again," the officer added.

After another exchange of confused glances, the two guards complied, each of them carefully following the officer's instructions.

The officer watched with great satisfaction, waiting until both men were completely disarmed before continuing. "Do you have families?" Neither man answered, again looking confused. "Is my Takaran incorrect?"

"Uh, no, sir," the guard on the right answered.

"Well, then... Do you have families?"

"Yes... Yes, I do," the guard answered.

The officer looked at the other guard. "And you?"

"A wife, sir," the other guard replied nervously.

"No children?"

"We are expecting... In three months," the guard said.

The officer nodded his understanding. "Return to your families, burn your uniforms, and look for new careers." The officer waited for a moment, but again, the guards looked confused. "That, or die here and now."

"But...we swore an oath to protect..."

"That is our responsibility now, not yours," the officer said, cutting the guard off mid-sentence. "However, if you wish to die this day in order to honor your oath, I can certainly respect that." The officer smiled coldly. "The choice is yours, of course, but I would consider how your needless deaths will affect those you love, before making your decisions."

One last look between them was all that was required.

"Yes, sir," the first guard said. "Thank you, sir," he added, as he stepped back away from his post. The other guard did the same, bowing respectfully to the enemy officer who had just allowed them to continue living. Both men quickly moved away, and then disappeared down a side ladder.

The officer turned back toward the shuttle, a satisfied grin on his face. There was nothing more rewarding than victory.

* * *

It had been a long and fitful night for Connor Tuplo. Images of their mission to Corinair made sleep almost impossible for him, especially with visions of Travon Dumar, a man he had never met, sacrificing

3

himself on Connor's behalf. And the dying man's last words... *You will find a way. You are Na-Tan.*

Being captain of a ship, one with a crew, all of whom depended on him to keep them alive and fed, had been a difficult enough responsibility for Connor to become accustomed to. But this?

I am not Na-Tan. Connor repeated this to himself again and again, but it didn't seem to stick. If anything, it reinforced the same question he had carried with him for the last five years. *Who am I?*

Connor walked up to the guest quarters building on the Ghatazhak base that accommodated those rescued from Corinair the day before. He was about to reach for the door, when it opened suddenly.

"Captain," Doran Montrose said with surprise. "It's great to see you again, sir."

Connor looked confused for a moment. "Uh..."

"From the rescue?" Doran quickly added, recognizing the young man's confusion. "I was among those you and your crew rescued."

"Ah... Of course."

"Thank you," Doran added, reaching out to shake Connor's hand. "Again."

"Again?" Connor asked without really thinking, as he shook Doran's hand.

"Yes, it's not the first time that you've rescued us from certain death." Doran suddenly realized the reason for Connor's confusion. "Well, the first time for *you*, I suppose. I know you don't remember the previous times." Doran smiled comfortingly. "Rest assured, though, that *I* shall never forget them. Nor shall all the others who made it home to their loved ones, because of you."

"But, I'm not *really* him, am I." Connor wasn't asking a question.

"I guess that depends on your point of view," Doran replied, a contemplative look on his face.

"Then you knew me before?" Connor asked. "I mean, you knew *him*?"

"Him, you... I've known you both. I served under you in the Alliance, and I was there when you woke... in your new body."

"Then, *you* consider me to be Nathan Scott," Connor surmised, trying to put the pieces of a puzzle together. "Even though I have no memory of that life?"

Doran looked down for a moment. "It is difficult to explain..." He chuckled. "It is difficult to understand, even for me." He looked at Connor. "To me, it does not matter. You are Nathan... You are Connor. You are both men... Different, and yet the same."

"Then, you also think I am this Na-Tan?"

Doran smiled broadly. "I have always believed you to be Na-Tan, and I doubt that I shall ever stop." Doran put his hands on Connor's shoulders. "He is in there, somewhere, waiting to be awakened. Of this, I am quite certain. Only you can decide the if, and the when." Doran sighed. "Regardless, I still appreciate what you, be you Connor Tuplo or Nathan Scott, did for myself and my family yesterday. This, too, shall always be remembered." Doran patted Connor on the shoulder again and continued on his way, leaving him more confused than before.

* * *

"All rise for our Lord Dusahn!" the guard at the entrance to the Takaran Hall of Nobles commanded in Takaran.

The line of Jung officers on either side of the hall snapped to attention. The Takaran nobles

5

who had been forced to attend were somewhat less enthusiastic, standing nonetheless.

Lord Dusahn strode confidently into the middle of the hall, dressed in his usual, form-fitting, black uniform trimmed in crimson. He stopped in the middle of the room, pausing to look upon the thirty-plus leaders of the noble houses of Takara. Although his face did not reflect it, he took great satisfaction in the knowledge that these men, the wealthiest, most powerful men in the Takaran system, as well as all that they owned, were now his to do with as he pleased. This knowledge was nourishment to his soul, feeding his long desire for conquest and power. He had spent the last thirty years in search of an empire to call his own. Now, sprawled before him, were the very seeds of that empire.

Lord Dusahn caught notice of two men who were not standing. They were both middle-aged, yet appeared strong and healthy. Unlike the other nobles, they wore the trappings of warriors, not statesmen.

A brief, almost unnoticeable glance to one of Lord Dusahn's officers to his right was all that was needed. Within seconds, four armed guards moved, weapons at the ready, toward the sitting men. Following them was an officer, obviously their senior.

"You will rise and show your respect for our lord," the officer instructed them sternly.

One of the men turned slowly to look at the officer before speaking. "We will show our respect, when we have been shown something worthy of it," the man said in a low, growling voice.

The officer snapped his fingers, and the guards instantly pointed their energy rifles at the two sitting men. "Rise, or die."

The two men stared at the officer, unwavering. Finally, they slowly rose to their feet, their menacing gaze never leaving the offensive officer.

The officer was steadfast. Once the two men had assumed a standing position, he gave them another order. "Bow to your lord."

Again, the senior of the two men who now stood as the rest, glared at the officer. "Ybarans bow to no one," he growled, looking as if he might bite the head off the officer at any moment.

Still undaunted by the Ybaran statesman's threatening posture, the officer, whose eyes were still locked on him, took a step closer, putting himself no more than a half meter away from the man's face. "Are you sure?"

"I am," the Ybaran replied without hesitation.

"And do you speak for all Ybarans?" the officer inquired.

"I do."

"Very well," the officer replied, finally breaking eye contact with the elder Ybaran. "Kill them," he ordered his men as he stepped back.

A split second later, four bolts of energy leapt from the soldier's rifles, all of them drilling into the heads of the two Ybarans.

Noblemen all around the Ybarans gasped in horror, jumping back as the two bodies fell to the floor. Smoke from the still-burning flesh of the statesmen wafted upward, quickly spreading through the room to remind everyone in attendance of what happens to those who disobey their new ruler.

The officer turned toward Lord Dusahn without looking at the fallen Ybarans. "Shall I dispatch their world, my lord?"

"Promptly," Lord Dusahn replied, without the slightest hint of remorse on his face.

Noblemen across the great hall exchanged glances of disbelief, as the gravity of the officer's inquiry, as well as his leader's response, hit them. They were all suddenly faced with a new reality.

Lord Dusahn took a deep breath as he looked at the faces of the nobles, measuring their reactions. Shock and horror, just as he expected. These men would be easy to control, just as his intelligence had indicated. "I am Lord Dusahn, ruler of the Dusahn Empire, of which you are now subjects." He spoke in a voice that was confident, but controlled. He did not yell, or attempt to intimidate them. He simply spoke as if he had no doubts that every word was absolute truth. "From this day forward, you shall all serve the Dusahn. Cooperate, and your businesses shall continue to profit, your industries shall continue to grow, and you shall all live in prosperity. Your worlds, your resources, and your technologies shall be added to ours."

"To what end?"

Lord Dusahn looked in the direction from which the question had come.

"To what end, my lord?"

"Identify yourself," the officer who had confronted the Ybarans demanded.

"Milas Christova, leader of House Christova," the man replied, standing. "I mean no disrespect, my lord," he continued politely, "and if I am speaking out of turn, I offer my sincerest apologies. But this is the first audience we have had with you, and we know not your empire's protocols in such matters."

The officer looked to Lord Dusahn, expecting a

subtle signal from his leader to end the man's life. But the signal did not come.

"A fair question," Lord Dusahn finally replied. "Speak your mind, Mister Christova."

"If you seek to utilize our resources, industries, and technologies, then surely you have a goal in mind?"

"The goal of any empire is to expand its influence as far as possible," Lord Dusahn explained simply.

"But again, to what end?" Mister Christova wondered.

"Humanity is scattered far and wide," Lord Dusahn continued. "They are weak, disorganized, and inefficient. They exist without purpose, accomplishing little. Advanced, industrialized systems such as yours are few and far between, connected only by loose strings of marginal colonies struggling to survive, let alone thrive. The Dusahn mean to connect them. Give them purpose and prosperity."

"By conquering them," Mister Christova pointed out.

A sinister smile came across Lord Dusahn's face. "My vision requires the participation of all inhabited worlds, Mister Christova."

"And those who do not share your vision?"

"They shall *learn* to do so," Lord Dusahn insisted.

"And if they do not?"

"Then they shall be eliminated. The Dusahn do not tolerate disobedience, as the Ybarans are about to learn. I trust you have no objections, Mister Christova?"

"No, my lord. Not from myself, nor from any of my fellow nobles, I suspect," Mister Christova was quick to reply. "But the Corinairans, as well as several

---

other worlds, are still members of the Sol-Pentaurus Alliance. It was my understanding that the Alliance and the Jung Empire had agreed to end hostilities years ago. When the Alliance learns of your presence in the Pentaurus cluster…"

"The Jung Empire has grown fragmented and weak," Lord Dusahn stated, his voice seething with disdain. "The Dusahn caste now stands apart."

"But the Alliance will come nonetheless," Mister Christova insisted. "Be you Jung or be you Dusahn, you will still be considered an unwelcome aggressor."

Lord Dusahn took in a deep breath, looking as confident as ever. "Do not concern yourself with the Alliance," he said dismissively. "Concern yourselves only with how each of your noble houses will profit by your cooperation with the Dusahn Empire."

* * *

Connor stood in the corridor outside Doctor Sato's quarters, staring at the door. Behind it were at least some of the answers he needed. The problem was that he wasn't sure he wanted to *know* those answers. He was happy with his life. It wasn't an easy one, since they were almost always living from job to job. And that would only get worse now that the Jung occupied the Pentaurus cluster.

All morning, Connor had been wondering if he had done the right thing by helping Jessica and the Ghatazhak. It was *possible* the Jung gunship that had fired on them during the Asa-Cafon rescue had not identified them. But now, that was even more unlikely. Had he refused, he might have been able to continue operating on the outer fringes of the Pentaurus sector, at least for a while. At the very least, the Seiiki would not be a *hunted* vessel.

Unfortunately, after yesterday's events, it most certainly would be.

Refusing to help would have been the logical choice, as it would have increased their chances of survival. The Ghatazhak fixed his ship, and had fueled and provisioned her. He could have taken his ship and headed for either the Torramire sector, or the Bednali sector. Both were sufficient distances away to ensure at least a few years of operation before the Jung came knocking at their doors, as well. And neither sector had been introduced to jump drive technology. He could have cleaned up enough to go even further out into the lost colonies of the core. Assuming they could protect themselves from pirates and the like. Rumor was that piracy was an even greater problem outside of the Pentaurus sector. Systems such as Sherma, Gaiperura, and Peabody, all of which were just outside the Pentaurus sector, had seen more than a few raids. Had it not been for the presence of the Ghatazhak, those raids might have been more frequent.

Connor wondered if his decision to stay and help was because it was the right thing to do, or if it was because he feared losing his ship to pirates, had he ventured further out into unprotected territories. He wanted to believe it was the former, but he wasn't sure.

He *was* sure of one thing, however... He had to speak with Doctor Sato. Whether he liked her answers or not, he needed to know.

Connor took a deep breath, then pressed the door chime button. He heard a muffled musical tone from within, which he found amusing, considering these quarters were meant to accommodate Ghatazhak soldiers who were spending the night on base rather than returning to their homes in the countryside.

"*Just a minute,*" he heard a voice call from inside. There was no turning back now.

A moment later, the door opened. Slowly, at first, with the demure doctor peeking through the crack. Once she recognized Connor, she smiled and opened the door all the way. "Captain Tuplo," she greeted him warmly.

Connor gazed at the young woman for a moment. He had only seen her face briefly during the rescue, as everything had happened so quickly. He remembered her vividly, however, from his recovery after the crash...

The crash! It just occurred to Connor that there had in fact, never *been* a crash. "You weren't helping me recover from injuries sustained during a crash, were you," he said, without so much as a greeting.

"Pardon me?" the doctor replied.

"I'm sorry," Connor apologized, realizing he hadn't even said hello. "Doctor Sato, right?"

"Yes, of course."

"I'm sorry," Connor repeated. "I thought... I mean, I was hoping..."

"I suspect you have some questions to ask me," Doctor Sato said, making it easier for him. "Please, come in," she added, stepping aside.

"Thank you, Doctor," Connor replied, entering her quarters.

"Please, Connor, call me Michi."

Connor nodded as he stepped inside and waited for Michi to close the door and lead him further into her quarters.

"Please, make yourself comfortable," she instructed,

gesturing toward the two sitting chairs in the corner of the suite.

Connor followed her lead, moving to the chairs. He peeked out the window as he took his seat, noticing the amount of activity outside. "They seem awfully busy out there."

"General Telles has decided to move the Ghatazhak to a new home," Michi explained.

"Really. To where?"

"I don't know," she replied. "But you didn't come here to ask about the Ghatazhak."

"No..." Connor suddenly found himself unsure of what to ask first. "Um..."

"I suppose they have told you that you are a clone of Nathan Scott," she began, wanting to break the ice for him, "and that you carry his memories locked up inside you?"

"Yes, they have."

"And you believe them, don't you?"

Connor scratched his head. "I have to admit... at first, I didn't. But now..." He looked down for a moment. "It's a lot to take in. I always thought I had parents, that I was born like everyone else."

"You were, just as I was, just as all clones were. Each of us was once born of two parents. We have simply been *reborn*, some of us many times over. But we are still the same people... Children born of parents. It matters not whether the body that currently carries our consciousness was grown inside a mother's womb, or inside a cloning bath. For it is not the host vessel that defines us. It is our consciousness, our memories, and our experiences. *Those* are the things that define who we are."

Connor stared at her for a moment. "Then, I am incomplete?"

"What?"

"If all that I have been told in the last few days is true, then I have only existed as Connor Tuplo for *five years*. I may share the same personality traits as Nathan Scott. I may even have the same consciousness. But without his experiences, I am *not* him. I am *not* Nathan Scott."

Michi sighed, leaning back in her chair as she gazed at the troubled young man. "Assume for the moment that the backstory we gave you was true. That you *were* Connor Tuplo, born of Amma and Jarrot Tuplo of Rakuen, and that you suffered a brain injury which caused complete amnesia. Would the fact that you could not remember any of the details of your life up until the moment the amnesia occurred make you any *less* Connor Tuplo? If we had named you Darus Myle, even though your birth name had been Connor Tuplo, would that make you any less Connor Tuplo?"

"Then, either way, I am incomplete," Connor concluded. "As either Connor Tuplo, *or* as Nathan Scott. Without the memories of one or the other, I am not yet truly who am I supposed to be."

"Correct." Michi sighed again. She leaned forward and took Connor's hand. "I am told you have had flashes of memories past."

"Yes," Connor admitted. "Bits and pieces. Nothing I could string together and make sense out of, really. Faces, images... But I couldn't tell you who or what they were. Sometimes, I think I know, but it's just a feeling, really. One that is still so full of doubt..."

"Your brain is trying to access those memories, Connor," Michi explained.

"If the memories are there, why am I unable to access them?"

"It has to do with the technology used to copy your consciousness and memories. It was designed to work on Nifelmians, not Terrans. Our brains have been restructured, over generations of cloning, to better facilitate the transfer from chemical to digital, and back to chemical." She noticed the confused look on Connor's face. "Think of it this way. A data bank is formatted in such a way that a computer can find the data it needs. The data bank has a directory, one that the computer's operating system knows how to read. It understands how the data bank is partitioned and tagged, thus enabling it to easily retrieve information. *Your* brain has had information put into it in a way that it does not understand, thus forcing it to find the information on its own." She noticed he still looked confused. "I'm not helping, am I."

"Not really," Connor admitted.

"Imagine your memories are like the pieces of an enormous puzzle, and those pieces are hidden within your brain. Your brain finds those pieces, without you even realizing it. But there is no image on the surface of those pieces to help you assemble them. They are blank. It is only when your brain manages to fit two pieces together that the images on the pieces appear. At that moment, your brain writes the location and nature of those images into its directory. The more pieces that come together, the more information displayed on the surface of the assembled pieces. When enough information appears, your brain will recognize the image for what memory it represents."

Connor shook his head and sighed. "And this is all going on without my being consciously aware of it?"

"Yes. Awake or asleep. In fact, more so when you are asleep, as your brain is not having to devote resources to sensory input and the tasks of daily life."

"Then, I will eventually regain my memories...or Nathan's, I mean."

"In time, perhaps," Michi replied. "But it is unlikely that you will ever regain them all, on your own."

"How much of them might I regain?"

Michi sighed, looking down for a moment. "We don't know." She looked back up at him. "You have to understand. Nothing like this has ever been tried before. You might regain them all, or you might regain none of them."

"I see." This time, it was Connor who let out a heavy sigh. "If you had to guess..."

"I don't know that I could," Michi insisted. "Not without more information, at least."

"Try?"

Michi paused, trying to think of what to say next. "The fact that you have had some flashes of unrecognized memory is a good sign," she said, taking careful measure of her words. "It tells me that your brain is at least *trying* to put the puzzle back together. But we are talking about *billions* of pieces, Connor. More likely, *trillions*. Considering how little of your memories your brain has recovered on its own over the last five years, I would say it is unlikely you'll recover more than a small percentage of them." She looked at him, noting his disappointment. "I'm sorry." When he did not react, she pressed further. "What is it, Connor?"

Connor did not respond at first. "It's like I'm being asked to choose between being the only person

I know myself to be, versus being someone else. And to make matters worse, that someone else is a man everyone considers to be a hero... A *legend*, in fact."

"No one is asking you to choose between being Connor Tuplo and being Nathan Scott," Michi assured him. "Transferring your consciousness and memories from your current body, into the new one, will not destroy *your* memories of your life as Connor Tuplo. It will simply be moving you into a host that is better capable of giving you access to *all* the memories you currently carry within you. Those of both Connor Tuplo *and* Nathan Scott."

"But then I'll have *two* personalities. Won't *that* cause a problem as well?" Connor wondered.

"Likely, yes. It may, indeed. Again, this has never been tried before."

"There's something else I don't understand," Connor continued. "If Nathan Scott's consciousness and memories were taken from his body by that device of yours, and then stored for two years while you grew *this* body, why can't you just restore them again from that same device, into the new body, and leave me out of it?"

"It doesn't work that way," Michi explained. "Yes, the device can *theoretically* store the subject's consciousness and memories for an indefinite period. But when it restores the consciousness and memories to a new host, it restores the *original* image. It does not retain a copy that can be used on another host at a later date."

"Why not?"

"Cloning of an entire human being has always been a moral and ethical issue of great contention among the many varied human cultures. The vast majority of them have always been against the cloning of an entire being. Some are even against the cloning of that being's organs to be transplanted later into the original host. When the Nifelmians began cloning humans, they had to deal with those moral and ethical issues. One of their decisions was that, although they would clone the host body, they would never allow a *copy* of that host's consciousness and memories to exist. It would always have to be unique, and original. That is how *our* culture reconciled with the moral and ethical implications of whole-human cloning. Therefore, the device was designed to move the host's consciousness and memories *between* bodies. In fact, it was only meant to store the host's consciousness and memories for two years. It was intended to be used in emergencies only, in case of accidental death. Therefore, it only had to store the consciousness and memories until a new body could be grown."

"I thought it took two years to grow a clone?" Connor said. "Isn't that cutting it kind of close?"

"On Nifelm, a clone can be grown to full maturity in just over a year, if need be. On Corinair, however, our facilities were very rudimentary at first. It was quite an accomplishment just to grow you to full maturity within two years, let alone to the age you were at the time of your death."

Connor looked surprised. "How old was I?"

"At the time of your death, you were twenty-nine Earth years of age."

"And how old was I when I was awakened on Corinair?"

"Your current host body was twenty-five Earth years of age when the restoration was initiated."

"Then I'm thirty now?"

"In Earth years, yes," Michi confirmed.

"I wonder what that is in Rakuen years," Connor mumbled to himself.

"So, you actually gained six years of life by dying," Michi pointed out, smiling wryly. "You would have been thirty-six Earth years old by now."

"I'm not sure the extra six years were worth it, Doc."

Michi nodded. "I can certainly see your point."

"So, if I agree to be transferred into the new body, I'll get all my memories back? I'll become Nathan Scott again?"

"It's a bit more complicated than that, I'm afraid," She admitted. "The body into which you would be transferred is still two generations away from being one hundred percent compatible with the transfer technology. Turi has written a conversion algorithm that should make the process more effective, but how *much* more effective has yet to be determined. And then, there is still the issue of how you will handle the memories of two different identities. You could end up seeing Connor Tuplo's experiences as if you were simply Nathan Scott *pretending* to be Connor Tuplo."

"Like some kind of undercover operative?"

"Perhaps."

"Or?"

"Or, you could end up with psychiatric disorders, such as dissociative personality, schizophrenia..."

"Great."

"Those are unlikely, in my opinion. From what I have learned about Nathan Scott, and from what I have seen of Connor Tuplo, I believe the melding of the two identities will not pose a problem."

"Why do you say that?"

"I have studied Nathan Scott in great detail.

Personnel files, mission reports, log entries, vid-files, personal accounts from Jessica and others who knew him. We even managed to obtain vid-files about Nathan and his family. They were public figures, after all. In fact, I feel as if I knew him quite well, despite the fact that we never actually met. When I see you, when I hear you speak, when I see how you think and carry yourself, I see Nathan Scott. There is no doubt in my mind that he is within you, waiting to be let out. And that is what I have been working toward for the last five years."

Connor shook his head in disbelief. "But why? Why all this effort, for one man?"

"Because you did not deserve to die," she replied. "And because humanity *needs* men like Nathan Scott."

"Then, you believe that I, that *Nathan Scott*, is Na-Tan?"

"I don't know about all of that," Michi admitted. "Na-Tan is, after all, just a legend. But, if a legend is what is needed, then I can think of no better man for the job."

* * *

Lord Dusahn walked out onto the rooftop landing pad, followed by his officers and guards.

"My lord, with all due respect, I do not believe you should let the nobles engage you in such a way," his senior advisor, General Hesson, said, continuing the conversation that had begun in the elevator on the way up.

"It is better for them to believe they are of value, and that their positions are respected by us," Lord Dusahn replied, as he paused to look out over the city of Answari.

"They will eventually realize that is not the case," General Hesson reminded him.

"By then it will be too late. We will have a firm grip on the entire sector...perhaps even beyond. By then, their fortunes will be so intertwined with our successes that they would not dare to rebel, or they would risk everything."

"Wealth is not the sole motivating force of men."

"Of these men, it is," Lord Dusahn insisted. He moved closer to the edge of the platform, looking out across the vast cityscape, into the country lands beyond. "These men know not what they have."

"Please, my lord, a single sniper could easily..."

Lord Dusahn dismissed the general's concerns with a wave of his hand. "To have so many hospitable worlds within easy reach of one another. Only one of them had the fortitude to turn it into an empire. And they let it fall to a boy-captain with a single ship. And when they realized their error and assassinated their leader's successor, they did *nothing* with it. *Nothing.* Seven years, and with jump technology. They should have controlled everything within a thousand light years of this world. But again, they were afraid of *one* ship." He gazed upon the city. "Their world is beautiful and rich, yet they do nothing with it. They are pathetic, and we would be better off by simply wiping their worlds clean of every last one of them."

"Agreed, but the Alliance," the general reminded him.

"Yes, the Alliance." Lord Dusahn shook his finger. "That is the only reason they still live. We need their industry and their work force to quickly build up our fleet, if we are to rid ourselves of the Alliance, once and for all." Lord Dusahn sighed as he continued gazing down on the city of Answari, admiring the sunset. "What a world, wasted on such men."

"I agree that we need their infrastructure and

their workforce, my lord. What I do not agree on is the speed at which they will be able to increase the size and firepower of our fleet. Their shipyards are meager, at best, with only four bays—one of which has been occupied with the same project for going on *eight* of their years."

"You and I both know that their fabrication technology supports a much faster production schedule," Lord Dusahn reminded his advisor. "Had it not been for the Avendahl, they likely would have created a dozen warships by now."

"Lucky for us that they did not," General Hesson said. "We are spread thin enough as it is."

Lord Dusahn turned away from the edge of the platform and headed back toward his waiting shuttle. "How many of their jump-enabled ships are still unaccounted for?" he asked the general as they walked.

"Eighty-seven at last count."

"And how many of those eighty-seven ships could we arm?"

"Upwards of half, based on current intelligence. Unfortunately, most of them are avoiding the cluster, for fear of capture."

"Then we must give them something they fear more," Lord Dusahn told him. He stopped at the base of his shuttle's boarding ramp. "You have access to their registries? Their crew rosters?"

"Indeed."

"Then round up their families, and feel free to be brutal about it. Once they learn that we have them, most will return immediately."

"And those who do not?"

"Kill their families; hunt them down and destroy them without mercy," Lord Dusahn instructed. "I may be willing to answer questions from men who think themselves important, but I will not tolerate disobedience."

"And what of Ybara?" the general wondered. "Did you really wish it cleansed?"

"I would have expected it already finished," Lord Dusahn said as he turned and headed up the boarding ramp.

* * *

"*Vids from all over Corinair have popped up on the global-net, showing families of the crews of jump ships being taken into custody, a consequence of those crews not responding to the Dusahn's demands to return and relinquish control of their vessels. In Aitkenna alone, fourteen families have been arrested, and six deaths have occurred among those families during the arrests. The fact that the Dusahn have allowed these vids to be distributed without restriction indicates that they wish the crews, of what the Dusahn are referring to as 'illegally operated jump ships', to see what is happening to their families as a result of their refusal to comply with the new Dusahn directive. We will continue to broadcast updates as allowed, but we strongly urge the captains of these 'outlaw' vessels to surrender their ships to the Dusahn, before more innocent people are incarcerated, or worse.*"

"My friend, Allaya... Her entire family was taken not more than an hour ago," Morri said as his father turned off the view screen on the wall in the store office. "She was away at the time. She called me in a panic."

"Where is she now?" Anji asked.

"I do not know. She is hiding. She said she would call back when she could."

"Tell her to come here," Anji instructed his son.

"But, she will be discovered. If the Dusahn learn her identity, we will all be punished."

"Then we must make sure they do *not* learn her true identity," Anji replied.

Morri looked at his father. "What are we going to do?"

"The same thing Corinairans always do," Anji replied. "We survive, and we'll be ready to fight."

"But how?"

"Any way we can."

* * *

Connor walked into the Seiiki's galley, finding Josh and Marcus sitting in the booth in the corner.

"Captain," Marcus greeted from the table.

"Marcus, Josh," Connor replied. "Is that *jina*?" he asked, pointing at the full decanter in its wall cubby. "Where'd we get jina?"

"From the Ghatazhak mess," Josh replied. "They dry it and grind it themselves."

"Don't know why they go to all that trouble," Marcus muttered. "Them beans are stronger raw."

"Maybe, but they're bitter and disgusting," Josh argued.

"But they keep you awake."

"I'll take brewed jina over fresh any day," Josh insisted.

"You and me both," Connor agreed as he poured himself a cup.

"You talk to the doctor?" Josh wondered.

"I did," Connor replied as he stirred his jina.

"And what did she say?" Josh asked. "If you do the transfer, will you still be you?"

"Will I still be me?" Connor shook his head as he moved over to the table. "If you mean, will I still remember my experiences as Connor Tuplo, then the answer appears to be yes, although there doesn't appear to be any guarantees on that."

"Then, are you gonna do it?" Josh wondered.

"I don't know." Connor sat down and took a sip of his jina.

"Don't you want to remember who you are? Where you came from? Your family?"

"Josh," Marcus scolded. "Give the man a break."

"I'd wanna know," Josh continued.

"Even if a lot of painful memories came along with it?" Connor asked. "Nathan Scott had to make a lot of difficult decisions. Decisions that caused people to die. A *lot* of people. There's got to be a lot of baggage that goes along with all that. A lot of guilt. A lot of pain. Do I really want to bring all of that back onto myself?" Connor took another sip of his jina. "Maybe I'm better off as Connor Tuplo."

"Then why don't you look very convinced?" Marcus wondered.

"That obvious, huh?"

"Yup."

Connor shook his head and sighed. "It's the way that old man looked at me when he died. Like a ghost from his past, or something. He really believed I was Na-Tan, and that I could save them all."

"We all do, Cap'n," Josh said. "Why the hell do you think we've been hanging around with ya all these years?"

"The Jung have jump ships, Josh," Connor said. "Lots of them. The Ghatazhak only have a handful of ships, and small ones at that. There's no way they can take on the Jung."

"It ain't about winning," Marcus told Connor. "It's about fightin'. Yeah, the idea *is* to win. But it's about standing up for what's right." Marcus chuckled. "Like I'm one to talk."

"Even if you don't stand a chance in hell?"

"Especially if you don't stand a chance in hell," Marcus insisted.

"Actually, the expression is, 'a snowball's chance in hell'," Josh corrected.

Marcus glared at him. "That's partly why Nathan Scott was such a legend," Marcus continued, turning his attention back to Connor. "You could always count on him to do the right thing, regardless of the odds."

"But I'm *not* him," Connor pointed out. "Not unless I go through with the transfer."

"I'm not so sure about that," Marcus argued.

Connor cast a quizzical look Marcus's way.

"You took the Rama job, didn't you?"

"We needed the money," Connor shrugged.

"The money was shit," Marcus argued. "Said so yourself. You took the Corinair rescue as well."

"Because they fixed my ship, fueled her, and loaded her up, including this jina," Connor pointed out.

"Bullshit. You still could've said no, and you know it," Marcus argued. "You took the run because it was the right thing to do. You took it because people who once meant something to you were in trouble."

"You took it because my best friend's wife and daughter were in trouble, as well," Josh pointed out.

Connor took another sip. "And here I thought I took it because a pretty girl asked me to." He looked at them both. "You know, I'm not as noble as you both seem to think I am."

"I'm bettin' you are," Marcus replied.

"So am I," Josh added.

Connor sighed, thinking for a moment. "And if I refuse the transfer, and set a course out of here?" Connor asked. "Are you two going to come with me?"

Marcus and Josh exchanged glances, after which Marcus spoke. "We won't like it, but we'll go. That's what family does. And crew *is* family."

Connor sighed again. "Yes, they are... They truly are."

* * *

Coln Augist stood on the edge of the crowd, listening to the voices of the protesters as they chanted their angry war dirges. It had only been three days since the Alliance super-weapons had obliterated Nor-Zerest, Nor-Tempali, and Nor-Jurost, along with several strategic posts in systems further away from the core of the Jung sector. Although civilian casualties had been relatively minor, more than a million of the Jung warrior castes had lost their lives in the blink of an eye. The devastation of the targeted worlds had been complete. In the case of Zhu-Dengari, there was nothing left. Nothing but debris.

Coln had not seen the people of Nor-Patri this angry since one of Nor-Patri's moons, Zhu-Anok, had been destroyed seven years prior. It had rained destruction down upon the very world on which he now stood. To this day, a ring of debris could still be seen in the night sky over the Jung homeworld.

He and his fellow spies had been inserted during the weeks of chaos that had followed. It had been relatively easy to blend into Jung society, as many of the data records had been destroyed in the attack. Millions of identities had to be rebuilt, and it was well known that more than a few of those identities had been false. Common criminals, people wishing to escape debt, even a few desperate to escape a loveless marriage...they had all used the confusion to start anew.

Coln had always expected to be caught. Time and again, he had wanted to send word to his father that he was alive. But doing so would, most likely, have led to his capture. And his presence on Nor-Patri was too valuable to the Alliance to risk for personal needs. He always told himself that the day would come when it would be safe to seek out his father, but with each passing year, that day seemed further away.

The crowds called upon their leaders to strike back at the Alliance for the unwarranted attack. They carried pictures of loved ones whose lives had been taken without cause. They carried banners of the various warrior castes, urging them to seize power from the leadership castes and destroy the Alliance once and for all. More importantly, they demanded to know why their leaders had not reacted to the attack upon the empire.

It was a question that Coln needed answers to, as well. And he needed them before he transmitted his next covert report back to the Alliance through the jump comm-drone that visited the Jung homeworld at random, but frequent, intervals in order to maintain communications between the two worlds.

He only hoped the jump comm-drone was still operating.

* * *

Twelve of the sixteen Dusahn ships in orbit around Takara disappeared behind flashes of blue-white light. A split second later, four of them appeared a few hundred thousand kilometers from the fifth planet in the Takar system, Ybara. The ships settled into orbit around the large, rocky world, spreading out evenly across the planet's middle latitudes, until the entire side of the planet was within range of the small task force's weapons.

Ybaran fighters, secured by services the Ybaran Ghatazhak had once performed for several noble houses of Takara, came up from the surface to challenge the Dusahn forces. The Ybarans were heavily outgunned, even though the Dusahn had sent four of their smallest warships. But the Ybarans were a proud people, and would not go down without a fight.

The Ybaran fighters were met with precise rail-gun fire from the Dusahn ships. Within the first minute of the engagement, the Ybaran forces were reduced by half. After another minute, they were cut in half again. By the third minute, there were only a handful of fighters left. The remaining fighters veered away, instead taking up positions to protect the more than twenty shuttles attempting to flee their doomed world. If their world was to die, at least some of their numbers might escape alive and start over elsewhere.

But the Dusahn were unwilling to let a single Ybaran escape. Their message to all the other worlds in the Pentaurus cluster, and beyond, was to be clear. Disobedience would not be tolerated.

Waves of Dusahn interceptors came streaming out of all four ships. Twelve, twenty-four, forty-eight. Within a minute, the Ybarans were outnumbered ten to one. Their fighters were quickly dispatched, as were the shuttles they fought to protect. Several jump-enabled shuttles managed to make it away, only to be pursued by the Dusahn interceptors. They too, would be hunted down and destroyed without mercy.

Once the skies above Ybara were clear of

resistance, the Dusahn ships went to work on the Ybaran ground defenses. One by one, missile bases and surface-to-orbit plasma cannons were targeted and destroyed by Dusahn surface-attack fighters. The fighters cleared a swath around the planet, leaving it wide open for orbital bombardment.

Weapons fell from the bays of the four Dusahn warships. Once through the upper atmosphere, their warheads separated, fanning out toward preprogrammed targets on the surface. The first lap around the planet saw the destruction of all the Ybaran surface defenses, as well as her major cities and infrastructure. The second lap destroyed all remaining pockets of civilization, as well as the limited Ybaran industrial capabilities.

By the time the Dusahn ships began their third attack pass around Ybara, little of significance was left to target, yet they continued to do so. Surface-attack fighters buzzed low over the surface of Ybara, taking care to stay clear of the orbital bombardment. They hunted in packs, searching for any signs of human life to extinguish. Once every Ybaran had been eliminated, they turned their attention to the few buildings still standing.

Eight hours later, the surface fighters and interceptors returned to their home ships, and the four Dusahn warships broke orbit and disappeared behind flashes of blue-white light, bound for other systems to join their fellow warships in further conquest.

All that remained on the surface of Ybara were the rubble of buildings, the thick smoke from countless fires, intense radiation, and the lingering smell of death, from pole to pole.

The world of Ybara was no more.

CHAPTER TWO

Connor sat atop the Seiiki, just aft of the windows that had once offered tremendous views from the owner's cabin below, but now opened into the upper passenger compartment. He sat gazing at the distant aurora, shimmering on the horizon. It was a phenomenon common to most of the worlds he had visited in his lifetime, yet it always amazed him nonetheless.

My lifetime.

It was a term that had confused him ever since he had awakened after the *accident*. And now, it confused him even more. His lifetime, everything that had occurred prior to waking in the hospital on Corinair, was still undefined to him. Unfortunately, recent events had further mired that past. Over the years, he had managed to come to grips with what he *thought* his past to be, despite the fact that all he had were tiny flashes of memory. He had desperately wanted to remember it all, but now, he was not so sure.

"Care for some company?" Jessica called out from behind as she topped the aft access ladder. When Connor did not voice his objection, she continued forward. "Nice view," she said, pausing to take in the vista. "We don't often see the aurora at this latitude." She sat down next to him. "Have you seen a lot of them?"

"A few," Connor replied. After taking a breath, he added, "In Angla, it means 'new dawn'."

"Kind of appropriate, huh?"

Connor looked at her, puzzled.

"Well, you're trying to decide whether or not to

go through with the transfer, and *become* Nathan again, right? That would be a new dawn of sorts. Not only for you, but likely for this entire sector."

Connor shook his head. "I think you put too much faith in me...or him."

Jessica smiled. "You're so much like him, you know. Even after all that he accomplished, Nathan never felt qualified to be the leader that he had already become. He always felt like he was pretending to be captain and that, sooner or later, everyone would find out the truth."

Connor sighed, looking down at the bow of the Seiiki in front of him. "I know the feeling. I never really felt like the *captain* of the Seiiki. The fact that I *owned* her was the only thing that made me feel even remotely justified to be in charge. Of course, now I know that she doesn't really belong to me..."

"But she does," Jessica insisted, cutting him off. "Deliza *gave* her to you."

"But her registration..."

"A bit shady, I'll admit," Jessica replied. "But there's no law that says you can't rename a ship. Marcus just did it in a way that would make it difficult for anyone to figure out that she was once the Mirai. The Seiiki *is* your ship, trust me."

Connor didn't respond at first. He looked up at the sky, this time gazing at the stars directly overhead. "And I can still take her and leave, anytime I wish?"

"That was the deal," Jessica replied.

Connor could hear the discord in her voice. "You know, rumor has it that there are hundreds, perhaps even thousands, of human-inhabited worlds out there," he said, still gazing at the stars overhead.

"It's not a rumor," Jessica assured him. "The Data Ark had records of at least three hundred colony expeditions intending to establish a colony well outside the Sol sector. And that doesn't include those who fled to escape the plague. The people who settled Corinair were on one of those ships. Their own history speaks of ships departing in droves. At least a few per week, and that was just on one core world."

Connor continued scanning the stars as he spoke. "Yup, I could spend a lifetime exploring them. I could probably make a good living, as well. They likely don't have jump drives."

"Then, why didn't you?"

Connor looked at her, puzzled again.

"You could have left this sector years ago," she continued. "Why did you stay?"

"I don't know. Expenses, upgrades, maintenance... They kept us taking jobs just to keep our heads above water."

Jessica smiled.

"What?" Connor asked, puzzled by her smile.

"'Head above water'. It's an Earth expression. You don't hear it much in this part of the galaxy." She poked him in the chest. "You see, he's in there. You know that, don't you?"

"Yeah, I suppose I do." Connor went silent again.

After several minutes, Jessica spoke. "What is it?"

Connor looked at her, embarrassed to share what he was feeling.

"Come on," Jessica urged, "tell me."

"I'm scared," Connor finally admitted.

Jessica laughed.

"Not exactly the reaction I was expecting," Connor said, shaking his head.

"I'm sorry," Jessica apologized. "Of course, you're scared," she continued. "Only an idiot wouldn't be."

"Nice to know I'm not an idiot, then."

"Connor, I get it. I really do. Being Nathan Scott is a *big* responsibility. Being a leader always is. But you gotta believe me when I say that you are *very* good at it. You *are* Na-Tan."

"You don't really believe in that Na-Tan crap, do you?"

"Not in the way the legend describes him, no," Jessica explained. "But I do believe in the power that Na-Tan has to lead...to inspire. Na-Tan is a role... like an actor playing a part in a vid-play. But only certain people can really do the role justice. *You* are one of those people."

"So, you want me to be an actor?"

"No, we want you to be yourself. Nathan."

Connor sighed again. "But it doesn't make any sense. General Telles is way more qualified to lead a rebellion. Why doesn't *he* play the role of Na-Tan?"

"Telles? Please," Jessica scoffed. "Granted, he is a brilliant and dedicated man, but he is hardly Na-Tan. He lacks the compassion that you have. Telles is a tactician. He's always calculating the possible outcomes of any action...weighing risk versus benefit."

"Isn't that what a leader is supposed to do?" Connor wondered.

"Sure, but we're talking about leading *people*. And *people* aren't just numbers. Nathan knew that. *You* know that."

"And Telles doesn't?"

"He does, but only because he understands human psychology and behavior. That's different than empathy."

"You're saying he doesn't *feel* what others feel?"

"He does, but he chooses to turn it off out of necessity. That's what the Ghatazhak do. It's why they're so effective. But that's not the sole reason that you're the only one who can be Na-Tan."

Connor looked at her.

"It's because of this," she said, putting her hand on his cheek. "This face... Those eyes. They engender trust. They engender confidence."

"Even with this beard?" Connor joked.

"Are you kidding? The beard has got to go. You look like some kind of hermit."

Connor forced a smile. After another minute, he spoke. "I don't know if I can do it, Jess."

"Fine, keep the beard."

"That's not what I meant."

Jessica sighed. "I know," she said, leaning closer to put her head on his shoulder.

* * *

"You asked to see me?" Commander Jarso inquired from the entrance to Captain Gullen's office.

"Yes, Commander," the captain replied, gesturing for him to enter. "I trust you and your men have gotten settled?"

"Indeed, Captain," the commander replied, taking a seat across from the Glendanon's captain.

"I wish I could provide you with better accommodations," the captain said apologetically.

"They will do nicely."

"I heard that only twenty-three ships made it aboard," Captain Gullen said. "I am sorry for the loss of your comrades."

"Twenty-one, actually," Commander Jarso corrected, "including myself. Ensigns Dutko and Cheval did not survive their injuries."

Captain Gullen frowned. "Again, I am sorry."

"Had you not come to our aid, more of us would have died," the commander pointed out. "On behalf of myself, and my men, I thank you and your crew. You all took a great risk to rescue us."

"The crew of the Avendahl, as well as their families, protected Corinair for nearly eight years, Commander. It was the least we could do."

"May I ask what your plans are, Captain?" Commander Jarso asked.

"For the moment, it is all we can do to stay one jump ahead of the Jung. They have been following our old light ever since we jumped from the Darvano system. They very much wish to find us."

"Because you rescued us," the commander surmised.

"Perhaps," the captain agreed. "However, it is more likely that they want this ship. The Glendanon is one of the largest jump-capable transports in the sector."

"How long can you stay ahead of them?"

"For as long as is necessary," the captain said.

"If I may make a suggestion, Captain?"

"Please."

"Jump to Camden Alpha Major."

"Big Blue?" the captain replied in shock. "Why?"

"She has a magnitude of two point two. If you move in close enough, the star's light and radioactivity should mask your jump and your departure track."

"An interesting idea," the captain said thoughtfully.

"Not too close, of course."

"Of course."

"If I might ask another question?" the commander wondered. After Captain Gullen nodded, the commander continued. "How long will my men and I be allowed to remain on your vessel?"

Captain Gullen leaned back in his chair, sighing. "You are, of course, welcome to remain as long as you like, Commander. Unfortunately, your fighters have a relatively short jump range. And we cannot spare much propellant, as we know not where we will be able to replenish our supplies."

"Then you do not intend to surrender your ship to the Jung," the commander stated.

"No, I do not."

"Then you have plans on how to proceed?"

"Yes," the captain replied. "My intention is to contact the Ghatazhak."

"You know where they are?" the commander asked, surprised.

"Yes," Captain Gullen replied. "I am one of the few who do. I have been hesitant to do so, for fear that I might lead the Jung to them. But, perhaps, by following your advice, we might be able to safely make contact."

"The Ghatazhak?" Commander Jarso said, surprised. "It was my understanding that they were disbanded."

"That is only what they wished us to believe," the captain replied. "Granted, their numbers are few, but if anyone is to stand in opposition to the Jung, it is the Ghatazhak."

* * *

Elam Jahal watched as his commanding officer examined the message. They had served together for many years, and his friend had always been difficult to read, holding his emotions in check better than most. But, on this night, the concern on the general's face was obvious...at least to Elam.

General Telles handed the message pad to his second in command, saying nothing.

Commander Jahal read the message, his own expression unchanged. "Surely, none of this comes as any surprise to you."

"No, it does not," the general admitted. "I had hoped that I would never again hear of such blatant disregard for life."

"The Ybarans will not be missed," Commander Jahal pointed out.

"No, they will not," the general admitted. "They were an offense to all that we are. Nevertheless, they did not deserve extermination. No one does."

"There was a time when we might have been the ones carrying out such orders," the commander reminded him.

General Telles sighed. "That time has long passed. We choose our own path now. No one chooses it for us."

"That is incorrect," Commander Jahal argued. "Fate chooses our destiny, and *you* decide which path we take to meet it."

General Telles looked at his friend. "You read the entire message?"

"Yes. If anything, it will make it easier to convince him to join us."

"Captain Tuplo, or Captain Gullen?"

"Either," the commander replied, "or both."

Both men turned as Jessica entered the Ghatazhak communications center. "You wanted to see me, sir?" she asked as she approached them.

Commander Jahal handed her the message pad.

"Shit," Jessica muttered as she read the message. "The whole planet?"

"Nothing left alive," the commander confirmed.

"How did we get this intel?" Jessica wondered.

"The Dusahn are actively broadcasting images of the aftermath throughout the cluster," General Telles explained.

"The Dusahn?" Jessica asked. "Who the hell are the Dusahn?"

"One of the Jung castes," the general replied.

"I've never heard a Jung caste identify themselves by caste name, and not as Jung," she commented. "Is it possible they are operating independently?"

"Anything is possible," the general said. "However, based on our understanding of the Jung, it would seem unlikely."

"Does it matter?" the commander wondered.

"At present, no," the general agreed. He turned to Jessica. "Are we still on schedule?"

"The first few loads have been staged off-world. Equipment and supplies mostly. But we've only got the one boxcar to work with, so it's slow going. At least we've got plenty of cargo pods to preload, so we can keep Solomon and his crew jumping, nonstop."

"What about the cargo shuttles?" the commander asked.

"You can only fit so much in a cargo shuttle," Jessica replied. "And they take time to load. It would help if we had more transports."

"Stick to the priorities, as planned," the general instructed. "I will find us the transports."

* * *

"As you were," Captain Taylor ordered as she marched confidently into the Aurora's command briefing room. Those in attendance, getting ready to stand, settled back into their seats.

Cameron moved to her place at the head of the conference table and sat down. "Seven days ago, the Sol Alliance launched a KKV strike against a dozen Jung tactical assets. The shipyards in the Dorgahn, Jasi-Tona, and Nor-Tendi systems were all destroyed, as were military bases in the Escari, Amarrari, and Lungdahl systems. These, along with half a dozen other assets, were targeted to send the Jung leadership a message. We will not tolerate any transgressions."

Cameron looked at the faces of her senior officers, each of them displaying controlled shock. "Millions of military personnel were killed," she continued, "as were millions of civilians stationed in those facilities. Although no civilian population centers were targeted, command expects the Jung population to demand wide-scale retaliation. Therefore, all Alliance ships will remain on full alert."

"Captain," Commander Kaplan started.

Captain Taylor held up her hand to silence her executive officer. "I know. We don't have a choice."

"We haven't spotted a single ship since Alpha Centauri," Lieutenant Commander Kono reminded the captain. "Maybe the Jung recalled their ships after the strike?"

"Maybe," Cameron admitted. "But it doesn't matter. Not to us. Our orders are to maintain alert status, and to continue to conduct detection patrols."

"Captain, my pilots are flying eighteen hours a day," Commander Verbeek, the Aurora's CAG, complained.

"Ground crews are burning the candle at both ends, as well, sir," Master Chief Warhl, the Aurora's chief of the boat, added.

"The crew is being pushed over the edge," Doctor Caro chimed in. "We can't keep feeding them stims forever, Captain."

"Command has promised more personnel," Captain Taylor assured them. "But it will take nearly a week to get us up to full staffing levels."

"Even with full staffing levels, we can't maintain full alert status indefinitely, sir," Commander Kaplan reminded her. "Sooner or later, someone is going to make a mistake...possibly a disastrous one."

"We can use the comm-drones," Commander Kamenetskiy suggested.

Cameron looked at him.

"Our patrols are for detection purposes, right? Why don't we just put sensor packages on them and jump them to take scans at strategic locations, then jump them back and collect the data?"

"That won't give us real-time response capabilities," Commander Verbeek argued.

"You were planning on attacking a Jung ship with a pair of Super Eagles?" Commander Kamenetskiy said skeptically.

"He's right," Commander Kaplan agreed. "That could work."

Cameron looked at her science officer. "Lieutenant Commander?"

"It could work," Lieutenant Commander Kono admitted. "We would need more comm-drones, though."

"How long would it take, from the moment they were picked up on sensors, to the moment we become *aware* of the detection?" Cameron asked.

"That depends on several things," the lieutenant commander explained. "How many times the drone stops to conduct scans before returning, how much time is spent scanning at each stop, and at what point along the drone's route the detection occurs."

"Rough guess?"

"As little as a few minutes, to as much as half an hour, I imagine."

"Wouldn't the target be long gone?" Doctor Caro wondered.

"Perhaps, but at least we would have a course projection to work forward from," Lieutenant Commander Kono said.

"And it *would* take some of the pressure off the crew," Commander Kaplan admitted.

"A pilot can pursue a contact," Commander Verbeek reminded the captain. "A drone cannot. We would be increasing our chances of losing the contact."

"Or, we'd be focusing our pilots on areas where contact is most likely. Like along a hot track," Captain Taylor said. "Lieutenant Commander Kono, work up some numbers for me."

"Yes, sir."

"Kamenetskiy, I'll need to know how quickly you can add the sensor packages to the drones, as well."

"Not a problem," Vladimir promised.

"Verbee, give me a revised flight schedule based on Kono's numbers," Cameron said. "I'll run the idea past command." She paused a moment before continuing. "With the Jung in the Pentaurus cluster, we have to assume that they now have jump drives."

"Captain, we have yet to see any evidence of jump drive usage by the Jung in *this* sector," Lieutenant Commander Kono pointed out.

"The message from the Ghatazhak in the Pentaurus sector clearly indicated that the Jung who invaded the cluster did so using jump drive technology," Cameron explained. "So, until proven otherwise, we are to operate under the assumption that the Jung here have jump drives, as well."

"It would explain how they were able to get so deep into Alliance space without being detected," the XO said.

"What bothers me is that they *were* detected," the captain said.

"You'd rather they weren't?" Vladimir wondered.

"They shouldn't have been," Cameron explained. "At least, not until they were in position to attack. We could jump into orbit above Nor-Patri, drop a nuke on her capital, and jump away again before the Jung could respond. If they have jump drive technology, then they should be able to do the same."

"Assuming they wanted to," Commander Kaplan interjected. "Maybe they just wanted us to know that they *could* get past our borders without being detected?"

"But to what end?" Cameron wondered.

* * *

Connor looked across the sea of the dead and dying that lay before him, their faces reflecting a shock and horror that no being should ever witness.

Compelled by some unknown force, Connor walked through the bodies. Some were whole, others were torn apart. Blood was everywhere, and the stench...the stench of death filled the air, making it difficult to breathe without retching.

Arms of victims reached out to him as he walked amongst them. Their unintelligible voices begged for him, their hands clutched at his trousers as he passed. Try as he might, he could not understand their pleas. *Were they asking for his help? Were they asking for salvation?*

Or were they asking him why?

Connor suddenly sat upright in his bunk, his eyes wide in horror, panting and out of breath. He stared straight ahead for a full minute before realizing that it had been a nightmare. He looked around the compartment. His bed. His desk. His jacket and gun belt hanging on the door. His cabin.

His breathing began to return to normal, and his terror faded. After another moment, he pushed his blanket back and turned, swinging his feet out over the side of the bed and placing them on the cold deck of his ship.

His ship.

The Seiiki had been all he had known for the last five years. It had been his refuge, his escape. It was the one thing he felt he had control over. On this ship, he was in charge. He decided where they went, what jobs they took. It had not been an easy life, but it had been a good one.

But why?

Why had it been a good life? Surely there were better lives to be had. So many worlds to live on. So many people. So many customs. So many careers. Why limit himself to this?

It was a question he often asked himself, and the answer was always the same.

Escape.

Connor rose from his bed and walked over to the door to his private head. He laid his hand on the tap, causing the tiny sink to fill with cool water.

The water felt good on his face, as if it were washing away the horrific images his mind had just conjured up to torture him.

Were the images real? Were they from his past? Nathan's past? Or were they what his mind *feared* he would see if he became Nathan Scott?

Connor suddenly realized what he was trying to

escape. It wasn't his past. After all, he had almost no memory of it.

It was his future.

* * *

President Scott sat watching the other members of the Alliance Council argue with one another. The meeting had been under way for several hours, and they were no closer to reaching an agreement than they had been at the start. If anything, they were becoming more divided.

He looked at Admiral Galiardi at the opposite end of the table. He, and the two junior officers who stood behind him, were the only ones other than President Scott not actively engaged in a heated debate.

Admiral Galiardi lowered his chin for a moment, his eyes locked on the president's, as if inviting him to take control of the situation before it escalated out of control.

President Scott sighed. It wasn't the first time that the leaders of the Sol Alliance worlds were in dispute. It seemed to be a monthly occurrence, which, as of late, became an almost daily one. "Gentlemen," the president urged. "Gentlemen!"

It did little good. Finally, the president picked up his gavel and started banging it on the table with all his might, continuing to do so until every last one of them was silent. Realizing that he may have taken it a bit far, he calmly placed the gavel on the table, straightened his tie, and began to speak. "This constant bickering is getting us nowhere. Here are the facts. The Pentaurus cluster has fallen to the Jung. The Jung ambassador denies any knowledge of such actions. Jung ships have invaded Alliance space, in blatant violation of the cease-fire agreement. They have attacked our ships. We have defended ourselves, destroying several Jung ships in the process. In retaliation, and as a warning, we have launched a tactical KKV strike, crippling a dozen of the Jung's key military assets. We estimate the death toll to be in the millions. Mostly military, but not all. Since the strike seven days ago, we have received no official communications from the Jung Empire, despite repeated attempts to open a discussion on recent events. Furthermore, we have not detected any Jung incursions into Alliance space since the KKV strike. However, intelligence indicates that the Jung population is calling for retaliatory strikes against the Alliance."

President Scott looked at Admiral Galiardi. "Admiral, in your professional opinion, can the Alliance afford to send ships to the Pentaurus sector to deal with the Jung invasion of Alliance worlds in that sector?"

"No, Mister President, we cannot," Admiral Galiardi replied with absolute conviction. "We do not know the total fleet strength of the Jung, nor do we know the exact positions of their ships. As evidenced by their deep incursions into the Sol sector, it is entirely possible that more of their ships are lying in wait within Alliance space. Until such time that we are certain that Alliance space is clear of Jung ships, we cannot afford to send a single gunboat, let alone larger vessels."

"And if we do not send ships to the Pentaurus cluster?" the president inquired.

"I'm afraid we must consider the Pentaurus *sector*, lost."

"And what does that loss mean to the Alliance?" the minister from the Tau Ceti system asked.

Admiral Galiardi looked to President Scott,

realizing that the Tau Ceti minister had spoken out of turn. When President Scott nodded, the admiral continued. "The Pentaurus sector is highly industrialized, and highly advanced. The Jung forces there will multiply quite rapidly."

"How rapidly?" the president asked.

"As you all know, the Takarans were the only ones with warships in the sector. As well as the Avendahl, which was protecting Corinair. Now that those ships are gone, there is little to prevent them from taking over the entire sector."

"How long will it take them to capture the Pentaurus sector?"

"Without exact fleet strength numbers, we are only guessing. But I would expect it to take less than a month, if not half that."

"Is there anything that we can do?" the president wondered.

"At present, nothing. There are still too many unknowns, both in the Sol sector, and the Pentaurus sector. The best we can do is to send equipment, supplies, and weapons to the Ghatazhak, in the hopes that they may be able to impede the Jung in some way. But sending ships at this time is out of the question."

President Scott sighed as several members of the council again began to protest. "Gentlemen!" the president demanded, raising his voice again. "We can spend no more time arguing. The time to vote is now. Do we, or do we not, send ships to the Pentaurus sector?"

* * *

Connor came walking into the galley, looking no more rested than when he had excused himself for the night hours ago. He paused for a moment, surprised to see his entire crew gathered at the table. "Why are you all up?" he asked as he headed for the refrigerator. "You guys have bad dreams, too?"

"Who needs bad dreams when you have real life?" Neli commented.

Connor poured himself a glass of juice. "What is it?" he asked, downing the juice.

"Ybara," Dalen said quietly. "They wiped it out."

"What do you mean, wiped it out?" Connor wondered, a puzzled look on his face.

"The Dusahn wiped them all out," Marcus explained.

"Glassed the entire planet," Josh added.

"What?" Connor couldn't believe what he was hearing. "All of them? Women and children... everyone?"

"Nothing left alive," Neli replied.

"Who are the Dusahn?" Connor asked.

"That's what the Jung are calling themselves," Josh explained.

"Wait... Didn't that guy say something about 'Lord Dusahn', when we were rescuing..."

"Yup," Marcus replied.

Connor still couldn't believe it. "The entire planet?" he muttered as he sat down next to Neli. "How do you know?"

"The Ghatazhak sent us the feed. The Dusahn have been allowing everyone to broadcast the images," Josh explained.

"Guess they want everyone to know what happens when you piss them off," Dalen muttered.

"What did the Ybarans do?" Connor wondered.

"Apparently, they refused to show respect for Lord Dusahn," Marcus added. "Not too surprising, for Ybarans."

Connor suddenly felt the weight of the galaxy on

his shoulders. Without a word, he rose and left the room, heading aft.

"Captain," Josh called after him, rising from his seat to follow.

"Let'm go," Marcus insisted. "I suspect he's got some thinkin' to do."

* * *

The door to the holding room opened, and a Dusahn officer walked in. He paused to look at the two women sitting at the table before him, appearing unimpressed, and wholly disinterested in his task. "You are Isa Gullen, wife of Edom Gullen, captain of the Glendanon. Is this correct?"

Isa looked at her daughter, unsure if she should answer.

"Please answer the question," the officer said impatiently, seeming irritated.

"Yes, I am Isa Gullen. What do you want from us?"

"I am the one asking the questions," the officer corrected. "And you are Sori Gullen, daughter of Edom?"

"You know that I am," Sori replied, a touch of rebellion in her voice.

"Very good." The officer placed his data pad on the table in front of him. "You are being recorded. This recording shall be transmitted throughout the Pentaurus sector, so that Captain Gullen will see it."

"Why are you doing this?" Sori demanded. "We have done nothing to you."

"No, but your father has refused to comply with a general order from Lord Dusahn."

"What order?" Sori demanded.

"Lord Dusahn has ordered that all jump-capable

ships immediately report to their homeworld, so they can be fitted for compliance."

"What are you talking about?"

"It is quite simple, young lady. Your father is to turn the Glendanon over to us, without further delay."

"Or what?" Sori asked, fearing the officer's response.

"Or you shall both be executed," the officer replied without the slightest hint of emotion. The officer turned to face the camera on the other side of the window behind him. "Captain Gullen, you have ten days to comply, or your wife and daughter shall pay for your crimes."

* * *

Jessica climbed out of the vehicle as it pulled to a stop in front of the Ghatazhak hangar at the Lawrence Spaceport. She paused for a moment, watching as three boxcars touched down a few hundred meters away. Once they landed and their engines began to wind down, she continued on to General Telles, who was standing near the door to the Ghatazhak flight operations office. "Where did you get the extra boxcars?" she asked, yelling to be heard over the whine of the engines.

General Telles pointed to the nearest boxcar. "Lorrel contacted us a few hours ago. Through him, we found Penski and Oresto."

"I'm surprised they haven't turned their ships over to the Dusahn," Jessica said, her volume returning back to normal now that the three boxcars had shut down their engines.

"Many have," the general said. "However, the life of a boxcar crew and that of a family man are not a good match."

"How did you convince them to help us?"

General Telles handed Jessica the data pad he had tucked under his left arm. "I showed them this." Jessica read the communiqué on the data pad, her eyes widening. "So, we're on our own, then," she concluded, handing the data pad back to General Telles.

"Quite possibly for some time," the general said. "They have promised to send equipment and supplies, but that may take weeks to arrive, by which time we will not be here."

"What are your plans?" Jessica asked.

"We are not prepared to fight the Dusahn. For now, we must concentrate on surviving, and building up our capabilities." He looked at Jessica. "Have you spoken with him since your return from Corinair?"

"Yes, more than once. He is still undecided."

"It will be far more difficult without him," the general reminded her.

"I know," Jessica replied. "Believe me, I have done all that I can. It is still *his* decision, however."

"Yes, it is." General Telles looked back at the boxcars. "See that the schedule is changed to utilize the three new boxcars," he ordered. "Then bring Captain Tuplo to my office. It is time for him to make his decision."

* * *

General Hesson's aide met him in the corridor on the way to see Lord Dusahn.

"His mood?" the general asked his aide.

"He was pleased with the annihilation of the Ybarans."

"Has he shown any indication of easing up on his timeline?"

"According to my sources, he has not."

The general's eyebrow shot up for a moment. "As I expected," he muttered as he stepped up to the entrance to Lord Dusahn's office. He pressed his hand against the scanner pad next to the door, and, a moment later, it opened.

"General," Lord Dusahn greeted, in his usual terse manner.

"The families of the missing jump ships are being detained as ordered, my lord. As of this morning, twenty-seven ships have surrendered."

"Out of eighty-seven," Lord Dusahn said to himself. "Not exactly an enthusiastic response, I'd say." Lord Dusahn picked up his mug, taking a long sip of his hot beverage.

"Perhaps we should give them a bit more incentive," the general suggested.

"Such as?" Lord Dusahn wondered.

"Execute a few of their families, perhaps?"

"That might have the opposite effect," Lord Dusahn warned. "They were promised six days, and it has only been one. Many of the ships may not have even received the message, as of yet."

"Fear, is an excellent motivator," General Hesson stated.

"Fear has already been provided," Lord Dusahn replied. "Trust is what we must now earn. We must show them that while disobedience shall not be tolerated, loyalty, on the other hand, shall be rewarded."

"Of course, my lord."

Lord Dusahn glanced at the digital display on the wall of his office, studying the map of the Pentaurus cluster, and the positions of his forces. "Any word on the jump ships that briefly visited the Darvano system?"

"The ship that aided the escape of the Avendahl's remaining fighters, the Glendanon, is still at large."

"You have not been able to locate her?"

"Not yet, my lord. Her captain is no fool. He spends little time resting between jumps, in an effort to stay one jump ahead of his pursuers."

"Then he knows he is being followed."

"He *suspects*," General Hesson corrected. "But he cannot maintain such frequent jumps forever. Eventually, he must pause to recharge his energy banks. When he does, we will find him."

"I would prefer that ship intact," Lord Dusahn reminded him. "She is a sizable asset."

"I understand."

"And the other ships?"

"One has been located. The other has not. We are preparing to move on the first, by the end of the day."

"I trust you will deal with them," Lord Dusahn said.

"We will send what forces we can, my lord," General Hesson promised. "However, our forces are spread more thinly than we would prefer. Perhaps, it would be best to wait until our dominance is more assured. After all, the target lies well outside this sector, and is unlikely to be a threat."

"If they have a jump drive, they *are* a threat," Lord Dusahn corrected, annoyed by the general's disagreement. "Maximum force."

"My lord," General Hesson pleaded.

"We must show these people that the Dusahn do not tolerate any disobedience. Directly or indirectly." He paused a moment, pondering the general's concerns. "You may use my personal legion," he finally said.

"The Zen-Anor, my lord?" the general replied, surprised by Lord Dusahn's decision.

"If anyone can strike fear in the hearts of men..." A sinister smile began to form on his face. "Besides, it will be a good training exercise for them."

* * *

Connor Tuplo walked down the Seiiki's cargo ramp and out onto the tarmac. He paused to take in the fresh night air of Burgess. Unlike most of the worlds the Seiiki regularly visited, the spaceport at Lawrence was more open. No sound suppression walls, no boarding tunnels, no underground facilities. Everything was on the surface, with far more room between its few buildings than necessary. It was as if its builders had felt that a need for expansion was yet to come.

Connor had done a little research during his brief stay on Burgess, if for no other reason than to distract himself from the decision he was about to make. At one hundred and nine light years from Takara, the Sherma system was well outside the Pentaurus sector. It had been settled during the rise of the Ta'Akar Empire under the reign of Caius. At the time of settlement, linear FTL was the only means of interstellar travel, thus its location kept it clear of Takaran influence. In fact, at the time, the closest inhabited world was at least a fifteen year journey. This had been exactly what its founders had wanted. To be removed from all external societal influences and restraints. To have the freedom to live as they saw fit.

Human interstellar history was replete with such dreams. To leave the world one did not like behind, to start over elsewhere. Dreams of utopia always seemed to plague humanity, despite the fact that such societies never came to be. They always demanded more compromise than humans were willing to give, and perfection could not be achieved by imperfect creatures.

However, the world of Burgess seemed as close as Connor could imagine a utopia to be. It lacked the technological sophistication of the more developed and heavily populated worlds, but that seemed to be its strength. The lack of complexity resulted in a more relaxed lifestyle, one where people took the time to enjoy the simple things, rather than trying to accomplish a week's worth of work in a single day.

But, like all things, Burgess was beginning to fall to the lure of progress. The design of the spaceport was evidence of that. The introduction of jump drive technology nine years ago had found its way to the Sherma system only a few years later, and it provided an opportunity that its citizens could not refuse. The result was the expansion of a simple airfield designed for local shuttle operations, to one that could accommodate ships such as the Seiiki, and larger, on a regular basis. The demand had not yet come to fruition, but its use had grown with each passing year.

Connor found it ironic, the parallel between his own desire to avoid a monumental change that had been put before him, and the desire of many of the Burgeans to keep their simple way of life intact. Especially since it had been Nathan Scott—the man from whom Connor had been cloned, and whose memories were locked up inside him—who had placed the specter of change in front of them.

You're thinking too much, again.

Connor sighed and cleared his mind. All around him, the Ghatazhak flight ops ramp was bustling with activity. There were now three boxcars being loaded, instead of the usual one that Connor had seen before. In addition, two rather ancient Palean deep space interceptors, both of which had been heavily modified, were in the process of refueling. It was by far the busiest Connor had seen the Ghatazhak ramp since his arrival a few days ago.

Connor wanted to turn around and march back up the ramp to his ship, fire up its engines, and jump away from this place...perhaps from this entire region of space, never to be seen again. But he could not. Although he still hadn't made up his mind, whatever he decided, he owed the face-to-face delivery to Jessica and General Telles.

He made his way across the ramp, pausing as vehicles drove across his path. There were hundreds of people, both Ghatazhak and Burgean civilians alike, working at a near-frantic pace to get the Ghatazhak, their equipment, and their families to another world, one further removed.

But would it be far enough?

The advent of the jump drive had been an undeniable boon to the worlds of the Pentaurus sector, and beyond. Before the jump drive, the interaction between worlds as far as Burgess was an annual event, at best. Even within the Pentaurus sector, such interaction was only a few times per year. But with the jump drive, such interaction occurred on a daily basis. Some of the more popular worlds saw arrivals and departures of jump-enabled transports several times per day. It was rumored that, within the Pentaurus cluster, one could visit every world within the cluster in a single day, assuming they had the means to pay for such passage. In the short, eight and a half years since the fall of the Ta'Akar Empire, the economic structure of the cluster had completely transformed. Economies were no longer tied only to a single world, or system. Now, the economies of multiple systems were not only bound together, but also dependent upon one another to survive. The agricultural world of Ancot in the Savoy system was a prime example. Its production had quadrupled, and it was now the primary source of consumable matter for more than a dozen systems within the Pentaurus sector. It was a delicate balance that was now under threat of destabilization from the Dusahn invasion.

Connor entered the Ghatazhak flight operations office, and immediately found Jessica, General Telles, and Commander Jahal waiting for him.

"Captain," General Telles greeted.

"General," Connor replied. He nodded at Jessica and the commander as well.

"Were you able to get some sleep?" the general inquired.

Connor chuckled. "Not enough to matter."

"Understandable. I imagine it is a difficult decision."

"You don't know the half of it," Connor replied.

"I take it you heard about Ybara?" Jessica wondered.

"Yeah, I did," Connor replied. "Are you sure about that? I mean, the *entire population*?"

"It was not just Ybara's population that was destroyed," General Telles insisted. "All life, including plants. All buildings, infrastructure...all traces of the Ybaran civilization...gone. Even half the atmosphere has been blown into space. It is now a barren, uninhabitable rock, scorched beyond all recognition. It will take centuries to restore, if ever."

Connor felt a cold chill go down his spine, as if

he had witnessed something terrifying. "Any word on why?"

"The Dusahn released this," Commander Jahal said, activating his data pad and handing it to the captain.

Connor watched the video of the Ybaran representatives refusing to stand, followed by aerial footage taken by robotic drones in the atmosphere of Ybara as it was being ravaged by Dusahn energy weapons from orbit. "All this, because two old men refused to show respect for a man they had just met?"

"Precisely," the general replied.

"It's unbelievable," Connor muttered to himself. He looked at Jessica. "Who does such things?"

"The Dusahn do such things," she replied. "The *Jung* do such things."

Connor felt the pit in his stomach growing in size with each passing moment. "And you really believe you can stop them? With a few hundred men, some boxcars, and a couple of modified, old interceptors?"

General Telles took a deep breath, letting it out slowly. Then he looked Connor in the eyes as he spoke. "It is true that we may fight and *not* win. But it is *more* certain that we will *not* win, if we do *not* fight."

"And you really think that me becoming Nathan Scott will make the difference?"

General Telles recognized that Captain Tuplo's question was just as much a challenge of that belief. "I only know that it will give us a better chance at victory."

"I am not a leader," Connor argued. "I am *not* Nathan Scott."

"But you *can* be," Jessica insisted. "Don't you see, Connor? You *are* the only one who can do it.

These people...the people of the Pentaurus sector; they have all heard of Na-Tan. He delivered them from oppression. He gave them the jump drive. He gave them freedom. We think they will believe in him again, and choose to follow him into battle once again."

"To their deaths, no doubt," Connor added. "You are asking too much of me," he said, shaking his head. "You're asking me to give up everything I know. My ship, my crew, my relatively safe life. All so I can take on the responsibility for hundreds, if not thousands, of lives?"

"We are not proposing an army, Captain," General Telles pointed out.

"But, if what you say about the Dusahn is true, it will be more than just the lives of those serving under me that I will be responsible for," Connor argued. "It may very well be the lives of entire populations, just like the Ybarans."

"I realize it is an incredible responsibility, Captain," the general assured him.

"No, I don't think you do, General," Connor insisted, cutting the general off. "No disrespect intended, but you're trained to look at things more analytically, and without emotion, are you not?"

"You are correct," the general admitted. "But I am also trained in human psychology..."

"I'm sorry, but it's not the same thing."

"Connor," Jessica interrupted, "*I* know the anguish you are feeling over this. Nathan felt the same way. He never wanted to be in command. He just wanted to be one of the guys, doing his job, and enjoying life as best he could. He *loathed* the responsibilities of command. He absolutely hated it, and he *never* felt qualified or deserving of such responsibility. But he took it on, nonetheless."

"Why?" Connor asked.

"Because it was his job," Jessica replied. "It was what he had sworn to do."

"That's it," Connor declared. "That's the difference. It's not *my* job. *I* never took such an oath. Maybe *Nathan* did, but *I, Connor Tuplo,* did *not.*"

"She is mistaken," General Telles said.

"What?" Connor replied.

"I am?" Jessica added.

"It was not his oath that bound him to step up and take command," General Telles explained. "There were others who could just as easily have taken command, had he declined. But he did not. Nathan Scott did it because it was the right thing to do. It is as simple as that."

Connor had no response.

"So, now, you must ask yourself the same question, Captain," General Telles continued. "Are you the kind of man who can step up and do the right thing?"

Connor looked at the general, then at Jessica. After a long moment, he sighed. "I'm sorry, I'm not that man. I'm not Nathan Scott, and I'm certainly not Na-Tan." He could see the disappointment in both their eyes, especially Jessica's. It pained him greatly to let them both down, since he knew that there had been a special bond between Nathan Scott and both of them. "I'm sorry," he repeated, as he turned to leave.

Jessica watched in disbelief as Connor Tuplo, who in her mind *was* Nathan Scott, disappeared through the doorway, quite possibly leaving her life forever. She turned to look at the general, her eyes welling up with tears. "What do we do now?" she asked in a hoarse whisper.

"Same as we had planned," the general replied, "only without Nathan."

CHAPTER THREE

Connor walked back across the Ghatazhak ramp, this time paying little attention to the activity around him. Every sight, every sound, every minute spent on this world amongst these people only reminded him of the guilt he felt from saying no.

Josh, Dalen, Marcus, and Neli all stood in the middle of the Seiiki's cargo bay, watching Connor as he ascended the ramp.

"How long until we can lift off?" Connor inquired as he reached the top of the ramp.

"Uh, an hour, maybe," Dalen replied, confused.

Connor stopped to look at his engineer. "Why so long?"

"Uh, cuz I'm calibrating the starboard shield emitters," Dalen answered. "I didn't think we'd be going anywhere soon. I can cancel the calibration if you'd like, Cap'n."

Connor thought for a moment. "An hour will be fine," he decided.

"Where we goin'?" Josh asked.

"Rakuen," Connor replied, as he continued forward.

"That's in the Rogen sector," Josh reminded his captain. "That's two sectors away, Cap'n."

"I know where it is, Josh," Connor growled.

"Beg your pardon, Cap'n, but why are we goin' to Rakuen?" Marcus asked.

"We should be able to pick up some work there, before we head further out," Connor explained, as he headed up the short ladder to the main deck.

"How far out are we goin'?" Marcus wondered.

"As far away from all of this as we can," Connor declared as he topped the ladder.

"Then you're not gonna..."

Connor turned and cast a menacing glance at Josh, cutting him off mid-sentence. "Become Na-Tan? Of course not. What kind of fool would take on such a suicide mission?" Connor put both hands on the rail, facing aft toward his crew gathered below. "I'm taking the Seiiki as far away from the Dusahn as we can go. There are plenty of inhabited worlds out there, most of which have never even heard of a jump drive. We'll work them as we work our way across the galaxy."

"And when do we stop?" Neli wondered.

"When we find a world we truly love," Connor replied. "One we're sure we want to settle down on. Then we'll sell the Seiiki to them, clean up, and we can all retire...in style. Hell, we'll be heroes without ever even getting shot at."

"But, Cap'n," Josh began, only to be interrupted again.

"I know, they'll still come. The Dusahn, the Jung, the Ta'Akar. It doesn't matter," Connor insisted. "Don't you see, Josh? There will always be *someone* who wants to rule us all. And there's nothing we can do to change that. With any luck, if we go far enough out, we can live out our lives in peace, before the Dusahn, or the Jung, or *whoever*, find us."

Connor paused, looking at the faces of his crew. They appeared surprised. He knew that they all expected him to stay and help the Ghatazhak fight the Dusahn, although, for the life of him, he couldn't understand why. "None of you have to come with me," he sighed. "You can stay here. The Ghatazhak promised they'd provide you safe passage home.

Although you may have to wait awhile, considering that they're in the process of relocation at the moment. I'll even give you a cut of the credits in the ship's account. It ain't much, but it should at least buy anyone who wants to leave a few weeks' lodging while you find work." Connor again scanned their faces, noting their disappointment. "Look, it's the best I can do. I'm not him. I'm not Nathan Scott."

"You are, Cap'n," Marcus disagreed. "We were there when they woke you up. You may not remember that you're him, but you are."

"No, I'm not," Connor insisted angrily. "I'm a fucking copy, and a broken one at that."

"But they can fix you, Cap'n," Josh urged.

"So that I can die again?" Connor argued. "For what? So that everyone else can live? What about me? When do *I* get to live?" Connor threw his arms up in frustration. "We lift off in one hour. Anyone who doesn't want to go should pack their stuff and be off this ship before then." Connor shook his head, as he turned to go through the hatch. "That's the best I can do."

Josh looked at Marcus in disbelief.

"You all heard the captain," Marcus said. "If you want off, start packing."

"What are you going to do?" Neli asked.

"This is my home," Marcus replied. "And that's my captain," he added, pointing toward the hatch that Connor had disappeared through a moment earlier. "The name he goes by makes no difference to me."

* * *

A tap sounded on Connor's cabin door.

"Cap'n?" Dalen called from outside.

"Don't tell me you broke something else, Voss,"

Connor chided as he rose from his bunk and made his way to the door.

"No, sir," Dalen said. "Someone..."

Connor swung the door open.

"...wants to... Uh..." Dalen stepped aside, revealing Jessica standing behind him. "She wanted to see you, Cap'n."

Connor looked at Jessica, then back at Dalen. "We on schedule for liftoff?"

"Yes, sir," Dalen assured him.

Connor continued to look at Dalen. "Shouldn't you go and make sure we *stay* on schedule?"

"Yes, sir," Dalen replied, backing away.

Connor returned to his bunk, leaving the door open. "If you've come to try and change my mind..."

"Not at all," Jessica assured him, stepping inside his cabin and closing the door behind her.

"Then why are you here?" Connor asked, not looking at her.

"I just wanted to say goodbye," Jessica said.

Connor finally looked over at her, if only for a moment.

"Look," Jessica began, taking a seat at the desk next to his bunk. "I understand why you don't want to become Nathan again."

"It's not *again*," Connor reminded her.

"Right." Jessica took a breath, starting over. "I understand why you don't want to *become* Nathan Scott." A small chuckle escaped her lips. "Hell, *Nathan* didn't want to be Nathan Scott. And he certainly never wanted the kind of responsibility he ended up getting. No *sane* person would. I get that. I really do."

Connor looked at her again, longer this time. "It's not that I'm afraid," Connor insisted. "It's just that I don't see it making any real difference in the grand scheme of things."

Jessica looked puzzled. "How do you mean?"

Connor sat up at the edge of his bed, facing her. "Say I *did* become Na-Tan, and say we *did* defeat the Dusahn, or drive them out of the sector, or whatever. In a galaxy with hundreds, if not thousands, of inhabited worlds, there have got to be dozens more just like them. Defeat one, and another will simply take their place, right? I've read some history. A lot of what was lost to us out here has made it back into circulation because of the Data Ark, you know. Human history is filled with such stories. Empires rising and falling. Hundreds, thousands, millions, dying because of one man's twisted vision. Time and time again." Connor swung his feet back up onto his bunk and leaned back against the headboard. "Seems the smarter play is to stay out of the way of it all."

Jessica looked down for a moment. "Someone once told me that there were two kinds of people. The ones who help themselves, and the ones who help others." She looked up at Connor. "Neither is better than the other. They just are who they are. The key to happiness is knowing which kind of person you are, and being able to accept that."

Connor sighed. "I thought you said you weren't here to try and change my mind."

"I'm not, Connor. Really," Jessica insisted. She reached out and took his hand. "Look, I know you don't see yourself as Nathan. I get that. But to me, you *are* Nathan, and you always will be. It's the only way I can cope with his death. By believing that he is still alive, in you. And as much as I want him back, the idea that *you*, Connor Tuplo, will be somewhere out there, living a full and happy life... Well, that works for me, too."

Jessica reached out with her free hand and touched his cheek. "Goodbye, Connor Tuplo."

Connor watched as Jessica rose, walked to the door, and without looking back, opened it and disappeared from his life forever.

* * *

Connor stared at the shipboard time display on the wall of his cabin. Fifty-seven......fifty-eight...... fifty-nine... He closed his eyes for several seconds, taking slow, measured breaths as he ran every possible scenario through his head. *Staying and becoming Na-Tan. Staying and becoming Nathan Scott, but not playing the role of Na-Tan. Playing the role without becoming Nathan. Becoming Nathan Scott, but still leaving.* Despite how wrong it felt, the only smart move seemed to be to leave. The question was, would he be going alone?

He was relatively certain that Marcus would stay aboard, which meant that Neli would likely stay, as well. He doubted that Neli felt any loyalty to himself, the Seiiki, or the rest of the crew, and she certainly didn't care much for Josh. But she seemed to care a great deal for Marcus, and Marcus for her.

Josh, on the other hand, was still a question mark in Connor's mind. On the one hand, he and Josh had become good friends over the last five years, and Josh had promised to stay on board. But Loki and Josh had known each other a long time, and had been much closer. In addition, Josh always seemed to crave excitement, which was something that life as a cargo ship pilot did not normally provide.

Dalen was a complete mystery. Although somewhat scatterbrained, the young man had proven to be loyal in the past. On more than one occasion, he had stepped up when needed, and was always ready to bring an extra gun into play on those rare occasions where it was needed. But like Josh, Dalen also enjoyed excitement. And young men such as Josh and Dalen often believed themselves invincible. The romantic notion of joining a rebellion might be more than Dalen could resist.

Connor had a sudden flash. Three young men. Each of them considerably intoxicated. They were calling to him, challenging him.

Connor, eyes still closed, tried to recall more of the memory. Old buildings. Ancient looking vehicles. The design did not match anything he had seen in the Pentaurus sector. The other three men were egging him on, daring him to do something. They were walking quickly along the storefronts, nearly slipping on the icy sidewalks. It was cold...very cold. The other three men stopped at a building, pointing at the sign in the window. He grew closer, laughing. *Join the fleet! Protect the Earth!* Then suddenly the images were gone.

After a deep breath and a long sigh, Connor opened his eyes and rose from his bunk. His decision had been made. He was Connor Tuplo, and that was who he intended to be. If he had to go it alone, so be it. The Seiiki could easily be flown by one, and he could pick up a new crew in the Rogen sector.

Connor exited his cabin and headed forward, stepping through the hatch into the forward port corridor. As he passed the galley entrance, he stopped. Standing in the galley to his left was his crew; Marcus, Neli, Josh, and Dalen.

"Ship is ready for departure, Cap'n," Marcus stated.

"Shall I start the preflight?" Josh inquired.

Connor smiled. "Sure." He stepped aside as Josh passed and headed for the Seiiki's cockpit. Connor looked at Dalen, who was holding a full duffel bag. "Is this goodbye, Dalen?"

Dalen looked confused, then glanced down at the bag he was holding. "Oh, no," he assured Connor. "This is just supplies and stuff. The Ghatazhak let me raid the kitchen in the flight ops office before they started packing it up. I figured the more food we had on board, the better, right?"

"Right." Connor smiled again. "I trust you finished the calibration?"

"You bet, Cap'n," Dalen replied. "We're good to go."

"Good. You and Neli stow those supplies," Connor instructed. "We liftoff in five."

"You got it," Dalen replied.

"I'll go raise the ramp and secure the cargo deck," Marcus said as he exited the galley.

Connor said nothing to the old man as he passed. Everything he wanted to say was conveyed in the glance that they exchanged. Then he looked at Neli.

"Crew is family," she whispered, as she leaned forward, kissed him on the cheek, and turned to help Dalen put away the supplies.

It surely is, Connor thought as he watched Neli and Dalen unpack the contents of the duffel and put them away. He sighed again, exiting the galley, heading forward. There was nothing he wouldn't do to protect his family, and at that moment, he felt a lot better about his decision.

Connor could hear the Seiiki's engines spinning up. He ran his hand along the curved bulkhead that surrounded the forward lift fan, feeling its vibrations as it spun to life. He bounded quickly up the short cockpit access ladder, and moved smoothly into the pilot's seat on the left.

"Preflight is complete," Josh reported. "Reactors are online, and we'll have full power in forty seconds."

Connor donned his comm-set. "Lawrence Control, this is the Seiiki on pad six. We're ready for departure."

"*Seiiki, Lawrence Control. Stand by for departing traffic on pad six.*"

"Seiiki, standing by," Connor replied.

"Full power," Josh announced. "All systems show ready for departure."

Connor looked out the side window. In the distance they were gathered; General Telles, Commander Jahal, Deliza, Yanni, Loki, his wife and child, the two Nifelmian doctors who had given him back his life...and Jessica. They did not wave, they simply stared at the Seiiki from afar. But Connor felt as if his eyes were locked with each of theirs.

"*Seiiki, Lawrence Control. You are cleared for departure from six. Depart on heading zero two zero. Cleared to jump at three thousand.*"

Connor did not reply, continuing to stare at the people who he should have considered family just as much as his crew.

"Cap'n?" Josh called.

Connor keyed his comm-set, his eyes still fixed on the people gathered in the distance. "Seiiki is cleared to depart pad six. Fly zero two zero, jump at three thousand."

"*Safe journeys, Seiiki.*"

Connor sighed, his eyes still gazing outside. "Take us out, Josh."

* * *

Jessica and the others watched as the Seiiki climbed away, eventually disappearing behind a distant flash of blue-white light in the night sky above Lawrence. No words were exchanged among those gathered to witness their departure, and silently, each of them went off in different directions to go about their duties.

"General," Commander Jahal called.

"Yes."

"Communications reports that one of the boxcar captains, Josan Donlevy, knows where the jump freighter Morsiko-Tavi is hiding out. He believes that, if asked, he would gladly support the Ghatazhak evacuation."

"I am not familiar with this ship," General Telles replied as he turned and started walking back to the flight operations office.

"A standard flatbed hauler," Commander Jahal stated. "Originally designed for interplanetary use. Dozens have been fitted with jump drives since the fall of the empire. They are not large ships, but they can carry at least eight to twelve cargo pods."

"Who commands her?"

"Effry Tobas," Commander Jahal replied. "Ex-Corinari pilot."

"He flew with the first group of Falcons that Dumar sent," Jessica recalled. "The ones that helped us destroy the battle platform. He was one of the few Falcon pilots who made it home alive."

"Then he can be trusted," the general assumed.

"He has no love for the Jung, that's for sure," Jessica assured him.

"And if he has family on Corinair?"

"Then he could be working for the Dusahn," Commander Jahal concluded.

"Not Tobas," Jessica insisted.

"Authorize the contact, but do not divulge our location. We will have one of our combat jumpers rendezvous with the Morsiko-Tavi elsewhere, and place a squad on her decks. If Captain Tobas wishes to join us, we will welcome his assistance, but only if the captain turns over his command codes to us. We cannot allow him to send word of our location to the Dusahn."

"He's not going to like that," Jessica warned.

"He does not have to like it," the general replied. "He only has to comply." The general paused for a moment, his attention piqued by several blue-white flashes of light, high above in the night sky. The first few were small enough to be boxcars, or even shuttles, but there were too many of them. Finally, he saw an even larger flash, much higher.

"Uh-oh," Jessica mumbled.

"I do not believe trusting Captain Tobas will be an issue," General Telles said.

"Ops reports a Dusahn assault ship has just jumped into orbit, along with a half dozen fast-attack gunships," Commander Jahal announced.

"Sound the alert," the general ordered. "Activate all defenses, and get all jump ships spun up and ready to depart."

Moments after jumping into orbit over Burgess, dozens of small shuttles began pouring out of the open bay on the underside of the Dusahn assault ship. The ships fell smoothly away, firing their deceleration thrusters as they descended on the planet. Once they reached their desired speed, each ship disappeared behind its own blue-white flash of light.

————————

"It will take the Dusahn no time to discern our location," General Telles warned as he donned the last piece of his combat armor. "Assuming they do not already know."

"Falcons are fueled and ready," Commander Jahal reported as he picked up his combat helmet. "Their flight crews are climbing aboard now."

"Tell them to get airborne without haste," the general instructed as he, too, donned his helmet. "How many combat shuttles do we have?"

"Three," Jessica replied. "The other three are due shortly. We still have four boxcars on the ground, as well as one cargo shuttle. The rest won't be back for at least an hour."

"We likely will not be here in an hour," the general said. He turned back to the commander. "Our automated defense systems?"

"Charged and ready," the commander replied.

Blue-white flashes of light illuminated the interior of the Ghatazhak flight operations office.

"Dusahn troops in the perimeter," Commander Jahal warned. "They're using some sort of jump-enabled, rapid-deployment shuttles. They're jumping in all over the place."

"Telles to all Ghatazhak," the general began after tapping the comm button on the side of his helmet. "Defense plan alpha seven. Maximum force." The general headed for the door. "Let's get to work."

Jessica followed the general and the commander toward the exit, but stopped at the comms station. She quickly typed in a brief connection string, and waited. "Come on, pick up."

————————

Three men in flight suits ran toward the first

Super Falcon, bounding up the port boarding ladder as blue-white jump flashes reflected off their ships and the front of the hangar. Earsplitting claps of thunder followed each flash of light at varying intervals. The sound of automated plasma and laser cannon fire immediately filled the air, adding to the cacophony around them.

One by one, the flight crew dropped through the topside hatch into their ship. Sergeant Nama, the ship's weapons and systems operator, was the first one inside, quickly moving to his station just behind the copilot's seat. He was already powering up his console as the ship's copilot, Ensign Lassen, moved forward past him and slid into the copilot's seat on the right.

Lieutenant Teison, the Super Falcon's pilot and commanding officer, was the last one in. He tapped the overhead hatch controls, causing the hatch to slide closed. By the time he reached the pilot's seat, his copilot already had the Super Falcon's reactors spinning up, and her systems coming to life. "Turn them over as soon as the reactors reach twenty percent," he instructed as he strapped himself in.

"Already at fifteen," Ensign Lassen replied.

"Two, you up?" Sergeant Nama called over his comm-set.

Lieutenant Teison glanced to his left. "They're climbing in now, Riko."

"Damn, talk about slow," the sergeant said as he continued to activate his systems.

"Twenty percent, turning over the mains," Ensign Lassen chimed in.

"Marso was probably taking a piss or something," the lieutenant chided. "Avionics are hot."

"*One, Two. You up?*" a voice called over the comms.

Several bolts of yellow flashed across their ship's nose.

"We're taking fire!" Ensign Lassen reported.

"No! They're strays!" the lieutenant exclaimed. "Who's got flight line defense?"

"About time, Marso," the sergeant quipped.

"*Falcon One, Jevers!*" a stern voice replied. The sound of ground weapons fire echoed loud and clear over the comms.

"Check the north! We're taking strays from the north!"

"*Then get the hell off the ground,*" the stern voice replied. "*We could use some cover fire.*"

"*Combat Two, we'll be up in thirty seconds. We'll provide your cover, Sarge,*" another voice announced.

"*Make it quick,*" Sergeant Jevers replied.

"*Three will be right behind you, Two.*"

"Forty percent," Ensign Lassen reported.

The Super Falcon shook as three energy blasts slammed into her starboard side.

"I'm pretty sure *that* qualifies as taking fire!" Ensign Lassen commented.

"You got shields yet, Riko?" the lieutenant asked.

"We're on the ground, Tees!"

"So are the guys firing at us!" Ensign Lassen pointed out. "Fifty on the mains. Takeoff power in twenty, jump in forty!"

"Raise them!" the lieutenant ordered.

"It'll sever the GPU cables," the sergeant warned.

"One to Ground! Get clear! We're raising shields!" The lieutenant reached up to the overhead panel between himself and his copilot, quickly killing several breakers. "We're no longer drawing power from the ground!" He glanced outside to see the ground crew running for cover. "They're clear! Raise the damned shields!" he ordered as several more blasts slammed into their starboard side.

"Coming up!" the sergeant replied.

"Fuck! They're jumping in all over the place!" Ensign Lassen swore, pointing at the sensor display that had just come to life in the middle of the forward console.

"Guns are hot! Shields are up!" the sergeant reported. "Targeting the hostiles to starboard!"

"Two! Raise your shields!" the lieutenant ordered.

"*Already coming up!*" the reply sounded.

"Takeoff power!" Ensign Lassen reported.

Lieutenant Teison looked to his left again, at the other Super Falcon. "Two, you ready to launch?"

"*Fifteen seconds!*" Lieutenant Eski, Falcon Two's pilot, replied over the comms.

"All ground forces on the ramp! Falcon One! Heads down!" the lieutenant ordered over the comms as he pushed the lift thrusters forward. The Super Falcon rose a few meters off the tarmac, just enough to allow her ventral guns to deploy. "Riko! Sweep left to right! I'll sweep right to left!" He leaned his flight control stick to the left, causing the ship to translate sideways, while maintaining its height above the ground. Narrow streams of energy weapons fire streaked out from under their nose as the two ventral turrets swept from left to right, sending deadly bolts of plasma energy into the enemy troops. As the ship slid to port to provide cover for Falcon Two, the lieutenant twisted his flight control stick and caused his ship to yaw from right to left, holding down the trigger on the Super Falcon's wing-mounted energy cannons. Several enemy landers exploded in bright orange and yellow balls of rapidly expanding burning gases, sending debris in all directions. "Come on, Eski! We gotta go!"

———————

"For cryin' out loud! Why does he always choose us?" Sergeant Torwell complained from the open side of the combat jump shuttle.

"I'm sure it's because he likes hearing you complain all the time," Lieutenant Latfee quipped from the copilot's seat.

"It's not that I mind being the general's favorite," the sergeant explained. "It's just that he doesn't behave like most generals. The man's always jumping into the middle of shit, and getting us shot at!"

"This is the first time we've taken fire in seven years, Torwell!" Commander Kainan pointed out from the pilot's seat. "And I'm pretty sure we're going to take fire today, whether the general's on board or not!"

Sergeant Torwell continued watching the distant battle while he scanned for any sign of an approaching vehicle that might be carrying the general. Blue-white flashes, followed by screeching thunderous claps, continued to pop off in every direction. "Man, it's only a matter of time before they start jumping in around..."

A blue-white flash appeared less than ten meters away, directly to the side of the combat jumper, announced by the sharp thunder and wave of displaced air that knocked the sergeant backward into the jumper.

"Shit!" Commander Kainan exclaimed as two more flashes appeared nearby. He grabbed his flight controls and jammed his thrust lever forward, causing the jump shuttle to leap into the air.

A small, boxy-looking, Dusahn lander, only

slightly smaller than their jump shuttle, hovered ten meters away, a meter off the tarmac, its lift thrusters screaming. Doors on all four sides disappeared into the hull of the tiny ship, and four soldiers jumped to the surface, their weapons firing in all directions. They were dressed in crimson and black combat armor that covered every centimeter of their bodies, complete with combat helmets similar to those worn by the Ghatazhak. Their weapons were bulky, requiring both hands to wield, but they did so with practiced ease and precision.

Sergeant Torwell, now on his back on the deck of the main compartment, felt himself pushed down hard. As he struggled to get to his feet, several energy blasts from Dusahn ground forces slammed into the underside of the rising shuttle. Without warning, the shuttle ceased its decent. The sergeant suddenly felt much lighter, scrambling back to his feet. As he managed to attain a standing position once again, the shuttle spun quickly to starboard. Torwell grabbed the gunner's chair hanging from the turret in the center of the shuttle's main compartment ceiling, to avoid being tossed out the open side hatch. The combat shuttle's side guns opened fire as the ship spun around, its discharges flooding the open compartment with red light.

Sergeant Torwell reached over to the side console and pressed a button, causing the side hatch to slide closed, before climbing up into his gunner's chair. "Back secure!" he announced.

"I've got at least a dozen jump flashes in the air!" Lieutenant Latfee reported. "Three two zero, twenty clicks, a thousand meters up. Inbound at high speed! They've got to be attack fighters!"

"Telles, Combat One!" the commander called over

comms. "We're taking fire! We had to launch! Give us your position and we'll pick you up!"

"*Negative!*" the general responded. "*It's too hot at our location! Will advise!*"

"Copy that! We'll start maneuvering and try to provide air cover!"

"*Protect the transports!*" the general ordered.

"Understood." Commander Kainan increased his ship's thrust, causing them to climb again as he pushed his flight control stick forward to begin maneuvering. "Get that gun up, Torwell."

"What the hell do you think I'm doing!" the sergeant shouted back as he strapped himself into the gunner's chair.

"*Come on, Eski! We gotta go!*" Lieutenant Teison urged over comms.

"I need some power here, Marso!" Lieutenant Eski begged.

"Ten seconds to liftoff power!" Ensign Marso promised.

"Jesus!" the lieutenant exclaimed as he watched Falcon One hovering in front of them a few meters away, sweeping the enemy positions with a fiery wave of plasma cannon fire.

"Got power!" Ensign Marso announced.

Seven more blue-white flashes appeared nearby, most of them to port, as the lieutenant jerked the Super Falcon's lift thruster throttles forward. "Two is up!" he announced over comms.

"Deploying ventral guns," Sergeant Tillem reported from his station behind the copilot's seat.

"Concentrate on the new arrivals to port!" the lieutenant ordered.

"*Two, One!*" Lieutenant Teison called over comms.

"Follow us up! We've got inbound fast movers to the northwest!"

"Right behind you, Jasser!" Lieutenant Eski replied.

"I got five of them!" the sergeant declared.

"Falcons One and Two," General Telles barked. *"Take out the fast movers and then climb to orbit! I need that ship out of my sky!"*

"Telles, Falcon One. We're on it, sir."

"Let's go hunting, Jasser," Lieutenant Eski said, as he guided his Super Falcon into position just behind Falcon One's right wingtip.

Laura Nash stood on her front porch, transfixed by the countless flashes of light on the horizon, and the distant sounds of battle.

"What are the pretty lights?" Ania asked, pulling at her grandmother's pant leg.

Before she could answer, her sons pulled in front of the porch in one of the farm trucks, skidding to a stop in the dirt driveway.

"Is it..." Laura began to ask.

"Why didn't you answer?" her nearest son said from the driver's seat, holding up his comm-unit.

"I didn't hear..."

"Jess just called. We have to get to the bunker and wait for extraction."

"Come on, Alek! Let's go!" Drew urged from the passenger seat.

"Mom, did you hear me?" Alek wondered, noticing that his mother was still transfixed by the blue-white flashes in the distance. "Where's Pop?"

"Fixing pump four," she answered. "I'll call him," she added, finally breaking her attention away from the distant battle.

"The bunker, Mom," Alek reminded her. "And don't wait for Pop. Understood?"

"I know what to do," Laura replied, annoyed by her second oldest son's demanding tone. "Go, gather your families. We'll see you at the bunker," she instructed, shooing them off with one hand as she grabbed Ania's hand with the other.

Two blue-white flashes appeared without warning, directly in front of the onrushing flight of Dusahn fighters, streams of red plasma energy bursting out ahead of them. Seven Dusahn fighters were annihilated before they even realized they were under attack. Two more were damaged and had to maneuver wildly to avoid destruction.

The remaining seven enemy fighters broke formation, turning out in all directions, maneuvering to get a shot at the two ships that had just appeared in front of them. But both targets disappeared behind blue-white flashes before they could return fire.

"We got four!" Sergeant Nama declared with glee.

"Bullshit! We got four! You got three!"

"Hits don't count, Len," Sergeant Nama insisted. "Only kills."

"Two, One," Lieutenant Teison called over comms from the Super Falcon's pilot's seat. "Opposite break, left right. Cross attack Zed Two, in thirty."

"Cross attack Zed Two in thirty," Lieutenant Eski, the pilot of Super Falcon Two, acknowledged. *"Breaking right!"*

"Breaking left," the lieutenant added, as he pushed his Super Falcon into a steep left turn. "We good?"

"Jump drive at forty percent and climbing,"

Ensign Lassen replied from the copilot's seat. "As long as we don't jump more than a few thousand clicks at a time, we should be fine."

"Good. Jumping," the lieutenant announced as he pressed the quick jump button on the side of his flight control stick. The Super Falcon's windows suddenly became opaque, clearing a moment later after the pre-programmed, one-hundred-kilometer jump was completed. Another push on his flight control stick rolled the ship into another tight left turn. "Ready all weapons," he warned, glancing at the time display on the center of his console. "Attack jump in ten..."

The remaining seven Dusahn fighters had wisely chosen to remain spread out after the first surprise attack. However, they continued their charge toward the Ghatazhak base less than ten kilometers ahead.

Two jump flashes again appeared, this time to either side of the loose formation of fighters. Red bolts of plasma energy flashed from either side, rather than from dead ahead. From the side, the Dusahn fighters were much bigger targets. Five of the enemy ships disappeared in fiery explosions, sending clouds of debris hurtling forward along their path of flight as the two attacking ships crossed paths from either side, directly through the middle of the two remaining Dusahn fighters. More energy weapons fire leapt out from the Super Falcons as they streaked away to the left and right, and the remaining two enemy fighters were just as easily dispatched.

"*Hell, yeah!*"

"Two, One," the lieutenant called. "Form up on me and prepare to jump to orbit. We'll vector well aft

81

of the target, then jump in from behind. I want his main propulsion down."

"*Chop off his legs, so he can't run!*" Lieutenant Eski replied. "*Sounds good to me!*"

"I hope their ground forces are as easy to kill as their air support," Ensign Lassen commented as he calculated the next jump.

"I have a feeling those were the only easy kills we're going to have today," the lieutenant said.

All across the Lawrence Spaceport, as well as the nearby Ghatazhak base, Dusahn Zen-Anor troop landers appeared behind blue-white flashes of light. The landers were small, rectangular boxes, with their corners cut at forty-five-degree angles, giving them the appearance of fourteen-sided boxes, with thrusters in all corners. They had no discernible cockpit for the pilot, and were barely large enough to accommodate the four men who leapt out of each one.

After jumping in to hover a meter above the surface, a door just large enough for one man would open up on all four main vertical sides of the lander, allowing its four passengers to jump to the surface. Once relieved of their payloads, the landers would begin ascending, and, only a scant ten seconds after first appearing, would disappear behind the same flashes of light.

Once on the ground, the incoming crimson and black troops would immediately open fire, and always with specific targets in mind. They appeared undaunted by the amount of retaliatory weapons fire being hurled their way by both ground troops and automated defense turrets. While their combat armor appeared to absorb most personal energy weapons fire with relative ease, they could not withstand the energy from the automated turrets. In the first minute of the attack, the first wave of troops on the ground was easily reduced by half, but the landers kept coming, in wave after wave, and never in the same location twice.

"Kellen, Telles," the general called over his helmet comms as he continued firing at the advancing Dusahn ground forces. "Sweep to my left, between the center group and the west group. Moran, sweep right. Triple tap your targets. Their armor is heavy."

"*Kellen, copy.*"

An energy blast ricocheted off the general's shoulder, jumping skyward, but the general did not flinch, only continued firing. "Moran, Telles! You copy?"

"*Moran's dead, General!*" another voice replied.

"Willem?" the general asked, recognizing the sergeant's voice.

"*Yes, sir!*"

"Take command of Moran's platoon, Sergeant!"

"*Yes, sir!*" the sergeant acknowledged. "*Charlie, circling right!*"

"Those landers must be automated," Commander Jahal said, as he also fired at the advancing crimson and black forces. "There's not enough room in them for four men and a pilot."

"And no one flies that precisely," Jessica added as she fired three quick shots from her energy rifle into the chest of a nearby Dusahn soldier, dropping him instantly.

Two more energy blasts slammed into the barricade the three of them were crouching behind, but again, the general did not flinch.

"You might want to duck once in a while," Commander Jahal suggested.

"Lazo, Telles!" the general called over his helmet comms, ignoring his friend's warnings. "Priority targets for all turrets are the landers! Ignore the ground troops for now."

"Our turrets can take out the troops much quicker than we can," Commander Jahal reminded the general.

"The ship in orbit isn't that big," the general explained. "They must be able to turn those landers around quickly. If we take enough of them out, we can slow their rate of reinforcement."

"What are you trying to do, win this thing?" the commander replied as he continued firing.

* * *

Captain Equin studied the tactical display of the attack on the planet below. His forces were still heavily outnumbered, but the landing operation had just begun. Although he was losing men to the resistance forces on the surface, the rate of attrition was still substantially less than the rate at which he could move his Zen-Anor troops to the surface.

"Major Ofrus reports that the resistance is better organized, equipped, and trained than we had anticipated," the captain's tactical officer reported calmly.

"I suspect their level of training will be woefully inadequate," Captain Equin said with a menacing smile.

"Of course," the tactical officer agreed. "However, Lord Dusahn's orders are that any resistance is to be met with maximum force."

"Very well," the captain agreed. "You may begin bombardment. Target their population centers and infrastructure for now. Once the Zen-Anor have defeated this world's pitiful military, they will march the streets, executing anyone who still draws breath."

"You do not wish to cleanse the surface?" the tactical officer inquired, surprised.

"That will come later," the captain insisted. "After the Zen-Anor have completed their little training exercise." He turned and smiled at the tactical officer, picking up his beverage to take a sip as he reveled in the chance for the overwhelming victory that his lord had bestowed upon him. "I would like footage of the carnage," the captain added as an afterthought. "Lots of glorious immersive footage, to be enjoyed again and again."

"As you wish, Captain."

* * *

"Helm reports we're ready to jump to the Sherma system, Captain," the Glendanon's comms officer reported over the intercom.

"I'll be there in a moment," Captain Gullen replied. "I guess that ends our game, for now," the captain said to Commander Jarso, who was sitting across the table from him.

"Too bad," the commander replied, still studying the game board. "I believe I would have had you in twelve moves."

"Doubtful," the captain replied with a grin as he rose from his seat. The old captain headed for the exit, the ever-polite commander following behind.

Captain Gullen had taken a liking to the commander. He had never cared much for Takaran nobility in the past, but men like Commander Jarso were different. They had given up everything by denouncing the legality of the new Takaran government that had risen from the assassination of

Casimir Ta'Akar eight years prior, and had dedicated their lives to the protection of the Darvano and Savoy systems. They were honorable, educated, and polite, yet still had the swagger and confidence of military men who were well aware of the destructive forces they controlled. He had seen many such men before, in his years in the service of the Ta'Akar Empire. But then, as a young Corinairan forced to serve the empire, the officers of noble blood were far less considerate.

The two men entered the bridge of the Glendanon. "All set, Jonah?" Captain Gullen asked his pilot, as he took his seat in the captain's chair near the back of the small compartment.

"Aye, sir," the pilot replied. "One, twenty-two-light-year jump left to Sherma."

Commander Jarso came to stand beside the captain, looking around the cramped space.

"Not exactly the bridge of the Avendahl, I imagine," the captain said, noticing the commander's surprise.

"It is smaller than I expected, I'll admit."

"We're a cargo ship, Commander," the captain explained. "Space is money."

"I've noticed," the commander replied.

"What will we have left after the jump?" the captain asked his pilot.

"Just under eight, Captain."

"Eight?" the commander asked, confused.

"Eight light years," the captain explained. "We find it easier to talk of our jump charge in range, instead of percent of total capacity."

"But, range is also based on your speed at the time of the jump, is it not?"

"This ship doesn't do much accelerating and decelerating. Just enough to adjust for the differences between stable orbit velocities from planet to planet. So we're usually within a thousand or so kilometers per second of our average cruise speed at all times."

"Seems an awfully inaccurate way to calculate a jump."

"Maybe, but cargo ships don't usually jump in close," the captain replied, "so we have a much bigger margin of error."

"Of course."

"Distance at transition?" the captain asked the pilot.

"Just inside the orbit of the system's furthest planet, Captain. I figured you wanted to take a good look from far away before we moved in closer."

"Good thinking, Mister Osso." The captain pressed the all-call button on the side console of his command chair. "All hands, this is the captain. Stand by to jump." The captain looked at his pilot. "You may jump when ready, Mister Osso."

"Aye, sir."

"I noticed that you always warn your crew before jumping," the commander said. "Might I inquire as to why?"

"Just a courtesy, really. Lets them know we changed locations. Gives the crew a sense of travel, and cuts down on the calls to the bridge asking where we are."

"Life aboard a cargo ship is much different than that of a military ship," the commander observed.

"We like to keep it a little more casual, whenever possible," the captain explained. "But when there is work to be done, every man knows his role, and his place in the chain of command."

"Starting the jump sequencer," Mister Osso

Ryk Brown

announced. "All emitters are green, jump field generators show ready. Jumping in ten seconds."

"You might want to close your eyes," the captain warned as his pilot counted down to the jump. "Our windows don't turn opaque."

"Three..."

"Thanks for the warning," the commander replied.

"Two..."

The captain, the commander, and all four of the bridge crew closed their eyes tightly.

"One......jumping."

A blue-white flash filled the windows of the Glendanon's bridge, washing over the interior with blinding intensity.

Mister Osso opened his eyes as the flash faded, his eyes immediately going to the jump control panel. "Jump complete," he announced as his fingers danced over the navigation section of the helm. "We are now in the Sherma system," he announced after a moment, "about three point seven billion kilometers from Burgess."

"Very well," the captain replied, rising from his seat. "Maintain course and speed. Mister Axon, send a message to the Ghatazhak, and let them know we've arrived. We'll wait to hear from them before we jump the rest of the way to Burgess."

"Maintain course and speed, aye," the pilot acknowledged.

"I'll get that message out directly, sir," the comms officer assured him.

Captain Gullen turned to the commander. "Now, let's see if you were right about those twelve moves, shall we?"

"Gladly," the commander replied, stepping aside and gesturing politely for the captain to lead the way.

Captain Gullen smiled as he headed for the exit, determined to show the young man a thing or two about the ancient game of chess. But he didn't make it past the hatch.

"Captain!" the systems officer called out. "I'm picking up a large ship in orbit over Burgess."

"What kind of ship?" the captain asked, pausing.

"Unknown at this time," the young officer replied. "I'm also picking up a lot of smaller ships near her. They appear to be coming and going from the larger contact."

"Cargo shuttles, perhaps?"

"Too small, sir." The systems officer's eyes suddenly widened as he stared at the sensor display. "Captain, it's a warship! They are bombing the surface!"

Captain Gullen was suddenly more interested. "Can you determine their target?"

"We're too far out, Captain. I'm also picking up two more ships. They appear to be attacking the larger ship." The systems officer looked at Captain Gullen. "I believe they are Palean four zero twos," he said in disbelief.

"The Alliance flew Palean four zero twos against the Jung back in the Sol sector. But they retired them once they had enough Super Eagles," Commander Jarso recalled.

"They gave the last three to the Ghatazhak," Captain Gullen told the commander. "They were non-functional when the Ghatazhak left Sol. They were among the cargo that I hauled to Sherma for them."

"Then it is the Ghatazhak who are under attack," the commander realized.

"They cannot survive an orbital attack," the

captain said. "Not with only a few four zero twos. Nobody could. Not even the Ghatazhak."

"They might," the commander disagreed, "with our help."

"You have no idea what that ship's defenses might be," Captain Gullen warned. "And you are only twenty ships, Commander. The chances of your survival..."

"Twenty-one," the commander corrected, cutting him off. "And, if the Ghatazhak are, as you say, the only ones who can stand against the Dusahn, then they are worth protecting. My men and I stand ready to assist them, Captain."

"This ship carries no armaments, Commander."

"I only ask that you remain at a safe distance, so that those who survive the battle have someplace to return."

Captain Gullen sighed. "I cannot promise how long we will remain in the system," he told the commander. "But I can promise that we will remain as long as humanly possible."

———

Alarms sounded throughout the ship. Twenty men, each of them once of the noble houses of Takara, ran out onto the Glendanon's massive cargo deck. They weaved their way between stacks of cargo pods that towered like buildings on city streets all around them.

Once they reached their rows of jump fighters, the pilots climbed up onto their ships, using the fold-out boarding ladders built into the sides of the fuselages.

As they boarded their ships, cargo techs scrambled about to ensure that the departure of the Takaran fighters would not be impeded. But they had little time, as the entire deck would need to be depressurized before the doors could be opened, and the long process had already begun. In a few minutes, the air inside the massive bay would be too thin for them to breathe.

Commander Jarso slid down into his cockpit, immediately activating the canopy. As it slid closed, he donned his helmet and checked that its umbilical was still attached. With his helmet on and sealed, he buckled himself into his flight seat and pressed the restraint lock on the side. The sides of the seat changed shape, coming up over his thighs and binding him snugly into his chair.

The commander flipped on his main power and immediately started up his ship's reactor plants. His console sprung to life, and his helmet comms crackled as they came online. He kept one eye on his squadron status display, green indicators illuminating as each ship powered up.

The commander glanced outside, noting that the last of the cargo deck technicians had left the area. Soon, the massive sections of the Glendanon's cargo deck would begin to roll aft.

"Glendanon, Raker Leader. All Rakers are manned and powering up. We'll be ready for departure in one minute."

"*Raker Leader, Glendanon. We copy. We're waiting for the all clear from the deck chief before rolling back the doors. Is there enough room for you to pass above the forward cargo, or do you need us to roll back and expose the mid deck?*"

Commander Jarso activated his sensors, scanning the stacks of cargo pods in the forward half of the ship. "We can make it as far as the second section," he told the Glendanon's communications officer. "Forward of that, the stacks are too high."

"Copy that. Deck chief has given the all clear. We're rolling back the doors now. Launch when ready."

"You might want to have the first three sections rolled back by the time we return," the commander warned him. "We might be pretty well banged up by the time we get back."

"Understood. Good luck."

Orange warning lights began to flash across the length of the cargo deck, warning all that it was about to be opened to space.

"Jarso to all Rakers. There appears to be some sort of assault ship attacking Burgess. We suspect that the Ghatazhak are under attack, as well. We do not have confirmation as to the identity of the attacking forces, but it's a good bet that it's the Dusahn. If we are to stand against the Dusahn, we will need the Ghatazhak. Our mission is to destroy that ship, then fly cover while the Ghatazhak evacuate to the Glendanon. We will divide into four groups, led by myself, Rio, Gio, and Sissy. Dumdum, Razz, Mother, and Hedge will go with Rio. Red, Sticky, Shooter, and Stringbean will go with Gio. Opie, Deaf, Peanut, and Rat will follow me. The rest are with Sissy."

"Come on, Rubber," Lieutenant Commander Sistone complained. *"Why do I get all the babies?"*

"Because you're so good with children, Sissy."

"Sissy, can we play a game?" Ensign Hux teased over the comms.

"Pipe down, Hux," the commander scolded. "This is serious business. Sissy, you and the children provide close air support for the Ghatazhak at the Lawrence Spaceport."

"Any idea where that is?" Lieutenant Commander Sistone quipped.

"It'll be where all the jump flashes are concentrated," the commander replied. The flashing orange lights outside his ship suddenly changed to red. "The doors are opening now, gentlemen. As soon as the first two are open, we can slide along the top to the exit. We launch by the numbers. Once outside, everyone form up on your leaders before we jump in." Commander Jarso fired his thrusters, lifting his ship up off the deck with ease, now that the Glendanon had decreased the artificial gravity in the cargo bay to minimums. "Let's get some payback, boys. Rubber is up," he announced, as he fired his forward translation thrusters and headed up over the stacks of cargo pods toward the not-yet-opened second bay door.

* * *

"Port dorsal shields are down to thirty percent!" Sergeant Nama warned. "You think maybe you could show them our starboard shields for a change, LT?"

"I'll do what I can," Lieutenant Teison promised, as he pulled the Super Falcon into a wide right turn. "How many more passes until that damn shield of theirs comes down?"

"None of their shields are below eighty percent right now," the sergeant replied.

"We'll never survive long enough to bring even one of those shields down," Ensign Lassen said in despair.

"How about a little positivity once in a while, Tomi," the lieutenant complained as he activated the next jump.

"Okay, I'm *positive* we won't survive long enough to bring their shields down," the ensign replied as the Super Falcon's windows cycled opaque and then clear again.

"Target their number eight shield again," the lieutenant ordered as he steered the Super Falcon directly into the incoming defensive energy weapons fire.

"When the hell did the Jung get energy weapons on their ships?" Sergeant Nama asked. "I thought they only had rail guns."

"They're not Jung, remember?" the lieutenant reminded him.

"Jung, Dusahn... Same thing, right?"

"Just unload on them, Riko."

"I am!" the sergeant assured them.

The ship rocked violently as several energy bolts slammed into their forward shields.

"Fuck! You can show them our starboard side anytime, LT!" the sergeant exclaimed.

"I am!" the lieutenant yelled back.

"Two is hit! Two is hit!" Sergeant Tillem declared over the comms. *"We lost all forward shields!"*

After a pause, the lieutenant keyed his comms. "How bad?"

"Fuck!" the panicked sergeant cried out. *"We're decompressed! They're dead! Eski and Marso are both dead!"*

"Two is headed right for that ship, LT," Ensign Lassen warned.

"Len! Can you get out?" the lieutenant asked over comms.

"Get out to where, Jasser?" Ensign Lassen wondered.

The lieutenant knew it was hopeless. Even if the sergeant was able to push himself away from his crippled ship, its momentum would carry him into the enemy ship's shields, killing him instantly.

"*I'm going to try to force a reactor overload,*" the doomed sergeant reported. "*If I can time it just right, I might be able to...*"

Super Falcon One continued to shake violently as incoming energy weapons fire impacted against the starboard shields. When the sergeant's transmission cut off, both pilots looked to the sensor display as the green icon indicating the position of Super Falcon Two suddenly disappeared.

"We can't take much more of this," Sergeant Nama warned, breaking the silence. "Half our shields are below twenty percent, LT."

Lieutenant Teison said nothing. He was a Ghatazhak. Like all other Ghatazhak, his training had begun as he entered puberty, and had lasted more than a decade. He had only recently become a pilot, but the same no-fail mindset that drove him as a Ghatazhak foot soldier dictated his approach to flying. Admitting defeat while they could still fight was a difficult thing to do.

"LT," the sergeant urged.

"If we can't stop them, at least we can provide cover while the others escape," Ensign Lassen reminded his commander.

"We can stop them," the lieutenant insisted. "Tillem had the right idea."

"They took him apart before he even got close, Jasser," Ensign Lassen said.

"He was dead stick," the lieutenant argued. "We're not."

"Jasser..."

"You all know that not even half of our forces will get out alive if we don't take that ship out," the lieutenant said, looking at his copilot. "And you can be damned sure that none of our families will make it out alive."

"Maybe they won't glass the entire planet?" Sergeant Nama said hopefully.

"Are you willing to bet your wife's life on that?" Lieutenant Teison asked, looking back at the sergeant.

No one spoke for several seconds.

"It's your call, Jasser," Ensign Lassen finally said. "I'm with you either way."

The lieutenant looked over his shoulder at Sergeant Nama.

"Let's do it," the sergeant agreed.

"Coming about," the lieutenant stated, bringing the Super Falcon into a tight left turn.

"I'll get the reactors as close to critical as I can without lighting us up," Sergeant Nama said.

"Be ready to dump all available energy into the forward shields," Lieutenant Teison instructed. "We'll fire as if we're making another attack run, then kill the weapons and dump the power into the shields when we cross the safe jump point."

"Wouldn't we have a better chance if we forgot about the weapons and dumped all the power into the shields?" Sergeant Nama suggested.

"Then they'd know we were making a suicide run," the lieutenant replied. "They'd train every gun on us. You got enough power to keep the shields up against every gun?"

"Jump point in ten seconds," Ensign Lassen announced.

It was the longest, quietest ten seconds of their lives. At the end of it, the last remaining Palean four zero two, nicknamed the Super Falcon, jumped back into the Dusahn assault ship's field of defensive fire. Again, the ship shook as enemy energy bolts slammed into their weakening shields.

"Open fire," the lieutenant ordered.

"Forward shields down to twelve percent," Sergeant Nama reported.

"Twenty seconds to safe escape jump point," Ensign Lassen announced.

"Stand by to kill weapons and dump all power into the forward shields," the lieutenant instructed.

"Reactors are at one hundred and thirty-seven percent. I'm overriding the safeties to keep them climbing. They'll light up at one-forty-two," the sergeant warned.

"Ten seconds!"

"One-thirty-nine."

"Five seconds."

"It's been an honor, gentlemen," the lieutenant said as he held their course.

"Jump flashes!" Ensign Lassen exclaimed. "Bearing zero eight five, up eighteen relative! Twenty clicks! Holy shit! They're Takaran fighters!"

Lieutenant Teison pulled back hard on his flight control stick, pitching the Super Falcon up and away from the Dusahn assault ship. "Nama! Dump all power into the ventral shields, and dial those reactors back down to safe levels!"

"Falcon One to incoming Takaran fighters!" Ensign Lassen called over comms. "Identify and state intentions!"

"Falcon One, Commander Jarso of the Avendahl! Approaching with a flight of twenty jump fighters looking for some action. You boys know where we might find some?"

"I'm passing over the target right now!" Lieutenant

Teison announced. "Have at her, Commander, and welcome to the party!"

"I'm picking up another target, way out by Aluria!" Ensign Lassen reported. "Database IDs her as the Glendanon!"

Lieutenant Teison looked back at the sergeant, a broad smile on his face. "Get on the secondary and inform Telles that help has arrived."

* * *

"General! They're pounding the shit out of us!" Commander Jahal yelled over the sound of energy weapons fire and explosions. "There are pockets of us cut off all over Lawrence! By my count, we've already lost one hundred men! And we've only been fighting for ten minutes! We cannot hold! We have to retreat!"

"To where?" the general challenged, as he continued to return fire.

Another blue-white flash appeared, accompanied by a deafening clap of thunder and wave of displaced air. Only this time, it was directly behind them.

The shock wave knocked them all over. As the general got back up, four crimson and black soldiers leapt from the hovering cube, landing only a few meters from General Telles, Commander Jahal, and Lieutenant Nash. The soldier facing them immediately took aim and fired repeatedly, striking Commander Jahal in the chest and face, sending him spinning to the pavement in a smoldering heap.

General Telles, still not on his feet, returned fire, triple-tapping the nearest enemy soldier in the middle of the chest, the third round finally making its way through the crimson and red armor and into the enemy soldier's torso. He quickly fired at the next soldier, who was turning to take aim at him, but caught his weapon with his first blast. The enemy soldier's weapon sizzled and popped as the infuriated soldier cast it aside, pulled a large combat knife from his side, and lunged at the general in one smooth motion.

Jessica fired repeatedly as she got to her knees, but the other two soldiers were facing away from her, and the back of their armor seemed impenetrable.

General Telles took the lunging Dusahn soldier low, driving his shoulder into the man's upper thighs. The blow caused the soldier to flip over as he swung his blade at the general. Telles felt the man's blade bounce off the armor on his left thigh as he passed under the toppling man. He tucked neatly into a roll, continuing forward at a run. Two steps, then a leap, and the general was on top of one of the soldiers that Jessica had fired upon before. His own knife already in hand, he found the weak spot in the body armor, between the chest piece and the neck. As Telles rode the man to the ground, his knife drove deep into his clavicle, severing the enemy soldier's subclavian artery. He pushed the knife across the man's neck, opening him up before stepping off and rolling to his right to avoid energy weapons blasts from another group of four Dusahn soldiers who had just jumped in behind them.

Jessica fired four shots into the man Telles had knocked over to finish him, then concentrated her fire on the final soldier from the first group, drilling slowly into his back with each bolt of energy. The man resisted, and even tried to turn to face her. That was his mistake, as his armor was not as thick on the sides, and her energy blasts finally found the flesh they sought. As the man fell, she saw General Telles single-handedly taking on four attackers in close combat. Twisting and dodging, stabbing and punching, all four men tried in vain to take down the general. She raised her weapon to open fire, when two more flashes appeared nearby, nearly knocking her back down again. She opened fire on the nearest lander to her left, managing to strike one of the thrusters on the corner of the small ship. The enemy lander tipped to one side as its four doors opened. Two of the men fell out, awkwardly landing on their sides. The third man managed to jump to safety, but the fourth was unable to get out before the lander struck the tarmac and exploded, killing the two men who had fallen to the ground.

Four more shots from her energy rifle dispatched the one survivor from the ill-fated lander. Jessica turned to check on the general, only to find a pile of dead bodies at his feet.

General Telles picked up the nearest Dusahn energy weapon and opened fire on the four men who had just jumped out of a nearby lander, taking them down one by one.

Jessica raised her weapon to fire on the departing lander, but it exploded before she could pull the trigger. She ducked instinctively as a combat jump shuttle streaked low over them, weapons blazing, firing into the forces advancing behind them. She turned back to the general, who was now standing amongst a second pile of dead Dusahn soldiers, firing at yet another lander that had just jumped in nearby. Four more Ghatazhak were running toward the general from the west, and Jessica finally felt as if she had a chance to catch her breath.

"General!" Sergeant Anwar yelled as he and his men approached. "What are your orders?"

General Telles looked surprised at the question. "We fight! What else?"

"*Telles, Falcon One! Do you read?*" Jessica's helmet comms crackled. "Falcon One! Go for Nash!"

"*Lieutenant! Twenty-one fighters from the Avendahl just jumped in to join the fight! They're attacking the Dusahn ship now!*"

"What?" Jessica called back. "Where'd they come from?"

"Did you not get the word?" Sergeant Anwar wondered.

General Telles checked his comms, but found them dead.

"*The Glendanon is here! Near Aluria! They are standing by to evacuate us!*" Ensign Lassen explained.

"The Glendanon is here!" Jessica told General Telles. "Twenty-one of the Avendahl's fighters are attacking the Dusahn assault ship in orbit."

"They must destroy that ship," the general said as he removed his damaged helmet, tossing it aside.

"*Nash! Combat One! Is the general all right?*"

"He's fine!" Jessica replied. "His comms are fried!"

"*We managed to push the bastards back a bit! And it looks like there's a lull in the landers for the moment. We can extract you now.*"

"General, Combat One says they can pick you up, but it's got to be now."

"Yes, yes. Now, we have a chance."

"Combat One, Nash! Go for extraction!"

"*Combat One, inbound!*"

"We will take to the air," the general decided. "From there, we can coordinate the evacuation."

The combat jumper streaked overhead again, blasting away at the nearest Dusahn troops before turning back to start their descent.

"One of the cargo shuttles is ready to depart," Sergeant Anwar told the general. "They are carrying Ghatazhak families."

"At least they now have a nearby destination," General Telles commented. "That should speed up the process."

The combat jump shuttle came down behind them, bouncing slightly as its gear touched the tarmac.

"I'm not going," Jessica told the general.

General Telles looked at her, ready to scold her for her insubordination, but knew what she was about to say. "Very well. See to your family. Get them back here if you can. If not, get them someplace safe, until we can come back for them."

"You know there's no place safe for them, none of them. Not on Burgess," Jessica argued. "Even if we destroy that ship, they'll send another! And just as soon as they can, they'll glass this world, and kill every living thing on it! All because of us!"

"Not because of us!" the general disagreed. "Because they are Jung!"

"*We gotta go!*" Sergeant Torwell called over Jessica's helmet comms.

"We will go with you," Sergeant Anwar told Jessica.

"What about *your* families?"

"I have no family on Burgess," Sergeant Anwar told her. "And neither do Jorsen or Basquer."

"What about you?" Jessica asked, looking at the fourth Ghatazhak.

"My wife and son are already on the cargo shuttle!" he replied. "Now, let's go and get this done so I can join them!"

"Retreat to the back side of the hangar!" General

Telles suggested. "Take one of the haulers!" He reached out and put his hand on her shoulder armor. "Good luck, Lieutenant!"

Jessica watched momentarily as the general turned and walked confidently to the combat jumper.

"Shall we, Lieutenant?" Sergeant Anwar urged.

"Let's move out!" she yelled over the sound of the combat jumper's engines as it lifted off a few meters away from them.

* * *

Five Takaran fighters appeared from behind five simultaneous flashes of blue-white light, only a few kilometers to starboard of the Dusahn assault ship. The ships began maneuvering erratically to avoid being tracked by the Dusahn defensive turrets. As they maneuvered, they fired their main plasma cannons, timing their shots to target the same shield, in the hopes of overloading the emitters that formed it.

But the Dusahn defenses were swift and accurate. Within seconds of appearing, the Takaran fighters were taking multiple direct hits on their own forward shields, forcing them to break off their attack run earlier than hoped, and jump to safety.

Undaunted, the pilots from the once-proud ship Avendahl, continued their attack, jumping in from multiple angles with the hope of confusing the Dusahn defenses. But their weapons were not powerful enough to disable even a single section of the enemy assault ship's shields.

———————

"This is getting us nowhere, fast!" Ensign Capra complained over comms.

Commander Jarso rolled right and pitched up, ending his latest attack run, activating his jump drive once he had a clear jump line. Eyeing his tactical display, he waited until the other four ships in his group jumped in behind him to reform before keying his comms. "They are channeling their power to the side we attack."

"*How the hell do they know?*" Ensign Defforo wondered.

"They do not. They are maintaining just enough power in all shields to prevent them from falling under a single attack pass. Once we jump in, they shift power to beef up that shield, replacing the drain as we jump out," the commander surmised.

"*What if we swarm attack?*" Ensign Oppert suggested. "*All twenty-one ships at once, on the same shield.*"

"The attack corridor on a single shield is too narrow," Commander Jarso explained as he completed his turn inbound. "We would be too clustered, and would be easy to target."

"*No room to maneuver, either,*" Ensign Dakus added.

"Precisely."

Commander Jarso sighed. "We must divide further... Attack from as many different angles as possible, simultaneously. We must make it impossible for them to accurately target our ships. We must force them to distribute power equally to all shields."

"*That will take forever!*"

"Deaf follows Opie and attacks ventral port side. Rat follows Peanut, ventral starboard."

"*What are you going to do, Rubber?*" Ensign Oppert wondered.

"I'll loiter until I pass the word to all Rakers, then I'm going to target those landers as they come and go. If we can't kill that ship, maybe we can impede her ability to put troops on the surface," the commander explained. "Break formation and get to work. I'm going in solo."

Commander Jarso did not wait for an answer, but tapped his jump button several times in succession to move ahead ten kilometers at a time. He much preferred the "skipping" method of jump combat, as it allowed him to be more creative.

A few more jumps, and he was bearing down on the Dusahn assault ship again, coming at her from behind and slightly above. As he opened fire on her stern, five jump flashes appeared below, to his left. He glanced at his tactical display to ID the Rakers as he jinked his fighter about to avoid being targeted by the Dusahn's defensive weapons. "Gio flight! Rubber! Next jump to delta tango four and hold for me."

"Gio to delta tango four and hold," Lieutenant Commander Giortone acknowledged. *"Gio flight, Leader. I have jump control."*

Commander Jarso pitched his fighter downward toward Burgess, sliding underneath the aft end of the Dusahn ship. With landers jumping in and out of the assault ship's ventral bays, the amount of defensive fire was greatly reduced to avoid taking out their own spacecraft. The commander picked his targets of opportunity, firing at landers as they dropped from the assault ship's bays. He picked off four of them with ease, before two of the forward ventral guns locked onto him and lit up his forward shields.

The commander rolled his ship to the right as his shields were quickly drained from the weapons fire, placing his fully charged port shields toward the incoming attack. As soon as he had a clear jump line, he pressed the jump button on his flight control stick, jumping toward the rendezvous point where he would relay the new attack plan to Lieutenant Commander Giortone and the rest of his flight.

The commander's new attack strategy would take a considerable amount of time to produce any tangible results, but it would keep the assault ship busy defending itself, instead of being free to pummel the planet below. Even better, it gave his men a better chance at survival. For it was now a numbers game, and since the enemy had more, he had to protect the few numbers they had.

"The next wave of landers is jumping in," Lieutenant Latfee told the general.

"Willem, Telles. You still alive?"

"*Are you kidding?*" the sergeant replied, the sound of multiple energy weapons fire nearly drowning out his voice. "*I'm just starting to get a good sweat on, sir!*"

"Good to hear, Sergeant," the general replied. "Move your men to the east side of the hangar. The next cargo shuttle will land there. I'm calling in another strike to the north of the hangar. Two passes by Two and Three. That should give you time to get the next group aboard the transport and away."

"*Understood,*" the sergeant replied. "*Moving now.*"

"Combat Two and Three, Telles. Strike! Pads four, five and six, to the north and west! Caution! Friendlies on the east side of the hangar. More friendlies moving from south of pad six to east side of hangar. Strike in two mikes!"

"*Combat Two, acknowledged.*"

"*Combat Three, acknowledged.*"

"Where do you want us, General?" Commander Kainan asked.

"Circle around the back side of the hangar, down

low, out of Two and Three's line of fire. Then pop up and provide cover for the cargo shuttle while they load."

"Got it!"

General Telles leaned to his right as the jumper started a left turn, the view out the port side hatch giving him a clear sight line to the nearby Dusahn positions that were about to be attacked by his combat jumpers. His forces had done well so far, managing to evacuate nearly half of their families. But his forces were rapidly dwindling.

As the combat shuttle rolled out of its turn back to level flight, the general caught sight of the city of Lawrence on the far side of the spaceport. Although the orbital bombardment of Burgess had been slowed considerably by the efforts of the Avendahl's fighters, there were still continuous plasma blasts descending from the sky. And they were not focused entirely on Lawrence, but on the surrounding areas as well. The Dusahn captain had parked his assault ship in geostationary orbit above Burgess, giving him the ability to pummel the area at will. Their only advantage was that the Dusahn captain had also chosen a low orbit, which restricted the area that his guns could reach. This meant that others on Burgess would be spared bombardment, at least for the time being. There was no doubt in his mind that, as soon as the Dusahn had gotten rid of the Ghatazhak, they would finish off the rest of the planet, making it an example, just as they had Ybara. Even if they somehow managed to rid themselves of that assault ship, more would follow, and the people of Burgess had neither the ability to defend themselves, nor sufficient transportation to evacuate even a tenth of their population in time.

Regardless of the outcome of this battle, Burgess

was doomed, and only because, eight years ago, the Ghatazhak had chosen it as their new home.

———————

Commander Jarso came out of his jump, headed straight for the underside of the Dusahn assault ship, on her starboard side. He rolled left and right, adjusted his pitch to vary his path of flight, and translated from side to side as an extra measure. His last two passes had earned him extra attention by the Dusahn defensive turrets, as he had managed to kill fourteen landers in only four passes. He rolled the jump range selector dial on his flight control stick two more clicks, taking it down to five-hundred-meter hops.

Just as the Dusahn ship's ventral and starboard defensive turrets were about to swing onto him, he pressed the jump button again, leaping ahead half a kilometer. Suddenly, the four landers that had just appeared under their host ship to return and reload were right in front of him.

Commander Jarso pressed his cannon trigger, sending blasts of plasma energy toward the helpless landers. They came apart in a rather unsatisfying fashion, as they were both low on propellant and empty of bodies. At least the Dusahn were now short four more landers.

Another press of the jump button got him clear of several volleys from the Dusahn defensive turrets, just before they impacted his already weakened shields. Four more flashes of light appeared just above and ahead of him. A glance at his tactical display identified them as Dumdum, Razz, Mother, and Hedge; Lieutenant Commander Riordan's group.

The commander rolled right, pulling his ship into a quick, ninety-degree turn, then pressed his jump button again, bringing him nearly to the nose of the assault ship. He twisted his flight control stick back to the left as he came out of his turn, swinging his ship around to face back toward the center of the enemy ship. Now flying backwards, he blasted away at three more landers that were departing the assault ship, but only managed to hit two of them.

As he was about to press his jump button to begin his evade and escape maneuvers, he saw eight Dusahn fighters fly out of the port side of the assault ship. They immediately pitched down toward the surface, then disappeared behind blue-white jump flashes. "Rio Flight! Rubber! You still nearby?" he called over his helmet comms.

"Rubber, Dumdum! We're still here!"

"Rio Flight, Rubber! New targets! Eight fast movers just launched out the port side and jumped down into the atmosphere. They have to be headed for Lawrence. Pursue and destroy."

"Understood."

Jessica held on tightly as the vehicle bounced violently, barreling down the dirt road at top speed. They were headed away from Lawrence Spaceport, into the hilly countryside where her family had established their farm when she had brought them here from Earth over six years ago...a decision she was now beginning to regret.

Though the battle was now falling far behind them, there was still the threat of plasma strikes from orbit, which even now occasionally landed nearby. Although the majority of the strikes seemed to be targeting Lawrence, its spaceport, and its surrounding infrastructure, the Dusahn seemed to have a penchant for sending every third or fourth volley into arbitrary locations. It was as if they were trying to ensure that everyone within the sound of the attack was equally terrified.

As they bounced along, she fought off visions of Ania huddled in the bunker her father and brother had built, clutching her grandmother in terror. The thought tore her up inside, a feeling she did not care for, as she knew it might inhibit her ability to make good decisions under fire. She had learned a lot over the last seven years, but she still lacked the emotional control that the rest of the Ghatazhak possessed. It was a fact that constantly annoyed her mentor, General Telles, although he himself admitted that there had been more than one occasion where her emotions had guided her toward an outcome that turned out to be more favorable than originally planned.

She feared that this would not be one of those times.

"Jump flashes," Sergeant Anwar said, his eyes gazing at the distant horizon as he drove.

Jessica scanned the horizon, unable to spot anything. A moment later she heard the screeching, thunder-like sound that always accompanied jumps into the atmosphere. "Sounds like multiple ships," she commented as she continued to look around. "There!" she exclaimed, spotting several small black dots passing low over the hilltops. They were firing at something on the ground, a fact that she almost missed as their energy bolts were disappearing behind the hills between her and the targets, only a split second after they were fired. "They're firing at..." It hit her. "They're firing at my family's farm!"

"Why would they fire at a farm?" Sergeant Anwar wondered.

"I don't know!" she replied. "Maybe they're clearing their guns or something!"

"More likely they have orders to fire at any target they see, regardless of its value," the sergeant surmised. "Poor strategy."

"Who cares about their strategy!" Jessica exclaimed. "They're shooting at my family!"

"They are shooting at everyone's families," the sergeant corrected.

His calm control of his emotions was pissing her off more so than usual. "Can't this thing go any faster?"

"It's a cargo truck, Lieutenant, not an assault vehicle."

Jessica turned and slid the back window open. "Fast movers dead ahead!" she yelled to the three men in the back. "Open fire as soon as they get in range!"

"You will only draw their fire, Lieutenant," the sergeant warned.

"That's the idea, Deno."

"More contacts to the west," Lieutenant Latfee announced. "Eight fast movers! ETA ninety seconds!"

"I was hoping that their fighter escort was more limited," the general admitted, as he watched two of his combat jump shuttles pass over the Ghatazhak flight operations ramp, blasting away at the Dusahn ground forces in an effort to keep them from advancing toward the hangar.

"Four more landers just popped in!" Sergeant Torwell warned as he swung his gun turret to the left. "Port side! Half a click!"

"Three more directly ahead!" Lieutenant Latfee reported.

"I've got them," Commander Kainan replied as

111

he opened fire with the combat jump shuttle's main guns.

"Bring us lower so I can get an angle!" the sergeant demanded.

"Dropping down!"

General Telles reached up to the side gun tucked into the overhead just above the side cargo hatch. One press of the release button and a slight downward pull brought the weapon from its storage position. Its automated deployment mechanism caused it to swing down into place, with its barrel well outside the port hatch.

The general stepped in behind the weapon and opened fire only a few seconds after the sergeant had done the same from his turret above. "Target the landers, Sergeant," he instructed as he fired on the Dusahn soldiers who had already dropped to the surface and were about to shoot at the cargo shuttle being loaded just behind the Ghatazhak hangar.

Two of the landers exploded as the other two disappeared behind blue-white jump flashes. Without instruction, the sergeant immediately joined the general in targeting the troops that the landers had delivered. In less than fifteen seconds, all sixteen of them were dead.

———————

The Ghatazhak in the back of the bouncing cargo vehicle opened fire as the eight Dusahn fighters closed on them. Plasma shots erupted on the roadway ahead, sending up massive amounts of debris as they tore the road apart. Shot by shot, the yellow balls of energy sped down the roadway toward them.

"Hang on!" Sergeant Anwar warned.

Jessica's eyes were on the approaching fighters. Her plan had worked. Their fire had lured them away from the helpless farmhouses on the surface, toward a target of at least some military significance. The sergeant's warning caused her to look forward. The rain of yellow fire was moving right toward them, and they had nowhere to go but directly ahead.

In a blinding flash of light and an ear-shattering thunderclap, they took a direct hit into the middle of their cargo bed. The force of the impact caused the vehicle to bounce into the air, coming down hard. The sergeant tried to maneuver the vehicle around the gaping holes in the roadway in front of them, but to no avail. He swerved around one, then another, but ended up nosing down into the third, the cargo truck coming to a sudden, violent stop as its nose slammed into the side of the crater, crushing it.

Jessica's ears were ringing, and her senses were blurred. Her eyes were open, but she couldn't recognize the images in front of them. Someone was yelling, but she couldn't make out what they were saying. And something was burning...nearby. She could feel the heat, and the acrid smoke burned her nose and throat.

"Are you injured?"

She finally understood the voices. "I... I don't know," she replied without thought. Another voice yelled in the distance. Something about someone being dead. And someone was missing. She felt a pair of hands pulling at her, followed by a sharp pain in her right leg, causing her to scream out in anguish.

"You're bleeding badly," the sergeant warned. "I must remove the penetrating object. It will not be pleasant."

"Just do it," she begged. She wished she hadn't. He pulled the object from her leg in a smooth, quick jerk before the last word left her lips. She screamed in pain again. A moment later, she felt cooling relief, and the pain subsided as the sergeant sprayed her leg wound with the analgesic healing compound that each of them carried.

"Two of them are breaking off and coming back around," another voice warned.

"We must find cover," the sergeant told her. "Can you move?"

"Try and stop me," she replied, summoning all her strength to climb out of the wreckage.

* * *

Connor Tuplo sat in the pilot's seat of the Seiiki, staring at the forward window as it cycled between opaque and clear with each jump in the series. A cold chill swept over him, and he turned and looked at Josh.

Josh didn't realize his captain was looking at him at first, but a moment later, he turned. "What is it?" he asked, noticing the concerned look on Connor's face.

"I'm not sure," Connor admitted. "I was just thinking..."

"About what?"

"A lot of things, I guess. But all of a sudden..." Connor stopped mid-sentence, his gaze turning downward.

Josh smiled. "You wanna go back, don't you?"

Connor looked back up at Josh. "How did you know?"

"I've known you for five years now, Cap'n. Nearly nine, if you count... You know."

Connor pressed the abort button on the series jump sequencer. "I'm turning us around," he announced, taking the flight controls.

"I'll plot a course," Josh added. His smile broadened. "You're still in there, aren't you, Nathan."

"Shut up and plot the course, Josh."

CHAPTER FOUR

Captain Tobas walked into the Morsiko-Tavi's mess hall, moving to the front of the room. Inside, his crew of ten, along with his first officer and chief engineer, were waiting patiently. "I've spoken with Josan Donlevy. He commands a boxcar, and is in orbit here above Passellus, a few thousand kilometers ahead of us. It seems he and a few other boxcars are assisting the Ghatazhak in their relocation. He's invited us to join them."

"I thought the Ghatazhak disbanded years ago," one of the crew said.

"I heard they were still on ice in the Takaran system," another mentioned.

"Apparently not," Captain Tobas replied.

"Where are they?"

"Donlevy wouldn't say, at least not until we agree to join him."

"How the hell are we supposed to decide if we don't know where we're hauling them?" his first officer asked.

"Donlevy assures me that the hops are well within our normal operating ranges," the captain told them.

"What's in it for us?" a crewman wondered.

"Well, you've heard that the Dusahn are demanding that all jump-capable ships surrender to them or face the consequences."

"What consequences?"

"Use your imagination," the captain replied. "Nothing good, I'm sure. If we surrender, we're likely out of work."

"But at least we'll be alive," one of the crew pointed out.

"Perhaps," the captain admitted.

"What are you thinking, skipper?" the chief engineer wondered.

"Well, we can't make port, unload, and get paid at this point. And we do have six days before the Dusahn start hunting us. So, I'm thinking we strike a deal with the Ghatazhak and help move them. They've got to have funds to operate, as well as propellant. After that, we decide whether to head deeper into space, or surrender to the Dusahn. Either way, at least we'll have funds in our pockets."

"What are we going to do with the cargo we have, Captain?" the load master wondered. "We've got a full load on board."

"We sell it cheap, at either the departure or destination points. Worst case, we leave it somewhere and come back for it. It's all raw ores anyway, so there are going to be buyers for it no matter where we go."

"So, you're telling us we have a say in this?" one of the more outspoken crewmen wanted to confirm.

"In this case, yeah," the captain replied. "You should all have a say. So, raise your hands if you want to surrender to the Dusahn now, and hope for the best." The captain waited a minute, but not a single hand went up. They had all seen the broadcasts from the destruction of Ybara. "Very well. At least that much is unanimous. All in favor of heading out of the sector now, and hoping to find a buyer for our cargo, raise your hands." He waited another minute, but only three hands went up.

"All in favor of assisting the Ghatazhak, and *then* deciding what to do next." The remaining hands went up. Captain Tobas sighed. "Very well. I'll call Captain Donlevy. We should be under way shortly.

Once we get a destination, I'm going to want all the acceleration you can give us," he told his chief engineer. "I'm pretty sure the Ghatazhak homeworld isn't nearby, and I want to get there with as much jump juice left over as possible, just in case."

"We'll use a good portion of our propellant," his engineer warned. "We're practically at max gross load, remember."

"*Propellant* we can *always* get," the captain replied. "*Time* can be a bit more difficult to find when you *truly* need it."

* * *

Corporal Volmara and Sergeant Anwar pulled Jessica up from the crater as the two Dusahn fighters dove toward them, opening fire. Blasts of plasma energy pounded the dirt roadway, sending debris in all directions as the explosive impacts flew toward them.

"Let's move!" the sergeant barked as he grabbed Jessica with his left arm, nearly dragging her toward the side of the road as he raised his rifle and joined the corporal in returning fire at the incoming fighters. The impacts barely missed them, the last one lifting all three of them off their feet, tossing them to the side of the road.

Jessica cried out in pain as she rolled to her side, clutching her wounded leg. Sergeant Anwar and Corporal Volmara both scrambled back up, opening fire again as the Dusahn fighters streaked overhead, then pulled up and disappeared behind flashes of blue-white light.

"They jumped away!" the corporal announced.

"They probably decided we weren't worth the extra effort," the sergeant guessed.

"They're headed for the spaceport," Jessica said, grimacing through the pain.

"Telles, Anwar," the sergeant called over his helmet comms. "You have the inbound fast movers?"

"*We have them, Sergeant,*" the general replied. "*Sit rep?*"

"We got our transport blown out from under us by those fighters. Jorsen and Basquer are gone..."

Two jump flashes appeared in the roadway, one above, and one below their position.

"Shit, we've got company," the sergeant said, raising his rifle to fire on one of the pods.

* * *

"Two more jumps, and we'll be in the atmosphere over Lawrence," Josh reported.

"You're keeping it above the transition altitude, right?" Connor asked.

"Of course," Josh replied, "although theirs is ridiculously high."

"They like their peace and quiet, I suppose," Connor said, as the windows cycled opaque, and then clear again.

"Last jump in five seconds," Josh reported. "Have you thought about what you're going to say to her?"

"To who?"

Josh smiled. "To who... To Jessica, that's who."

"I don't know," he began, as the windows cycled again. "Maybe something like..."

The windows cycled clear again, as the ship rocked and bounced at the sudden introduction into the Burgean atmosphere. Below them was the city of Lawrence and her spaceport, but both were dotted with fires and the occasional explosion, and the atmosphere was clouded by the multiple columns of smoke rising from the city. Their sensors began screaming alerts, just as a bolt of plasma energy streaked past the starboard side from above.

"...what the hell!" Connor grabbed the flight control stick and put the Seiiki into a wild, spiraling roll, just as two Dusahn fighters appeared directly behind him and opened fire. "Raise our shields!" he ordered, as he punched the intercom button. "Everyone, hang on! We're under attack!"

"Shields are coming up!" Josh replied.

"Jesus, there's four of them stuck on my ass!" Connor exclaimed. The ship shook violently as several plasma shots slammed into them. "Please tell me the shields are up!"

"They're up!" Josh assured him. "We're good!" Josh glanced at the sensor display in the Seiiki's center console. "You need to split-s to port, then twist it down to shake them!"

"Split what?"

"Let me!"

"I've got it," Connor insisted.

"Captain! Let me!" Josh urged. "It's what I do!"

"Take it!" Connor finally agreed, releasing the controls.

Josh grabbed his flight control stick and the throttles, then began his maneuvers. Their nose came right, then left, as they rolled over in ways that Connor didn't know his ship could. Finally, he put them into a spiraling dive. As they dove, each revolution became wider, and the spaceport below drew closer.

"Josh! You need to pull up!" Connor warned.

"Not yet!" Josh refused.

"If this doesn't work..."

"I know, I'm fired! Relax, Cap'n! I got this!"

"*Shit, we've got company,*" Sergeant Anwar reported over the general's comm-set. The general could hear the sound of his men's weapons firing in rapid succession.

"*Fucking landers!*" the sergeant added angrily.

"How many?"

"*Two! No, three!*" the sergeant reported. "*Above and below us. We're going to get caught in a crossfire!*"

"Can you get to cover?" the general asked.

"*Not a lot of options, sir! And Nash is injured!*"

"New contacts!" Lieutenant Latfee announced as Combat One turned hard left to avoid incoming fire from the Dusahn fighters.

"How many?" General Telles asked, continuing to fire at any Dusahn soldiers on the ground who came into his field of vision.

"Five! Four more fast movers! But they're ours!" the lieutenant exclaimed. "From the Avendahl! They're engaging the Dusahn fighters!"

"*Cargo One is lifting off,*" the pilot of the cargo jump shuttle reported.

"What about the fifth one?" the general wondered as he continued firing at enemy troops below.

"Too big and slow to be a fighter," the lieutenant reported. "Wait, four more contacts just came out from behind... Christ! What the hell?"

General Telles stopped firing, turning toward the cockpit. "What is it?"

"They're diving! They're in a spiraling dive right for us!"

"For us?"

"For the spaceport, I mean! Jesus, General. I think the other four are attacking..."

The combat shuttle suddenly banked a hard

right, as a larger ship streaked over them, heading off low, toward the city.

"It's the Seiiki!" Sergeant Torwell exclaimed from his turret at the top of the combat shuttle.

"What?"

"He's right!" Lieutenant Latfee agreed. "I'm picking up her ID codes!"

———

"Any idea what frequency the Ghatazhak use?" Connor asked as the Seiiki cleared the city and headed into the low hills to the west.

"It's in the database," Josh told him. "Under Lawrence SP Ground Two."

Connor looked at Josh, as he scrolled through the frequency data base. "Got it."

"*How bad is she hit?*" the comms crackled, the voice nearly drowned out by the sound of plasma cannon fire.

"*Leg wound!*" another voice replied. "*Bleeding controlled, but she can't move well.*"

"*Leave me here and get my family out!*"

"That's Jess," Josh realized in horror.

"*I think we can hold, as long as no more... Damn it! Two more landers!*" More weapons fire was heard over the comms.

"I've got two flashes dead ahead, in the hills," Josh said. "That's gotta be them, Cap'n."

"*God damn it, Telles! You order them to leave me here and get my family off this fucking rock!*" Jessica demanded.

"Jess! This is Josh! We're five clicks out, skimming the treetops. We'll be there in thirty seconds! Keep your heads down!"

"What are you doing, Josh?" Connor asked, not sure he wanted to hear the answer.

"Nothing I haven't done before, Cap'n."

"*Josh? Is that...*"

"Yes, it's us!" Connor answered. "Just do as he says!"

"There!" Josh declared, pointing forward. He rolled the Seiiki over on her port side at a forty-five-degree angle, then slipped the ship sideways into the narrow valley through which the roadway ran.

"Oh, shit," Connor declared, as Josh moved them down even lower. He looked forward at the troops advancing toward Jessica and the two Ghatazhak soldiers, their weapons firing. The closest group didn't even turn to look, unaware of the Seiiki's approach. Connor looked out his side window and slightly aft at the port nacelle, which was now only two meters above the road. "Oh, my God!" he said, turning back to look forward briefly. The far group of Dusahn soldiers stopped firing at Jessica and her men, and instead, targeted the Seiiki. "You're insane!"

"Hang on!" Josh yelled.

———

There was a whoosh of displaced air and several sickening thuds, followed by a blast of heat and the earsplitting scream of the Seiiki's main engines as she climbed into the sky, twisting and rolling, still pursued by two Dusahn fighters.

Jessica raised her head again, just in time to see the lifeless bodies of two Dusahn soldiers, their heads and shoulders ripped from their torsos, tumbling down the roadway toward them.

Sergeant Anwar and Corporal Volmara jumped up and opened fire on the remaining Dusahn soldiers, charging toward them as they fired.

"Jesus, Josh!" she exclaimed over her helmet comms. "You took their fucking heads off!"

Josh rolled the Seiiki to starboard as he looked over at Connor, smiling. "Heh, heh, heh," he giggled maniacally.

"You're a sick little guy," Connor declared. "You know that, don't you?"

"So I've been told."

"*Seiiki, Raker Five!*" Ensign Auklud called over the comms. "*Take the valley to the north! We're on the other side of the ridge. We can jump them from above as they follow you in!*"

"Raker Five, Seiiki!" Josh replied. "I'll line'em up, and you take'em down!"

"*Anwar! Telles! Sit rep!*" the general called over comms.

"*We're good for now!*" the sergeant replied. "*The Seiiki shook them up, and we finished them off.*"

"*You need to find cover before more landers show up,*" the general warned.

"*Cargo Two, inbound,*" another pilot reported.

"*Cargo Two, Telles. Land behind the hangar.*"

"*Cargo Two, copy.*"

"Jess!" Josh called out as he turned into the canyon, just as Raker Five had instructed. "We'll swing back and pick you up as soon as we get rid of these two pests on our back."

"*Make it quick!*" Jessica shouted back.

"*Arm up and get to the cargo bay,*" Connor instructed over the loudspeakers.

Marcus burst through the forward hatch of the cargo bay onto the landing, leaping down to the cargo deck. As he headed aft, Dalen entered the bay from the starboard landing.

"What the hell is going on?" Dalen asked in a daze, looking like he had just woken up.

"*We're going to come in low and fast, and touch down just long enough to pick them up,*" Connor continued over the loudspeakers. "*Bring the ramp level, then drop it as we land. Touchdown in thirty seconds.*"

"Land where?" Dalen asked. "Are we already at Rakuen?"

"We're back at Burgess," Marcus replied as he activated the ramp. Air rushed into the back of the Seiiki, filling the cargo deck. "Wake the hell up, kid!" he added, as he opened up the port weapons locker and pulled out two rifles.

"*The LZ is cold now, but more Dusahn landers could jump in at any moment.*"

Dalen slid down the access ladder, coming down beside Marcus. "What the fuck is going on?" he asked again, as he took the rifle that Marcus handed him and flipped on the weapon's power switch.

"The Dusahn are attacking Burgess!" Marcus yelled over the sound of the rushing air and the Seiiki's engines. He pressed the ramp controls again, stopping the ramp when it was level with the cargo deck.

"And we came back to help?" Dalen asked, still in disbelief as he donned his safety harness and headed across the cargo deck to the starboard side. Once across the deck, he hooked up his lifeline to the side safety track, then donned his comm-set. "*How the hell did he even know?*" he asked over the comms.

"Just be ready to shoot at anything that shoots

at us!" Marcus instructed as he stood, ready to drop the ramp to the surface.

———————

Jessica looked up as the Seiiki crossed only a few meters over their heads, kicking up dust and debris with her lift thrusters. Sergeant Anwar grabbed the collar of her chest armor and pulled her up, helping her climb back up onto the side of the roadway.

Two blue flashes appeared directly behind them, their thunderous claps barely audible over the sound of the Seiiki's engines. Corporal Volmara spun around and opened fire on one of the two Dusahn landers hovering a meter above the roadway, only twenty meters away from them. His first two shots hit the sides of the lander on the left, causing minimal damage. The doors on the lander slid open, revealing a Dusahn soldier directly facing him. The corporal's next four shots struck the Dusahn soldier square in the chest, burning through his armor. The soldier jerked, slumped, and fell forward from the lander as his other three comrades jumped safely to the ground. "Go!" the corporal yelled over his shoulder to Sergeant Anwar and Jessica. He continued firing as both landers began to climb, disappearing behind jump flashes a few seconds later. He quickly dropped two more soldiers, but the other five made it to cover, returning fire as they ran.

Corporal Volmara stood fast, firing with pinpoint accuracy, but he was one against five, and was without adequate cover. Yellow bolts of energy fired from three different Dusahn weapons slammed into his torso and legs, but he continued to stand and fire, covering the escape of his fellow Ghatazhak. He managed to place two shots into the face of a Dusahn soldier who poked his head up a bit too high, just before the corporal's stand was ended by three more shots to his chest, neck, and head.

Jessica struggled to keep up with the sergeant as he dragged her toward the landing Seiiki. Through her tactical helmet's face shield, she could see the Seiiki touchdown ten meters ahead of them, its cargo ramp dropping to the ground a second after. She could also see the green icon identifying the position of Corporal Volmara flash orange, then disappear completely.

Marcus and Dalen saw the corporal go down, and opened fire from either side of the top of the Seiiki's cargo ramp. Firing over the top of Jessica and the sergeant, they pounded the Dusahn position with as much fire as they could muster, but it was not enough. Their rifles were no match for the Dusahn body armor, and the Dusahn knew it. They rose from their positions, emboldened by the new attackers' lack of firepower, opening up on the Seiiki itself, no longer concerned about the two combatants the ship was attempting to rescue.

Jessica and Sergeant Anwar reached the bottom of the Seiiki's cargo ramp. The sergeant dumped Jessica onto the ramp, tossing her nearly a third of the way up in the process, after which he turned and opened fire on the advancing Dusahn soldiers.

Marcus ran down the ramp toward Jessica, still firing his woefully underpowered rifle at the advancing enemy line. Two more flashes of blue-white light appeared behind them as he reached down and grabbed Jessica by her chest armor.

Sergeant Anwar raised his rifle slightly, taking aim at one of the landers that had just jumped in, destroying the lift thrusters on either side and toppling it over. It struck the ground and exploded, just as four Dusahn soldiers were jumping from the second lander. The explosion sent the descending soldiers flying, and knocked the soldiers already on the surface to the ground.

That was what the sergeant needed. He stopped firing and ran up the ramp, grabbing Jessica by the arm and helping Marcus drag her along.

"*Go, go, go!*" Marcus yelled over their comm-sets.

Josh pushed the lift throttles forward, and the ship began to rise quickly off the surface. He glanced at the monitor at the top of the center console and noticed, on the cargo hatch camera, that Marcus and the others were having a difficult time making it up the ramp as the Seiiki climbed. Josh decreased the thrust level on the ship's forward lift fans, allowing the back of the ship to rise more quickly than its nose. Another glance at the monitor showed the three of them tumbling along the ramp toward the cargo bay as Dalen ran across the deck to activate the ramp controls.

Connor watched in amazement as his copilot flew his ship with a level of expertise he had not realized the young man possessed. Weapons fire from the Dusahn soldiers on the ground had resumed, and they were taking repeated hits in their aft ventral shields as they climbed. At the same time, four contacts suddenly appeared on the sensor display, all four moving toward them from the starboard side at considerable speed. Yet, despite all of this, Josh was grinning from ear to ear, as if he were having the time of his life.

"*Get us to my parents' farm!*" Jessica pleaded over the comms.

"Just tell me where it is," Josh replied confidently.

"I know where it is," Connor replied as he started scrolling the ground map to locate it.

"*Seiiki! Raker Six! Two bogeys at your four high, five clicks!*"

"Raker Six, Seiiki! I have four on my scope!" Josh replied.

"*Seiiki, Six. We're spoofing so they can't tell friend from foe. We'll have them in ten. Suggest you turn hard left and climb like hell.*"

Josh pushed his throttles to full power, yanked out his forward lift fans, and pitched up and left, just as four yellow bolts of plasma energy shot past them to their right.

———

"*Combat Three is down hard!*" the pilot of Combat Two reported.

"Any survivors?" General Telles asked over comms as Combat One began a climbing right turn to evade weapons fire from the ground.

"*Negative!*" Combat Two replied. "*There's no way anyone survived that impact.*"

"*Telles, Willem. I think they've stopped their advance!*"

"Kellen, Lazo, Todd! Can you confirm?" Telles inquired.

"*We seem to be holding our own on the west side,*" Lieutenant Commander Kellen replied.

"*Same to the northeast,*" Sergeant Todd added.

"*I haven't seen any more landers in the last few minutes,*" Master Sergeant Lazo reported. "*You don't suppose we shot them all down, do you?*"

"Unlikely," the general admitted.

"I'm picking up jump flashes outside of the

spaceport perimeter," Lieutenant Latfee reported from the copilot's seat. "Just inside Lawrence proper."

"Circle back to the north," the general ordered. He moved back to the side door as the jump shuttle began its turn. Squinting to see through the wind and smoke, he could barely make out Dusahn troops to the north of the Ghatazhak flight operations ramp. They were moving away from the Ghatazhak positions, back toward the city. "They're retreating," he realized. "Those pods are to pick them up!"

"That means they'll have to land to load up," the lieutenant said. "That means they'll be sitting ducks!"

"It also means the Dusahn are going to start glassing the planet!" the general concluded. "Raker Leader, this is General Telles of the Ghatazhak. Are you on frequency?"

"Telles, Commander Jarso. Affirmative."

"Jarso, Telles. The Dusahn are recalling their ground forces. Suspect they intend to glass the planet. I need you to take down that ship!"

"Telles, Jarso. We're trying, sir, but their shields are too damned powerful. The lowest we've been able to get any one section is twenty-eight percent. We just don't have anything big to throw at them!"

"Understood," the general replied. After a moment, he spoke again. "Commander Jarso, have half your forces continue the attack on the assault ship. Send the other half down to cover our evacuation, in case those ground forces change their minds."

"Understood," Commander Jarso replied.

"Telles to all Ghatazhak forces. Disengage any Dusahn forces that are withdrawing. Repeat, do not pursue withdrawing forces. Concentrate on getting our people out of here. Lazo, call the boxcars in while we have fighter cover. We need to get all our people off this world before the Dusahn glass it."

"*Understood,*" the master sergeant replied.

Lieutenant Latfee turned to look at the general. "There are at least a million people on this planet, General."

"I am well aware of that, Lieutenant," the general replied solemnly.

———

Jessica's parents sat quietly in the family bunker located on the far side of their farm. Her mother, Laura, sat with little Ania and her other grandchildren, trying to keep them distracted in the cold, poorly lit facility.

"I don't know why we even left Earth," Alek's wife muttered woefully.

"Enough," Alek said. "Besides, you know you don't mean that. You love it here, just as much as everyone else."

"A lot of good that does," she argued. "Look where we are now."

They heard a low rumble from outside.

"Did you hear that?" Drew asked.

"It came from outside," Drew's wife said.

"It's getting louder," their father realized.

The rumbling increased, then quickly turned into the distinct sound of spacecraft engines, screaming as they strained to keep something aloft. The sound quickly became overwhelming, and Jessica's father motioned for his sons to get their weapons. As they armed themselves and moved into position, Laura, along with Alek and Drew's wives, herded the children toward the back of the bunker behind the storage crates.

There was a thud, and the scream of the engines

quickly subsided. All three men prepared themselves, taking aim at the entrance to their hiding place.

A minute later came the sound of metal striking the door from outside. *"Nash family!"* a voice called from outside. *"I am Sergeant Anwar of the Ghatazhak! I was sent by your daughter, Lieutenant Jessica Nash, to rescue you!"*

"How do we know you are who you say you are?" Alek yelled back.

After a moment, the voice yelled back. *"Am I speaking with Alek, or Drew?"*

"Why would I tell you?"

Another moment passed. *"If it's Alek, Jessica says her nickname for you when she was a child was 'Butter Butt'!"*

Alek's father looked at his son in confusion. "Butter Butt?"

"Don't ask," Alek replied, lowering his rifle with obvious relief. "We're coming out!" he shouted back to the sergeant. "Please don't shoot us!" Alek went to the door, unlocked it, and pulled it open.

"Why would I shoot you?" Sergeant Anwar asked, his weapon hanging at his side.

"Sorry. But you Ghatazhak are a bit on the scary side."

"After all these years?" the sergeant retorted.

"Where's Jessica?" Laura asked, as she came out from hiding, carrying little Ania.

"She is aboard the Seiiki. You will see her momentarily."

"Why didn't she come?"

"She is injured, but she will be fine. I will take you to her now, but we must move quickly."

"Where are we going?" Alek's wife asked as they moved past the sergeant.

"*This way!*" Marcus yelled from outside.

"Away from this world."

"What?" Alek's wife said, pausing. "Why?"

"The Dusahn are about to destroy it," the sergeant explained, helping her up out of the bunker. "Please, we must hurry. We do not know how much time we have."

General Telles jumped from the combat jump shuttle as it came to a stop, hovering two meters above the Ghatazhak ramp. As soon as his feet hit the ground, the shuttle rose and started forward again, its engines screaming, pulling it into a climbing left turn, back toward the city.

"General!" Master Sergeant Lazo called out as he jogged up to his commanding officer. "All of our immediate families have been evacuated. We are now working on getting the last of the critical equipment and supplies."

"What about our civilian personnel?" the general asked. "What about *their* families?"

"I assumed that you would want the equipment and supplies first."

"Our fabricators are already safely off-world," the general reminded the master sergeant. "Our civilian support must come first. We owe them no less consideration."

"Yes, sir," the master sergeant replied. "I'll make it happen."

Lieutenant Commander Kellen walked up to the general, falling in beside him on his way to the hangar. "Getting soft in your old age, Lucius?"

"Elam was killed," the general said as he walked, ignoring his friend's wisecrack.

"I heard."

"That makes you my second, Soron."

"I know."

"It doesn't mean you get to call me Lucius, though."

"Sure it does," the lieutenant commander replied, smiling. "The last of the Dusahn troops have left the surface. I suspect the bombardment will begin shortly."

"As do I," the general agreed. "Have the men help get people into the cargo shuttle."

"Yes, sir."

"And find some commander's bars," the general added as he reached the flight operations office door. "You've just been promoted."

———

Laura and Ania ran up the Seiiki's cargo ramp toward Jessica, who was sitting on the floor, leaning up against the port bulkhead. Ania raced into Jessica's outstretched arms, wrapping her little arms around Jessica's neck, holding on as tightly as she could.

Laura Nash also hugged her daughter, then looked at the wound on her thigh. "Are you all right?"

"I'm okay, Mom."

"My God, Jess, it looks terrible. Are you sure?"

"Trust me, I've had much worse."

Explosions rocked the ship as bolts of plasma energy began to strike the surface nearby.

"*Is everyone in?*" Connor asked over the comms.

"Almost, Cap'n," Marcus replied. "Let's go, people!" he urged them as Alek and Drew guided their families up the ramp. Marcus moved over to the ramp controls on the side of the cargo bay hatch as Sergeant Anwar and Dalen came running up.

"That's it! Let's go!" Marcus said over his comm-set as he pressed the button to raise the Seiiki's cargo ramp and seal up the bay.

———

The building shook as bolts of plasma energy fired from orbit smashed into the surface all over the spaceport. Four impacts sounded in rapid succession, with the last one coming extremely close to the hangar. There was a sudden explosion outside, and the office shook violently. There was a terrible sound, like the tearing of metal, followed by two more secondary explosions.

"*Two is down!*" someone cried out over comms. "*Oh, my God! Cargo Two!*"

Telles ran back outside. The far corner of the hangar was gone, and the entire eastern side of the building was ablaze. He ran over to Commander Kellen, who had been knocked from his feet by the explosion. "Are you injured?" he asked as he reached down to help the commander to his feet.

"I am fine," the commander insisted, shaking the effects of the blast off. He looked over at the burning wreckage mixed in with the burning building. He could see several bodies, flailing helpless in the fire, as they were burned alive. Men ran toward the fire, scrambling to help those who had survived, many of whom were badly injured. "My God, it was fully loaded. Two hundred people."

"Jarso! Telles!" the general barked over his comm-set. "I need that damned ship out of my airspace! I don't care how you do it! Just get it out of here, or none of us are going to make it off this rock alive!"

"*Telles, Box One. We're empty. Put your people in a cargo pod and we can come down and snatch them up quickly.*"

"Negative," Telles replied. "We cannot afford to

lose any more transports. This LZ is closed until further notice!"

Wave after wave of fighters appeared behind blue-white jump flashes as the Avendahl's pilots pitted their ships against the shields and guns of the Dusahn assault ship. No longer was she launching and receiving jump landers. Either she was out of fighters, or had simply decided they were not necessary, as her guns were proving effective.

"*I'm hit!*" Ensign Defforo reported.

Commander Jarso looked back and to his right, where he knew the ensign to be. The young man's fighter was in a tumbling spin, and was on a collision course with the enemy ship. "Punch out, Defforo!" the commander urged, as he fired his last volley and pitched up to get a clear jump line.

"*I'm initiating an overload and ejecting my reactor!*"

"There's no time!" the commander warned.

"*I can make it!*"

Commander Jarso waited, postponing his escape jump, hoping to see the ensign's emergency beacon on his tactical display after ejecting. Unfortunately, the Dusahn's point defenses had other plans. They had locked onto his ship and were pounding his port dorsal shields. He waited until his shields were down to ten percent, then pressed the jump button on his flight control stick.

The commander's tactical display went blank as his ship jumped to safety, only to repaint a few seconds later, albeit with information that was now a minute old. He could see the icon for his own ship on the display, making its attack run. As he brought his fighter around to jump back to the target, he saw the icon representing Ensign Defforo's ship turn yellow, indicating it had been hit. As he finished his turn and pressed his jump button again, the icon changed from yellow to flashing orange, then disappeared completely.

As his canopy cycled back to clear, he watched his tactical screen repaint. There was no icon for Ensign Defforo's emergency beacon. "Defforo! Did you get out?" he cried out, but heard no response. "Leader to all Rakers! Did anyone see Defforo punch out?"

"This is Shooter. He punched out at the last minute, sir, but he didn't get clear in time. He probably got fried by his reactor overload."

Commander Jarso glanced at his sensor screen, noticing that the Dusahn assault ship's shields were only marginally impacted by the ensign's reactor overload. Quick math told him that all of their reactors combined would not be enough. "Falcon One, Raker Leader. Four zero twos use antimatter reactors, right?"

"Falcon One, affirmative."

The commander could tell by the sound of the Falcon pilot's voice that he knew what the commander was thinking.

"We don't have ejection systems, you know," Lieutenant Teison added.

"I seem to remember as such," the commander replied solemnly.

"I'll jump out toward the Glendanon and put my crew adrift first," the lieutenant said. *"No need for all three of us to die."*

"Rubber, there's got to be a better way," Lieutenant Commander Giortone urged.

"I'm open to suggestions," the commander replied.

"Me, too," Lieutenant Teison added, half-joking.

"You know, if any of us had the hardware..." the commander began.

"*Don't sweat it,*" the lieutenant insisted. "*I'm Ghatazhak. It's what we do.*"

"*That's it! Let's go!*" Marcus said over comms.

"Get us out of here, Josh," Connor ordered.

Josh had already started pushing the throttles forward, causing the Seiiki to ascend before the captain had finished giving the order.

"Ramp is coming up," Connor reported.

"I'm taking her through the canyon to the right," Josh told him. "They'll try to zero in on us as soon as they pick up the heat of our engines. We're far enough north that the mountains might hide us from their scanners."

"They're too high, Josh," Connor argued. "They'll see us no matter what you do."

"It's just until the back is buttoned up," Josh promised. "Then I'll jump us the hell out of here."

"Bullshit, Jasser!" Ensign Lassen exclaimed. "We fight together...we die together. We are Ghatazhak as well, you know."

"Which is why you must let me do this alone, Tomi," the lieutenant insisted. "The general will need every Ghatazhak he has left to defeat the Dusahn. We die if we must, but only if we must. To do otherwise is *not* the way of the Ghatazhak, and you know it."

"Jesus, LT," Sergeant Nama begged. "You know what you're asking of us?"

"I'm not asking," the lieutenant reminded them both. "It's my call. Now gear up! Every moment you waste means more people die. More Ghatazhak die!"

* * *

"Jump complete," Mister Das reported from the Morsiko-Tavi's helm station.

Captain Tobas turned to look at his communications and systems officer, Baen Kellog. "You see anything?"

"One big contact, a few thousand kilometers ahead, just inside the orbit of Aluria. Looks like a cargo ship... A big one at that. Running her profile through the database."

"Why is she holding so far out?" Captain Tobas's executive officer, Quarren Glenn, wondered. "There's nothing on Aluria."

"Registry shows her as the Glendanon, sir," Mister Kellog reported. "I'm also picking up a cargo shuttle, Corinairan design. It just jumped in next to the Glendanon... Captain! Burgess is under attack! There's some sort of assault ship in orbit. They're bombing the hell out of Burgess! I'm picking up Takaran fighters as well! They're attacking the assault ship!"

"Are they having any effect?" the captain wondered, his concern growing.

"Not that I can see. Christ, they just lost one of their fighters! Went up like a bomb! Must've hit his reactor plant!"

"This ain't what we signed up for," the XO said to the captain, under his breath.

Captain Tobas responded with only a glance. "Any immediate threats in the area?"

"Negative, Captain," Mister Kellog replied. "The only ships nearby are the Glendanon, that Corinairan cargo shuttle, and a few boxcars that appear to be operating from the Glendanon's decks."

"Alert me of any changes," the captain instructed. "Helm, load an emergency escape jump, just to be safe. Maintain our current position relative to all targets, and maneuver as needed to maintain a clear jump line at all times."

"What do you intend to do?" Mister Glenn asked his captain.

"I intend to find out what the hell is going on," the captain replied. "Mister Kellog, use the frequency Donlevy gave us, and see if you can raise the Ghatazhak."

"Aye, Captain."

"Assuming any of them are still alive," the XO grumbled.

* * *

"*This is Captain Tobas of the jump cargo ship, Morsiko-Tavi,*" the captain announced. "*We have come to the Sherma system at the request of Captain Donlevy, to assist in your relocation.*"

"Captain Tobas, this is General Telles of the Ghatazhak," the general replied, yelling to be heard over the impacts of the Dusahn plasma weapons pummeling the surface. "Are you able to take class three cargo pods onto your decks?"

"General," Commander Kellen interrupted. "I've just received word that Lieutenant Teison is going to set his crew adrift for the Glendanon to rescue, and he is going to ram the Dusahn ship and set off his antimatter reactor."

General Telles looked at his newly promoted commander. "Then Commander Jarso is unable..."

"He has lost four ships already, and is still unable to make acceptable progress," the commander explained. "Teison is right. If he forces his reactor to destabilize as he strikes the target, it will not only take down their shields but will likely destroy the entire assault ship."

"We are carrying twelve fully loaded class one cargo pods," Captain Tobas replied, *"but we can set them adrift temporarily in order to accommodate your immediate needs."*

General Telles held up his hand. "Morsiko-Tavi, Telles. What are you carrying?"

Commander Kellen looked impatient. "General, we have little time..."

"We may not need lose another ship, *and* another good man," the general told him.

"Telles, Morsiko-Tavi. We are carrying assorted heavy ores, from the Haven system, crushed and compacted."

"That's what, forty to fifty thousand metric tons?" the general surmised, looking to the commander.

"Per pod," the commander pointed out. "At normal cruise speed for a cargo ship, that's got to be enough."

"Tell Lieutenant Teison to keep his crew aboard and stand by," the general instructed. "Morsiko-Tavi, Telles. I have a mission for you."

"That's all the more reason we should all go," Ensign Lassen argued before putting on his helmet. "What if you take a hit on the way in? What if you get injured and can't fly the ship?"

"That's what auto-flight is for," the lieutenant argued.

"Auto-flight can't take evasive action worth a damn, and you know it," the copilot continued to argue. "If it's worth one Ghatazhak life to save the rest, then it's worth all three of our lives to make *sure* the rest are saved."

"He's right, Jasser," Sergeant Nama agreed.

Lieutenant Teison did not respond. He knew they

were right. Their chances of completing the task and destroying the enemy assault ship were much better with the entire crew aboard.

"Falcon One, Kellen! Negative on the suicide run! Keep your crew and return to the engagement area in orbit. The general has another plan."

"Are you kidding me?" Ensign Lassen said in frustration. "That's twice in one day!"

"Is he kidding?" the Morsiko-Tavi's first officer wondered in dismay. "That's impossible! Does he realize the accuracy required to make that work? He does know we're a cargo ship, right?"

"Actually, it's not impossible," the pilot, Mister Das, said thoughtfully. "Our jump-nav computers use the same software that the military uses. We can jump to within a few meters accuracy. We just never do."

"But the course and speed calculations have to be perfect," Mister Glenn continued to protest. "And we'd have to know the exact course and speed the target is traveling. And what if we miss?"

"All cargo pods are fitted with self-destruct, in case they accidentally fall from orbit," the captain said. "You know that, Quarren."

"The Ghatazhak can give us the target's orbital trajectory and speed," Baen Kellog, the Morsiko-Tavi's systems and communications specialist, said. "It would be just like calculating the expected tracks of other ships in orbit in order to avoid a conflict. That's something we do all the time, Captain."

Captain Tobas sighed. "Get the target's orbital trajectory and speed."

"Yes, sir."

"Effry, are you forgetting how much all that ore is worth on the open market?"

"We're talking about lives here, Quarren," the captain replied sternly.

"Lives that are going to be lost, regardless. If we take down that ship, the Dusahn will just send another one. Not to mention the fact that by helping to destroy her, we'll move to the top of their shit list."

"Feel free to take an escape pod and go it alone, Mister Glenn," the captain said, becoming annoyed.

"Target data is coming in now, Captain," Mister Kellog reported.

"Captain, think about what you're doing," his first officer begged. "That's all I'm asking."

"I have, Quarren. I have."

"I should have an intercept course in a minute," Mister Kellog added.

"Mister Das, go to full power as soon as you have an intercept heading," the captain ordered.

"Aye, sir."

"Mister Vika," the captain called over the intercom.

"*Yes Captain,*" the load master replied.

"Prepare for emergency, simultaneous release of all cargo pods."

"*What?*"

"You heard me, Paton."

"*Yes, sir. What spread?*"

"Minimal energy," the captain explained over the intercom. "I just want them released. We'll thrust away from them gently."

"*Yes, sir. May I ask why, Captain?*"

"The Morsiko-Tavi just became a warship."

———————

"Jump complete!" Josh declared triumphantly, as the Seiiki's cockpit windows cleared, revealing the star-filled blackness of space.

"Scanning for any signs of pursuit," Connor said, looking intently at the sensor display.

"*Attention, all ships attacking the Dusahn assault ship,*" Commander Kellen's voice ordered over comms. "*Disengage and remain clear until fifteen thirty. At fifteen thirty-one, re-engage and destroy.*"

"Two jump flashes directly astern," Connor reported.

"*Attention, all ships attacking the Dusahn assault ship...*"

"Jumping!"

The windows cycled opaque, and then clear.

"Laying it over," Josh reported. He pushed the Seiiki's nose back down, bringing the ship on a new course ninety degrees off their previous track. "Jumping again."

"*Attention, all ships attacking...*"

Connor waited for the sensors to update after the second jump. After several seconds, he reported, "Nothing on our tail."

"*Attention, all ships attacking the Dusahn assault ship...*"

"All I'm picking up is the Dusahn assault ship and the fighters attacking it."

"*Disengage and remain clear until fifteen thirty. At fifteen thirty-one, re-engage and destroy.*"

"What do you think that's about?" Josh wondered.

"I don't know," Connor replied, looking at the time display. "But we're going to find out in two minutes."

"I'm going to do a few more evasive jumps, just to make sure," Josh decided. "But where do we go after that?"

"I don't know," Connor admitted. "I haven't thought that far ahead, yet."

"*You will need to jump in close before you release your cargo pods,*" General Telles advised over the Morsiko-Tavi's comms.

"How close?" Mister Glenn wondered out loud.

"Close enough so that the target doesn't have enough time to maneuver and avoid the impact, but enough time for us to maneuver to avoid the collision," the captain said. "Tell them we understand," he added, nodding at his communications technician.

"What about their guns?" Mister Glenn inquired.

"I suspect they will be more concerned with targeting the cargo pods, once they realize that we are maneuvering to avoid them," the captain explained.

"You hope."

"Mister Das, once the pods are released, you will need to quickly translate down and away, then fire the deceleration thrusters at full power as we turn. Understood?"

"Aye, sir," the pilot replied, his voice tense.

"How's our speed?" the captain asked.

"Holding at one seven zero."

"Jump point in ten seconds," Mister Kellog announced.

"Once you get a clear jump line, don't wait for my order, Mister Das. If this works, we do not want to be anywhere *near* that ship when those cargo pods hit it."

"Understood," the pilot assured him.

"Five seconds to jump," Mister Kellog began. "Three......two......one......"

"Jumping," Mister Das announced from the Morsiko-Tavi's helm.

The cargo ship's bridge had simple windows, requiring them to all close their eyes tightly during the jump. It was something they had now learned to do on instinct.

"Jump complete..."

The target they were aiming for was still too far away to be seen, but the planet it orbited was coming toward them at an alarming rate.

"Release the pods!" the captain ordered over the intercom.

"*Pods away!*" the load master replied.

"Translating down and away," the pilot reported.

The captain and his bridge crew watched in fascination as the massive cargo pod stacks began to drift upwards in unison. As their separation rate increased, the pods began to drift apart slightly.

"Firing deceleration thrusters at full power!" Mister Das announced.

"Point of no return in fifteen seconds," Mister Kellog reported.

Captain Tobas and his first officer gazed out the forward windows of the Morsiko-Tavi's bridge, as the cargo pods drifted up and ahead of the ship. With each passing second, the distance between the pods increased.

"Initiating turn to a clear jump line," the pilot announced.

"Ten seconds!"

"If they spread too far apart, half of them will miss the target," the first officer commented under his breath.

"Five seconds!"

"There's nothing we can do now but pray," the captain said, more to himself than anyone else.

"Three......two..."

"Clear jump line!" the pilot reported.

"...one..."

"Jumping!"

Captain Tobas closed his eyes tightly, holding

them that way for a full two seconds. When he opened his eyes again, the approaching ship and the planet below were gone, and only the inky, star-filled blackness of space remained.

"Oh, my God," Connor exclaimed, staring at the Seiiki's sensor display. "Did they just do what I think they did?"

Josh laughed. "They just tossed a dozen cargo pods at them!"

"Those things must weigh a few thousand tons each," Connor exclaimed. "You know how much kinetic energy that is?"

They continued to watch the sensor display, knowing that what they were seeing was at least thirty seconds old. The icon representing the Morsiko-Tavi disappeared, leaving only the cluster of smaller icons that represented the drifting cargo pods. Twenty seconds later, the icons for the cargo pods and the larger icon for the Dusahn assault ship merged.

"She's still there," Connor said in disbelief.

Commander Jarso's canopy cycled back to clear again as he came out of his jump. A quick glance at his tactical display told him that at least eight of his ships had also jumped in nearby. He did a quick scan of the Dusahn ship, and his jaw almost dropped open in shock. "Raker Leader to all Rakers! Target has no shields and is heavily damaged! Finish her off!"

"*Gio flight, follow me in,*" Lieutenant Commander Giortone ordered his pilots.

"*Rio flight, right behind you.*"

Four more ships jumped in to the commander's

port side. "Sissy! Target has no shields! Follow Rio flight in and let her have it!"

"*Hell, yeah!*" someone declared.

Commander Jarso turned to starboard, then brought his ship around to follow Gio flight toward the target. "Telles, Jarso! Target's shields are down! She's heavily damaged, and her propulsion systems appear to be offline!"

"*Raker Leader, Falcon One! Mind if we join in the fun?*"

"One, Leader! Join up and follow me in!"

"*Jarso, Telles! Finish them off, Commander!*"

"With pleasure, General. With pleasure."

Minutes later, the icon representing the Dusahn assault ship disappeared from the Seiiki's sensor display, followed by the victorious cries of the pilots who had finally finished her off.

"Hell, yeah!" Josh exclaimed with excitement. He looked over at Connor, noticing that he didn't seem as happy. "What's wrong, Cap'n? We did it!"

"All we did was buy a little time," Connor replied. "As soon as the Dusahn realize what happened, they'll send more ships. Bigger ships. And when they do, there will be nothing left."

"Take joy in every victory, for at times they may come infrequently."

Connor looked at Josh. "That sounds familiar."

"Some famous person from Earth said it," Josh replied. "From a few hundred years ago, or something."

"I didn't know you were an expert on Earth history."

"I used to read to pass the time on long recon missions during my time in the Alliance," Josh explained. "Books *you* gave me."

CHAPTER FIVE

Connor Tuplo stood at the forward end of the Seiiki's cargo deck, watching as Sergeant Anwar, a Ghatazhak med-tech, and Jessica's brothers placed Jessica on a stretcher, hoisted her up to waist level, and then carried her down the ramp. Her leg was a mess, with armor and flesh fused together. He wanted to go with her, but his responsibilities lay elsewhere.

General Telles walked up the ramp, exchanging respectful glances with Jessica as they passed each other. "She will be fine," he told Connor as he approached, noticing the concern on his face. "Thanks to you and your crew," he added, nodding in appreciation to Marcus and Dalen.

"She looks terrible," Connor replied, unconvinced.

"She has lost a lot of blood, and she will require some surgical intervention to separate her leg from the melted body armor. But her nanites will speed her healing. She should be back to full active duty in a few days."

"Nanites?" Connor wondered. He knew of the Corinairan nanites. His doctors on Corinair had used them to assist in his own recovery, after the crash. Or so they had told him. Since the fall of the empire, the Corinairan nanite technology had spread rapidly to other systems, although it was still unaffordable to most. But he had never heard of them being used prophylactically.

"All Ghatazhak maintain therapeutic levels of nanites at all times. It helps prevent illness, and speeds recovery when injured. She will receive a booster, of course, to speed her recovery even further."

"Don't they cause pain to non-Corinairans?"

"The Corinairans resolved that issue several years back, thanks to research and development sponsored by Ranni Enterprises."

"Speaking of the princess, where is she?" Josh asked as he dropped the last few rungs down the forward ladder behind the captain. "And where's Loki?"

"They were evacuated only minutes before the attack," the general replied. "They are safe aboard the Glendanon."

"For now?" Connor asked.

"The Dusahn are obviously aware of our existence, and they clearly want to be rid of us. Even more so now, I suspect."

"Yeah, I'm pretty sure taking out one of their ships pissed them off," Josh said, a small chuckle added for good measure.

"You don't seem terribly upset about all this," Connor commented.

"The loss of life and assets are regrettable," the general admitted. "But what we have learned about the Dusahn is invaluable."

"What you've *learned*?"

"They have taken control of eleven systems, and a week later, they can still only afford to send one vessel to deal with a potential military threat. This tells me that their forces are likely spread too thin, and that they expected less resistance after taking control. Their destruction of the Ybaran civilization supports this. The Ybarans were skilled warriors, but they possessed no transportation assets. They were completely reliant on Takaran ships. They were no threat to the Dusahn. The Dusahn simply used them to strike fear in the populations of their newly acquired worlds."

"How does that help?" Josh wondered.

"It means there is hope," Connor realized.

A rare smile appeared on General Telles's face. "You are in there, somewhere."

"What's next?" Connor asked.

"The Dusahn will return," the general sighed.

"How soon?" Josh asked.

"Minutes; hours; days... Impossible to tell," the general replied. "We must step up our evacuation efforts."

"You can't possibly hope to evacuate the entire planet," Josh argued.

"I have no intention of trying," the general replied in a matter-of-fact tone.

"What? Women and children, or something?" Dalen wondered.

Connor shook his head. "Only those with essential skills," he said with a somber expression on his face.

"And their immediate families, for morale purposes."

"That's awful!" Dalen protested.

"This is much bigger than one world," the general explained. "We cannot allow ourselves to think in such limited fashion."

"So you're just going to let hundreds of thousands of people die?" Dalen said in disbelief.

"He's right," Connor admitted. "This *is* much bigger than one world. It's bigger than *one sector,* in fact." He turned to General Telles. "What do you need us to do?"

"Allow us to use your ship to ferry our people from the surface to the Glendanon. Her docking arm

The Frontiers Saga Part 2: Rogue Castes - Episode #3: Resurrection

is compatible with your boarding hatch. This will speed up the evacuation process greatly."

"We can handle that," Connor replied. "People only, or do you want to move cargo as well?"

"People," the general responded. "Cargo is much easier to deal with, and at this point, is less valuable to the resistance."

The Resistance. It was the first time that Connor had thought of it in such an official fashion. He looked at Marcus.

"I'll clear the bay to make room for more passengers," Marcus assured him.

"I can have us ready to take the first load in a few minutes," Connor told the general.

"Can your crew handle the assignment without you?" the general asked.

Connor looked at Josh.

"Nothing personal, Cap'n, but I can probably fly her better by myself."

"Are you sure? She really does require two people to manage her properly."

"I can get her to the Glendanon in one piece," Josh promised. "Then, I can get Loki to fly right seat again."

"Very well," Connor replied. He looked at the general again. "What do you need me to do?"

"We need to talk, you and I."

* * *

"*The number of cargo pods we can take aboard is not the issue,*" Captain Tobas explained over the Glendanon's vid-comm. "*You're asking us to stack class one pods, filled with people, on an unshielded deck.*"

"Class one pods are pressurized," Captain Gullen

151

reminded him. "They have their own life support *and* shielding."

"*Which weren't designed for the occupancy level you're talking about,*" Captain Tobas argued. "*And their shielding isn't worth a damn. You know that.*"

"But it's only for a short time."

"*Can you truly promise me that?*"

Captain Gullen lowered his head for a moment, staring at his desk. "No, I cannot," he finally admitted.

"*The Glendanon has a closed deck. One that can be pressurized. You also have much better shielding,*" Captain Tobas said. "*Our deck is clear. Open your bays, and we will pull up alongside. You can transfer twelve of your class three pods that you wish to keep to my deck. That will give you room to accommodate at least a few thousand people. Set the rest adrift, and we'll come back to pick them up later. Let us haul the gear, Captain. You haul the lives.*"

"He has a point," the Glendanon's executive officer commented. "We also have greater power generation capabilities. Which means those class one pods don't have to run on their own reactors the whole time. That gives us more options in the long run."

Captain Gullen sighed. "Stacks of pods, filled with people packed in like sardines...with no way out."

"We can rig connector tunnels between the pods," the XO suggested. "Chain them all together, then to the ship. That will give them access to medical, the galley, the heads, everything. And it will make it a lot easier to move them off the ship through the docking arm later."

"That will take time," Captain Gullen reminded him.

"We already have five or six class one connector tunnels aboard, as well as three empty pods. We can

152

stack them at the aft end, and attach the middle pod to the hatch at the second level. That will feed directly into our crew deck."

"We'll need security to keep them from flooding into the ship and interfering with ship's operations," Captain Gullen said.

"Surely we can get a few Ghatazhak to provide security?" the XO suggested.

"I'll ask General Telles," Captain Gullen agreed.

"Have his people check to see if there are any more connector tunnels on the surface. The more the better," the XO added.

"*What do we do if the Dusahn show up?*" Captain Tobas asked over the vid-com.

"Not if, Captain," Captain Gullen replied. "When."

* * *

"This is the first time I have ever watched my ship leave without me," Connor commented as he watched the Seiiki disappear behind a blue-white flash in the waning daylight of Burgess.

"An unusual feeling, I am sure," the general said. "Walk with me?"

Connor and the general walked across the debris-strewn flight operations ramp, toward what was left of the Ghatazhak hangar. All about them were craters both big and small, scars of the battle they had just won.

"What was it you wanted to speak to me about?" Connor asked as they walked.

"I think you already know, Captain." After a few more steps, the general continued. "You see those people?" he began, pointing at the group boarding one of many cargo pods lying in the spaceport.

"Yes."

"Do you know why they are willing to climb into a giant metal box and go into space?"

"Because they have no choice?" Connor surmised.

"Precisely. Because the Dusahn left them no choice. They are being punished because they welcomed the Ghatazhak to their world. They welcomed warriors who had been cast aside by the worlds they defended. They did so not because they were warriors, but because they were people. People who needed a place to call home. Nothing more."

"And why are you telling me this?" Connor wondered.

"Because *they* are the ones who need Na-Tan," the general said, coming to a stop. "Not the Ghatazhak. The Ghatazhak follow me, because that is what they are sworn to do. They do not need hope, because they have courage. They have the courage to stand up and fight. They have the courage to do horrific things, when such things are necessary. The Ghatazhak do not fight to protect the weak, or to right injustices. We fight to protect our own. We fight to protect one another. We fight to protect our interests. We fight because we cannot live in a galaxy ruled by thugs and dictators. The Ghatazhak will never truly know peace until all such threats have been eliminated."

"I was under the assumption that the Ghatazhak were programmed to remain loyal to a particular person, or civilization," Connor said.

"We once were, it is true," the general admitted. "But that practice ended years ago. We now decide who, and what, we fight for. Today, we choose to fight for you."

"Me, Connor Tuplo, or me, as in Nathan Scott?"

"Technically, both. You see, we understand the *power* of an inspirational leader. And it is a power that we will desperately need in the coming days. The Ghatazhak now number only three hundred and forty-seven. The Dusahn likely number in the tens of thousands, at the very least. We will need them," the general said, pointing to the people boarding the cargo pods, "and others like them—thousands, if not tens of thousands of them—if we are to defeat the Dusahn."

"So, you want me to be some sort of symbol for your rebellion?"

"No, I want you to lead this rebellion."

"But I am not qualified. You and I both know that."

"Connor Tuplo may *not* be qualified, but Nathan Scott is. In fact, he is uniquely qualified." General Telles looked at Connor. "If you go through with the transfer, you will be even more qualified than Nathan Scott ever was. For you will have the memories and experiences of both men. Nathan Scott, *and* Connor Tuplo."

"But Connor Tuplo is just a cargo ship captain," Connor replied.

"One who has plied the outskirts of the Pentaurus cluster, as well as those systems that surround it. Because of this, you have a unique insight into this area of space. That, combined with Nathan's training, experience, and his ability to read a situation and react on instinct, are what we need. We need a natural-born leader, which is precisely what you are."

"Me, Connor Tuplo, or me, as in…"

"You know precisely what I mean, Connor," the general said.

"Yeah, I suppose I do." Connor stroked his beard, feeling unsure. "I'm just not sure I'm what everyone thinks I am."

"Why did you come back?" the general asked.

"Uh... I guess I just felt like it was the right thing to do."

"*That* is what makes you the *right* man."

* * *

"I hear you're looking for a copilot," Loki said, as he climbed up the ladder into the Seiiki's cockpit.

Josh turned in the pilot's seat to look aft, a big smile on his face. "I didn't think I'd be seeing you again so soon."

"Don't you mean *ever*?" Loki corrected, as he climbed into the copilot's seat.

"Something like that," Josh agreed, returning his attention to his console.

"You didn't cycle the APUs again," Loki scolded him.

"I was going to."

"Right," Loki replied doubtfully, cycling the auxiliary power units himself.

"I'm surprised your wife let you out of her sight, considering all that's happened the last week."

"I assured her we would just be doing simple passenger transfers. Nothing risky."

"And she believed you?" Josh laughed. "Has she forgotten who I am? All the adventures we had?"

"She doesn't know about most of those, Josh, and I'd like to keep it that way," Loki warned, casting a stern glance Josh's way.

"How's it going, Neli?" Josh asked over the comms.

"*Everyone's off. We're closing up now,*" she replied.

"You already do the separation checklist?" Loki asked.

"Yes, I did the separation checklist," Josh moaned. "You're as bad as Connor with all your checklists. *Real* pilots don't *need* checklists."

"Perhaps," Loki replied. "But *real* pilots use them anyway."

Josh laughed again. "You should fly with Connor. You two would get along great."

"Glendanon, Seiiki. Ready to disconnect," Loki called over the comms.

"*Seiiki, Glendanon. Disconnect in three......two...... one......*"

There was a clang of metal, followed by the hiss of escaping air as the docking clamps that held the Seiiki against the Glendanon's docking collar released their hold on the smaller ship.

"Pushing off," Josh reported as he fired the separation thrusters.

"How is he?" Loki wondered as he scanned the Seiiki's systems, checking for any anomalies.

"Nervous, unsure, freaked out," Josh replied. "Wouldn't you be?"

"*Seiiki, Glendanon. Clean release.*"

"See you on the next one," Loki replied.

Josh fired the separation thrusters again, increasing their rate of separation from the much larger cargo ship.

"Why did he change his mind?" Loki wondered.

"Not sure he did," Josh replied as he twisted his flight control stick to swing the Seiiki's nose away from the Glendanon.

"Then why did he decide to come back?"

"I don't know, to be honest," Josh replied. "He just suddenly decided to turn us around. You got the jump down ready?"

"We're jumping down?" Loki asked, surprised.

"Connor likes to save every drop of propellant we can, since we never know where the next drop is coming from."

"I guess I've been spoiled flying corporate."

"Give me fifteen down, and reduce your forward speed to fifteen hundred," Loki instructed.

"Fifteen hundred? We'll drop like a rock."

"We'll burn less fuel slowing vertically because of the forward lift fan," Loki explained.

"You sure?"

"It's just math, Josh."

"Never did like math much," Josh mumbled. "Setting her up to fall from the sky."

Loki finished entering the jump back down to Lawrence Spaceport into the jump-nav computer.

"So, is he going to do it?"

"Become Nathan?"

"What else?"

Josh sighed. "I really don't know." He looked at Loki. "I sure hope so. Think of all the new adventures we'll have."

Loki rolled his eyes. "Yeah, I'm sure Lael will *love* that."

* * *

Connor walked into the Ghatazhak medical ward, but was unprepared for what he saw. What had probably been a clean, orderly, efficient facility was now in complete chaos. The wounded were everywhere. Ghatazhak soldiers and civilian medical technicians scrambled to administer booster doses of Corinairan nanites to aid in the healing. Those who were beyond the capabilities of nanite therapy were given pain killers and sedatives, to ease them peacefully into an eternal sleep.

An image flashed in his mind. A medical bay. A young doctor, struggling to tend an overwhelming number of the wounded. A dying man. Someone important to him. His father? His brother?

His captain.

Connor exchanged glances with both Doctor Sato and Doctor Megel, both doing their best to lend aid, despite the fact that neither of them were even remotely qualified.

From a connected room, the only true doctor the Ghatazhak had stepped forth, calling for the next patient. He too was covered with blood, unable to take even a moment to clean himself from the previous patients.

Connor turned to General Telles, whom he had followed inside. "Why isn't anyone helping them?" he wondered, pointing to the people lying nearest to the entrance.

"Priorities," the general stated in hushed tones. "We must first treat those who are salvageable, those who may yet still be of service."

"Still be of service?" Connor couldn't believe what he was hearing, or what he was seeing. "How can you..."

"What you see here is but a fraction of those dead and dying, and of those soon to join them. This world is doomed. We cannot save them."

"But most of these people are still alive," Connor said, being careful to keep his voice as low as the general's.

"For now." General Telles could see the horror in Connor's eyes. "Our effectiveness, our ability to adapt, react, to fight... It would be adversely affected if we tried to evacuate these people and care for them. We barely have the ability to care for our own, let alone the tens of thousands scattered all over Lawrence."

Connor looked around again. "It's not fair."

"Life rarely is." General Telles looked at Connor again. "You are angry."

Connor thought for a moment, biting his lip. "Yeah, I'm angry."

"How angry?" the general asked.

Connor looked at him, a puzzled expression on his face.

"How angry are you?" the general repeated.

"Very angry," Connor replied, sounding uncertain.

"Who are you angry at?"

"At the Dusahn, of course."

"Angry enough to kill one of them, if he walked through the door right now?"

Connor stared at the general. He could feel his anger and frustration welling up inside him, and he felt like he was about to explode. "Yeah. Fuck, yeah."

General Telles could see Connor's emotions swelling in his eyes. He reached down and drew his sidearm from its mount on his hip, and held it up, handle-first, offering it to Connor. "So you could use this, to take the life of another man, simply because of the uniform he wore?"

"If it's the uniform of the Jung... Easily."

"You mean, of the Dusahn," the general corrected.

"Jung, Dusahn... Same thing, right?"

"Nothing is ever that black and white. As I am sure you are well aware." He again offered the weapon to Connor. "Take it. I suspect you'll need it."

"Thanks, but I have one," Connor replied.

"Consider this a needed upgrade, Captain."

"Very well." Connor checked that the weapon was powered down, then tucked it in his belt, pulling his jacket down over it. "Where is she?"

"Through that door," the general said, pointing.

Connor turned to head in the direction the general had pointed.

General Telles put his hand on Connor's shoulder

to stop him. "The anger that you feel is a potent weapon... *If* you can control it. If you cannot, then it is best that you walk away now, lest you take many others down with you."

Connor looked at him. "You're not much of a salesman, are you?"

"I will not lie to you, Captain. Not as Connor, or as Nathan. Should you choose to assume the role of Na-Tan, you will carry great responsibilities, ones that will change you forever." General Telles looked deeper into Connor's eyes. "But, I suspect that you are well aware of this fact."

Connor did not respond. He merely pulled away and continued to the door that the general had pointed toward.

He opened the door slowly, peeking inside to find Jessica sitting in a chair, her leg wrapped from hip to mid-calf in a bloody, makeshift bandage. The room was littered with more soiled bandages, and on the table next to her was a tray filled with bloody surgical instruments. On the floor next to her were the remnants of the body armor that had previously been fused with her own tissues. "Jesus," he muttered, half to himself.

"Yeah, the housekeeping here sucks," Jessica replied jokingly.

"Are you okay?" Connor asked. "You look really pale."

"Yeah, they don't have enough SPR to go around, so I passed on it. I guess I'll just have to wait for my body to make its own blood."

"Shouldn't you lie down, or something?"

"Where?" she asked, looking around the blood-spattered room. "I'm fine here. Besides, they gave me a whopper of a nanite booster. Doc says I should be ready to go in a couple days."

Connor looked at her leg, remembering what it had looked like when they carried her off his ship only an hour ago. "Doesn't seem possible."

"Yeah, well, those fifth-gen nanites are pretty remarkable. Better yet, they don't hurt at all, which is a big improvement, let me tell you. How is my family doing?"

"Fine, I suppose. General Telles sent them to the Glendanon. Something about not wanting you to be distracted."

"How's your ship?" she asked.

"Remarkably, still in one piece. Josh and Loki are shuttling people up to the Glendanon as we speak."

Jessica smiled, wincing as she adjusted herself in her seat. "It's good that they're flying together again. They're a hell of a team."

"So Josh tells me."

After an awkward silence, Jessica asked, "Why did you come back?"

"Telles asked me the same thing."

"Great minds, I suppose," she joked. "And what did you tell him?"

"That it just felt like the right thing to do."

"Just like that?"

"Just like that."

Jessica noticed the Ghatazhak weapon tucked into Connor's belt. "Nice gun."

"Yeah. Telles gave it to me. Said I was going to need it."

"He's right," Jessica agreed. "Whether you stay or go, you're still going to need it, sooner or later."

"I'm thinking I'm going to need it soon," Connor told her, a smile creeping out from behind his beard. "Real soon."

Jessica reached out and took Connor's hand, smiling back at him. "Finally."

CHAPTER SIX

"We have moved all our cargo forward, and are in the process of casting the containers adrift in orbit over Burgess, as ordered," the Glendanon's cargo master reported.

"Damn, that's a lot of credits being tossed out into space, Captain," the Glendanon's first officer pointed out.

"With any luck, we can come back and retrieve most of it later."

"We stacked the empty pods up against the aft bulkhead of the cargo bay, and joined them together with connector tunnels," the cargo master continued. "The first two class one pods full of evacuees have already been loaded and joined."

"Are we going to have enough connector tunnels?" Captain Gullen wondered.

"No, sir," the chief engineer replied. "There were only four more on Burgess. But I've got my men taking apart one of the empty class three pods and cutting it up. We can use the panels to weld together pass-through tunnels and connect the pods vertically."

"Why can't we do that to connect them side to side as well?" the first officer asked.

"The stacks can move as much as five centimeters from side to side under way, depending on how we're maneuvering. That's enough to break the welds. The pods don't move in relation to other pods in the stack, though. That cuts down on the number of connector tunnels we need."

"Just use the tunnels to connect the uppermost pods," the captain instructed.

"That's what I was thinking," his chief engineer

assured him. "People in the lower pods will have to go up to move to another stack, but that's a lot better than being completely sealed in."

"Make sure the first pod in every stack is an empty one," the captain added. "That will guarantee them a little room to spread out, at least."

"We're rigging up some makeshift heads, as well," his engineer explained. "They won't be pretty, but they'll work for now."

"How long are we expecting to have all these people on board?" the first officer wondered.

"I have no idea," Captain Gullen admitted. "No more than a few days, I hope. Just long enough to find a world to safely put them on, I imagine."

"Who's going to want them?" the first officer asked.

Captain Gullen looked at him with reproach. "They're refugees, Masel."

"They're fugitives in the eyes of the Dusahn," Masel argued. "Ones who are attempting to escape punishment for aiding and abetting those against the Dusahn. They might be afraid of suffering the same punishment. That *is* why the Dusahn do such things, isn't it? Wiping out entire worlds just to scare the shit out of everyone, to make people think twice about opposing them?"

"He's got a point, Captain," the engineer agreed. "They might even turn them over just to prove their loyalty."

"The two of you sure paint a bleak picture of humanity in the Pentaurus sector, don't you?" Captain Gullen commented.

"I'm sorry, Captain, but I'm inclined to believe that it's going to be every world for itself...at least in the foreseeable future."

Captain Gullen sighed. "Do what you can, gentlemen. And pray that we don't have to set them off on an uninhabited world."

* * *

Connor stepped out of the medical facility and into the cool night air. The area around the building was still littered with the bodies of the wounded, mixed in with those of the dead. The smell of blood and flesh, mixed with the scent of nearby fires, created an acrid aroma that seemed as if it were burning the very soul with each breath.

The medical staffing had been low inside. Out here, it was practically nonexistent. Those caring for the wounded were obviously civilians, each doing what they could to help one another. Connor wondered why they were even trying. *Surely they realized they were doomed? Surely they realized that the Dusahn would return and finish what they had started?*

Connor tried to avoid witnessing the suffering, instead looking out across the battle-scarred tarmac at the chaos outside the medical facility. There were now four boxcars being loaded, and at least a dozen class one cargo pods nearby that people were fighting to enter. Such a dichotomy.

Connor spotted General Telles, standing next to a small ground vehicle, guarded by two Ghatazhak. Next to the general was a Ghatazhak officer holding a full-immersion camera. The general signaled Connor, and he welcomed the reason not to stay and help.

"What are you doing?" Connor asked, pointing at the cameraman as he approached.

"Documenting. Propaganda is a powerful weapon," he explained. "There is something that we must do".

"What's that?" Connor asked, coming to stand in front of the general.

"There was a woman, one you probably do not remember. Jalea Torren. She was a member of the Karuzari."

"The rebels who opposed the Ta'Akar Empire," Connor said, recognizing the name. "I remember reading about them."

"She was a vile creature. Manipulative and deceitful, willing to do whatever was necessary to accomplish her goals."

"Isn't that what was needed at the time?"

"Yes, but she cared nothing for the people they were trying to liberate, nor any who fought beside her. Vengeance was her sole motivation. Vengeance for the death of her husband and child."

"Why are you telling me this?" Connor asked, raising his voice to be heard over the sound of a combat jump shuttle landing nearby.

"It was she who conjured the legend of Na-Tan to rally support for the final push that defeated the empire."

"I have read that legend as well, General," Connor said. "It says he led a fleet from the decks of a great and powerful ship. The Seiiki's a nice ship, but she's hardly great and powerful. And as for a fleet? Two cargo ships, a half dozen boxcars, and a few jump shuttles aren't going to cut it."

"I have an idea," the general said, his voice lowering in volume now that the combat jump shuttle was spooling its engines back down to idle. "But it does present some risk."

"To who?"

"To you, and to those who will care greatly about you, once you become Nathan again."

"I'm not sure I like the sound of that."

"Come, I will explain on the way. We must get someplace more quiet."

* * *

Cameron sat in her ready room aboard the Aurora, studying the latest readiness reports. "Any word on the next resupply?" she asked her executive officer.

"Command promises later today," Commander Kaplan replied. "They're finishing loading her as we speak."

"Are we getting jump missiles this time?"

"Yup. And spreaders, anti-FTL, sensor drones, comm-drones... Everything we need except crew."

Cameron sighed.

"I talked to a friend of mine from the academy. He said that command is trying to crew two more destroyers that are coming off the line in a couple days."

"Those ships haven't even been through flight trials," Cameron protested.

"Trial by fire, I suppose. Anyway, he said they're pulling ten percent of the crew from each ship in the fleet in order to crew them. Bottom line is, we're lucky they're not pulling any of *our* crew."

"So, we're stuck at seventy-five percent staffing levels then," Cameron stated irritably.

"Probably for a few more weeks, at least. My friend said he might be able to get me some new recruits who just finished basic, but we'd have to train them from the ground up."

Cameron leaned back in her chair, frustrated.

"What is it?" Commander Kaplan asked.

"We're running ourselves ragged out here, and we haven't spotted a single Jung ship in days. Not even an unconfirmed FTL trail."

"You'd prefer that we *did* find more Jung ships?" the commander wondered.

"At least it would justify all the hysteria," Cameron replied. "Have you watched any of the news broadcasts from Earth lately?"

"I try not to."

"Galiardi has the entire planet whipped into a frenzy. People are marching in the streets, demanding that we put an end to the Jung threat once and for all, before it's too late."

"What do you mean, too late?"

"The so-called experts are saying that if the Jung *do* have jump drive technology, then they obviously have just gotten it and haven't outfitted their entire fleet yet, because if they had, they would have launched an all-out attack, instead of sending a few ships in to test our response."

"Why the hell would they reveal they even *had* jump drives in the first place?" the commander wondered. "Surely they would expect us to take action."

"That's what they're saying," Cameron continued. "That the Jung *wanted* us to launch a KKV strike, so they could get the support of their own people."

"None of this makes any sense," Commander Kaplan said, throwing up her hands in frustration.

"No, it doesn't, and that's what bothers me the most," Cameron said. "You don't send ships out to be detected *and* destroyed, just to stir up a war. Not if you're the Jung." Cameron shook her head. "There is something else going on here. *Someone* doesn't want us to send ships to the Pentaurus sector. *That* much is obvious. Yet no one in command, from Galiardi on down, is saying that. Hell, the media isn't even saying that! It should be obvious to anyone with half a brain!"

"People believe what they want to believe, Cameron."

"Unfortunately, they want to believe the time for revenge has come."

* * *

"How long are we gonna keep this up?" Dalen wondered as he jogged up the Seiiki's cargo ramp.

"Until the Dusahn return, or there's no one left to evacuate," Marcus replied as he activated the ramp.

"You're kidding, right?"

"Nope."

"There's, like, a few hundred thousand people on this world, Marcus."

"You're just figuring that out now?" Marcus turned toward the people packed into the Seiiki's cargo bay behind him. "This here's a fast ride, not necessarily a smooth one. So everyone grab hold of something. A rail, your neighbor, whatever."

"How long is the trip," a nervous evacuee wondered.

"About five minutes," Marcus answered as the ramp closed and locked. "We're good back here," he reported over his headset.

―――――――

"*Good forward, as well,*" Neli reported over comms.

"Jump to orbit is loaded and ready," Loki reported.

"Lawrence Control, Seiiki. Ready for takeoff, north side of Ghatazhak hangar." Josh turned toward Loki. "Or what's left of it."

"Must've been one hell of a battle," Loki commented as he checked the ship's systems again.

"Lawrence Control, Seiiki. Ready for takeoff," Josh repeated. He looked at Loki, puzzled. "Lawrence

Control, Seiiki?" Still nothing. "Lawrence Control, anybody there?"

"I guess they have better things to do," Loki said.

"Yeah, like get in line to get off this rock, while the gettin' is good," Josh replied. "Lawrence Traffic, Seiiki is taking off from the north side of the Ghatazhak hangar. Cover your ears, we're jumping out low."

***

Ground crew and soldiers near the Seiiki moved quickly to the sides as the ship's main thrust nozzles swung downward, and, along with her forward lift fan, began spinning up to takeoff power. The wash of thrust swept over the tarmac as the ship lifted quickly off the ground. It did not execute the usual, leisurely climb and turnout that most ships did when leaving the Lawrence Spaceport. Instead, it tipped slightly left as it rotated to port, while still only a few meters off the surface. It began sliding in the direction of its turn, pitching up and accelerating as it came onto its departure heading. Then, less than thirty seconds after it had taken off, it disappeared behind a blinding flash of blue-white light that lit the spaceport up for a split second. It rocked the nearby buildings with the screech from the jump and the sound of air rushing to fill the void that the ship's departure had created in the atmosphere.

Without missing a beat, those on the ground assisting with the loading and departure of the Seiiki, immediately ran to nearby ships to help them, as well, while two boxcars appeared in the sky above them from behind their own flashes of light.

***

"Jump complete," Loki reported.

"Seriously, Loki... We've talked about this so many times."

"Sorry, old habit," Loki apologized as he switched frequencies on the Seiiki's primary comms. "Glendanon, Seiiki. Inbound for docking, in three."

––––––––––

"We'll be docking with the Glendanon in a few minutes!" Marcus barked from the forward catwalk. "Everyone needs to disembark in a quick and orderly fashion! If you see someone having a hard time negotiating the ladder, help them out. If you are unable to negotiate the ladder, step aside and let others out first! We will help you once the other passengers have passed! You will have to wait for the passengers in the forward section, and those standing in the corridors, to move off the ship before you will be able to follow! Anyone causing problems will be knocked the fuck out and dragged off the ship in an unconscious state! Please, everyone work together, so that I do not have to knock anyone the fuck out! Once on board the Glendanon, follow the instructions of her crew so that *they* do not have to knock you the fuck out!"

"Is that really necessary?" a woman complained.

"Watch it, lady," Marcus warned. "I've been known to punch women, too." Marcus looked at Dalen, who was smiling on the other side of the cargo bay.

––––––––––

"Five meters," Loki reported as the Seiiki translated slowly to port toward the Glendanon's extended docking arm. "Four......three..."

Josh pushed the base of his flight control stick gently to the right for a split second, causing the port thrusters to fire briefly, slowing their closure rate.

"Two meters..." Loki glanced at the displays. "All greens on alignments. One meter."

Josh fired the docking thrusters again. A split second later, there was a metallic thud, and the ship rocked gently.

"Contact," Loki reported. "Docking thrusters safe. Mains safe. Mag locks active. Glendanon, Seiiki has contact."

"*Positive locks. Positive seals,*" the Glendanon replied. "*Seiiki, you're go to pop the hatch.*"

"Copy that," Loki replied.

"Open up and get'em off," Josh instructed over his comm-set.

———————

"Popping the hatch," Neli replied over her comm-set. "Alright, people! Don't start moving until I call your group. When I do, move quickly toward the exit, and help each other out. Work together so we can get everyone moved off quickly. Anyone gives us any problems…"

"We heard," someone called from the back of the port corridor. "The guy in the back will knock us the fuck out!"

"Exactly!" Neli agreed. "Port side corridor! You're first! Let's go!"

The people lined up in front of her in the port corridor began moving forward single file, stepping through the boarding hatch and into the tunnel that connected the Seiiki to the Glendanon.

"Good that you can keep your sense of humor at a time like this," Neli told the man who had yelled back as he passed her on his way out.

"What else can you do?" the man replied with a shrug as he helped the young lady in front of him step through the hatch.

———————

"What's that? Twenty or thirty trips, so far?" Josh wondered, as he leaned back and stretched.

"More like fourteen, Josh."

"Really? Damn, this is going to take forever."

"Think of how the people still on the planet feel."

* * *

"*Ghatazhak! This is the Glendanon! Three Dusahn ships have just jumped into orbit over Burgess!*"

The building suddenly shook violently, and the few windows still intact in the Ghatazhak's flight operations office blew out from the shock wave.

The sudden nearby explosion nearly knocked Connor off his feet.

"We must leave, now!" General Telles shouted.

"Are we done here?" Connor asked.

"Yes! Telles to all Ghatazhak! Evac protocol Zeta One!"

"What the hell is Zeta One?" Connor wondered as another bomb impacted on the far side of the spaceport.

"You do not want to know," the general replied.

"*Telles, Combat One! We'll be there in two minutes to pick you up, General!*"

"One, Telles! Orbit until I signal!"

"*Understood!*"

"Captain, I must see to the evacuation of my men. Go to medical and get Jessica, Sato, and Megel ready to depart. I will send the other combat jumper to pick you up in a few minutes."

Another bomb struck nearby, rattling the building again. "Are we still going to be here in a few minutes?" Connor exclaimed nervously as the bombs continued to fall.

"They are testing us; checking for retaliatory defenses," the general warned. "Once they have

173

determined that there are none, they will move their larger ships into position and begin dropping nukes. If we are not gone by then, it will be too late," the general said as he headed for the exit.

"One, Telles! Orbit until I signal!"

"Understood!" Lieutenant Latfee acknowledged. He glanced at the sensor display. "Based on their initial firing pattern, if we circle west, then come south and across, we should be able to avoid the incoming...for now."

"This is going to get a lot worse," Commander Kainan said as he pulled the combat jumper into a tight left turn.

"Hey, at least they haven't launched any fighters," Sergeant Torwell commented.

"Yet," the commander said as he steered his shuttle away from the stream of energy bolts raining down from orbit.

"Jesus!" Lieutenant Latfee exclaimed, looking out the side window. "Boxcars on the ground! That stream of fire is marching directly toward you! You need to launch now!"

In the distance, streams of bright yellow plasma rained down, one after another, marching toward a row of three boxcars that were still loading evacuees. Dust rose as all three boxcars heeded the lieutenant's warnings and began spinning up their engines for takeoff. Beneath the boxcars, the hanging loading ramps into the cargo pods retracted upwards, people still scrambling to get inside. Those who were unable to get onto the ramps before they rose went running in all directions to escape the destruction that was coming rapidly toward them.

The line of energy bolts slammed into the ground,

one by one, sending chunks of concrete, dirt, and rock flying in all directions. Finally, the line of destruction reached the first boxcar as it was lifting off the ground, its boarding ramp only half raised. The bolt of energy slammed into the top of the boxcar, barely missing its flight deck, but finding one of its externally mounted propellant tanks. The tank exploded, the force tearing into the cargo pod directly below. The next two tanks to either side went a split second later, followed by the fourth on the far side. The boxcar, and its cargo pod below, fractured into half a dozen chunks, falling to the ground and breaking apart. Bodies were tossed in all directions; some of them whole, some dismembered, most at least partially ablaze.

The next boxcar was slightly higher above the ground when it was struck. First, by sections of the first boxcar as it came apart nearby, then by two plasma salvos from above. It too exploded in a series of near-simultaneous flashes of orange, yellow, and red, sending debris and bodies flying.

The captain of the third boxcar had been smarter, and managed to jump away before being struck. The ground below where the third boxcar had been a split second earlier erupted in a cloud of smoke and debris, the bodies of those who had not gotten clear igniting along with it.

"My God!" the lieutenant exclaimed in disbelief. "The boxcars..."

"Did you see that?" Sergeant Torwell asked.

"Did any of them get away?" the commander asked as he rolled the shuttle out of its turn.

"One, maybe," the lieutenant replied, as he watched the bolts of energy continue their path of destruction toward the Ghatazhak base on the far side of the flight apron.

———

"We can at least try to slow them down!" Commander Jarso insisted as he swung his fighter around the Glendanon and turned back in the direction of the enemy ships.

"*Negative,*" General Telles ordered over comms. "*We've already lost too many of you, and you are the only offensive spaceborne weapons we have! Your orders are to protect the Glendanon! Without her, we are doomed! Is that understood?*"

"Yes, sir," the commander replied. "Raker Leader to all Rakers. Anyone who still has jump power and propellant, form up on me. The rest, return to the Glendanon, before she is forced to jump away."

"*What about you guys?*" Lieutenant Commander Sistone asked.

"We'll stay up until the last ship escapes. If we don't make it back before the Glendanon jumps, we'll jump to the rendezvous point on the outskirts of the system and go cold. With any luck, you can send someone to pick us up later."

"*Assuming the Dusahn don't find us first,*" Ensign Viorol commented.

"You worry too much, Shooter," Commander Jarso joked.

"*That's because I've got Stringbean as my wingman,*" Ensign Viorol replied.

"*The way you fly, I'm the one who should be worried,*" Ensign Sanko muttered.

Commander Jarso glanced at his tactical screen, counting the number of fighters joining up on him as ordered. "You low, Sissy?" he called out, noticing that Lieutenant Commander Sistone was not among them.

"*Sorry,*" Sissy replied. "*Chasing after the children is tiring work.*"

"If we don't make it back, you're the new wing commander."

"*Just make it back, Rubber,*" Sissy replied. "*I'm not fond of responsibility.*"

"Disperse and withdraw! Or we will use deadly force!" the Ghatazhak sergeant warned the desperate crowds of civilians trying to get past the barricades and fences in order to board the last boxcar.

Blasts of energy continued to rain down on the spaceport, the city of Lawrence, and the surrounding areas. The landscape danced in the flickering yellow light of the descending bolts of plasma, only to mix with the reds and oranges of the explosions and fires that erupted with nearly every impact. Smoke filled the air, burning nostrils and obscuring the horizon.

The sergeant's warning fell on deaf ears. The citizens of Lawrence wanted off their doomed world, and nothing would keep them from the boxcar that had just landed and was now lowering its ramp to take on the small group of passengers waiting nearby.

A section of fence finally gave way to the force of the crowd pushing against it. One of its poles pushed up the soil around it, coming loose and leaning inward. Desperate men and women began climbing up the leaning fence, their weight pushing it over even further.

Seeing the breach, the crowd pushed toward it. Bodies climbed over one another, crushing those below. An apocalypse was upon them, and it was every man and woman for themselves.

The Ghatazhak sergeant heard the sudden roar of the mob and turned to his left to see the fence come toppling over and the crowd rushing into the spaceport. "To the left!" he barked. "Open fire!"

A dozen Ghatazhak soldiers responded, opening fire with their energy rifles as they moved toward the advancing crowd. In a wave of energy weapons fire, they mowed down more than one hundred civilians in the first few seconds.

But the crowd kept coming.

More Ghatazhak ran over to join them, adding their firepower. Hundreds more innocent men and women, all wanting to escape unjust annihilation, were quickly added to the pile of dead bodies.

While a single frigate maintained position over Lawrence, showering it with plasma weapons fire, two larger cruisers moved into position on either side of the planet's equator, in order to provide even coverage. As they moved into attack position, one of the cruisers launched a wave of fighters that quickly jumped away after clearing their host ship.

Connor ran across the spaceport as bolts of plasma pounded the Ghatazhak base ahead of him. He could see people carrying the wounded out of the medical building, trying to get those who had a fighting chance to survive to the cargo shuttle that was waiting only fifty meters away. As he drew closer, he could see Doctor Megel and Doctor Sato helping Jessica down the steps.

Then it happened. A series of plasma shots slammed into the ground to the right of the waiting cargo shuttle. One by one, the shots smashed into the ground, throwing up dust and debris behind each fiery explosion, inching their way toward the cargo shuttle and...

One of the shots struck the cargo shuttle as the wounded were being carried up the back ramp. The shuttle exploded, throwing bodies and torn metal in all directions. The explosion rocked the ground, causing Connor to stumble and fall. He could feel the heat wash over him, and the concussion made his ears feel as if someone had stabbed knives in them.

He rolled as he hit the ground, coming up to see the plasma shots flying past the exploding shuttle, slamming into the line of wounded evacuees and those helping them, and across the medical facility itself, before continuing to tear through the buildings on the other side.

The medical building came apart in a series of internal explosions caused by the immense heat of the plasma charge. The windows blew out, and the roof came crashing down, followed by the walls. Two more explosions from within the pile of debris sent shards of glass, metal, and bodies flying across the spaceport.

"NO!" Connor screamed. He jumped to his feet. There were only a few people moving. Those who could, were stumbling away from the burning building, dazed by the explosions. As he ran toward the destruction, he could see movement. People trying to get up. Broken bodies, burnt beyond recognition, summoning every ounce of strength within them in a vain attempt to find safety. But he couldn't see anyone who had escaped intact.

———

"Hurry the fuck up!" Josh demanded over his comm-set. "There are people dying down there!"

"We're getting them off as fast as we can, Josh," Neli protested.

"Their cruisers are moving into position, Josh," Loki warned as he watched the Seiiki's sensor display. "They're going to start glassing the surface any minute."

"They'll wait until they settle into stable orbits!" Josh argued. "The fucking Jung are nothing, if not methodical! We can get one more load!"

"Josh."

"Either way, we gotta disconnect, right? The Glendanon can't jump with us attached."

"Yes, but..."

"If you wanna go be with your family, that's fine. I'll make the last run myself."

"Telles will get them off in one of the shuttles, Josh," Loki tried to assure him.

"You don't know that, Loki," Josh retorted.

"Last group is heading off now," Neli reported. *"We'll be closed up in less than a minute!"*

Josh glared at Loki. "Are you staying or going?"

Loki did not respond at first. After a moment, he keyed his comm-set. "Glendanon, Seiiki. Stand by to cut us loose."

"Copy that. Standing by."

"You're going to get us killed, you know," Loki said as he started checking the Seiiki's systems in preparation to jump back down into the atmosphere over Lawrence.

"I haven't yet, have I?" Josh replied as he checked his flight control systems.

———

"*Seiiki is away,*" Loki's voice announced over the commander's helmet comms.

Two jump flashes appeared on the commander's tactical display as two boxcars jumped from the Lawrence Spaceport below, to nearby the Glendanon in orbit above Burgess.

"Looks like they're settling into orbit to begin their attack," the commander announced, watching the two Dusahn cruisers on his display screen.

A swarm of jump flashes appeared all around him, their light nearly blinding him. Threat alarms began to sound, and red icons appeared all over his tactical display. "Bandits all around! Odds and evens! Break and jump!"

The commander rolled his ship to port and brought his engine to full power. A split second later, he pressed his jump button just as two energy blasts came hurtling toward him.

One second later, his canopy cleared, and he was several kilometers away from his original position. Three more flashes of light appeared from behind him. A quick glance at his tactical display showed that three of his fighters had turned to port and jumped, just as he had instructed. "Break right and jump again!" he ordered without hesitation.

Another press of his jump button, and his canopy turned opaque, then cleared a second later. Again, three more flashes appeared behind him. He checked his tactical display, noting that half of the enemy targets had turned to follow their first jump, and were now at the location they had just jumped from. "Hard about and prepare to engage targets as they jump in," he ordered as he rolled into a tight left turn.

"*I'm with ya,*" one of his pilots replied.

"Turning."

"Let's go get'em!"

As he came about, six flashes of light appeared in front of him. Oddly shaped, black and crimson ships appeared, headed directly for him. He opened fire, sending bolts of energy from both his wing cannons and his belly turret. Two enemy fighters disappeared behind orange-red explosions, their icons disappearing from his tactical display.

"Jump!" he ordered, as he pitched up slightly to get a clear jump line and pressed the jump button on his flight control stick again. A moment later, his canopy had cleared, and the threat was behind him. But only two friendly icons were near him. He looked back and to his right, just as another jump flash appeared. It was an abnormal flash, uneven and with odd secondary flashes. Only the back half of a Takaran fighter, and several large pieces of a Dusahn fighter, appeared from behind the abnormal jump flash.

Damn.

Another glance at his tactical display offered little solace. Only a few kilometers away, the Glendanon now had nearly a dozen Dusahn fighters bearing down on her. "Glendanon, Raker Leader! There are too many of them!"

Six jump flashes appeared behind him, followed by streaks of plasma, two of which struck his rear shields, causing the back end to pitch up. "Rakers break and jump!" he ordered as he rotated his jump distance selection wheel two clicks and pressed his jump button again.

His canopy cleared. He looked around for jump flashes, but saw none. He checked his tactical display and saw that the Glendanon was under attack. "Glendanon, Raker Leader! You've got to jump!"

"Rakers, Glendanon! We'll be back!"

Commander Jarso watched his tactical display as the Glendanon's icon disappeared. He and his men now had no ship to land on, and the only habitable planet within range was about to be glassed.

———

Connor ran up to the pile of bodies and debris that was once the Ghatazhak medical facility. The bulk of the now-demolished building was on fire. He looked at the rubble. Bodies were strewn about, mixed in with the debris. A few of them were still moving. A woman reached out toward him, begging incomprehensibly for help.

Connor scanned right and left desperately searching...hoping... "JESSICA!" he cried out at the top of his lungs. "JESSICA!"

"Tuplo, Telles!" the general called over Connor's comm-set. He didn't hear him at first, over the sound of another string of plasma shots that walked across a row of buildings nearby.

"Tuplo! Are you there?" the general called again.

"Yeah! I'm here!" Connor replied. "I can't find her!"

"I'm coming to pick you up," the general told him.

"I have to find her!" Connor exclaimed, as he started pulling up pieces of rubble, hoping to uncover her, and praying for a miracle.

"She's gone, Connor," the general said. *"We have to get out of here. Be ready."*

"I can't go without her!" Connor shouted desperately. "I can't!"

"Connor!" a voice cried from nearby.

Connor turned to his right, spotting Doctor Sato,

183

crouching down beside a cargo vehicle, its top half ripped off by the force of the explosions. The sheared-off roof of the vehicle was half covering both her and Doctor Megel, and...

"Jessica!" Connor ran toward them, grabbing the damaged truck roof and pushing it to one side. "Are you all right?" he asked as he dropped to his knees next to her.

"I think so," she replied rather unconvincingly.

"I found them!" Connor cried over his comm-set. "All three of them! They're alive!"

———————

General Telles stood fast as the thrust blast from the descending combat jump shuttle threatened to knock him over.

"*All three of them! They're alive!*"

"*Breach! Fifteen Alpha! Civilians are pouring in!*"

"How many?" the general asked as the shuttle touched down nearby.

"*Hundreds!*" the sergeant replied. "*Hundreds more behind them!*"

"How many men do we have left on the ground?" Telles asked as he climbed aboard the shuttle, and closed the door behind him.

"*Twenty-four! There's no way we can hold them!*"

"Connor," the general called over his comm-set. "Move them into the open for extraction, away from any obvious targets."

"*Understood.*"

"We'll be there in two minutes."

General Telles leaned forward between the engine bulkheads that separated the combat jump shuttle's cockpit from its main cabin. "Fire mission! Fifteen Alpha! Zeta Protocol!" he ordered the flight crew.

The two pilots glanced at one another as the shuttle lifted off the ground and accelerated forward.

"Be ready topside, Sergeant," Commander Kainan instructed.

For once, Sergeant Torwell had no clever retort as he climbed back into his gunner's chair. "This sucks," was all he had to say as he swung his turret forward.

"You sweep left to right, we'll sweep right to left," the commander said. "Ten seconds, General."

"Telles to all Ghatazhak! Orderly withdrawal! Heads down! Evac, evac, evac!"

The combat jump shuttle swung into position behind the line of Ghatazhak soldiers who were attempting to slow down the advance of the desperate crowds. As they settled in low behind them, the soldiers stopped firing and ran in a low crouch to their right.

Sergeant Torwell swung his turret to the far left. "This sucks!" he repeated as he opened fire on the advancing crowds.

The shuttle pivoted slightly right, then opened fire. As they fired, they brought their nose slowly from right to left, sweeping their torrent of fire across the front of the crowd.

All three men tried not to look at the faces of the innocent people they were slaughtering. But those faces somehow found their way into their memories, and would be with them forever.

As they fired, the last of the Ghatazhak forces on the ground ran up the loading ramp into the boxcar's under-hung cargo pod.

As the boxcar's engines began spinning up again, more fences began to cave against the sheer weight of the crowds. Within seconds, thousands of people were rushing toward the boxcar.

"More to the right!" Sergeant Torwell warned, noticing the new influx of those wishing to escape. He swung his turret toward them and opened fire again.

Lieutenant Latfee watched as the last boxcar rose slowly off the ground, desperate civilians clinging to her gear. A second later, she jumped away, leaving several dozen dead bodies, and numerous body parts, on the surface below.

Another string of plasma blasts made its way across the spaceport, blowing apart everything it touched, sending chunks of red-hot concrete and melted rock flying into the air in all directions.

There was a sudden thud, and the shuttle rocked violently, as if it were going to tip over to its port side.

"We're hit!" the lieutenant called out. "I'm losing reactor two! Hydraulics are dropping!"

"Climbing!" the commander reported, pushing his throttles to full power as he struggled to keep the shuttle aloft.

"Energy banks one and three are offline!" the lieutenant reported, continuing with his damage assessment. "I'm losing jump power! We gotta jump!"

"We must pick up the others!" the general insisted.

"We can't!" the commander warned.

"I order you to..."

"If we don't jump now, we never will!" Lieutenant Latfee said, cutting the general off.

"We're losing propellant as well!" the commander exclaimed. "We've got to jump to orbit, now!"

"Do it!" the general ordered without hesitation.

The combat jump shuttle's windows turned opaque before the words left the general's mouth.

"Raker Leader to all Rakers," Commander Jarso called as he twisted his fighter to the right, rolling repeatedly to avoid the plasma bolts coming at him from behind. "Shake your tails, then jump to your designated recovery points and go cold."

"*See you soon, Rubber,*" Ensign Baylor replied.

"*It's been an honor flying with you, Commander,*" Ensign Sanko added.

"The honor's all mine," the commander replied. He spun his jump distance selector wheel on the side of his flight control stick several clicks, then pressed the jump button. Before his canopy even cleared again, he pulled a tight turn to the left and pitched down slightly. He rolled the wheel a few more clicks and jumped again. Another maneuver, another change in jump distance, and another jump, repeating it several more times.

Finally, after eight jumps and maneuvers to shake any pursuers from his tail, he jumped to his designated recovery point, on the outskirts of the Sherma system. There, he would shut down all his systems to avoid detection, and wait for rescue. He had enough life support, food, and water to last several days. If no help came by then, he would use his emergency stasis gear to put himself into the same cold sleep that had been used in ancient sleeper ships to cross the galaxy. That would buy him years of hope. And if rescue never came, he would be none the wiser.

"*Find cover. Do what you can to survive. We will come back for you,*" General Telles told them.

Connor looked at Jessica. "What are we going to

do?" Jessica was still shaken by her ordeal. "I don't know!" she cried.

"What about that bunker?" Connor asked, getting an idea. "The one on your parents' farm?"

"It's too far away," Jessica said, shaking her head as the plasma shots continued to pound the area nearby. "We'll never make it in time."

"There's got to be something we can do!" Connor insisted, refusing to give up.

"There's nothing," Jessica told him, sorrow in her eyes. "I'm sorry, Connor. I shouldn't have dragged you into this." She put her hand on his cheek, looking into his eyes. "I had no right."

"You saved me," Connor told her, putting both his hands on her face. "Seven years ago, and today! I was just going through the motions!" Several plasma bolts struck the ground nearby, a few hundred meters away. Debris sprayed over them, and he used his body to protect her. "I'd rather die, here and now, for something...for *someone*, than live decades for nothing."

A blue-white flash of light washed over them, accompanied by a screeching thunder and a wash of displaced air. The sound of explosions was suddenly covered by the scream of engines, as the Seiiki set down no more than fifty meters away from them, its thrust wash throwing dust and bits of debris against them as they huddled next to the crippled cargo vehicle.

Marcus and Dalen jumped from the Seiiki's cargo ramp as it came down, dropping the last meter to the surface and running over to them.

"Need a ride, Cap'n?" Dalen yelled, reaching down to help Jessica up.

"You bucking for a raise, Voss?" Connor said, grinning from ear to ear as he rose.

"Let's get a move on, people," Marcus shouted as he helped Doctor Sato and Doctor Megel to their feet as well. "Those cruisers are getting ready to glass this rock!"

As Connor headed toward his ship, the distant night horizon lit up with several blinding flashes of light.

"*Nukes!*" Loki warned over their comm-sets. "*We gotta go, now!*"

"Takeoff!" Marcus replied as they ran up the cargo ramp.

Connor came to a stop just inside the Seiiki's cargo bay, holding Jessica. They turned and looked out the back of the cargo bay as the ramp came level and continued upward. They could see more flashes on the horizon as the ship turned away from the direction of the nuclear bombardment, climbing as fast as it could, until its cargo ramp clanged shut, and she jumped away.

* * *

President Scott sat in his office, looking out the window at the city of Winnipeg.

"Are you even watching this?" his daughter asked as she entered from the door of the adjoining office. She walked over to his desk and picked up the remote. "Why is he still campaigning?" she wondered, turning down the volume.

"Galiardi is *always* campaigning," President Scott said wearily, still gazing out the window.

"I know, but the decision has been made, and he got his way. No ships to the Pentaurus cluster. Why doesn't he move on to more important topics?"

"In his mind, there is nothing more important

than protecting us against the Jung. That's what built his political base."

"He shouldn't *need* a political base," Miri argued. "He's an admiral, not a politician."

"Once you get to a certain level, everyone is a politician, Miri," the president said. "You should know that by now."

"Knowing and accepting are not the same thing," she commented. She looked at her father. "You're not happy with the decision, are you?"

"The Corinairans saved our lives eight years ago," he said. "We owe them."

"I know," Miri admitted with a sigh. "But as much as I hate to admit it, the admiral has a point. Can we really afford to send ships to the Pentaurus cluster when Jung ships are showing up unannounced, right here in our own part of the galaxy?"

"Can we afford not to?" the president countered. "If we end up at war with the Jung again, we're going to *need* allies like the Corinairans, and even ones like the Takarans. What better way to strengthen our support from the Pentaurus cluster than to help *them* in *their* time of need? That *is* how we became allies to begin with."

"If only we had *more* ships," Miri said.

"We kicked the Jung out of the Sol sector with far fewer ships than we have now," the president pointed out. "And they were quite firmly entrenched at the time."

"That was before they had jump drives," Miri argued.

"And *do* they have jump drives now?" the president asked. "No one really seems interested in answering that question. Instead, they just prefer to 'play it safe' and assume the worst."

"Isn't that for the best?"

"For us, yes," the president agreed. "But we are not alone in this galaxy."

"Which is why you need to read this," she said, changing the subject and handing him his briefing pad.

"Interstellar Trade Agreement?"

"You depart in a few hours, remember?"

"That's today?"

"Yes, it's today," Miri said.

An aide entered from another side entrance, handing her a note, and a small data chip. She read the note, and a puzzled look appeared on her face.

"Anything I should know about?" her father asked as he activated his digital briefing pad.

"Nothing, just a personal call. Probably one of the kids being overly dramatic again," she said, as she headed for her adjoining office.

"Give them my love," he told her as she left.

Miri stepped through the door, closing it behind her so as not to bother her father. She moved to her desk, sat down, and logged into her workstation. She inserted the data chip into the reader and waited. A few seconds later, a message came on her screen.

Message encrypted. Enter code key.

"A code key," she said to herself. She noticed the 'hint' button, and touched it. Another message appeared.

Missed opportunities...

"What?" Now she was even more puzzled. After a few moments, she typed, 'are lost advantages.' The decryption process started, and a few seconds later, a vid-file opened and began to play.

Miri's eyes widened, and her mouth dropped open. "Oh, my God."

"*Hello, Miri. I bet you weren't expecting to hear from me again.*"

CHAPTER SEVEN

Captain Gullen's eyes were wide, his jaw slack, as he stared in disbelief at Captain Tuplo walking into his wardroom. "Gentlemen," he finally managed to mumble, gesturing for everyone to take a seat. As he sat, he leaned toward General Telles, who was taking a seat to the left of him. "Is that...?" he started to ask under his breath.

General Telles put his hand up, silencing Captain Gullen. "Gentlemen, I want to thank you all for your help. We lost many friends today, and without the help of your ships, and your crews, even more of us would have perished. I see no way to repay this debt, save one. The Ghatazhak *will* rid the Pentaurus sector of the Dusahn, or every last one of us will die trying."

"*Forgive me, General,*" Captain Tobas said over the vid-comm link from the Morsiko-Tavi nearby. "*I mean no disrespect. We all know of your skill, cunning, and ruthlessness, as well as your dedication. But your numbers were few before the attack. Surely, they are considerably less now?*"

"Our numbers have been cut in half," the general replied evenly. "We now stand at two hundred and thirty-seven traditionally trained Ghatazhak, as well as another ninety-three civilian specialists, technicians, and support personnel."

"There are more than three hundred and thirty people in our cargo bay, General," Captain Gullen pointed out. "A *lot* more."

"We are working on getting an accurate count," the general said. "Our current estimate stands at one thousand and eleven, most of whom are the families of the Ghatazhak and our support personnel."

"The Ghatazhak have families?" Captain Tobas asked in disbelief.

"More than half of my men took wives during our time on Burgess. Many of them fathered children as well." General Telles informed them.

"Does that not weaken their combat effectiveness?" Captain Gullen inquired.

"Nothing weakens the combat effectiveness of a Ghatazhak, except serious injury," the general replied confidently. "Even then, the reduction is negligible."

"How did you manage to survive all these years?" Captain Donlevy asked, also over vid-comm. *"Where did you get funding?"*

"Teams of us took assignments for private concerns, on numerous worlds outside the Pentaurus sector."

"You became mercenaries?"

"The term 'private security' would be more accurate," the general replied. "Although, I will admit that many of our clients were of questionable repute."

"Jesus," Captain Donlevy exclaimed. *"Am I the only one who shudders at the thought of Ghatazhak mercs?"*

General Telles's eyebrow went up at the captain's remark. "Captain Donlevy, have not many Corinari sought similar employment? I believe my people encountered them on occasion."

"Encountered them, or fought against them," Captain Donlevy retorted.

"When one has a particularly unique skill set, is it not in one's best interest to seek employment

193

that utilizes those skills? Would you suggest the Ghatazhak become farmers? Bakers? Bankers? Perhaps politicians, or even cargo ship captains?"

Captain Donlevy had no response.

"The fact is, the galaxy still does, and always will, need the services of people such as ourselves. Humanity may not like to admit that fact, but it exists, nonetheless. The invasion by the Dusahn is evidence of this. Humanity needs people to fight for them, and to inspire them to stand up and fight for themselves alongside us."

"*And how do you propose to do that?*" Captain Tobas asked over the vid-comm, trying to take the heat off his friend.

"Allow me to introduce Deliza Ta'Akar," the general replied, gesturing to Deliza sitting to his left. "She is the daughter of Casimir Ta'Akar, the sole survivor of the Ta'Akar family, rightful heir to House Ta'Akar and the throne of Takara. I have pledged the loyalty of the Ghatazhak to her."

"*To do what?*" Captain Donlevy asked, almost laughing.

"I plan to reform the Karuzari, and drive the Dusahn from our homes," Deliza said confidently.

"*She is a child!*" Captain Donlevy exclaimed, still chuckling, "*and a woman at that!*"

"Funny, I never noticed Corinair to be particularly sexist," Deliza stated flatly, her reply directed at Captain Donlevy over the vid-comm.

"*I misspoke,*" Captain Donlevy apologized. "*I did not mean that you were incapable because of your gender. It is just that Corinairan women do not involve themselves in the military. They use their brains, not their brawn.*"

"Then I am well suited for this role," Deliza replied

smartly. "And rest assured, Captain, that I do not intend to charge into battle, gun in hand. As the general has said, one must play to their strengths. I intend to play to mine."

"As the daughter of the original founder and leader of the Karuzari, she is a natural successor," Captain Gullen informed them.

"*Perhaps,*" Captain Donlevy said, "*but I doubt that many will find her a compelling leader.*"

"I have known Miss Ta'Akar for more than seven years, now," Captain Gullen said, interrupting Captain Donlevy. "She is a well-spoken, young woman, with great business skills, and her intellect borders on genius, just like her father."

"*But her father was a natural leader,*" Captain Donlevy reminded them. "*Regardless of her genius, I do not see this young woman inspiring thousands to lay down their lives and follow her into battle.*"

"Which is why we have enlisted Captain Tuplo, of the Seiiki," Deliza replied, "formerly known as Captain Nathan Scott, of the Aurora."

The room suddenly became quiet. A smile formed on Captain Gullen's bearded face, but the faces of the others showed nothing but astonishment.

"*Impossible,*" Captain Donlevy said, although with some uncertainty. "*Captain Scott surrendered himself to the Jung and died in their custody over seven years ago!*"

"Or so the galaxy was led to believe," Deliza replied, a satisfied look on her face.

"*How is this possible?*" Captain Tobas wondered over the vid-comm. It was obvious that he seemed more willing to believe their claims than Captain Donlevy.

"Myself and Lieutenant Nash rescued Captain

Scott on the eve of his execution," General Telles explained.

"*From the Jung homeworld?*" Captain Donlevy questioned, refusing to believe it. "*Images from his memorial service on Earth have been rebroadcast throughout the galaxy. We all saw his body!*"

"What everyone saw was a *clone* of Nathan Scott," the general replied calmly. "One placed there by us."

Deliza glanced momentarily at the general to her right. It was an instinctive glance, one of puzzlement. Afterward, she hoped that it had been discrete enough to hide her surprise at the general's bending of the truth.

"*Cloning is illegal,*" Captain Donlevy sputtered angrily.

"On Corinair, perhaps," General Telles admitted.

"*Then how did you manage to clone him?*" the captain demanded. "*And where? And how did you manage to clone him so quickly?*"

"The details are not important," the general said, dismissing his questions. "However, if you require proof as to his identity, we will be happy to provide you with it."

"*You realize what the Jung will do when they discover he is still alive, don't you?*" Captain Donlevy asked. "*You think the Dusahn are a threat? Wait until the entire Jung fleet comes calling, looking for Captain Scott there...*"

"The cease-fire between the Alliance and the Jung has already broken down," Connor explained, trying to sound as confident as he imagined Captain Scott would. "Jung ships have been detected as deep as a few light years from Sol. Limited battles have ensued, and several Jung ships have been destroyed. As of yet, no Alliance ships have been lost. However, the Alliance has also launched a limited KKV strike against Jung military assets deep inside the Jung sector, resulting in the loss of millions of lives."

"*Oh, my God,*" Captain Tobas exclaimed. "*You're saying the galaxy is at war?*"

"More accurately, on the verge of galactic war," General Telles corrected. "Our last message from Sol before evacuation indicated that they were currently in a 'standoff'. No Jung ships have been detected in Alliance space since the KKV strike a week ago."

"*A week ago?*" Captain Donlevy realized the significance. "*That's when the Dusahn invaded the Pentaurus cluster, as well. Surely there is some significance to the timing of the two events?*"

"We have no evidence that supports or refutes that hypothesis," the general replied. "However, it is a logical assumption at this point."

"*Then, we are not merely facing the Dusahn, but the Jung Empire, as well,*" Captain Tobas surmised.

"That is a possibility," the general admitted. "However, I do not believe it to be true. Were we facing the entire Jung Empire, none of us would be talking right now. The Jung Empire has hundreds, if not thousands, of ships. And they have fabrication technology that, although inferior to our own, would still enable them to outfit far more ships than the few they have sent to conquer the Pentaurus cluster."

"*Or they only recently acquired jump drive technology, and are still in the process of outfitting their fleet,*" Captain Donlevy suggested, in opposition to the general's theory.

"Were that the case, the Jung would have waited to invade the Pentaurus cluster," the general argued. "The Jung prefer to attack with overwhelming numbers. The Dusahn used the element of surprise to offset their *lack* of such numbers. The Jung Empire is caste-based," General Telles explained further. "We believe the Dusahn to be operating of their own volition."

"*Like some kind of rogue caste?*" Captain Tobas wondered.

"Precisely."

"*Wouldn't they fear punishment by their own people?*" Captain Donlevy asked. "*After all, their actions are likely to cause a galactic war.*"

"Not if the *Dusahn* acquired jump drive technology, but the Jung did not," Connor suggested.

"Now I'm confused," Captain Gullen admitted.

"Many of the Jung castes do not see eye-to-eye," General Telles explained. "It is even rumored that some castes were expelled from Jung space for their failure to comply with the directives of their collective leadership. The Dusahn may be just such a caste."

"*But you said that Jung ships have been detected deep within Alliance space,*" Captain Tobas reminded them. "*To do so, wouldn't they need jump drives?*"

"One would think so, yes. Unfortunately, we have no information on the method of their insertion," General Telles replied. "However, given our experience with the Jung, the rogue caste theory makes the most sense."

"Even if the Dusahn *are* acting alone, if Jung ships are popping up deep inside Alliance space, the Alliance is unlikely to send aid," Captain Gullen said.

"That is a distinct possibility," General Telles admitted. "In the meantime, however, we must prepare. And our first order of business is to find safe accommodations for the souls we carry."

"Indeed," Captain Gullen agreed. "The Glendanon

is not designed to support so many. Our cargo bay is not adequately shielded for long-term occupancy, even from within class one pods."

"Can the shielding be improved?" Deliza asked. "The Ghatazhak have fabricators."

"I was not aware of this," Captain Gullen said.

"They were moved to a secure location on an uninhabited world, at the start of the evacuation."

"Then you're planning on joining them," Captain Donlevy said, surprised.

"I see no other alternative."

"Don't you have family on Corinair?" Captain Donlevy asked.

"I do," Captain Gullen replied. "The general has agreed to attempt their rescue."

"Attempt?"

"I cannot guarantee it will be a success," General Telles admitted.

"Then why not give up your ship?" Captain Donlevy wondered.

"Because, as it stands, these people are our best chance at regaining that which, once again, has unjustly been taken from us. The Karuzari drove the Takaran Empire out of the Pentaurus sector, back into the cluster, and with the help of Nathan Scott, liberated us all from the reign of Caius. I believe they will do the same with the Dusahn."

"And you are willing to bet your family's life on that?" Captain Donlevy asked.

"Do I have the right to possibly condemn billions, perhaps trillions of innocent people, simply to save those most dear to me?" Captain Gullen asked Captain Donlevy. "How could I be worthy of my family's respect if I did so? How would I live with myself?"

"*Did the Ghatazhak have the right to condemn the citizens of Burgess?*" Captain Donlevy wondered.

"The Ghatazhak had no way of knowing..." Deliza began to argue.

General Telles held up his hand, cutting her short. "The captain has a valid point. And to that comment I answer no, I did not. No one has the right to condemn others to death. Not one, not millions, not trillions. Unfortunately, such decisions often must be made, and made by the few, or even just one. This is precisely why the Ghatazhak exist."

"*No offense, General,*" Captain Donlevy said, "*but I'm not so sure I want the Ghatazhak making such decisions. And I suspect most people would agree with me on this. It's too easy for you to turn your emotions off and on. You may feel remorse for those who died on Burgess, but we do not feel your pain is genuine. People want to know that their leaders care about them, that they feel pain when they lose men in battle, or when they fail to protect societies.*"

"I completely understand your sentiments, Captain. And were I like you, I suspect I would feel the same. This is precisely why we have asked Captain Scott to come out of hiding, and lead the rebellion."

The room became quiet for several moments.

"Captain Donlevy," General Telles began, breaking the uncomfortable silence. "As you have been the most critical of our proposal, I will ask you first. Will you join us?"

"*Why doesn't Captain Scott ask me himself?*" Captain Donlevy wondered.

"Very well," Connor said. "Captain Donlevy, will you join us to fight the Dusahn?"

Captain Donlevy thought for a moment. "*I served*

with you in the Sol sector, Captain. There are few men I would trust more to care about the well-being of my crew, my ship, and myself than you. Therefore, I will join you. But on one condition. If any of my crew do not wish to join your cause, you must allow me to return them to their homes, as best I can."

"Agreed," Connor replied. "And thank you." Connor turned his attention to the other view screen. "Captain Tobas, will you join us?"

"I will also have to ask my crew, and I ask for the same considerations, should any of them choose differently. But I will pledge myself, and my ship, to you and the Karuzari, Captain."

"Thank you," Connor replied. He turned his attention to Lieutenant Commander Sistone.

"I cannot make such a decision until I know the status of Commander Jarso," the lieutenant commander stated stubbornly.

"We have already dispatched Falcon One on a cold-coast recon through the Sherma system," General Telles replied. "Once the system is clear of the Dusahn, we will send a boxcar back to retrieve any pilots who survived."

Lieutenant Commander Sistone nodded his appreciation.

Connor and the general both turned their attention to Captain Gullen of the Glendanon.

"I believe I made myself clear," Captain Gullen said.

"Nevertheless, I should formally ask for your help, Captain," Connor replied. "Will you join us?"

"On one condition," Captain Gullen replied. "You must promise me you will shave off that ridiculous beard of yours. Not all of us can pull off that look."

"Soon," Connor promised with a grin.

"Very well, gentlemen," General Telles said. "Captain Donlevy, Captain Tobas, I believe you need to meet with your crews."

Both captains voiced their confirmation and quickly signed off.

Connor suddenly seemed to relax a bit, breathing a sigh of relief. "I wasn't sure I could pull that off," he said in a heavy exhale.

"You did well," General Telles said.

"Well?" Deliza exclaimed. "I wouldn't have known the difference!"

Captain Gullen looked puzzled. "Now I'm confused again."

"I'm afraid things are a bit more complicated than we led Captains Donlevy and Tobas to believe," General Telles admitted.

"I do not understand."

"The original *body* of Nathan Scott died in that cell," the general explained. "We were only able to rescue his consciousness." General Telles put his hand on Connor's shoulder. "This man is the clone of Nathan Scott, but he is not yet Nathan."

* * *

Doctor Chen exited exam room four, closing the door behind her as she left. "Four will need interior scans of the left arm and shoulder," she told the nurse who met her in the corridor.

"I'll get started on it, Doctor," the nurse replied. "Five is female, mid-thirties, lower right abdominal pain times forty-eight hours."

"Thanks," the doctor said, noticing a man standing just past the door to exam room five. "Who is that?" she asked the nurse under her breath. "Husband of five?"

"If so, he sure doesn't act like it," the nurse

replied, shrugging as she entered the exam room the doctor had just exited.

Doctor Chen headed down the corridor to the next examination room, nodding politely at the serious gentleman standing quietly near the door. She opened the door and walked inside as she read the next patient's chart on her data pad. "Miss Everson, I'm Doctor Chen. What seems to be the problem?"

The patient waited for the door to close. Without speaking, she pulled a small electronic device out of her purse, set it on the side table, and activated it. Two seconds later, the indicator light on the device turned from yellow to green.

"I assure you that these rooms are private," Doctor Chen promised as she pulled up a stool to sit in front of the nervous patient. Miss Everson wasn't the first patient who had brought a surveillance protection field generator into the exam room. "Even the man outside the door cannot hear anything we say."

"I apologize for the precaution, Doctor Chen," the patient began, now satisfied that no one would be able to hear them. "Before I begin, I must confirm that you are Doctor Melei Chen, former chief medical officer of the Aurora, at the time under the command of the late Captain Nathan Scott?"

"Uh... How did you... Who are you?"

"Again, I apologize, but please, I must confirm your identity before I say anything else."

"Well, I suppose you already know that I am, otherwise you wouldn't be here," Doctor Chen said.

"What year of your EDF training were you at the time?"

"Uh, fifth year, I think. Yes, fifth year."

"And the rotation prior to the Aurora?"

"Surgical. And my mother's maiden name was

Liang, if that helps," she added sarcastically, tired of the incessant questioning.

"Thank you for your patience, Doctor," the woman said. "I'm afraid I'm rather new to this cloak and dagger stuff."

"What's going on?" Doctor Chen wondered. "Who are you?"

"My name is Miri Thornton," the patient revealed. "Miri Scott-Thornton."

Doctor Chen suddenly put two and two together. "The President's aide... You're Captain Scott's sister, aren't you?"

"Yes, I am."

"I don't understand. Why are you here? And why are you pretending to be a patient?"

"I needed to speak with you, in private, which is not an easy task in my position."

"I imagine not."

"You're still in the reserves, right?"

"For two more years, yes. Then, I'm finally free." Melei suddenly became suspicious. "Why do you ask?"

"I'm afraid I have a very big favor to ask of you."

"What kind of favor?" the doctor wondered, one eyebrow going up skeptically.

"I need you to volunteer to return to active duty."

Doctor Chen laughed. "Why the hell would I do that?"

"Because I need you back on the Aurora," Miri explained.

"Have you been watching the netcasts, Miss Thornton? We're on the verge of another war with the Jung. Being a doctor aboard a warship is not exactly a smart career move right now."

"What if I told you that the Alliance was going to

be activating you anyway, and that by agreeing to help me, I can make sure you end up on the Aurora instead of some other ship?"

"Which ship hardly makes a difference," Doctor Chen said, unimpressed. "They're all going to get shot at, sooner or later."

"But if you are assigned to the Aurora, then you can deliver a message to her captain for me. A message of vital importance to the security of the entire Alliance, and perhaps even the entire galaxy."

Doctor Chen looked at her, squinting in suspicion. "Why do I get the feeling that I'm not going to like where this is going?"

"Trust me, Doctor, if what I think is about to happen is in fact what *is* about to happen, then you may very well *prefer* to be on the Aurora. And if not, I can see to it that you get transferred back to surface duty as soon as possible." Miri opened her hand, revealing a small data chip. "Will you deliver the message to Captain Taylor?"

Doctor Chen looked at the data chip for a moment. "Fate of the galaxy, huh?" She sighed, picking up the chip. "What is it with you Scotts? You're always in the middle of it all."

"It is vitally important that no one knows about this," Miri warned.

"Am I doing this for you, or for the president?" Doctor Chen wondered.

"Neither," Miri admitted.

"Then for whom?"

"I cannot tell you," Miri said apologetically. "But, if I could, I believe you would agree to help. For now, let's just say you're doing it for all of humanity."

"Oh, is that all?" Doctor Chen put the data chip

into her pocket. "I don't suppose you really have abdominal pain, do you?"

"No, but it might be best if you put me through the usual examinations, just for the sake of appearances," Miri suggested.

"Of course," Doctor Chen said, picking up her medical scanner to begin the examination. "You do realize you've just ruined what was shaping up to be a pretty good day, don't you?"

* * *

"But, once the transfer is complete, he will be Nathan Scott again?" Captain Gullen asked, trying to make sure he understood the general's explanation correctly.

"If all goes well, yes. There may be some memory loss, such as incomplete or fragmented memories, but both Doctor Sato and Doctor Megel are confident that the fifth-generation clone will be successful."

Captain Gullen looked at Deliza. "And this process has been going for seven years? It must have cost you a small fortune."

"A small price to pay, considering," Deliza replied. "Captain Scott did save my life on more than one occasion."

"Yes, as he did for us all," Captain Gullen said. He took a deep breath and sighed, then looked at Connor. "Do you truly understand the responsibility you are choosing to accept?" the captain asked him. "The risks you will be taking? If you become Nathan Scott, you will become *the* most hunted man in the galaxy. The Jung will not rest until they can hold your severed head high for all to see."

"You're not exactly helping, Captain," Connor replied.

"I'm not trying to," Captain Gullen admitted. "I

just don't understand how any man can willingly accept such a challenge."

"Didn't you offer your ship, knowing full well that doing so might condemn those you love to execution at the hands of the Dusahn?" Connor asked.

"Yes, but..."

"Both are difficult things to do. Most would say that yours is even more difficult. I am only putting my own life at risk."

"And the lives of those willing to follow you," the captain pointed out.

"Only if they choose to do so. I'm not making the decision for them. You, on the other hand, are making the decision for your wife and daughter." Connor could see the anguish on the captain's face. "I realize you are doing what you believe is the right thing to do...not for them, but for everyone. *That* was a difficult decision to make, just as mine was."

"It is what men such as us do," General Telles added.

Connor squinted a moment, as a memory flashed in his mind. "That which other men cannot do."

General Telles looked at Connor, a wry smile on his face. It was not the first time that one of Nathan's memories had found its way out of the depths of Connor Tuplo's mind.

"And the procedure must be done in the lab on Corinair?"

"Yes," Deliza replied. "To rebuild and regrow the clone, using DNA from Captain Tuplo, would take another five years, at least. And because of the Dusahn, we will not have access to the markets that created the revenue streams that funded the effort. The clone is waiting in that underground lab, along

207

with all the equipment necessary to complete the transfer."

"Although the lab is secure, it is only a matter of time before it is discovered," the general explained. "The Dusahn have already started searching every technology company and manufacturing facility on the worlds they have seized. We must reach that lab *before* they discover it."

"How do you intend to get onto Corinair, and into that lab, without being detected?" Captain Gullen wondered. "And how do you plan to get *off* Corinair once the transfer is completed?"

"Getting to the lab is not as difficult as one might think," the general replied.

"We can't jump in there like before, not even into a cave," Connor warned. "It didn't take them long to find us. Next time, they'll just bomb the entire area and be done with it. We'll never get out in time."

"I do have a plan," the general replied, "not only to get you into that lab and out again, but to rescue your wife and daughter, Captain Gullen. However, without a warship, our chances of success are somewhat limited."

"Perhaps we should wait for word from Captain Taylor?" Connor suggested.

"Every day that we wait we run the risk of losing Nathan Scott," the general said. "Quite possibly forever."

* * *

"I've been hounding command for more personal time for nearly a week now, and this is what I get for it," Commander Kaplan complained as she entered the Aurora's ready room and plopped down in the chair across the desk from Cameron.

Commander Kaplan had always been a bit on the

informal side. It was something Cameron had come to accept about her. Although she normally did not prefer such informality among her officers, there were times when she appreciated the ability to talk openly with someone. And, as long as the informality took place in private, it did little harm; although, at times, she did wonder if push came to shove, if the commander would carry out an order that she did not agree with, or if she would argue the order. She hoped she would never have to find out.

"Executive Officer: Aurora: Fleet Command: Blah blah blah... The immediate transfer of Commander Caro, Megan H., M.D., serial number blah blah to the ESS Chennai at earliest. Replacement CMO to arrive shortly, blah blah blah... Can you believe this?"

"They're taking our chief medical officer?" Cameron said in disbelief. Commander Kaplan handed Cameron her data pad. "Did they say who will be replacing her?"

"Someone named Chen," the commander replied. "This is unbelievable."

"Melei Chen?" Cameron asked, scanning the data pad. "Oh, yes, there it is."

"Wasn't she the newb who took over as CMO when the rest of the medical staff was killed, back during the Aurora's super jump?"

"Yes, she was," Cameron said. "She did a pretty good job, too."

"Well, at least she should be fully trained by now. But that's going to leave us without a doctor for half a day."

"As long as we don't go into battle, we should be all right," Cameron comforted her. "If anything serious comes up, we can jump shuttle the patient back to fleet medical."

"I suppose," the commander reluctantly agreed. "I thought the Chennai wasn't due for launch for another month?"

"I guess they moved it up," Cameron surmised. "Can you blame them?"

"The early launch of the Chennai means it's just going to be that much more difficult to fill out our crew. We're going to be working double shifts till Founders' Day!"

"It's not like we're the only ship working doubles, you know."

"I just hope this Doctor Chen of yours has a better bedside manner than Caro does."

"I assume you haven't told the commander yet?"

"No, I wanted to tell you first, in case you wanted to protest it to Fleet."

"Not interested," Cameron said. "Besides, Caro will like life on a destroyer better. Smaller crew, fewer staff to manage. She's not exactly a people person."

"I'll tell her to start packing, then," the commander said, rising from her seat. "Let's just hope they don't swap anyone else out," she added on her way toward the hatch. "With all these doubles, who has time to break in someone new if we don't have to?"

* * *

Connor walked through the boarding ramp from the Glendanon to the Seiiki, wondering how he was going to pitch his idea. He had asked a lot of them over the last ten days, and yet they had stuck with him every step of the way. They truly were his family.

He got to the Seiiki's outer hatch and punched in his security code, stepping into the Seiiki's airlock once the outer door was open. It was standard practice never to allow the ship to be directly open to another ship's environment, when docked, for the simple reason that docking collars were never one hundred percent reliable. The fact that his crew had been left with no choice but to do so, while quickly transferring passengers to the Glendanon during the evacuation of Burgess, made him shudder.

The inner hatch slid open, and Connor stepped inside and activated the mechanism, causing it to close behind him. He followed the sound of his crew, a few steps aft in the Seiiki's compact galley.

"Cap'n," Josh called out in greeting. "How did your meeting of the minds go?"

"It went well, thank you," he replied, pulling an empty water bottle out of the cabinet. "You guys finish running all the diagnostics?"

"Yes, sir," Dalen answered. "Other than a few burnt-out relays, and a slightly singed port shield generator, we're in pretty fair shape, all things considered."

"That's good to hear," Connor said as he filled his water bottle from the cold tap in the refrigerator door. He took a long drink, then turned to face his crew sitting at the booth in the corner. "Listen, I wanted to thank all of you for sticking by me the last couple weeks. I know I've probably made some questionable choices in your minds, and I appreciate that you always put your faith in me, even if you don't necessarily agree with me. It means a lot." Connor swallowed hard. "I just thought you deserved to hear it from me."

"Wow," Neli said. "That's the most emotion I've heard you use since that time you came home drunk off your ass back on Perinorimo."

"No, it wasn't Perinorimo," Josh disagreed. "It was Little Bastone."

"No, it was Perinorimo," Neli argued.

Ryk Brown

"You're both wrong," Marcus interrupted. "It was Barklin. That little dive bar around the corner from the spaceport. Finny's, or something."

"You're all wrong," Connor told them. "It was the Morrisay Inn, on Hondori. And for the record, I wasn't drunk off my ass. I was under the influence, I'll admit..."

"Port security brought you back in a shopping cart, Cap'n!" Josh reminded him. "You were singing some song... What was it?" Josh turned to the others. "Something about lost loves and sunsets?"

"The sun has set on love," Marcus started singing.

"Yeah! That's it!" Josh agreed excitedly. "Oh, man, it was pitiful! Singin' is not your strong suit, Cap'n!"

"Enough," Connor insisted, embarrassed. "Enough."

"We're just giving you a hard time, Cap'n," Josh grinned.

"Enjoy it while you can," Connor told him. "Once I become Na-Tan, you're all going to have to bow down to me whenever I walk into the room," he joked.

"Oh, really?" Josh challenged.

"So, it's been decided?" Marcus asked. "You're going through with it?"

"It appears so," Connor admitted, as the airlock proximity alarm sounded.

"How are you plannin' on gettin' on and off the planet?" Marcus wondered, calling after Connor as the captain headed forward to the airlock.

"Oh, I'll just swoop us in and drop him off, then jump back in when he's ready to go," Josh declared confidently.

"Just like that?" Dalen wondered. "On a planet full of Dusahn jump fighters?"

"Man, I'll jump in and out so fast they'll never even know I was there," Josh bragged.

212

Connor returned, along with Doctor Sato, Doctor Megel, and General Telles with several Ghatazhak, each of them carrying several equipment bags.

"Seriously, Cap'n, how *are* we going to pull this off?" Marcus wondered.

"The general has it all figured out," Connor promised.

"I'm all ears," Marcus assured him.

"I'll explain it later," Connor replied. "We have some training to do."

Marcus leaned to his right, noting General Telles and his men, followed by the two Nifelmian doctors.

"We going somewhere?" Josh asked.

"Innis, fourth planet," Connor instructed.

"Why? There's nothing there. It's a dust bowl."

"But, apparently, it's got the right gravity," Connor explained vaguely. "Let's get going."

* * *

Cameron walked into the Aurora's medical department, looking for her new chief medical officer. "Hello?" she called, surprised that no one was there to greet the captain. "Doctor Chen?"

"Captain Taylor," Doctor Chen replied, coming out of one of the exam rooms. "My apologies, I was with a patient, and apparently we are short-staffed. It seems my only two nurses both just came off doubles, and my only med-tech is at lunch at the moment."

"We can reschedule, if you'd like," Cameron suggested. "I'm feeling fine, after all."

"Thank you, no," Doctor Chen replied. "As your new CMO, I am required to personally establish the baseline medical condition of all senior officers within seventy-two hours of assuming command of the ship's medical department."

"Yes, I'm well aware of the regulation," Cameron replied. "I just thought that, considering the circumstances, a little leeway might be prudent."

"The circumstances are exactly why it is imperative that I see to the health of the ship's senior officers," Doctor Chen insisted. "After all, we are at a state of alert, and the crew and the senior officers have all been working double shifts for more than a week now."

"Of course, you're right."

"We'll use exam two, Captain," the doctor said, gesturing toward the open door.

"You know, I was surprised to see you returning to shipboard duty," Cameron said as she entered the exam room. "I thought that, after your last tour, you would have had enough. At least that's the impression I had when you departed."

Doctor Chen closed the door behind them and locked it. "Your impression was correct, Captain," she admitted, her tone suddenly becoming more personable. "I'm not here out of choice. Hell, this morning I was having coffee at my favorite little shop near the hospital, enjoying the view of the ocean, and now I'm God knows how many light years away from home."

"What's going on, Doctor?" Cameron asked.

"I have no idea," she replied. "All I know is that Captain Scott's sister, Miri, came into my hospital emergency department, pretending to be a patient, just so she could talk to me *covertly*. Me! Of all people! And now, ten hours later, I'm here talking to you."

"What did she say?" Cameron wondered.

"That I was being activated, and that if I agreed to deliver a message to you in secret, she would see that I was reassigned back to Earth just as soon as possible."

"What message?"

Doctor Chen reached into her pocket and pulled out the data chip that Miri had given her. "I don't know. I just know that I'm supposed to give you this, and I'm not supposed to tell anyone about it."

"Then you don't know what's on this chip?" Cameron asked as she accepted it from the doctor.

"She wouldn't tell me, and believe me, I asked," Doctor Chen explained. "All she would say is that, if I knew what was on that chip, I would be happy to help. Oh, and that the fate of humanity might depend on getting it to you. So, not that big a deal, right?" she added, rolling her eyes in frustration.

Cameron looked at the chip, noticing that it had no markings, which in itself was unusual. "Are you sure she didn't say anything else?"

"Nothing."

Cameron sighed, looking down at the data chip in her hand. "I guess I'd better take a look at the message, then," she said, as she started to get up.

"Actually, I do have to give you a check examination, Captain," Doctor Chen said. "Regulations. Besides, it's the only way I could get the chip to you in secret."

"Of course," Cameron replied, sitting back down. She thought for a moment as Doctor Chen opened the cabinet and got out a medical scanner. "I wonder what the message is," Cameron said, more to herself than to the doctor.

"I have a feeling I don't want to know."

* * *

"I want them dead!" Lord Dusahn demanded, his voice echoing throughout his headquarters on Takara. "Do you understand me?"

"Yes, my lord," General Hesson replied. "Might I inquire as to how you wish us to best accomplish this task?"

Lord Dusahn looked at his trusted general and lifelong friend. He knew full well the general was asking only to point out the futility of his leader's outburst. He took a deep breath, letting it out slowly, after which he nodded recognition of his friend's masterful calming of his lord's demeanor. The outburst had not been befitting of the leader of the Dusahn caste, and they both knew it. Such occasional outbursts of rage were Lord Dusahn's weak point, one he had tried for decades to master, but as of yet had failed.

"If I may offer my counsel?" the general suggested, now that his leader had calmed down.

Lord Dusahn simply nodded in agreement, saying nothing.

"It is an isolated incident, one that should be of no concern as of yet."

"I have heard stories of these *Ghatazhak*," Lord Dusahn said, his voice low, despite the fact that he and the general were alone.

"As have I, my lord. They are formidable warriors, but they are surface warriors, nothing more. And their numbers are insignificant compared to your Zen-Anor, let alone our standard ground forces."

"You once told me that such men should not be underestimated," Lord Dusahn reminded his general. "Such was Captain Equin's fatal error, was it not?"

"Indeed it was, my lord."

"Then see that it does not happen again."

"Of course, my lord."

Lord Dusahn sighed again. "I don't suppose there is anything we can do to *find* these Ghatazhak, and rid ourselves of them once and for all?"

"Tracking their old light would likely be difficult, if not impossible," the general admitted. "Evasion of such techniques is a simple matter. And we have too few ships to conduct a comprehensive search of the *entire* sector, let alone beyond. However, there is one thing that might yield results."

Lord Dusahn suddenly looked interested.

"We believe the ship that aided the Ghatazhak in their escape is the same ship that assisted in the evacuation of the surviving Avendahl fighters during our initial invasion of the Darvano system."

"The Glendanon?"

"Indeed, my lord."

"Don't we have his wife and daughter in custody?"

"Indeed, my lord."

Lord Dusahn smiled, leaning back in his seat. "A man who is away from home so much will not return for his wife, but he might, for his child."

"My thinking, as well," the general agreed, although without the obvious pleasure.

"Execute his wife," Lord Dusahn instructed. "In public, first thing in the morning."

"As you wish, my lord," the general promised, bowing respectfully and backing away to exit.

* * *

Cameron sat in the middle of her quarters on the Aurora, staring at the blank view screen on the wall in front of her, just as she had been for the last half hour. She had isolated her personal terminal from the rest of the ship prior to inserting the data chip. Surprisingly, the chip had only required Cameron's thumbprint in order to decrypt its message. Considering the lengths to which Miri Scott-Thornton had gone to get the chip to her in secret, she had expected more elaborate safeguards.

The chip had been in her possession for several hours now. She had waited until the long workday had finished, in the hopes that she would be able to watch the message in its entirety, without interruption. She had no idea how long, or how short the message might be, but she was sure of one thing. Whatever the message was, it deserved her undivided attention, which was exactly what she was about to give.

Cameron picked up the remote, and pressed the button to play the message. The image was black at first, then faded into view. It was a small, nondescript room, something akin to an operational office at a military base, but she could not be sure. There was communications gear on the counter along the far wall, and a map of an airfield on the wall above the comms gear. The room was properly lit, although not too bright, and by the small amount of light coming through the one window that she could see, it was night.

Then the room suddenly illuminated for a moment. Brilliant blue-white light that was gone a split second later.

A distant jump flash.

A second later, her suspicions were confirmed by the customary clap of thunder that always occurred when a large ship displaced the air by its sudden arrival into the atmosphere. It was a unique, unforgettable sound.

A spaceport.

A voice mumbled in the background, along with some chatter on the comms gear. She could hear some movement off camera, and could see some shadows moving to the left. Then a man stepped into view. As he turned to look into the camera, Cameron's mouth fell agape.

"Oh, my God," she exclaimed, both hands coming up to cover her mouth. She could not believe what she was seeing. The man appeared younger than she remembered, especially considering that seven years had passed since she last saw him. His hair was noticeably longer, and his face was covered with a thick, poorly trimmed beard. But it *was* Nathan, of that she had no doubt. She could see it in his eyes. The kindness, the determination, the confidence... and the feeling of trust they always engendered when you looked into them.

"Nathan," she whispered.

"*Hello, Miri. I'll bet you weren't expecting to hear from me again.*" he began. "*Yes, it's me under all this. It's your baby brother.*" He touched his beard. "*Pretty good disguise, huh? Well, it is if no one is really looking for you, I guess.*" He took a deep breath before continuing. "*I guess I should apologize for not getting in touch with you sooner. But, as you might expect, it's complicated. You see, I haven't really been myself for a long time. I wish I could explain it all to you, but there's not enough time. To be honest, I don't really understand it all myself just yet, but I hope to very soon. Just know that I am incredibly sorry for what I must have put you all through. I hope you know that I was only doing what I felt I had to do, in order to save you all.*"

There was another voice, one that was deeper and more official in syntax. Cameron thought she recognized the man's voice, but could not quite place it. Nathan was looking at the man off camera, nodding his head.

"*Look, Miri, I don't have a lot of time to explain, but I need your help. By now you know that the Dusahn have invaded the Pentaurus cluster, and they control all of the worlds within it. Soon, we fear that they will expand their reign to include the entire sector, and beyond. This gives them a vast industrial base,*" *complete with all the resources and technology, as well as the economy and work force needed, to rapidly expand their fleet."*

As if on cue, to emphasize the point, another jump flash filled the room, followed by the customary clap of thunder. Nathan looked away from the camera momentarily, caught off guard.

"And Miri, they have jump drives. Lots of them. But here's the thing. They call themselves the Dusahn, and they claim to be acting separately from the Jung. We have no way of confirming this, but everything we've learned thus far supports this."

The man's voice from off camera spoke again. Cameron couldn't hear him well enough to understand what he was saying, but it seemed as if he was reminding Nathan of something.

"I know that things back in the Sol sector are not ideal right now. I know that Jung ships have been showing up deep within Alliance space. I have no explanation for this, but I am positive that all is not as it appears. There is something far more complex, far more sinister going on. I suspect that Galiardi is using these sudden intrusions into Alliance space as justification for KKV strikes, and to rally support for his dream of building a space faring military of epic proportions."

Another jump flash filled the room, but this time, Nathan ignored it.

"Anyway, to the point of this message. I need you to get the following message to Captain Cameron Taylor, commander of the Aurora. You need to do it without anyone knowing. I know that's asking a lot, but trust me, I wouldn't ask if it wasn't a matter of life and death, for billions, maybe trillions of people, both in the Pentaurus cluster, and back in the Sol sector

as well. *Again, tell no one about this message, and for now, tell no one that I am alive. I suspect everyone will know soon enough.*"

Nathan paused for a moment, as if marking the end of the first message, and the beginning of the second portion intended for Cameron.

"*Hi, Cam,*" Nathan began. "*I'll make this short. General Telles, Jessica, Deliza Ta'Akar, and I are resurrecting the Karuzari in the hopes of fighting the Dusahn. Josh, Marcus, and Loki are with me, as well, along with what is left of the Ghatazhak.*"

Another jump flash washed over the room, but Nathan continued.

"*Less than an hour ago, we were attacked by a Dusahn assault ship. By some miracle, we survived, but with heavy losses, and we expect the Dusahn to return shortly to finish the job. We are evacuating now, in the hopes of saving what little is left. The Dusahn invasion was too precise. They must have had good intelligence prior to the attack. However, the general does not believe they were aware of the Ghatazhak until after the invasion. We have no delusions of being able to defeat them, as we have no warships, other than a few combat jump shuttles, and two Falcons. What we are hoping to do is to harass and impede the Dusahn at every turn, in the hopes of preventing them from becoming any stronger prior to the arrival of Alliance ships. Unfortunately, we cannot hope to accomplish this task without help. We have received word that the Alliance is willing to send us aid in the form of weapons and supplies, but is unable to send what we really need, which is a ship. But not just any ship.*"

Nathan paused. The look on his face told her what was coming next.

Ryk Brown

"*Cam...... We need the Aurora. With her, and with Na-Tan at her command, General Telles believes we can not only rally support, but we might actually have a chance at defeating the Dusahn.*" Nathan stopped and sighed. "*I know I'm asking a lot. I know that this goes against everything you believe in, and that it puts everything you've worked for at risk. But do you really want to be a part of the world that Galiardi is trying to create?*"

Nathan looked off camera for a moment before continuing.

"*Believe me, Cam, I would not be asking if I thought there was any other way. Unfortunately, there is not. The Pentaurus sector needs Na-Tan, they need the Aurora, and they need her crew. I know you never liked the whole Na-Tan thing. But Telles says the people need hope. They need inspiration. They need a leader they can believe in. The same is as true now as it was nine years ago. If we save this sector again, we will likely be saving the Sol sector, as well. If the Dusahn are acting on their own, then they are even more dangerous. And if they are acting under Jung authority, then that means the Jung in your part of the galaxy also have jump drives, in which case one ship is not going to make a bit of difference there. Out here, at least you have a chance to make a difference.*"

"*Ghatazhak! This is the Glendanon!*"

The voice was coming from the comms gear, and it caused Nathan to turn to look behind him. "*Three Dusahn ships have just jumped into orbit over Burgess!*"

The image on the view screen shook violently, and a nearby explosion erupted, followed by the sound of windows being blown out by the shock wave. It caused Cameron to flinch, gasping as her hands returned to her mouth again.

222

"Cameron, the Aurora must be in the Darvano system at zero six thirty hours, Corinairan mean time, six Corinairan days from the date stamp on this message. Jump in, guns blazing! Kill anything that you can't ID as friendly! If you don't, it is unlikely that I will survive!"

"We must leave, now!" the man off camera insisted.

The camera shook as another bomb exploded nearby.

"I wish I could explain!" Nathan said, struggling to remain standing as the building shook. *"You just have to trust me!"*

"Telles to all Ghatazhak! Evac protocol Zeta One!"

"What the hell is Zeta One?" Nathan asked, as another explosion knocked over the camera, and he disappeared from view, heading out of the building.

"You do not want to know," Telles replied off camera, as the camera suddenly tilted to one side, then switched off.

Cameron sat there, her hands covering her mouth, staring wide-eyed at the blank view screen. Finally, she picked up her comm-set from the table in front of her, and placed it on her head. "Vlad, you there?" she asked, her voice shaking. "Vlad?" She couldn't remember the last time she felt this overwhelmed.

"Yes, I am here. Are you all right?" Vladimir asked over her comm-set.

"I need you to come to my quarters, right away."

"I will be there in five minutes."

"Thank you." Cameron removed her comm-set and placed it back on the table. After wiping the tears from her eyes, she picked up the remote and queued the message for replay.

CHAPTER EIGHT

"Isa Gullen", the woman said, barely able to speak as she wept. She and seven others stood in the middle of the public square on Aitkenna.

"Larso Gavin," the next man in line proclaimed.

The gathered crowd tried not to stare. Many even attempted to appear as if they just happened to be passing by.

"Forrel Evans," the last man in line stated, his lip quivering in fear.

A Dusahn officer carrying an immersive vid-cam moved slowly down the line of prisoners as each stated their name, then turned to move to one side. Once in position, he turned back around to face the line of prisoners, as well as the Dusahn soldiers who were about to become their executioners. "By order of Lord Dusahn, leader of the Dusahn Empire, you are hereby condemned to immediate execution, for the crimes committed against the Dusahn Empire by your kin." After barking out the sentence, the officer looked to the sergeant in charge of the firing squad and nodded.

Three unintelligible words came from the mouth of the officer in charge of the firing squad, with a pause between each. As the third word rang out, all four soldiers opened fire with their energy rifles, sweeping back and forth across the row of prisoners. Their bolts of energy pierced the prisoners' bodies, instantly burning gaping holes in their torsos, dropping them all to the ground.

Another order was given, and the firing stopped, the guards returning to the position of attention, weapons at their sides.

The crowd gasped in horror at the sight of the smoldering bodies, covering their faces to avoid the stench of burnt, human tissue. Within minutes, the crowd began to disperse, and a team of unlucky Corinairans moved in to dispose of the bodies.

There would be no burials. There would be no last rites. There would be no acknowledgment of any of the last wishes of the deceased. The bodies would be incinerated without ceremony, and the only notification to their next of kin would be the immersive video of their loved ones' executions.

The message was clear. The Dusahn did not tolerate disobedience.

* * *

General Telles and Captain Tuplo stood behind Josh and Loki in the Seiiki's cockpit, gazing out the forward windows at the surface of the planet below them.

"See, I told you," Josh said. "Nothing but dust and rock."

"Perhaps, but the gravity is nearly identical to that of Corinair," General Telles stated.

"But the air isn't even breathable," Josh reminded them.

"The atmospheric pressure is adequate," the general assured him. "We will be fine, as long as we all wear face masks with supplemental oxygen and filters. Just find us at least twenty square kilometers of level area, with an atmospheric pressure of approximately twelve hundred millibars."

"Whatever you say," Josh replied, shaking his head.

"Once down, remain in the cockpit and be ready to launch again," the general instructed. "We will be conducting a series of training hops." General Telles turned and headed down the ladder to the main deck.

Connor looked at Josh and Loki. "This should be fun."

* * *

Vladimir sat on the couch next to Cameron, staring at the blank view screen in disbelief. Finally, he turned to look at her. "Nathan is alive?"

Cameron said nothing, just nodded her head and sniffled.

"He has been alive all these years?"

"Uh-huh."

"And Jessica knew?"

"I'm not sure, but it looks like it. That would explain why she suddenly quit and moved to the Pentaurus cluster."

"And they didn't tell us?"

Cameron shook her head, sniffling again.

Vladimir looked back at the blank view screen. "I'm going to kill them both." He looked back at Cameron again and asked, "When do we leave?"

"What?"

"We have to depart immediately."

Cameron looked surprised. "We can't just go, Vlad."

"Of course we can," he argued. "You're the captain, aren't you? You say go, we go. That is how it works."

"We are on the verge of war, remember?"

"You heard him, Cameron. He needs us. The entire Pentaurus sector needs us."

"The Sol sector needs us!" Cameron exclaimed.

"We haven't seen a Jung ship in nearly a week. Besides, the Alliance has plenty of ships."

"The Alliance has thirteen ships, Vlad. That's hardly *plenty*."

"Are you forgetting about the three hundred and fifty gunships?"

"No, I'm not. Because they are *gunship*s, not full-sized warships."

"They can take down full-sized warships when they hunt in packs."

"Vlad..."

Vladimir threw up his hands, rising from the couch to pace around her living room. "You heard Nathan, Cam. The Dusahn are the threat, not the Jung. Just the other day, you told me you thought things were not as they seemed. You said, 'there is something else going on here.' *This* is that something else!"

"You're talking about disregarding our oath and making off with a fifteen-hundred-meter warship!"

"Our oath was also to the people of the Pentaurus cluster," Vladimir pointed out. "A fact that Alliance Command *and* our political leaders seem to have conveniently forgotten!"

"You're asking me to disobey orders!" Cameron protested.

"I'm asking you to *help* the *one man* who saved all of us seven years ago!" Vladimir shouted at the top of his lungs.

"Calm down, Commander," Cameron pleaded, throwing in his rank to remind him that she was still in charge.

"Don't you see?" Vladimir continued, taking his voice down a few notches. "If we do not go, the Dusahn quickly become a far more dangerous threat than the Jung will ever be."

"But if the Jung already have jump drives..."

"You don't believe they have jump drives any more than I do," Vladimir said. "And like Nathan said, if they do, then one more ship isn't going to make a difference. Besides, if they *were* going to attack, don't you think they would have done so by now? We just took out a dozen targets and killed millions of their people! If that wasn't a good enough excuse to send a fleet of jump ships in to annihilate us, what is?"

"But I'd be in direct violation of our orders, for crying out loud!"

"Then you'd go down in history again, wouldn't you," Vladimir argued. "The first female to captain a warship, the first female to lose a warship in battle, and the first captain to steal her own ship and go rogue."

"It would be akin to defecting, wouldn't it?"

"The worlds of the Pentaurus cluster are still our allies," Vladimir argued. "Except Takara, that is. So you wouldn't be defecting, you'd simply be upholding the Earth's obligation to help defend the Pentaurus cluster."

"I'm not so sure Galiardi is going to see it that way."

"Screw that old man," Vladimir said with a wave of his hand. "You and I both know he's playing the whole Jung angle for all it's worth, so he can drum up enough support to become the next president of the Alliance. I think he even *wants* us to go to war with the Jung again, so he can become the hero who defeated them. That would *guarantee* him the election." Vladimir sat back down on the couch next to Cameron. "You know you want to do it."

"Storm off across the galaxy to save our long lost friend? Of course I do," she admitted. "He'd do the same for us."

"He *did* do the same for us."

"What about our crew?" Cameron wondered. "If we go, we'll be on our own, cut off from the Alliance, and we'll be flying into who knows what. I would be asking my crew to put themselves in harm's way, to dishonor their oaths to the Alliance, and become criminals... Fugitives who might never be able to return home."

"Unless Nathan is right, and we end up saving everyone," Vladimir pointed out. "Then, we'd be heroes... For a second time, too!"

Cameron sighed, her face tense with indecision. "I just don't know if I can do it."

"If you don't, I'll mutiny and do it for you."

"Promise?"

"Anything for a friend," Vladimir joked.

"I have to think about it, Vlad," Cameron explained. "It would be grossly irresponsible if I did not."

"More irresponsible than stealing a warship?"

"Vlad..."

"I'm sorry," he said, taking her hand. "Of course, you should think about it. Take all the time you need." He leaned back on the couch. After a few moments, he looked at his watch. "Okay, it's been thirty seconds. Have you decided?"

"How about we talk about it in the morning?"

Vladimir sighed. "You're the captain," he finally conceded. "But remember, it will take us nearly a week to get there, so you must decide soon." Vladimir leaned over and kissed Cameron on the cheek. "Thank you for telling me he's alive," he told her. Then, he rose from the couch and headed for the door. "I will make plans to seize control of the ship from you while you think about it, just in case."

Cameron watched her old friend disappear

through the door, happier than she had seen him in years. And she understood why. She had also carried the guilt for Nathan's sacrifice for all these years... Always wondering what they could have done differently, or how they might have rescued him from execution.

Apparently, one of them did. And now she had to decide if she was willing to sacrifice everything she had worked for her entire life.

Her entire life.

That was when she made her decision.

* * *

Connor, Doctor Sato, and Doctor Megel stood on the barren, dust-blown surface of Innis Four, watching General Telles and his men carefully pacing out measurements and pushing long marker poles into the ground.

"What are they doing?" Doctor Sato asked from behind her breathing mask.

"Marking out the target area," Connor explained.

"I don't understand," Doctor Sato said, still confused.

"I don't think I want to," Doctor Megel added.

After a few more minutes, General Telles came walking toward them while his men finished stringing colored ropes around the nearby marker poles.

"Before you is the city of Aitkenna," the general began, speaking extra loud to be heard from behind his breathing mask. "Those four shorter poles, with the green rope around them, are the landing pad at Ranni Enterprises. The taller poles to the south, the ones with the red ropes strung between them, are the north wall of the Ranni Enterprises building. The poles to either side are the neighboring buildings, and the row of poles to the north are the elevated rail tracks that run east to west along the north side of the landing pad. Your goal is to land on the pad, secure your canopy, move as quickly as possible to the entrance to Ranni Enterprises, and gain entry. You must do all of this within one minute of jumping."

"Jumping?" Doctor Sato wondered.

"You will be conducting a low-level, low-surface speed jump from the back of the Seiiki, from a height of one hundred meters."

"One hundred meters?" Doctor Sato exclaimed. "We'll be dead!"

"You will be using parachutes," General Telles explained.

"Uh, General," Connor began, "Aren't parachutes usually used from a little higher up?"

"These are special parachute systems, designed for extremely low-level use."

"We can't jump out of a flying spaceship," Doctor Sato protested. "We're doctors, not soldiers."

"Can you teach Lieutenant Nash how to conduct the transfer?" the general asked.

"Given enough time, probably," Doctor Megel said.

"Can you do it in five days?"

"Maybe," Doctor Megel replied. "Maybe not... Okay, probably not."

"Then I suggest you pay attention," the general advised.

"General, I have no experience in this type of thing," Connor said. "None of us do. And that landing pad looks to be an awfully small target. And judging by the way you laid out those buildings, we're going to have to be awfully precise. Isn't there a less risky way to get us on the surface?"

"The systems are self-navigating," the general

explained. "They are accurate within one meter, under winds of less than five kilometers per hour."

"We lived on Corinair for seven years," Doctor Sato said. "Aitkenna is pretty windy this time of year."

"But the winds are normally out of the southwest, which means that the Ranni building will be blocking it during the last sixteen meters of your descent," the general explained.

"The last sixteen meters," Connor commented sarcastically. "I feel so much better."

"This plan has the highest probability of getting you all on the surface without significant injury," the general informed him.

"Oh, why didn't you say so," Connor replied. He looked at Michi and Tori. "I feel better. How about you guys?"

The two Nifelmian doctors did not reply.

"We will start by gearing you all up, then practicing your vessel exit procedures. After that, we will execute our first practice jump, starting at five hundred meters."

"We?" Connor wondered.

"I will be jumping in place of Lieutenant Nash."

"Then you'll be going with us?" Doctor Sato asked.

"I shall not. Lieutenant Nash will be well enough to lead your team on this mission," General Telles explained.

"Doesn't she need the practice?" Connor wondered.

"Lieutenant Nash has made many such jumps," the general assured them. "She requires no practice."

"Good to know," Connor said dryly.

"With each successive jump," the general continued, "we will decrease our jump altitude. Once you have mastered the techniques required and are able to land within the target area, we will conduct all subsequent jumps at the planned jump altitude."

"How many jumps are we going to do?" Doctor Sato wondered.

"As many as it takes," General Telles replied.

Doctor Sato looked at Connor, then turned to look at her fellow Nifelmian.

"Don't look at me, Michi," Doctor Megel said. "Leaving Nifelm was your idea."

* * *

Cameron sat at the small table in her quarters, studying both the old Earth Defense Force and the Sol-Pentaurus Alliance regulations, hoping to find a loophole that would give her the authority to take the Aurora to the Pentaurus cluster against orders.

So concentrated was she that it took three alerts from her door buzzer before she went to answer it.

"You wanted to see me?" Commander Kaplan said as she entered Cameron's quarters.

"Yes, come in," Cameron said, closing the door behind the commander as she passed into the room. "I apologize for the late hour," she said as she made her way to the sitting area. "I hope I didn't wake you."

"I was just finishing up some reports," the commander replied as she took a seat at the table. She glanced at the data pads in front of her. "Regulations?" she asked. "I thought you had them all memorized."

"I do," Cameron replied, sitting down. "I was hoping I'd find one that I'd forgotten."

"Is this what you do when you can't sleep?" the commander wondered. "Study regs? Because those would put me right out."

Cameron turned off both data pads and pushed

them aside. "I wish it were something as simple as insomnia," she began.

"What's going on, Captain?"

"Please, Lara, this conversation is unofficial, and off the record. So, if there was ever an appropriate time to be informal with your commanding officer, this is it."

"How ominous," Lara replied, leaning forward to listen. "Now, I'm intrigued."

Cameron took a deep breath, letting it out slowly, unsure of how to begin. Her mouth contorted from side to side, as she contemplated exactly how to ask the question that was on her mind.

"Cam, come on," Lara urged. "It can't be that bad."

"Hypothetically speaking, if I decided to do something that was not only a breach of regulations, but was also directly against orders, but I was doing it because I truly believed it was the right thing to do, would you back me?"

"Without hesitation," Lara replied immediately.

Cameron was taken aback. She hadn't expected such a quick response. In retrospect, she realized that she should have, as the commander had always been impulsive, making decisions on instinct rather than taking the time to think it through, like Cameron usually did. At that moment, she realized her executive officer was much like Nathan in that sense. That was probably why Cameron had always felt comfortable with Lara as her second in command. "Just like that?"

"Just like that."

"Without thinking it over first?"

"Why would I? I trust you, Cam. I always have. More importantly, I know how carefully you think things through. I *also* know that you don't break the rules without a *really* good reason. So, if *you* feel it's important enough to risk your career, then so do I." Lara smiled, adding, "Hypothetically speaking, of course."

Cameron breathed a sigh of relief. "You don't know how happy I am to hear that."

"So, what are you thinking...hypothetically?"

Cameron took a deep breath before replying. "I'm going to take the Aurora to the Pentaurus cluster." She suddenly felt as if a weight had been lifted from her, having finally shared her decision with someone, especially the one person she truly needed to back her. If anyone would be able to successfully oppose her, and rightfully so, it would be the ship's executive officer.

"Hot damn!" Lara exclaimed. "Jesus, Cam. When you decide to break a rule, you don't fuck around, do you?"

Cameron suddenly remembered the other old friend Lara reminded her of. "You know me," Cameron replied sheepishly. "Do it right, or don't do it at all."

"So what made you decide to go rogue?" Lara asked excitedly.

"I've got something I need you to see," Cameron replied, picking up the remote from the table, and pointing it at the view screen.

Cameron watched her XO as the video started.

"Where is this?" Lara asked. "And who is that?" she added as Nathan stepped into the shot and began to speak. "Wait, did he say Nathan?" she asked, glancing at Cameron.

"Yup."

Lara looked at her again. "As in Nathan Scott? Captain Nathan Scott?"

"The one and only."

"Oh...my...God," Lara gasped as she continued to watch the video. "I thought he was dead."

"We all did," Cameron replied.

"This is unreal," Lara said, her eyes never leaving the screen. "I've seen plenty of video footage of him. Take away the beard and the long hair..." She looked at Cameron again. "When did you get this?"

"Recently."

"*How* did you get this?"

"That, I cannot say."

"Did the President's aide send it to you?"

Cameron didn't answer.

"You can't say that, either," Lara realized.

"Correct."

"Wait, he's talking to you now," Lara said.

A minute later, the explosions started, surprising Lara the same way they had startled Cameron the first time she had watched the video. When the message ended, the commander sat there speechless and in shock, just like Cameron.

Finally, Lara turned to her. "You think it's legit?"

"Well, there's no real way to be sure, other than to go to the Pentaurus sector," Cameron admitted. "But yeah, I believe it's really him."

"If anyone should know, it would be you," Lara agreed. "But you should still have Shinoda's people look at it."

"I plan to," Cameron agreed.

"Has Commander Kamenetskiy seen this?" Lara asked, remembering how close the Aurora's chief engineer had been to the former captain of the Aurora.

"Yes. I showed him immediately after I saw it."

"I'm gonna go out on a limb here and guess that

he's totally on board with going to the Pentaurus sector."

"Oh, yeah," Cameron assured her. "He's probably overriding the jump range safeties as we speak, just to be ready."

Lara leaned back in her chair, the reality of the situation sinking in. "Jesus, Cam... This is big. I mean, *really* big. Fucking *huge*, in fact. It's Nathan Scott... *Na-Tan*."

"Please, don't call him that. I hate that stupid name."

"What's your plan?"

"To be honest, I don't really have one yet. That's why you're here."

"Outstanding," Lara grinned in anticipation. "I'm your girl. I know exactly what we need to do."

"You do?" Cameron relied, surprised.

"Are you kidding? I've run such scenarios a thousand times. It's my job as XO to keep an eye out for such things."

"I thought that was Shinoda's job," Cameron pointed out.

"Well, technically. Okay, so it's my job to keep an eye on *you*, to make sure *you* don't go rogue."

"In that case, you're doing a lousy job, Commander."

"I'll take that as a compliment," Lara replied, grabbing one of the data pads to get started planning.

Cameron shook her head. "Jess is gonna *love* you."

* * *

Connor stood at the aft end of the Seiiki's cargo deck, waiting for the Seiiki to make what would be their fourth training jump of the day. To his left was

General Telles, and standing behind him were Michi and Tori, the two Nifelmian cloning specialists.

The first jump had been easy. At first, he wasn't sure if Doctor Sato was going to be brave enough to exit the ship. It had seemed so low, despite the fact that it was the highest jump of the day. But once the jump was completed, and they were on the ground, even Michi had to admit that the jump had been exhilarating. And, as promised, the jump system had automatically navigated them right to the target, every one of them landing with ease.

The second jump had also gone well, although Tori had lost his balance while landing and tumbled over. They had all been better about recovering their canopies as well, which required them to brace while the pack reeled in their lines and canopy. At first, Connor had wondered why they couldn't simply drop their gear and run, but the general had explained that leaving the gear out in the open might alert the Dusahn that someone had jumped out of the ship, and that it wasn't just spreading leaflets warning the citizens of Corinair of the impending attack.

The third jump had been even lower than the first two, and to Connor, it seemed as if they were traveling a bit faster upon landing. Just like the previous two jumps, Connor had felt more at ease than he expected, and almost felt as if, as Nathan Scott, he had done this before. Only now did he realize that Nathan must have made many training jumps during his time as a fighter pilot.

Loki's voice counted down the last few seconds before their fourth practice insertion jump. This time, they were jumping at the planned mission jump altitude of one hundred meters, one third of the height of their last jump, which Connor had already thought was impossibly low.

The count reached zero. Connor imagined the windows in the Seiiki's cockpit turning opaque, as there were no windows in her cargo bay where they waited.

"Jump complete," Loki announced, as the cargo door began to swing quickly downward.

Air rushed in. The Seiiki's ground speed was quite low compared to her normal rate of travel, but it was enough to fill the cabin with blustering currents of air from all sides as the cargo ramp fell open. When the ramp passed the level, General Telles held up his right hand, signaling that they would jump in five seconds.

Despite instructions to the contrary, Connor glanced at the ground below that rushed past them. It was too low, too fast.

Four seconds after putting his hand up, the general's open hand became a fist, and a second after that, he pointed forward and ran out toward the aft end of the ramp, jumping into the air.

Connor ran right beside him, leaping into the air less than a step behind the general. Three seconds later, he heard and felt the dispersal charges in his pack firing, sending his chute upward and away from his back. The charges directed the four corners of the canopy away from him, forcing it to catch the air as quickly as possible. Once open, the lines yanked at Connor's harness, pulling him backwards. As his feet swung down and under him, then out in front, the force spun him around one hundred and eighty degrees, in the direction of travel.

There, not fifty meters below and one hundred meters ahead of him, was the landing site the general and his men had marked out with poles and colored ropes.

High over the elevated rails, stay down the center, flare just before you cross the near side of the landing pad. Connor repeated this to himself at least three times on the way down. The nav-system might be able to steer him to the landing sight, but he had to control his rate of descent, as well as his flare, to land.

Twenty seconds into the jump, and with his canopy fully deployed, Connor reached up and grabbed his control rings. He glanced to his right, spotting the general only ten meters away and two meters ahead of him. The general looked calm and relaxed, like he had made such jumps hundreds of times.

Connor could feel his heart racing, his breathing speeding up. He pulled at his control rings as he glided over the poles which marked the location of the elevated railways. Connor wondered if the poles were set to the height of the actual rails, with or without a tram car running along them.

He cleared the poles. Five seconds later, he pulled again to flare, slowing both his rate of descent, as well as his forward ground speed, as he crossed the near side of the simulated landing pad. His flare was a touch high, and he landed harder than the previous jump, but he was down safely, only forty-six seconds after jumping from the Seiiki.

Connor continued running forward and to his left, making room for Doctor Sato, who would be landing behind him only five seconds after he touched the ground. As he ran, he grabbed the big retract knob at the center of his chest piece and gave it a twist to his left, activating his pack's canopy retraction system. He could hear the winch whirring, and could feel the increased drag pull him backwards slightly as his canopy, still partially inflated, tried to pull him backwards. He leaned forward as he ran, adjusting his angle and stride as the canopy was reeled in and the pull against him decreased.

Once his canopy was fully retracted into his pack, he changed course and ran toward the two poles marking the main entrance to Ranni Enterprises as a gust of wind came up from behind. A shadow crossed over him as he ran, and he looked up to see Doctor Megel sailing over the general and into the red ropes strung between the poles. The Nifelmian had flared too late and had overshot the landing pad by more than twenty meters. The doctor plowed through the red ropes, pulling them off their poles, landing in a tangled mess more than ten meters past.

A few seconds later, Connor arrived at the poles marking the entrance to the building, coming to a stop next to General Telles. A few seconds later, Doctor Sato came up behind him.

"You just crashed into the building," General Telles said flatly as he walked over to help Doctor Megel untangle himself from the red marker ropes.

"So, I'm dead then?" Tori asked sheepishly.

"Doubtful," the general replied. "You would probably survive the impact. However, you would likely be injured, which would create an additional burden on your team, thus jeopardizing the success of the mission, as well as the survival of your teammates."

"Sorry," Tori said as he got to his feet.

"Do not be sorry," the general said. "Identify the problem, and learn from it. Why did you flare so late?"

"I wasn't expecting to have to flare so quickly. I

forgot that, because we were jumping from a lower altitude than before, our descent time would be considerably less."

"Very good. Remember that next time. Think of the site picture, not the time it takes to get to the ground. That is why we have marked everything out for you. Learn from your mistake, and correct the error on your next jump."

"I'll get it right next time," Doctor Megel promised the general.

"Do not be ashamed, Doctor. As your colleague pointed out, you are doctors, not soldiers. And for doctors, you are doing quite well."

"And as soldiers?" Connor wondered, wishing he hadn't before the question left his lips.

"Not so well," the general admitted, heading toward the Seiiki that was landing fifty meters away.

Connor looked at the two Nifelmians, both looking as tired as he felt. "Not so well," he echoed.

"I don't know," Michi said, "I think I did pretty well that time."

* * *

Captain Taylor and Commander Kaplan marched down the corridor of the Aurora's command deck toward the command briefing room, two ship's security personnel in tow. As the captain entered, Commander Kaplan paused and whispered instructions to the senior of the two guards. As she followed the captain into the briefing room, the guard discretely relayed her instructions into his comm-set.

"Attention on deck!" the guard inside the room barked as the captain and the executive officer entered the compartment.

For the first time since any of them could

remember, the captain did not immediately order those in attendance to remain seated. More than a few worried glances were exchanged among the command staff as they waited for their captain to get to the head of the conference table and give the order, 'As you were.'

Captain Taylor reached her spot at the head of the conference table, Commander Kaplan standing at the chair to her right. The captain nodded at the guard inside the door, who then stepped out, securing the door behind him, as did the guard on the aft entrance.

The officers exchanged more concerned glances when the status lights on the door control panels changed from green to red, indicating that the doors were now locked...from the outside.

Captain Taylor looked at each of her senior officers, all still standing at attention. "Before we begin, I must warn you all that what you are about to learn must be held in the strictest of confidence. I am about to trust each of you with information that only a handful of people in the entire galaxy know. The decisions you make in this room in the next hour will not only change your lives, but those of your families, friends, and quite possibly the futures of countless others. If any of you have any doubts as to whether or not you are comfortable with such responsibility, I beg of you to dismiss yourselves now, without repercussions." She looked at her officers again, noting that not one of them so much as flinched.

She was not surprised.

"As you were," she finally ordered, taking her seat.

The officers in attendance glanced at one another

again as they took their seats. Only this time, looks of curiosity were mixed with those of concern.

"Before I continue, I would like to assure you that I thought long and hard before I made my decision, considering every possible angle and outcome. I regret that none of you will have that luxury, as I will require *your* decisions by the end of this meeting. I also regret that I cannot reveal to you the information that prompted my decision, until *after* I have each of yours. Rest assured, I am doing this as much for *your* protection, as for that of the mission."

Captain Taylor scanned the faces of her officers again, looking for indications that any of them might already have doubts, but found none. "As you all know, ships of Jung design have been detected and intercepted at various locations within Alliance space, and the deepest penetration thus far has been just outside the Sol system. The Alliance has successfully repelled each intrusion, and has even destroyed a total of six ships to date. In response to these clear and blatant violations of our standing cease-fire agreement with the Jung, the Alliance has destroyed several key military assets belonging to the Jung, using super-JKKV strikes. Each of these assets was well within Jung space. As you might expect, the reaction of the Jung population has been a general call for retaliation. However, since the KKV strike, no Jung ships have been detected within Alliance space. If the Jung were violating Alliance territory, they appear to have stopped doing so, at least for the time being."

Cameron paused for a moment, again checking the faces of her officers, and giving them a chance to question her, if desired.

"You also know that on the same day Jung ships

started appearing in Sol space, Jung ships invaded both Takara and Darvano, destroying the Avendahl and at least eight other warships. Those forces now control the entire Pentaurus cluster, and local intelligence expects them to expand their area of control to include the entire sector before long."

"Local intelligence?" Lieutenant Commander Shinoda wondered.

"I'll get to that," Cameron promised, continuing. "What most of you do *not* know is that local intelligence has discovered the Jung ships in the Pentaurus sector are operated by a Jung caste known as the *Dusahn*."

"Captain," Lieutenant Commander Shinoda interrupted, "the Dusahn caste left the Jung sector centuries ago. We don't really know why, but we suspect they had some sort of a falling out with the Jung leadership caste at the time. There is even speculation that they attempted to seize control, but failed."

"I don't suppose any of this is verified?" Cameron wondered.

"No, sir. But, if I might ask, how did *you* get this information, but Fleet Intelligence did not?"

"I don't know that they didn't," Cameron replied. The reactions she saw to her accusation were as she had expected.

"Fleet Intelligence shares all pertinent information with the security and intelligence department of each ship in the fleet, as well as with their captains," the lieutenant commander reminded her. "The identity of the caste operating in *any* sector is *always* pertinent, as battle tactics are known to differ from caste to caste."

"I am well aware of this, Lieutenant Commander,"

Cameron replied. "Which begs the question: Why didn't command share this information with us? Why did *I* have to receive it through personal back channels?"

"You *didn't* get this intel from command?" Lieutenant Commander Shinoda asked, surprised.

"I did not," Captain Taylor replied. "In fact, I received this information in a personal message from a trusted friend residing *in* the Pentaurus sector. Furthermore, it was carried on a jump comm-drone sent directly *to* Fleet Command nearly a day ago. I checked with a friend in communications at Fleet Command. There was also an intelligence report transmitted from that jump comm-drone, one from General Telles of the Ghatazhak, directed to Alliance Command. I find it hard to believe that the general was *not* aware of the contents of the message. Therefore, I can only conclude that command *knows* the Jung ships in the Pentaurus cluster are operated by the Dusahn, and have decided not to release that information, not even to us."

"By 'command', you mean Galiardi," Lieutenant Commander Shinoda clarified.

"That would be my first guess," Cameron confirmed. "However, I admit that I have no way to be sure."

"Surely, they have their reasons," Commander Verbeek said.

"No," Lieutenant Commander Shinoda disagreed, "they *should* have disclosed this to us in the daily intelligence updates."

"Maybe it's going to be in tomorrow's updates?" the commander suggested.

"If there was enough time for the captain to get the

info through back channels, then what is command's excuse?" the lieutenant commander argued.

"I'd like to know what the captain is thinking," Lieutenant Commander Vidmar, the Aurora's chief tactical officer, interrupted.

The other two lieutenant commanders looked to their captain, equally interested.

"I don't really know," Cameron admitted. "But it's what I *suspect* that concerns me."

"What do you *suspect*?" Lieutenant Commander Vidmar asked.

"That command is purposefully hiding that information from us... *All* of us."

"Why?" Commander Verbeek wondered.

"Because then we'd realize it's not really the Jung who are sneaking around the Sol sector," Commander Kaplan said.

"That would pull the rug out from under the admiral's supporters, wouldn't it," Commander Kamenetskiy mumbled.

Everyone at the table looked at Vladimir, shocked by his comment, despite the fact that most of them were likely thinking the same thing.

"I'm sorry. Did I say that out loud?"

"You gotta be kidding me," Commander Verbeek exclaimed. "The man's an admiral, for cryin' out loud..."

"The man is a power monger..." Lieutenant Commander Vidmar argued.

"You really think he'd launch a KKV strike if he didn't think the Jung..."

"Enough!" Cameron yelled, cutting off her CAG and ending the debate before it got out of control. "I don't care what the truth is at this point, because there is really no way for us to know. I am only

247

certain of two things. First, something more is going on here, something that command, for whatever reason, is not sharing with us. More importantly, our allies in the Pentaurus cluster desperately need our help, and command has chosen to ignore them, despite the fact that a strong Jung industrial presence out *there*, poses a grave threat to our security back *here*." Cameron paused, taking a big breath and then sighing. "For that reason, I have decided to go against orders, and take this ship to the Pentaurus cluster, in order to help General Telles and the Ghatazhak *fight* the Dusahn, and prevent them from taking over the entire Pentaurus sector."

"Jesus, Captain," Lieutenant Commander Vidmar cried. "You're talking about mutiny."

"It's not mutiny," Lieutenant Commander Shinoda argued, "it's her ship, for Christ's sake!"

"It's not *her* ship," Commander Verbeek replied, "it belongs to the Alliance."

"You know what I mean," the lieutenant commander said, waving the commander off dismissively.

"Gentlemen," Cameron interrupted, raising her voice to get their attention. "I will not let this meeting turn into a debate. Is that clear?" Cameron looked at her three most opinionated officers. "Lieutenant Commander Shinoda is correct. This is *my* ship. That's why the OD announces 'Aurora arriving' when I come on board. This ship is an extension of my will, a fact that is supported by numerous regulations I would be happy to quote, if you'd like. In a nutshell, they give me the authority to do what I think is right. But they also make me responsible when I'm wrong."

"They also empower us to relieve you of command if we think you're wrong," Commander Verbeek reminded her.

"They do," Cameron admitted. "But I honestly feel it is the *right* thing to do."

"They'll hunt us down..." Commander Verbeek realized.

"Oh, don't be so dramatic," Commander Kaplan said. "If Galiardi is telling everyone the Alliance can't afford to send *one* ship, then how is he going to justify sending *another* one? Besides, do you *really* think they're going to blow a trillion dollar warship out of the sky?"

"More likely they'll cover it all up by claiming to have sent us themselves," Cameron said.

"Regardless, our careers will be over," Commander Verbeek pointed out.

"Which is why I am giving each of you an opportunity to opt out of this illegal mission. Anyone here who does not wish to be party to this will be provided safe passage back to Earth, prior to our departure."

"Are you going to extend the same courtesy to the crew?" Master Chief Warhl, the chief of the boat, asked.

"Of course."

"Well, I for one, would like to know more about this message you received, Captain," Commander Verbeek commented.

"I cannot share the message with you unless I know you are going with us to the Pentaurus sector," Cameron told him. "There is information contained within the message that I cannot allow to be carried back to Earth. It is too sensitive."

"If Fleet Command already has this information..."

"They don't have *this* information," Cameron assured them. "Trust me."

"When it gets right down to it, that's what you're

asking us all to do, isn't it, Captain?" Commander Verbeek said. "Trust *you.*"

"Yes," Cameron admitted.

"I trust her," Vladimir announced without hesitation.

"And why doesn't *that* surprise me," Commander Verbeek replied dryly.

"I trust her, as well," Commander Kaplan added.

"Another shocker," Commander Verbeek remarked.

"I trust her, too," Master Chief Warhl declared.

"As do I," Lieutenant Commander Kono added.

"Me, too," Lieutenant Commander Vidmar chimed in.

"And me," Lieutenant Commander Shinoda announced, joining the others.

"Look, I trust you as much as any of them, Captain," Commander Verbeek explained. "But we're talking about *stealing the Aurora.*"

"I know, Verbee. That's why I'm giving you all a chance to opt out. And in case any of you are wondering, this meeting will not be in the official logs, so if you do opt out, command will never know that you had prior knowledge of my intent."

"Wouldn't it have been easier just to lie, and tell us all that command ordered us to the PC?" Commander Verbeek suggested.

"I have too much respect for all of you to lie to you, especially about something this big." Cameron looked at the commander. "Even you, Verbeek."

Commander Verbeek chuckled, shaking his head. "What the hell. I guess I'm in, too."

"Very well. Just to be clear, anyone who is *not* willing to violate orders and follow me to the Pentaurus sector to fight the Dusahn, please rise, and security will escort you to your quarters until such time as you can be transported back to Earth." Cameron stared at Vladimir, who was sitting at the other end of the conference table, avoiding eye contact with any of her other officers. She could not blame them if they wanted to go, and she was not willing to put any undue pressure on them. She was quite sure they were already feeling enough pressure. But after a full minute, not one of them had risen.

Cameron breathed a sigh of relief. For this to work, she needed her command staff behind her. "Thank you," she said. "What I am about to show you reveals highly sensitive information. Information that could start a galactic war. However, I believe that in order for you all to put your hearts and souls into this mission, you need to know the real reason for my decision." Cameron picked up the remote from the table in front of her, and activated the main view screen on the wall. Another press of a button, and the video of Nathan began to play. A minute later, every mouth in the room, with the exception of hers, her executive officer's, and her chief engineer's, dropped open.

Five minutes later, Cameron turned off the view screen, the message now over. "The best man I have *ever* had the honor of serving with is going to *once again* risk his life to save us all. *I* intend to help him any way I can, and *nothing* is going to stop me."

* * *

"Captain?" a voice called from Captain Gullen's office aboard the Glendanon.

"Mister Gammon," the captain greeted. "What can I do for you?"

The young man looked guilty, almost afraid to speak.

"What is it, son?" the captain urged him.

"Comms just picked up this transmission from a jump comm-drone. It jumped into the system about three light hours away, did a blast transmission, then jumped away again. Mister Dolentz thinks it was a Dusahn comm-drone. We got reports of them jumping around to every system, broadcasting Dusahn propaganda. That's how we first learned that they took out Ybara, remember?"

"I remember."

"Anyway, the drone broadcast this before it jumped away," the young man explained, handing a data pad to his captain. "I'm really sorry, Captain."

Captain Gullen turned on the data pad, noting that the video broadcast being played on it was paused. He pressed play. Someone was carrying a camera down a line of frightened men and women, gathered in the main square of Aitkenna, on his homeworld of Corinair.

"*Jorsell Inman...*" the next man in line reported for the passing camera.

"What is this?" Captain Gullen wondered.

"A Dusahn execution line," the young man said, his own voice trembling at the thought of sharing the news with his captain.

"*...Ezri Danson...*" the next man in line reported as the camera passed him.

"Why are you..." Captain Gullen stopped mid-sentence as he recognized the next woman in line. "God, please, no... What have I done..."

"*...Isa Gullen...*"

CHAPTER NINE

Cameron stepped out onto the starboard catwalk from the Aurora's command deck, into her main hangar deck. Gathered below her were all the men and women on her crew, except for her bridge crew, whom she had already vetted, and a few specialists needed in engineering who had been cleared by Vladimir.

She was uneasy, knowing that only twenty people were currently running her ship. She thought back to a time nine years earlier, when the Aurora had operated with just as many hands. They had managed to pull off the impossible then, and in the two years that followed. She hoped for a similar miracle now.

She tapped her comm-set. "Lock it down, and put me ship-wide."

"*Security is locking it down now, Captain,*" Ensign deBanco replied from the bridge.

Cameron glanced below to her left and right, noting that security guards had entered the main hangar deck and were taking up positions at all the exits. The nearly two hundred crew members gathered below also noticed, many of them becoming concerned.

"*Ship-wide is active.*"

"Attention, crew of the Aurora. I have asked you to gather here for security reasons, since I have an announcement that affects you all. As you all know, the Jung have seized control of the Pentaurus cluster, destroying the Avendahl and the Takaran fleet in the process. You also know that our leaders have decided that the Alliance cannot afford to send even a single ship to honor the Sol-Pentaurus

Alliance charter...the very same charter that saved our world nine years ago, and led to the very same Alliance that protects our worlds today. I believe this decision to be a grave error, and I intend to do something about it."

Cameron could see the disturbed looks on the faces of her crew below. She had seen the same expressions on several of her senior officers when she first told them of her intentions.

"I realize that our primary duty is to protect the people of Earth, before the people of our allied worlds. But I believe that the presence of the Jung in the Pentaurus cluster is a much greater threat to the Sol sector than the Jung nearby. For I do *not* believe the Jung here *have* jump drives. If I am wrong, then we are outnumbered *and* outgunned, and the Aurora will make little difference if the Jung decide to attack the Sol sector with force. However, if I am right, we have a chance to stop what could be the greatest threat we have ever known, *before* that task becomes impossible."

Cameron took a deep breath. "In two hours, I am taking this ship to the Pentaurus sector, to join forces with General Telles and the Ghatazhak, where we will fight to once again liberate the Pentaurus cluster. This will be in direct violation of orders, so any of you who do not wish to continue to serve under my command are free to board those shuttles behind you, and you will be returned to Earth."

Another deep breath, and she ended with, "You have ten minutes to decide," after which she returned to the command deck.

* * *

Environmental warning horns echoed within the Glendanon's massive cargo bay. As they sounded, the lighting in the bay changed from red to a normal white light, signaling that the long repressurization cycle had been completed.

The Seiiki's cargo ramp lowered slowly to the deck. Connor, Michi, Tori, and General Telles and his men came walking out to greet the handful of technicians coming toward them.

"Good afternoon," the lead technician greeted as he and his team approached.

"Good afternoon," General Telles replied.

"I trust your training went well?"

"Well enough," the general responded, continuing past the technical team.

The lead tech said nothing. After the Ghatazhak had walked away, he turned to Captain Tuplo. "That bad, huh?"

"We did okay," Connor replied with a shrug. "I think he just wishes we had more time to prepare."

"We'll do our best to finish ahead of schedule," the lead tech promised.

"Just see that it's done right," Connor insisted.

"Yes, sir," the lead tech replied. "We'll get started removing the overhead windows over the upper and lower passenger decks."

"You're sure this is all going to work?" Connor asked.

"We've been working out the engineering side of it all day using the Glendanon's computers," the tech informed him. "It'll be a lot of work, but we'll get it done, Captain. We'll give her some real teeth for you."

"Thanks, I think," Connor replied uneasily.

Marcus came down the ramp next, passing the techs on the way as they headed up into the Seiiki. "Nervous?" he asked Connor.

"A little," Connor admitted. "I mean, they're opening up my hull."

"They're just windows, Cap'n. If you like, I'll see that they crate them up nice and safe."

Connor sighed. "Don't bother. I have a feeling the Seiiki won't be running passengers ever again," he said, patting Marcus on the shoulder. "At least not the kind who want to look out the windows."

"I can't believe we're gettin' plasma cannons!" Josh exclaimed with excitement as he and Loki came down the ramp.

"Don't get too excited," Connor warned. "They're only mark ones."

"Better than throwin' rocks," Josh replied. "Oh, wait; we couldn't even do *that* before."

"If you'll excuse me, Captain?" Loki said, nodding toward his wife walking toward him, carrying their baby daughter in her arms.

"Might as well start pulling all the passenger seats too," Connor instructed. "But save those. I'm sure we can do something with them, somewhere. Besides, we paid a lot for them, if I remember correctly."

"Don't remind me," Marcus said, as he turned to go back up the ramp.

* * *

Cameron stood in the flight operations center, staring out the large windows facing into the main hangar bay, as the last few members of her crew who wished to depart boarded the waiting cargo shuttle.

"Better half a loyal crew, than a whole crew that's only half-loyal," Commander Verbeek said from behind the captain.

Cameron glanced over her shoulder at the commander. "I was really hoping more of them would stay."

"If it makes you feel any better, I recognized quite a few of them as having families back home. They were probably afraid they'd never see them again."

"What about you, Verbee? You have a wife, don't you?"

"She doesn't like me much, to be honest. She'll probably be more than happy to divorce my sorry ass."

Cameron smiled at the commander.

"Look, Captain, I'm sorry I busted your butt this morning. But you really tossed a live one into the middle of the room, you know that."

"Yeah, I know." She smiled at him again. "I'd rather have you speak your mind, Verbee. You know that."

"That's why I did."

"How many pilots did we lose?"

"Are you kidding? Pilots are a glory-hungry bunch of idiots. They're already starting a pool on who will get the most Jung kills."

"Speaking from personal experience?"

"Damn right. I was just as dumb, once."

Cameron watched as the cargo shuttle closed its boarding ramp and began to roll into the transfer airlock on the port side.

"Nothing but the good ones left, Captain. Now, why don't you go and tell them the real reason we're going rogue?" Commander Verbeek suggested.

"I wish everyone would stop calling it that," she chuckled. "Makes us sound like a bunch of space pirates."

"Commander Verbeek, Pirate CAG. I kind of like the sound of that."

Cameron smiled and headed out of the flight operations center. She stepped into the corridor and to the port side, then back out onto the catwalk. With fewer than one hundred of her crew remaining, she chose to make her way down the side gangway to talk to them at deck level. They deserved that, at least. "Comms," she called over her comm-set as she headed for the port forward ladder, "play the message, ship-wide, every view screen, including the status screen on the forward bulkhead of the main hangar deck."

"*Aye, sir,*" Ensign deBanco replied.

Cameron made her way down the steep steps to the main hangar deck below.

"*Hello, Miri. I'll bet you weren't expecting to hear from me again,*" Nathan's voice echoed throughout the ship as the message reached every screen, every speaker, and every comm-set aboard the Aurora.

Cameron studied the faces of her assembled crew as she approached; all were transfixed by the image and words of a hero everyone thought was long dead. She waited to the side, not wanting to distract them, as the message played out. Nearing the message's end, the sounds of explosions began to fill the hangar bay, and Cameron continued toward the center, coming to stand directly in front of her crew when the video ended.

"The bravest, most dedicated, most selfless man I have ever known is about to risk his life again, to save not only the Pentaurus cluster, but quite possibly the entire galaxy. And the Aurora is going to help him."

"Company, A-TEN-SHUN!" Master Chief Warhl barked.

The men and women of the Aurora snapped to attention.

"Dismissed," Cameron said proudly. "And thank you."

Cameron stood still, feet shoulder width apart, hands clasped behind her back, making eye contact and nodding at every crew member who passed on their way back to their duty stations. Those who had stuck by her would never be forgotten.

She would make damned sure of it.

* * *

Connor walked between the stacks of massive cargo pods, up the center of the Glendanon's cavernous cargo bay, headed aft. As he approached the makeshift airlock, fashioned to join the starboard and port stacks to the aft entry into the cargo ship's inhabited areas, he could see workers high above him, welding sections of cargo pod hulls into place along the inner frame of the aft-most cargo bay doors. They started work within hours of their initial meeting, and had already torn apart two whole cargo pods. Unfortunately, their work was interrupted by the long depressurization, and repressurization, of the Glendanon's cargo bay, an event that rarely occurred on such a ship. Connor had no idea if their efforts to protect those forced to reside inside the cargo pods would do any good. There had been some debate about waiting for the Aurora to arrive. She would have additional space for the refugees, as well as dedicated fabrication facilities to create proper shielding panels. Although the Ghatazhak had a few fabricators, they were dedicated to completing the combat modifications to the Seiiki.

The Seiiki...a combat ship. The idea made Connor laugh. Sometimes he just had to pretend like none of this was real...like it was some kind of a dream. It was all happening so fast. Despite his inherent nature to make decisions on instinct, as of late, he had developed the annoying habit of overanalyzing things prior to making a decision.

Connor reached the entrance to the makeshift airlock. The airlock itself was nothing more than a metal shipping container, just big enough to hold a half dozen people. The Ghatazhak technicians had installed hatches taken from a few of the Glendanon's escape pods—a fact that made the crew somewhat unhappy—and a pressurization system from one of the pods, as well. After sealing the whole thing up, they connected it to the main hatch from the cargo bay into the inhabited area, then to the port and starboard cargo pod stacks via expandable rescue tunnels. They then wrapped them in carbon-sheathing in order to stiffen them up and provide additional strength. It wasn't a pretty setup, but it worked.

For now, however, movement through the airlock was quick. Although Captain Gullen required the airlock doors to remain closed at all times, with the cargo bay pressurized, there was no delay waiting for pressurization cycles to complete.

Connor entered the lowest class one cargo pod in the port stack. It had been hastily turned into a medical bay, and was packed with the wounded. Although it was still a busy place, full of pain and suffering, it was not the chaos and despair he had witnessed back on Burgess just over a day ago. Still, there were far too many patients, and too few real doctors to tend their wounds. There were, however, plenty of volunteers willing to do what they could. Anything to pass the time, and get away from the gloom and desperation of the cargo pods packed full of refugees above.

"Do you know where Lieutenant Nash is located?" Connor asked one of the volunteers. "Black hair, pretty, the only female Ghatazhak?"

"Oh, her," the lady replied, turning to point to a row of curtains along the forward side of the massive pod. "Third curtain."

"Thanks," Connor said, continuing on. He carefully made his way around the cots and the piles of bloody debris. A minute later, he pulled back the third curtain slowly, and found Jessica lying on a cot inside. "Nice room," he said, pulling the curtain closed behind him.

"Yeah, ain't it?" Jessica said as she sat up. "I have no idea why they put me in here. I told them I could go back and hang with the Ghatazhak. I can give myself the nanite boosters."

"I don't think conditions are much better anywhere else than they are right here. At least, not from what I've seen so far."

"So, how did the jump training go?" she asked, looking for any reason to keep talking. "You and the docs low-level insertion experts now?"

"Far from it, I'm sure," Connor replied. "I have to admit though, it *was* kind of fun. Not as hard as I thought, either."

"You've done it a few times before," Jessica reminded Connor. "As Nathan, I mean. Well, not actually the low-level stuff, but the parachute stuff."

Connor nodded. "I figured as much."

"Did you have a memory of it?" Jessica wondered, encouraged by his recognition.

"No, it just stood to reason. He *was* a military-trained pilot, after all."

"It's still kind of weird to hear you talk about

yourself in the third person," Jessica told him. "I mean, I know *why* you do it, but it's still weird."

"He still *is* someone else to *me*," Connor reminded her.

"I know, I know. The beard and the hair help, a little."

"Yeah, I was wondering the other day if my clone... I mean, *his* clone... The fifth-generation clone..."

"I got it..."

"I was wondering if *he* has a beard."

"Does it matter?"

"Not really," Connor admitted. "It was just a thought that crossed my mind. I mean, after I transfer *into* him, will I look any different?"

"Well, beard or no beard, you *will* be five years younger than you are now."

"I will?"

"Yeah," Jessica replied. "They only grow them to the age of twenty-five."

"Earth years, or Corinairan years?" Connor wondered.

Jessica looked puzzled. "You know, I don't think I ever really asked. It could be twenty-five Nifelmian years, for all I know."

"I guess I'll ask Doctor Sato when I see her again."

"Call her Michi," Jessica suggested. "She hates being called 'doctor'. So does Tori."

"I'll try to remember that."

Jessica pulled herself up a little, wincing.

"How's the leg doing?" Connor wondered, noticing her discomfort.

"It's a little sore," she admitted. "Mostly because of all the physical therapy they've got me doing. There's no equipment here, so they have to come up with some interesting ways to exercise my leg. Other than that, it's coming along nicely. I should be able to get up and walk around in a couple of days."

"I heard they have a gym on board," Connor told her. "I don't know how good it is, but you might want to check it out."

"Yeah, I'll do that."

"Are you going to be ready in time to escort us down to Corinair for my 'coming out party'?" Connor joked.

"Are you kidding?" Jessica smiled. "I've been waiting seven years for this."

* * *

"We cleared the Sol sector on our last jump, Captain," Commander Kaplan reported across the conference table in the Aurora's command briefing room. "Technically, we are now in Jung-controlled space, although there are no known outposts out here, and we are following the established outbound transit route from Sol to the Pentaurus cluster. I've ordered deep space scans and have asked Commander Verbeek to have his people conduct extended recon patrols during every recharge layover. We're also keeping the shields up, but at minimal power, so that they don't slow down the recharging process any more than we have to."

"Very well," Cameron replied.

"Commander Kamenetskiy is running all four antimatter reactors at one hundred and thirty-five percent to compensate for the additional power drain by our shields. But that's *fifteen percent* over their maximum short-duration rating, and he's running them that high around the clock. He insists it is safe, but I'm not so sure. I think he'll do anything to get back to his friend."

"If the commander says it's safe, I believe him,"

Cameron insisted. "He knows we won't do Nathan and the Karuzari any good if we blow ourselves up before we get there."

"Yeah, well, I'm surprised that he didn't propose we try to recreate your original *super jump,*" the commander said.

"He did," Cameron replied. "I'm pretty sure he was kidding, though." Cameron exchanged glances with her XO as Lieutenant Commander Shinoda and Lieutenant Commander Vidmar both came into the room.

"Captain, we've finished reviewing everything we have from Fleet Intelligence about the invasion of the Pentaurus cluster. Of course, their reports are still referring to them as 'the Jung', even the intel updates we received just before departure."

"What have you found?"

"Well, not a lot, I'm afraid. As soon as they received word, Fleet sent a few surveillance drones back to the PC. Out of ten drones, only four made it back."

"What happened to the other six?" Commander Kaplan asked.

"We don't know," the lieutenant commander replied.

"The Dusahn probably shot them down," Lieutenant Commander Vidmar commented.

"The Ghatazhak did collect some old light from the initial invasion, as well as a lot of civilian broadcasts... mostly news stuff. But it gave us additional images, many of them much better quality than we could hope for, collecting old light from afar."

Lieutenant Commander Shinoda stuck his data chip into the slot on the conference table, then picked up the remote and activated the view screen on the wall of the briefing room. "These pictures are from satellites in orbit over Corinair. And I think a few of them are from shuttles that were probably in orbit at the time of the attack. So far, we've been able to determine that there were at least four ships that invaded the Darvano system. Two were most likely frigates, as their images were not large enough to be destroyers. One was a cruiser, and another was either a heavy cruiser, or a battleship...we're not sure."

"You can't tell?"

"The problem is that the Dusahn ships, although obviously of Jung design, are likely much *older* than anything we've seen, and have probably been modified over time. For all we know, they aren't even the same ships they departed with. They could have conquered some industrialized worlds along the way, and used them to build new ships."

"Or captured some and modified *them.*" Commander Kaplan added.

"In order to take out the Avendahl, at least one of those ships would have to be a battleship, if not a battle platform," Lieutenant Commander Vidmar remarked.

"They didn't start building battle platforms until about a century ago," Cameron reminded them.

"A battleship then."

"Even with the element of surprise, the Avendahl should have been able to defend against a battleship," Commander Kaplan insisted.

Lieutenant Commander Shinoda pressed the remote again, putting up several new images. "Not if the Dusahn have large-scale energy weapons."

Cameron and the others looked at the pictures.

Brilliant red bolts of energy appeared to be traveling between the Dusahn ships and the Avendahl.

"Plasma cannons?" Cameron wondered.

"That would be my guess," the lieutenant commander agreed. "Or some other type of directed energy weapon."

"If the Dusahn were cast out, it would make sense for them to develop large-scale energy weapons," Commander Kaplan pointed out. "Better than having to carry around a few billion rail gun slugs everywhere you go."

"So how many ships will we be facing when we jump into the Darvano system?" Cameron wondered.

"We examined all the intel we received from Fleet prior to going rogue..." Shinoda looked at the captain. "Sorry, prior to departure. Anyway, the greatest number of ships we have seen in the Darvano system at one time is four, but usually only three. But, we don't have any *recent* data. Everything we have is from four days ago. And, since the PC is only ten light years across, they could have twenty ships in the cluster, all of which could jump to Darvano within minutes."

"All you really need to hold the cluster is one big-ass warship, and a bunch of frigates...or even gunships," Lieutenant Commander Vidmar observed. "Really, once they were rid of the Avendahl, they pretty much owned the entire sector, Captain."

"There's something else to consider," Lieutenant Commander Shinoda said. "The attack on the Darvano system occurred thirty minutes *after* the attack on the Takar system. And the attack on the Takar system was basically over in about twenty minutes, twenty-five tops."

"So, they may have used the same ships for both attacks," Cameron realized.

"Or, at the very least, a few from the first attack were sent to join the second attack," the lieutenant commander suggested. "Our intel on the attack on the Takar system is pretty weak. We don't even have any good IDs on the ships the Dusahn used. Just some basic ship size and count stuff. So what we originally thought to be at least six to eight ships, could in fact be four to six."

"Or even just four," Lieutenant Commander Vidmar commented.

"I'm betting at least six," Lieutenant Commander Shinoda said. "We sent a recon drone to the Burgess system just after you told us about the message. It came back less than an hour ago."

"What did it find?" Cameron asked, afraid of the answer.

Lieutenant Commander Shinoda shook his head. "Burgess was glassed. Nothing left alive. It will be uninhabitable for centuries. The drone collected old light, and we identified the attacking ships. An assault ship was first, but somehow the Ghatazhak managed to take it out. Then, about ninety minutes later, three more ships arrived. Two small, one large. I'm guessing two frigates and a heavy cruiser or battleship. If I'm right, and they started with six ships, then they're down to five now."

"Unless they have ships in reserve somewhere," Commander Kaplan commented.

"Do we have any estimates on the Dusahn's jump range?" Cameron wondered.

"We don't really have any information on that," Lieutenant Commander Shinoda admitted.

"Best guess," Cameron urged him.

Lieutenant Commander Shinoda hesitated. "There are just too many unknowns, Captain. They could be using four jump drives per ship, each with a range of thirty light years. They could be using two with fifty-light-year ranges. Or one that jumps one hundred and twenty. It's a wild guess at this point. For all we know, they could have staged ships nearby before attacking Sherma, although that would be an uncharacteristic strategy for the Jung."

"But perhaps not for the Dusahn," Cameron said.

"Like I said, too many unknowns," the lieutenant commander replied. "All we know for certain is that Dusahn reinforcements arrived at Burgess an hour and a half *after* the Ghatazhak defeated the first ship they sent. So one would have to assume that they have at least a ninety-minute response capability of at *least* one hundred and twelve light years."

"That's a scary thought," Commander Kaplan said.

"Yes, it is," Cameron agreed, leaning back in her chair. "We need to plan for battle," she said, looking to her officers for advice.

"Like Scott said, jump in guns blazing, and shoot anything that doesn't look like a friendly," Commander Kaplan said.

"I don't see how we can plan for anything else," Lieutenant Commander Vidmar agreed. "Not with what little intel we've got."

Cameron sighed. "Send recon drones to both Takar and Darvano. Park them outside both systems to collect data. Old light, comms, whatever. But they are *not* to penetrate either system. Program them to return and rendezvous with us at our final recharge layover prior to arriving at the Darvano system. I'd like to try to get a more accurate ship count, if possible. We've got a finite number of jump missiles on board, and I'd like to be smart about how we use them."

"Yes, sir," Lieutenant Commander Vidmar replied.

Cameron shook her head. "Keep working on the problem, people. I want something a little better than 'jump in guns blazing.'"

* * *

Captain Donlevy climbed into the pilot's seat of his Keenan-class cargo pod hauler, more commonly referred to as a boxcar. Secured beneath his ship was an empty, class one cargo pod, large enough to hold up to six Takaran jump fighters, if properly arranged.

"*Boxcar Seven, Falcon One,*" Ensign Lassen called over comms. "*We're ready whenever you are.*"

Josen looked at his captain. "You ready?"

"Ready as I'll ever be, I suppose," Captain Donlevy replied as he strapped himself in.

"Falcon One, Boxcar Seven," Josen responded. "Give us a few minutes to get on course and speed for the jump."

"*Copy that,*" Ensign Lassen replied. "*We're going to jump back to Burgess to make one final check. If we don't return before you're ready to jump, it means the system is still clear.*"

"Understood," Josen said.

"Take us out, Josen," Captain Donlevy instructed. "I don't feel much like flying today."

"No problem," Josen replied. It wasn't often that the captain let him fly the ship. But he fully expected this trip to come up empty.

Josen fired up the main engines and turned the ship slightly to its plotted jump course. He then tied the auto-flight system to the jump-nav computers and set the jump window for plus five minutes, which would give Falcon One plenty of time to return and warn them in case the Dusahn had returned to the Sherma system unexpectedly.

———————

Commander Jarso woke suddenly, jarred awake by his timer alarm. It had been three days, now, since the Dusahn had glassed Burgess, and he had been waiting at his assigned recovery point since then.

He had no way of knowing if the Dusahn were still in the system since all systems were shut down, and he had nothing but his eyes to scan the heavens in hope of rescue.

It was cold in his tiny cockpit. The emergency chemical heating system in his suit was barely enough to keep him from going into hypothermia. It had felt wonderful at first, since he waited as long as possible to activate it, for fear that his recovery might take longer than anticipated.

He had rationed both his food and water, as well, and consumed only the absolute minimum needed to survive. When he could no longer swallow, he would trickle a bit of water into his mouth. When his stomach became so angry that it hurt, he would eat one quarter of an energy bar. At the very least, he would be a few pounds lighter when rescued.

He could not help but long for the old Takaran jump fighters. They, like the Falcons, could jump repeatedly, achieving seemingly limitless ranges. But Captain Navarro had chosen to modify his fighters to follow the example of the Earth's Super Eagles. The result had been faster, more maneuverable, and more deadly for a multi-role attack craft, but it sacrificed its range. Just like the Super Eagles of Earth, his fighter carried only enough jump energy for a cumulative range of two light years, and he had used up a significant portion of that in battle. The fact was, he had almost no jump energy left, and what little there was, he planned to channel into the ship's environmental system once his ship's emergency batteries were depleted.

Commander Jarso had actually been surprised when no help had arrived after the first day. By his calculations, it would have taken the Jung no more than six hours to completely glass the planet, if that. That meant they had maintained some kind of presence within the system, beyond ending all life on Burgess. Why, he was not sure. The message was clear enough. Stand against the Dusahn, and suffer the consequences. Hanging around in case a ship returned to assess the damage to Burgess seemed a complete waste of time to him. Yet, he was well into his third day drifting in the frigid cold of deep space.

As planned, he made sure that he was awake every hour, on the hour, for five minutes. He rubbed his eyes, then pressed the power button on his comms, listening for a friendly voice.

———

Falcon One appeared on the outskirts of the Sherma system behind a blue-white flash of light. It was a tiny speck against a sea of stars, and was cold-coasting when it arrived. If anyone was in the system and wasn't looking their way when they arrived, they would be unlikely to detect them now.

———

"Jump complete. Approaching recovery point Echo Seven," Ensign Lassen reported. "Checking passive sensors." The ensign studied his sensor display for several minutes, also keeping an eye on the time display. "Still looks clear."

"Give him a call," Lieutenant Teison instructed.

"Rubber, you out there?" Ensign Lassen called over the comms. If the Dusahn were in the system, then they were far enough away that it would take at least a few minutes for them to pick up the radio call. Even if it did, it would make little sense to them.

Ensign Lassen looked at the lieutenant, waiting. He glanced at the time display again. Only a minute left in the comm window. "Rubber, Lassen. Make a sound, any sound. Show us you're alive."

As usual, Commander Jarso heard nothing but static. 'The sound of the cosmos' some called it. The commander thought of it as 'the sound of death'.

There was a crackle. Louder than usual. For a moment, he thought he heard a voice. Then it came again.

"*Rub.........sen.........Make.........any sou............ you're ali...*"

Commander Jarso's eyes widened in disbelief. He glanced at his clock. There were only twenty seconds left until procedure called for comms to shut down again. "Hello!" he called out. He realized he had forgotten to press his mic button, and tried again. "Hello! This is Rubber! I'm here! I'm here!"

"*Is......at......u, Jars......*" the voice called.

"Yeah, it's me! It's Jarso!"

"*Power......and stand.........You're ri.........a few min.........away, Comman...*"

"What about the rest of them?" the commander asked. "Did you find the others?"

"*You were.........first stop. We're loo.........for them now.*"

Commander Jarso felt a wave of relief wash over him.

"*Sit tight.........ready,*" Ensign Lassen instructed.

"Understood," the commander replied. "Just tell them to hurry the hell up."

———————

"Jump complete," Josen reported.

"Well, I'll be a..." Captain Donlevy declared, looking at the sensor display. "I've got a Takaran fighter at our ten, about twenty down, maneuvering slowly." The captain keyed his comm-set. "Handel! Cortesh! Open her up, we've got company coming!"

* * *

Cameron turned off the vid-com, ending the recording. She then typed in an encryption code, and encrypted the message she had just recorded. After that, she typed in a message in the hint field of the decryption prompter. 'What does your little sister call you?'

Cameron transferred the encrypted message to the outbound message queue, addressing it to Captain Robert Nash, Commanding Officer, ESS Tanna. She then set the message for secure deletion after it was sent.

Cameron pressed the intercom button. "Comms, Captain."

"*Comms, aye,*" Ensign deBanco replied over the intercom.

"Priority message in the outbound queue, bound for the ESS Tanna. She is currently patrolling near Chi Draconis."

"*Return destination for the jump comm-drone?*" the ensign asked.

Cameron thought for a moment. "Haven system."

"*Yes, sir.*" After a few seconds, the ensign reported back. "*Message is away, Captain.*"

"Thank you." Cameron turned off her intercom

and leaned back in her seat, satisfied that if things did not go well, at least someone would know the truth.

* * *

"How's it going?" Jessica yelled up at them from the deck.

Connor walked across the top of the Seiiki, headed aft toward Jessica's voice. "We're installing the port gun now," Connor called down to her as he reached the aft edge of the ship. "The starboard gun is already done. You want to see?"

"Sure."

Connor walked to his left, toward the starboard engine nacelle, climbing down the ladder rungs cut into the side of the inner edge of the nacelle itself. After dropping down the last meter, he headed back toward the cargo ramp to meet Jessica.

"Looks like you've made that climb before," she commented.

"Once or twice, yeah," Connor replied as he approached. "After you," he said, gesturing for her to head up the cargo ramp.

Jessica headed up the ramp, with Connor by her side. "I see you got the door guns installed," she commented, noticing the same guns that were mounted inside the side doors of the combat jump shuttles.

"Yeah, they even beefed up the power output a bit when they assembled them. I guess they had to tone them down inside the combat jumpers. Something about too much heat in a small compartment." Connor noticed that she was no longer limping. "I see your leg is healing nicely."

"Yup. Still a little sore at the end of the day, but I've been working the hell out of it. Telles has the suit tech adjusting my suit to give me a little more assist on my bad leg, just in case."

Connor waited for Jessica to ascend the ladder at the front of the Seiiki's cargo bay, to the landing one level above. After she passed through the forward hatch, he quickly climbed up after her, and followed her into the main passenger bay.

"Wow, this is different," Jessica commented, looking around. The passenger seats were gone, as were the big windows that had once been above them. Instead, there was only empty space. "What's going to be in here?" she wondered.

"Eventually, plasma generators and a couple of fusion reactors to power them. But there's not enough time to install them now. Besides, we don't really need them for this mission. The good stuff is up top," Connor said, pointing to the next landing above them.

Jessica headed up the newly installed access ladder leading to the center of the upper landing, then passed through the hatch into what had once been the upper passenger deck. The passenger seats had been removed from that compartment as well. On either side, there were new bulkheads that protruded nearly all the way to the center of the compartment, rising a little over a meter from the deck. Aft, and to either side, were two mark one plasma generators, as well as two small fusion reactors to power them.

Connor entered the narrow space behind her. "Go ahead," he urged, pointing to the left. "The starboard turret is fully functional."

Jessica climbed up the short ladder and sat in the gunner's chair. She strapped herself in, then activated the turret power, taking care not to arm the guns themselves. She twisted the control sticks on either side, tracking the guns back and forth, and up and down, taking note of the maximum fields of fire. "Not bad," she admitted. "As long as they come at you from above."

"Yeah, well, for this mission, that's probably where they'll be," Connor replied, "above us. Eventually they're going to put automated turrets on our underside, on either side of the cargo bay. They're also talking about putting another manned turret topside, between the cockpit and the forward lift fan, but that one will be smaller, like the ones in the top of your combat jumpers. We might even be able to squeeze another automated turret into the underside of our nose," Connor added excitedly. "But they're still working on the engineering for that one. They'll have to reconfigure the sensor package to make room for it."

Jessica smiled as she climbed down from the gunner chair. "Well, you're awfully happy about all this."

"Yeah, I'm kind of surprised, myself," Connor admitted. "At first, I was panicking at the thought of cutting holes in my ship, but then, I started thinking. Without the guns, we might not make it back in one piece. So..."

"Yeah, well, once this baby is done, she's going to pack a hell of a punch," Jessica said.

"I certainly hope so," Connor agreed. "For all our sakes."

Jessica noted the slight concern in Connor's last remark. "You're not getting cold feet, are you?"

"Getting?" Connor laughed. "Trust me, I've had them since the moment I turned the ship around and headed back to Burgess."

Jessica looked at Connor.

"What is it?" Connor wondered.

Jessica sighed. "You are *so* much like him. Sometimes, it's hard to believe that you're *not* him."

"Yeah," Connor replied. "You know, with each passing day, I start to feel more *like* him. I don't know if it was being under fire on Burgess, or the jump training, or putting in these guns... I mean, I still don't have access to his memories, but I almost feel like I *know* what he felt."

"I'm not sure I follow," Jessica admitted.

"What it feels like to live your life for a *purpose*. One that isn't centered around what *you* want, but what's best for *others*. For people you don't even *know*. For the last five years, I've been pretty much taking care of myself."

"You've been taking care of your ship, and your crew as well," Jessica reminded him.

"Not really," Connor said. "I mean, yes, I have been, but it's not the same. If I keep the ship flying and getting work, then I'm not only taking care of myself, but also my crew. It's not really a selfless act." Connor scratched his head. "Besides, I'm pretty sure that Marcus and Josh have been taking care of *me*."

"Yeah, that's probably because five years ago I told them I'd kill them both if they let anything happen to you."

"That would explain a lot," Connor admitted.

* * *

Cameron walked down the row of four Super Eagle jump fighters, her CAG, Commander Verbeek, behind her to the left, and her XO, Commander Kaplan, one step back on the right. On her right were the starboard launch tubes. Each of them had a fighter loaded and ready to deploy. All they needed were pilots. On her left were four more fighters, referred to as the 'second-up ready-birds'. Once the 'ready-birds' in the tubes were away, the second-ups could be loaded and launched within minutes. The minimum time required by Fleet operational standards was three minutes. Commander Verbeek's men had it down to two, a fact they had successfully demonstrated to her an hour earlier.

As she walked the line, she noticed something unfamiliar on one of the Super Eagle's nose gear. She stopped, moved closer, and squatted down to inspect the gear, in particular the two red bars that were stuck at angles through the deck grating, pinching in on either side of the nose gear. "What the hell are these?" she asked, standing again.

"Holding pins, sir!" the young deck tech standing nervously at attention next to his spacecraft replied.

"These aren't standard issue, are they?" Cameron stated, suspicion in her tone.

"No, sir!" the young man replied.

Cameron looked at the other fighters, noting that every one of them had the same two red bars sticking out on either side of their nose gear. "Whose crazy idea was this?" she demanded.

"Mine, sir!" the deck tech answered.

"Explain yourself, Mister..."

"Tosen, sir!" the young man replied. "They work better than the standard holding gear, Captain."

"I find that hard to believe, Mister Tosen," Cameron challenged. "Suppose you tell me why these red bars work better than the gear the engineers designed to hold down these spacecraft."

"Beg your pardon, sir, but the gear provided is a pain in the ass...uh, sir. They may hold the ships down nice and snug, but they're difficult to remove and weigh a ton."

"These don't look like they could hold down squat, Mister Tosen," Cameron remarked. "Are you telling me that these birds are gonna stay put if we're under attack and maneuvering hard?"

"I believe if we're under attack, these birds are already going to be out killing Jung, Captain," the young deck tech replied confidently. "And if not, we can turn up the gravity on this deck to keep the birds in place while you turn and burn, sir."

Cameron looked at Commander Verbeek.

"Shaved at least thirty seconds off our load and launch time," the commander told her.

Cameron nodded, then looked at the nervous young deck technician. "Good thinking, Mister Tosen," she told him, before moving on.

Commander Verbeek smiled at Mister Tosen as an obvious wave of relief washed over the young man, then continued to follow the captain.

* * *

"You asked to see me?" General Telles said, as he entered Captain Gullen's office aboard the Glendanon.

"Yes, General, thank you for coming," Captain Gullen said, rising to greet him. "I apologize for the inconvenience. I know you and your men must be busy preparing for tomorrow's mission."

"Not at all, Captain. The Ghatazhak are always prepared. Most of my men are already asleep for the night."

"You can sleep the night before a mission?" the captain wondered. "I was never able to do so when I was in the service. I was always running through every possible scenario, reviewing what I would do for each possible thing that could go wrong."

"The Ghatazhak constantly train," the general explained. "To the point that much of our reaction is automatic. Decisions that normal men might struggle with for hours, Ghatazhak are trained to make in a tenth of a second. Therefore, there is nothing for us to lose sleep over the night before."

Captain Gullen looked at the general. "I find that hard to believe, General. With all the terrible things that you and your men are called upon to do... Does not guilt ever rob you of sleep?"

"It does not."

"So, you felt nothing when you gunned down those innocent people on Earth eight years ago? Or on Burgess a week ago?"

"You are not the first to misunderstand the Ghatazhak, Captain," General Telles explained. "We are men, same as you. We feel, the same as you. We do not like the things that we must do. However, we are able to accept that we must do such things, in order to accomplish our mission."

"But what if your mission is not just?" the captain wondered. "Surely, there were missions performed under the reign of Caius that you would now find distasteful?"

General Telles sighed. "Again, it is difficult for most men to understand. When I served Caius, I was programmed to be loyal to him. I was programmed to make his goals my own. As long as I was performing to the best of my ability, pride in my efforts and my dedication enabled me to see past any guilt over the distasteful things that I had done. Because *I* knew that *I* had not chosen to do those things. *I* had been *ordered* to do them. My pride was in my ability to do such things. What I *feel* must be controlled. Anger must be converted into strength. Sorrow must be converted into determination. Guilt must be converted into pride. To do otherwise would only weaken the individual, and therefore, the collective unit. *That* cannot be allowed."

"What about now?" the captain wondered. "Your programming is not permanent. Whom do you serve now?"

"Now, the *Ghatazhak* choose," General Telles said with conviction, "and we choose to fight anyone who would threaten our survival."

"Regardless of right or wrong," Captain Gullen said.

"Right and wrong is subjective. Whatever threatens the peaceful existence of the Ghatazhak is considered *wrong* by the Ghatazhak. The Dusahn attacked us without provocation. Therefore, they are a threat to our survival. It is as simple as that. Whatever I must do to defeat them, I can live with."

Captain Gullen sighed, looking down at his desk.

"You are troubled by this?" General Telles asked, noticing the captain's distraught expression.

"I envy you, General," Captain Gullen admitted. "I would give anything for my conscience to be as clear as yours."

"What is it that troubles you?" General Telles inquired.

"The mission you are about to embark upon. I fear that many of your men may die trying to save my daughter, when all of your resources *should* be devoted to getting Captain Tuplo into that lab, and getting Captain Scott out. What right do I have to ask for special consideration for my child? Especially when it is I who put her in jeopardy to begin with."

"If it makes you feel any better, Captain, we are not attempting the rescue of *your* daughter alone. We are attempting to rescue all who have been imprisoned because brave men such as yourself refused to bow down to the Dusahn. Those are the people the Ghatazhak choose to serve. The ones who are willing to stand and fight for their own survival, even in the face of impossible odds." General Telles rose from his seat to depart. "And for the record, Captain, the Ghatazhak would be attempting to rescue your daughter even if we were not already going there to rescue Captain Scott. It just so happens that both objectives stand a better chance of success if simultaneously executed."

Captain Gullen looked at the general. For the first time, he saw the humanity in the general's stern features, and the honesty in his steely eyes. "Thank you, General... For everything."

"You are most welcome, Captain," General Telles replied with a respectful nod. "Now, I suggest you try to get some rest."

* * *

Cameron sat on her couch, watching the message from Nathan for the tenth time since she had sat down an hour ago.

"*Captain, Commander Kamenetskiy is here to see you,*" the guard outside her door called over the intercom on her side table.

"Let him in," Cameron replied. She sat, still watching the message, not bothering to get up to greet her friend. "I was wondering when you were going to get here," she said as he closed the door behind him.

"Why the guards?" Vladimir wondered as he walked over to the couch.

"Kaplan's idea," Cameron answered. "Just in case Galiardi's got an agent on board."

"Even Galiardi is not that paranoid," Vladimir insisted as he sat down next to her. "Do you have anything to eat?"

Cameron pointed to the vegetable plate and dip on the table in front of them.

"I meant *real* food," Vladimir said.

Cameron pointed at the same food again.

"How many times have you watched this?" Vladimir wondered, as he reached for the tray.

"A dozen, maybe. I lost count."

"Learn anything you didn't already know?" Vlad wondered, as he picked up a stick of celery and scooped up some dip.

"That Nathan doesn't look good with a beard."

"Nobody looks good with a beard," Vladimir replied. "They only *think* they do."

"He's got an accent now," Cameron said. "Takaran, like Dumar and Tug. You think he's been speaking Angla, or Takaran?"

"Not Takaran, that is certain," Vladimir said as he chewed his food thoughtfully. "You know, this dip is not that bad."

"It's hummus."

"Okay. This hummus isn't that bad," Vladimir corrected. "What else have you learned?"

"That I am relieved it will be Nathan who will be in command for this, and not me."

Vladimir almost choked. "Really?" he asked, once his throat was clear. "You? I thought being in command was always your dream."

"It was," Cameron admitted. "But of a ship and a crew. Not of an entire rebellion. Not when countless lives are at stake." She pressed pause on the remote, then turned to look at Vladimir for the first time since he had entered her quarters. "Honestly, I never understood how he was able to do it. For nearly a *year*, it was *all* on him. And not *once* did I ever see him hesitate when making a decision."

"I've never seen you hesitate when making a decision either," Vladimir said, scooping up more hummus, this time with a carrot stick.

"Maybe, but that doesn't mean I don't second-guess myself afterward."

"What makes you think Nathan didn't?"

"If he did, he didn't show it," Cameron said.

"He couldn't afford to," Vladimir comforted her. "Especially not with you always questioning his decisions."

"I didn't always question his decisions," Cameron objected.

"Of course, you did," Vladimir insisted. "At least in the beginning...and pretty much in the middle, as well."

"I was only making sure that he had considered all the angles."

"Which is probably what bothered him," Vladimir explained. "Nathan always made his decisions on instinct, not analysis."

"Which is a dangerous way to make decisions," Cameron argued.

"Not if you have good instincts," Vladimir replied. "And Nathan has excellent instincts."

"But what happens if his instincts are wrong?" Cameron challenged.

"Then he bears the responsibility," Vladimir explained. "That's what being in command is about. It's not about making the *right* decisions, it's about *making* the decision, and being able to live with the guilt when you're wrong."

Cameron sat for a moment, thinking. "Did Nathan have doubts?"

"Constantly," Vladimir replied. "He never felt deserving, or even remotely qualified, to be in command. He just didn't show it."

"So, he confided in you about his doubts?"

"Constantly," Vladimir complained. "To be honest, it became rather annoying after a while." Vladimir picked a celery string from his teeth. "But at least *he* ate meat."

Cameron did not respond. Instead, she just pressed play again, and rested her head on her friend's shoulder.

* * *

Josh moved slowly down the dimly lit corridor that ran along the Seiiki's port side, from her aft section where the crew's cabins were located, along the main passenger section, to the galley forward. His hair was a mess, and he was dressed in an old t-shirt, baggy shorts, and thick socks.

He made his way past the passenger bay, which had now been stripped of its seats, and into the galley just forward of the now empty compartment. Without turning on any lights, he opened the refrigerator door and started digging around inside, looking for something to eat.

"Early morning snack?" Connor asked from somewhere behind him.

Josh jerked back, startled, a half-eaten porshak roll in his hand. "Jesus, Cap'n," he exclaimed. "You scared the shit out of me!" Josh closed the refrigerator door and turned to look at Connor, sitting in the dining nook in the corner of the galley. "How long have you been sitting there?"

"A few hours, at least."

"Have you considered turning on a light?"

"I think better in the dark."

Josh moved over and sat down across the table from Connor. "Want a bite?" he asked, holding out his sandwich.

"No thanks," Connor replied. "I'm not hungry."

"Couldn't sleep again?"

"Didn't even try," Connor admitted.

"Why not?" Josh wondered. "After all, we've got a big day tomorrow... Uh, today, I mean," Josh corrected, glancing at the clock on the wall.

"I figured I'd stay up and enjoy my last night as Connor Tuplo."

Josh stopped chewing for a moment, the captain's comment sinking in. He started chewing again, then said, "I hadn't really thought of it like that, to be honest." Josh finished chewing and swallowed. "But you're still going to remember everything that happened over the last five years, right?"

"That's what they tell me," Connor replied. "But it's not going to be me, not really. It won't even be my body. Hell, I'll be five years younger."

"And you're complaining?"

Connor looked at Josh, a smirk on his face.

"Sorry," Josh said, taking another bite of his roll.

"In my head, I'll still be me," Connor said. "But I won't be alone. I'll be Nathan as well."

"What, like some kind of split personality?"

"Maybe. I don't really know."

"What did the clone docs say?" Josh wondered.

"They don't really know either. This is all new

territory for them. Hell, they're not even sure that I'll get *all* of my memories back."

Josh grinned as he chewed his food. "Well, at least you're admitting that you're Nathan."

"Genetically, I am. I can't deny that. But I'm still Connor Tuplo up here," Connor said, pointing to his head. "I guess I'm having a hard time coming to grips with the idea of having both identities swimming around in my head."

"Maybe it will be like when you're an undercover spy. You know, pretending to be someone you're not. Answering to another name, even though you know it's not really your name."

"I think you watch too many vid-plays, Josh."

"Probably."

Connor sighed. "You know, for the last five years, I've been struggling to remember things about myself. Anything at all. Then, when I found out *who* I really was, the thought of *remembering* all of that scared the hell out of me."

"Then why did you decide to go through with the transfer?" Josh asked.

"I guess the part of me that wanted to remember was stronger than the part that didn't," Connor replied.

Josh snickered. "Sure."

"What?" Connor asked, noticing Josh's expression.

"You decided to go through with it, because it's the right thing to do," Josh explained. "You see, memories or not, you're still Nathan Scott. It's in your genes."

"That simple, huh?"

"That simple," Josh insisted, taking another bite of his roll.

"What's that simple?" Loki asked as he and Jessica entered the dimly lit galley.

"Long story," Connor told him. "What are you two doing here? We don't depart for two more hours."

"The Glendanon's chief engineer wanted time to fully depress the bay before launch," Loki explained. "Seems he doesn't want to waste a single molecule of oxygen."

"With all the people aboard, can you blame him?" Connor replied.

"Shouldn't both of you still be asleep?" Jessica wondered.

"Well, wonder-boy here only needs four hours a night, or so he says," Connor replied. "As for myself, well, I'm trading this body in for a newer model in a few hours, so..."

"Hey," Loki said, looking at the porshak roll in Josh's hand, "isn't that my roll?"

CHAPTER TEN

The roof of the Glendanon's massive cargo bay began to roll back slowly, from fore to aft, gradually exposing the ships in her forward section. The combat jump shuttles were first to depart, sliding gracefully through the gap that slowly widened between the first roof section and the forward edge of the cargo bay. Immediately after, sixteen Takaran jump fighters, followed by a single Super Falcon, exited single file and turned to starboard as they cleared the retracting roof sections.

Eventually, the first roof section finished sliding under the second, and the second roof section tracked along with the first, both of them continuing their journey aft, sliding in unison underneath the third section. After a few minutes, the sequence stopped, leaving the forward quarter of the Glendanon's cargo deck exposed.

The Seiiki was next to depart, rising slowly off the Glendanon's deck. Immediately to the Seiiki's left, the Ghatazhak's last remaining cargo shuttle also began to rise. The Seiiki pitched up slightly as she climbed, turning a few degrees starboard and accelerating, while the cargo jump shuttle turned to port.

Finally, two boxcars lifted off the Glendanon's deck and climbed away, both continuing ahead of the Glendanon before turning onto their departure course.

Minutes later, several kilometers to the Glendanon's starboard side, the ships once stored within the Glendanon's hold converged on the Morsiko-Tavi. Her flat, open deck now empty of all cargo, the sixteen fighters landed on the cargo hauler to hitch a ride to the engagement area.

Once the fighters were secure on the deck of the Morsiko-Tavi, all eight ships disappeared behind near-synchronous flashes of blue-white light, bound for the Karuzari's first official offensive against the Dusahn Empire.

*   *   *

"*We'll be at full charge in seventy-three minutes, Captain,*" Commander Kaplan reported over the intercom in Cameron's ready room. "*Commander Verbeek reports all Eagles and Reapers are fully fueled, armed, and ready for deployment.*"

"Are the Reapers carrying maximum missile loads?" Cameron asked.

"*Yes, sir, as instructed,*" the commander replied. "*I reminded the CAG to reconfigure the first four Reapers that return for atmo ops, as well.*"

"I'm sure the commander didn't care for the reminder," Cameron joked.

"*No, sir, he did not,*" the XO replied, clearly enjoying herself.

"Very well," Cameron replied. "We'll go from alert to general quarters ten minutes prior to full recharge."

"*Aye, sir.*"

Cameron turned off her intercom and leaned back in her chair. Other than the few encounters with Jung ships over the last couple weeks, she and the Aurora had not seen any real combat since the attack on Nor-Patri seven years ago. That was when she lost the Celestia. Had it not been for Nathan's best friend, Luis, she likely would've gone down with the ship.

She looked around the captain's ready room.

She had made very few changes to the decor. A few pictures on the counter behind her, an updated diagram of the Aurora after her previous refit five years earlier, and a few pieces of art that soothed her. She wondered how she would feel once she handed this office over to Nathan. Although she enjoyed being in command, she had always missed the day-to-day challenges of running a ship and her crew that was the task of an executive officer. Captains spent more time thinking about the bigger picture, and deciding where the ship needed to go and what it needed to do. XOs thought about how to make that happen, in the most efficient way possible.

She would be fine. They just needed to survive the next couple of hours first.

* * *

General Telles sat patiently in the back of Combat One, along with Corporal Elken, Sergeant Morano, and Corporal Rossi. They had been sitting in the four corners of the combat jump shuttle for just over four hours. The first hour was spent in successive jumps that carried them across one hundred and fifty light years of space. The last three they spent waiting for the slower Morsiko-Tavi to catch up.

"Jump flash," Lieutenant Latfee reported from the cockpit of the combat jump shuttle. "Morsiko-Tavi, two hundred kilometers to starboard."

"Finally," Sergeant Torwell exclaimed with relief.

"What are you complaining about, Torwell?" Sergeant Morano asked from below the gunner and to his left. "You've got a great view up there, after all."

"A view of nothing," the sergeant said wearily. "Blackness and stars. Oh, and don't forget, we have been in Dusahn-controlled space for the last three hours, so that wonderful view you speak of also has the potential to be a Dusahn ship jumping in by surprise and blasting us into oblivion."

"You've got a gun," the corporal teased. "Shoot back."

"Anything?" General Telles asked the lieutenant.

"No, sir," the lieutenant replied. "But the Aurora would be coming in from the opposite direction, General. We wouldn't detect her for months."

"I was referring to unfriendly targets," the general clarified.

"Oh, sorry. Nothing but friendlies for as far as we can see."

General Telles glanced at the mission time in the upper right corner of the tactical display on the inside of his helmet visor. "Telles to all units. One minute."

———

"One minute," the general announced over Connor's helmet comms as he stood at the back of the Seiiki's cargo bay, facing aft.

"How are you doing?" Jessica asked.

Connor looked at Jessica to his left. "I'm good."

Jessica smiled. He looked scared to death. "How about you two?" she asked, turning to speak to Michi and Tori behind them.

Neither of the Nifelmian doctors answered, both nodding instead.

"You will all do fine," Sergeant Anwar assured them. "At least there will be no one shooting at you."

"Thanks," Connor replied dryly. "I feel so much better."

"Mission zero in thirty seconds," Loki called from the Seiiki's cockpit.

Connor took a deep breath, his eyes closed. "Crew

of the Seiiki. In case I don't get another chance to say this... Thanks for everything."

"*See you on the way back, Cap'n,*" Josh replied.

"Ten seconds," Ensign Lassen announced from Falcon One's cockpit.

"Guns are hot, targeting systems are online, missiles are armed in the bays," Sergeant Nama reported from the back of the Falcon.

"Five seconds."

"Here we go," Lieutenant Teison said under his breath.

"Three......two......one......jumping."

The Falcon's windows turned opaque, clearing a second later to reveal the planet Corinair directly ahead of them, and approaching rapidly.

"Multiple contacts!" Ensign Lassen reported.

"Locking onto all four surveillance sats over Aitkenna!" the sergeant reported from the back.

"One cruiser and two gunships!" Ensign Lassen exclaimed. "Looks like we got lucky!"

"Not for long, I'm sure," Lieutenant Teison mumbled.

"Good locks! Opening missile bays!"

"We're being painted!" Ensign Lassen warned.

"Jamming!" the sergeant replied. "Launching four! Weapons away!"

Four missiles streaked ahead of Falcon One, disappearing into the red-orange glow of the propulsion plant in their tails. Only a few seconds after they cleared the nose of the Falcon, all four missiles disappeared behind blue-white jump flashes.

"Weapons have jumped!" the sergeant added.

"More jump flashes!" Ensign Lassen warned.

"Dusahn fighters! Six of them at our two! Six clicks and closing fast, slightly high!"

"Taking evasive!" the lieutenant announced, as he twisted his flight control stick and put the Falcon into a steep, diving left turn.

"Bandits are launching missiles!"

"Direct hits on sats one and four!" Sergeant Nama exclaimed.

"They're jump missiles!" Ensign Lassen added urgently.

"Jumping!" the lieutenant announced. Two seconds later, they were much closer to the planet, which now filled their windows. The lieutenant immediately pulled the Falcon's nose up until it was pointed directly ahead, at Corinair's horizon.

"Flashes! Missiles are still tracking!"

The Lieutenant pressed his jump button again, causing the Falcon to jump ahead a few kilometers.

"Targets two and three destroyed!" Sergeant Nama added with satisfaction.

"The planet's gravity has them!" Ensign Lassen reported. "They can't turn hard enough to hold track. Nice move, Jasser!"

Lieutenant Teison eased the Falcon's nose back down toward the planet below. "Let's go start some trouble in Aitkenna, shall we?"

In groups of four, Takaran jump fighters rose smoothly off the deck of the Morsiko-Tavi, each group turning forward as they accelerated away from the flatbed cargo hauler. As they cleared the bow of the ship, they disappeared behind blue-white jump flashes. Once all sixteen fighters were away, the Morsiko-Tavi also jumped, but unlike the fighters, she was jumping to safety.

Commander Jarso felt a thud outside his fighter, which began to shake violently from the sudden entrance into the lower atmosphere of the planet. When his canopy cleared a split second later, it was daybreak, and the rising sun was at his back.

A quick glance at his tactical screen told him that the other three fighters in his group had jumped in with him, as expected, and all four of them were still in perfect attack formation.

A quick glance outside verified what his flight dynamics display was telling him-that he was flying a mere fifty meters above the sprawling metropolis of Aitkenna, the capital city of Corinair. His terrain-following sensors activated a second later, realizing that the ship was no longer flying in space but was hurtling along at breakneck speeds, towards buildings that were taller than their flight path.

"Terrain, terrain, terrain," the system prompted through the commander's helmet comms. The system immediately drew red dotted paths around the obstacles rushing toward them, indicating safe routes for the commander to fly without having to climb.

The commander kept his ship on the left-most track as he selected his ground targets. A security checkpoint. A military vehicle compound. Two precinct stations. All of them likely locations for Dusahn troops and assets.

His display lit up, indicating which targets he had selected, and which ones the other three ships in his group were targeting. It also indicated that his ship, being the lead ship, had priority firing control.

Without a word, Commander Jarso armed his nose turret and opened fire, the turrets on the other three fighters following his lead. His turret jumped from target to target, firing several volleys of red-orange plasma at each, before switching to the next target and continuing the attack. Once all four targets had been struck, the commander pitched up ten degrees and pressed his jump button.

Only fifteen seconds had elapsed.

Captain Donlevy's pod hauler shook violently after jumping into the upper atmosphere of Corinair. Although the air was much thinner at such a high altitude, his ship was not the least bit streamlined.

"We're over south Aitkenna!" his copilot, Josen Mullen, announced with excitement.

"Dump that shit!" the captain ordered over the ship's intercoms.

"I can't believe we're doing this," Josen exclaimed.

"Wait until we get to the next part, kid," the captain replied.

The aft door of the massive cargo pod slung under Captain Donlevy's hauler began to open. The weak light of dawn began to spill through the widening crack along the top of the door, illuminating the cavernous interior of the pod as it opened. Wind rushed in through the ever-widening opening, causing leaflets to tear free of the stacks lined up near the door, ready to drop.

Once the door was opened and angled down thirty degrees, the four men inside began rolling the stacks of leaflets out the back. As each stack fell, tiny dispersal charges fired, breaking the bindings around the stacks and spreading the leaflets far and wide, the wind dropping them throughout the city below.

Once all the leaflet stacks were safely unloaded, rows of smaller crates, each of them fitted with automatic parachute systems, were also rolled out the back.

The cargo master stood by the back door of the cargo pod, watching as the small parachutes opened below and behind them, one by one, and drifted downward toward the surface, their automated navigation systems steering them left and right in an effort to disperse the packages evenly around the city.

The cargo master watched the last package roll out the door, then slapped the close button with his open palm, after which he tapped the comm-button on his helmet. "Drop complete!" he reported as he walked toward the center of the empty pod. Half a minute later, the massive ramp slammed shut, sealing up the pod once again. A few seconds later, the bouncing and shaking stopped as the hauler jumped back into space, a full light year away from Corinair.

"Let's get this place ready for phase two!" he barked at his men.

———

Two young men came running out of their building, still wearing their sleep attire. They could hear the sounds of ships jumping in and out of the skies overhead, and the distant explosions calling them out into the chaos.

"*Look!*" a voice called out. One of the neighbors was pointing at four flashes of light to the west, just above the buildings. Four tiny fighters disappeared behind a row of buildings, and when they reappeared on the other side, they were firing their plasma cannons at targets on the ground ahead of them.

"*What is it?*" someone else called.

The first young man looked up, spotting tiny pieces of paper floating down toward them. Higher up were hundreds of small containers dangling under black parachute canopies.

The young man grabbed a leaflet as it descended, lifting it to his face to read. His eyes widened as he scanned the paper, and he shouted out in excitement. "The Karuzari are attacking the Dusahn! And Na-Tan is leading them!"

The other young man ran toward one of the crates that had landed nearby, his friend following closely behind. Both men dropped to the ground and pulled away the deflated canopy to get to the crate underneath. They unbuckled it and swung the lid open. Both men were taken aback at the contents.

Energy rifles.

"What the hell?" the first young man said.

The second young man was more alert and had his wits about him. "Quickly! We must get these into hiding, before the Dusahn come!"

"What are we supposed to do with these?" the first young man asked, confused.

"We're going to fight!"

———

The Seiiki's cockpit rattled as it jumped into the atmosphere of Corinair, only sixty-five meters above the surface of Aitkenna's industrial district. The shaking settled down a few seconds later, after the initial air displacement subsided, and the ship cruised along in the calmness of the early dawn.

"Jesus," Josh said under his breath, looking out toward downtown Aitkenna to his left. Jump flashes were appearing all over the center of the city as the Avendahl's sixteen surviving jump fighters slipped in and out of the atmosphere, attacking targets on the ground. The attack was less than a minute old.

"Drop point in twenty seconds," Loki reported over his comm-set.

The Seiiki's rear cargo ramp settled into position, sloping downward from the deck by a few degrees. Connor could see factories and streets passing under them as his ship flew low over Aitkenna. He knew his ship was only traveling at about one hundred kilometers per hour at the moment, but from such a low altitude, and with a parachute strapped on his back as he prepared to jump out of the ship, it seemed much faster.

"*Drop point in twenty seconds,*" Loki's voice announced over Connor's helmet comms. He looked to Jessica to his left. She gave him a thumbs-up gesture, which, despite the fact that he felt completely unprepared, he returned. He glanced over his left shoulder, spotting Doctor Sato. She looked odd, all dressed up in her jump gear. She was a petite woman, and looked overloaded by the weight.

"*Ten seconds!*" Loki warned.

Connor pulled at his harness, checking it one last time before jumping.

"*Five...*"

Connor looked at Jessica again. She appeared amazingly calm and relaxed.

"*...Four...*"

He wasn't sure that made him feel any better.

"*...Three...*"

The realization that this was it suddenly hit him. If he jumped, there was no turning back. He would become Captain Nathan Scott, Na-Tan, the man who defeated the Ta'Akar Empire, liberated Earth from

Jung rule, and ended an interstellar war before it really even began.

"...*Two*..."

And he would be the man who would lead the Karuzari rebels and drive the Dusahn from the Pentaurus cluster.

"...*One*..."

Or die trying.

Jessica was the first one out the door, running out onto the cargo ramp and leaping into the air. Connor followed her out, not more than two steps behind her. He leapt off the end of the ramp, his pulse racing and his breathing rapid. He spread his arms and legs out to stabilize for a few seconds, then, as he had been taught, he withdrew them as the dispersal charges fired, spreading his black parachute canopy above him.

His canopy filled with air, and his lines yanked at his harness, pulling back and upward with incredible force. The air was much thicker on Corinair than it had been on Innis Four, and he felt as if his shoulders had been pulled from their sockets.

His body twisted around to face the direction that the Seiiki had been flying when they had jumped, and he swung back and upward. As he swung back down under the canopy, he could see the Seiiki jumping away only a kilometer ahead.

When the Seiiki's jump flash disappeared a second later, Connor realized something that he had not anticipated. The breaking dawn provided little illumination, and with the Ranni facility abandoned, the exterior lighting was not on.

As if the Ghatazhak tactical helmet that he wore had read his mind, his visor suddenly painted with lines representing the obstacles surrounding his touchdown zone. General Telles had told them about the feature, but had not let them use it during their brief training, instead wanting them to learn to control their descent without the aid of digital navigation guidance. Not only were the obstacles clearly represented on the inside of his visor, so was the path he needed to follow to his touchdown point, along with a countdown timer to landing and his elevation above both the terrain below him, as well as the landing pad he was descending toward.

Connor reached up and grabbed his control lines, quickly gaining directional control. He was already slightly left of course, which he quickly corrected. He glanced to his right, spotting Jessica, barely illuminated by the light of the early dawn, riding smoothly beneath her canopy only a hundred meters ahead of him.

He turned his attention back to his visor, realizing that there were icons on it that represented Jessica, as well as Michi and Tori. At first, the visor was difficult to use, as he felt like he wanted to focus on the inner face of it. But he remembered Jessica's advice, and looked past it, letting the data appear as an overlay.

A moment later, his feet passed over the elevated transit tracks as he continued to descend toward the landing pad. Both the images on his visor, and the dimly lit pad in front of him, seemed to grow at a frightening pace.

Connor adjusted his grip, then pulled to flare as his feet crossed the near side of the landing pad. Two seconds later, he was on the ground and running forward. He grabbed the retract knob on his chest plate and twisted it as he ran, activating the canopy retraction winches in his pack. As he felt the pull of the canopy behind him, he leaned forward as he continued to run toward the Ranni Enterprises building fifty meters away.

Five seconds later, the pull of his retracting canopy was gone, and Connor followed Jessica across the compound, staying low as he ran. By the time he reached the building, Jessica was already punching in the security bypass code that Deliza had given her.

"We're in," Jessica announced as the status light on the keypad turned green. She swung the door open. "Let's go!"

Connor moved quickly inside, followed by Michi and Tori, who had both landed without incident. Jessica was the last one in, taking a moment to secure the door behind her. She scanned the area outside with the sensors in her tactical helmet, checking for any signs of pursuit. Luckily, they had none.

———————

"We've got incoming," Commander Jarso announced as he opened fire on a new set of ground targets. "Ten clicks, one thousand up..." The contacts on his tactical display faded out. "Alpha flight! Jump, jump, jump!"

As the commander slid his finger onto his jump button, the inside of his canopy lit up with blue-white flashes, several Dusahn fighters jumping in to his right and opening fire. Yellow bolts of energy slammed into his starboard shields as he pressed his jump button, causing his ship to shake violently as his canopy turned opaque, and he jumped away. "Well, that didn't take long," he said as his canopy cleared, and he pushed his fighter into a steep left bank. "Alpha! Evasive! Rally Blue Seven in one!"

Two more jump flashes appeared behind him,

and the commander pressed his jump button again. As his canopy cleared, he rolled his ship right and pitched up, spinning his jump range selector wheel two clicks before jumping again. Another turn, another range adjustment, and another jump, and his six was clear. He pitched up, jumped to an altitude of several kilometers, then glanced at his time display. He still had twenty seconds to get to rally point Blue Seven, so that he and his teammates could regroup and start their next attack run.

———

The Seiiki's cargo bay filled with blue-white light as it came out of its next jump. Sergeant Anwar and the other seven Ghatazhak lined up in two columns of four, standing ready to exit the open cargo bay.

"*Ten seconds to jump point,*" Loki's voice announced over their helmet comms.

———

The Seiiki raced between the buildings of Aitkenna's city center, following the main boulevard leading past the Walk of Heroes, right up to the central square outside of Aitkenna's hall of justice.

Four Takaran jump fighters appeared on either side of the Seiiki, accelerating past them and attacking the city center itself, pummeling the guard stations and Dusahn security barracks with energy weapons fire, before they disappeared behind jump flashes.

Eight Ghatazhak soldiers fell from the back of the Seiiki as she pitched upward, their black canopies popping open a split second after leaving the ship. As the Seiiki disappeared in a flash of blue-white light, four more Takaran fighters appeared, opening up on the Ghatazhak soldiers' intended landing site ahead, softening it for their approach.

Twenty seconds after jumping out of the Seiiki, all eight Ghatazhak, led by Sergeant Anwar, touched down at a run, disconnecting their canopies as they ran toward the security points about the square, their weapons firing with uncanny precision.

Two more flashes of blue-white light appeared, revealing two combat jump shuttles flying between the buildings. Two seconds apart, the shuttles passed over the central square, the first from east to west, the second from north to south, both firing at the ground targets as they passed. Once they cleared the other side of the central square, the shuttles pitched up and disappeared behind more flashes of blue-white light.

The attack was now two minutes old.

Jessica and Connor ran down the underground corridor of Ranni Enterprises, following Michi and Tori to their secure cloning lab. Once at the entrance, Tori placed his hand on the scanner pad, and his face against the eyepiece. The door popped open a second later, and they ran inside.

"Quick, take off your armor, and your clothes," Jessica instructed as the lights in the lab started coming to life.

Connor pulled off his helmet, staring in disbelief as he came face to face with... *Himself.*

"It's all true," he mumbled.

"Of course, it's true," Jessica declared. "Now take off all your gear and your clothes."

There, in the middle of the lab, hanging vertically in a clear tank full of viscous fluid, was the fifth-generation clone of Nathan Scott. He had a bundle of tubes connected to his chest, just below and left of his neck. His hair and beard were shifting lazily in the circulating fluid in which he was submerged, as was his...

"Why am I naked?" Connor asked awkwardly. "I mean, why aren't I... I mean, him... I mean, the clone. Why is he naked?"

"It's a comatose clone," Jessica replied. "What does it care?"

"*I* care," Connor insisted, as he started removing his body armor.

"We have to monitor the condition of the clone's body during the growing process," Michi explained. "It's much easier if the clone is naked."

Connor looked at Jessica. "Why am *I* removing *my* clothes?"

"You aren't exiting this building in your body," Jessica reminded him, as she helped him off with his chest piece. "You're going to be in *that* body. You want to run out of here naked? Or worse yet, without any body armor? There's a war on, remember?"

"Good point," Connor agreed, as he pulled off his shirt.

"We'll be ready in a couple minutes," Tori announced.

"What do I do?" Connor asked as Jessica pulled off his boots.

"Lie down over there, and put on that head gear," Michi instructed.

"Are you sure this is going to work?" Connor wondered, as he pulled off his pants.

"Reasonably sure, yes," Michi replied. "Normally, we'd run a full diagnostic, as well as baseline signal testing prior to starting the transfer procedure, but..."

"But what?"

"There's no time," Jessica reminded him.

"What's the rush?" Connor said nervously, as Jessica ushered his mostly naked body over to the transfer bed.

"War? Guns? Shooting? Death? Take your pick," Jessica told him.

"But, if no one saw us come in..."

"We can't be sure of that," Jessica reminded him, as she pushed him down on the table. "Besides, the process takes at least ten minutes. The longer we wait, the greater the chance the Dusahn bust down the door and kill us all!"

"We're in an underground lab, for crying out loud!" he cried, sitting up again.

"Connor, please!" Jessica insisted, trying to push him back down.

Connor looked at her, realizing she was right. "Okay, okay," he said, lying back down.

Jessica placed the transfer cap onto his head and fastened it in place. Then she bent down and gave him a long, deep kiss.

"What was that for?" Connor asked, obviously caught off guard.

"Just in case," Jessica replied, stepping back.

"In case of what?" Connor asked, starting to panic again.

"Hit it, Doc," Jessica ordered.

* * *

"Final decel burn complete," the helmsman reported as she shut down the Aurora's deceleration engines. "Closing decel thrust doors."

Cameron turned to face her tactical officer directly behind her. "What's the final tally?"

"Long range scans from the recon drone indicate the constant presence of a single ship. Best guess would be a heavy cruiser. However, we have seen a battleship come and go at least three times over the past four days, so we have to assume that it is within quick response range of Corinair. Other than that, only various gunships, and a few cargo ships."

"Has the cruiser maintained a steady orbit?" Cameron wondered.

"Yes, sir." Lieutenant Commander Vidmar replied. "Based on that, we should be able to plot a pretty close intercept course, if you'd like to jump in close."

"Negative," Cameron replied. "We'll jump in two light minutes out, take a quick passive scan, then jump to intercept. No reason to push our luck."

"We have no way of knowing how accurately our time is coordinated with the Ghatazhak," the lieutenant commander reminded his captain. "We're only coordinated with Corinairan time to within a single Corinairan minute of accuracy."

"Understood," Cameron replied. "Mister Bickle, plot the insertion jump."

"Aye, Captain," Ensign Bickle replied.

"Comms, ship-wide."

"Ship-wide, aye," Ensign deBanco replied.

"Crew of the Aurora," Cameron called, her voice echoing throughout the entire ship. "In a few moments, we will be joining the Karuzari and Captain Scott in an attack against the Dusahn. We do this not because of Captain Scott, but because Corinair, and other worlds of the Pentaurus cluster, are our allies. They were there to help Earth when we needed them. They fought and died alongside us when we needed them. Therefore, we will not abandon them when *they* need *us*. Our own world may call us traitors. Our comrades may call us deserters. But those who truly understand what loyalty means will respect our convictions. We know not what we are about to face, but we shall do so with honor, with courage, and the strength of knowing that those we help today, will be there for us tomorrow." Cameron paused a moment, before giving the order. "General quarters."

"General quarters, aye," Lieutenant Commander Vidmar replied.

The trim lighting all around the Aurora's bridge changed from orange to red, signifying her upgraded combat readiness status. Reports began to flood in from all over the ship as each department reported their readiness for combat.

"XO is in combat," Ensign deBanco reported. "Chief of the boat is in damage control. Flight ops reports ready-birds and second-ups are manned and ready to launch."

"All point-defenses are charged and ready," Lieutenant Commander Vidmar reported from the tactical station. "All plasma cannons are charged and ready. Torpedo cannons charged and ready, broadsides ready, and rail guns are deployed. Shields are at full strength."

"All stations report general quarters, Captain," Ensign deBanco reported from the communications center at the back of the Aurora's bridge.

"Very well." Cameron took a deep breath. It was probably the last time she would be taking the Aurora into battle as her captain. "Mister Bickle, jump us in."

"Jumping to Darvano in, three......two......one...... jumping," the navigator replied.

The interior of the Aurora's bridge was temporarily illuminated by her jump flash, despite the filter on the main view screen.

"Jump complete," Ensign Bickle reported.

"Launch ready-birds and second-ups," Cameron ordered.

"Running passive scans," Lieutenant Commander Kono announced.

"Ready-birds and second-ups, aye," Ensign deBanco acknowledged.

"Multiple contacts!" Lieutenant Commander Kono reported. "I've got a Dusahn cruiser in orbit, shields up. Four gunships trailing. The cruiser is launching fighters. Captain! I've got multiple jump flashes in the atmosphere over Aitkenna! Takaran fighters, combat jumpers... and the Mirai!"

"The Mirai?" Lieutenant Commander Vidmar wondered. "Isn't that..."

"Deliza Ta'Akar's ship," Cameron finished for him.

"What the hell is it doing in the middle of a battle?"

"I have no idea," Cameron admitted.

"Ready-birds away," Ensign deBanco reported.

"The Mirai has just jumped away, Captain," Lieutenant Commander Kono reported. "Wait, I've got her again, about five hundred thousand kilometers from Corinair, maneuvering."

"This is all two minutes old," Cameron muttered. "Looks like the party has already started."

"Intercept jump plotted and ready, Captain," Ensign Bickle reported.

"Double shoot'n scoot. Take us between the target and the planet. Get a good scan of the surface as we pass. Triplets on all forward tubes, and broadsides. Shield busters in the rail guns."

"Double shoot'n scoot, planet side, aye," Lieutenant Dinev answered from the helm, as she entered the maneuvers into the helm's queue.

"Triplets on all forward tubes and broadsides,"

Lieutenant Commander Vidmar acknowledged. "Shield busters in the rail guns."

"Second-ups away," Ensign deBanco reported. "Red Leader reports sixteen birds ready for action."

"Tell Red Flight to jump with us. We'll give them targets on the fly," Cameron ordered.

"Aye, sir," Ensign deBanco replied.

"Mister Bickle. Take us in," Cameron added.

"Jumping in five seconds," the navigator replied. "Three..."

"Here we go, people," Cameron said.

"...one......jumping..."

General Telles and Corporal Elken leapt out of the combat jump shuttle, descending the last four meters to the surface, as Sergeant Morano and Corporal Rossi did the same from the other side. At the same time, four more Ghatazhak jumped from the other combat jumper on the far side of the building. Before they could take more than a few steps, both combat jumpers had jumped away.

Telles ran toward the building, hugging the side of it as he sprinted toward the sounds of the firefight in front. As he and his three men rounded the corner, Commander Kellen and his three men did the same on the opposite side.

In the open square before them, upwards of twenty Dusahn soldiers were holding off the advance of Sergeant Anwar and his seven men, who had parachuted in only moments earlier.

General Telles glanced at the mission time display in the upper right corner of the tactical display on the inside of his visor. He was ten seconds early.

Luckily, Falcon One was five.

A flash of blue-white light appeared from high

behind them, and Falcon One jumped in less than a kilometer away from the backside of the building. It strafed the rooftop, taking out the half dozen Dusahn snipers who were taking up positions.

"Roof is clear!" Ensign Lassen declared as the Falcon streaked overhead and pitched upward toward the rising sun.

Four more flashes of light appeared to the right, and four Dusahn fighters turned to pursue Falcon One, but a second later, four Takaran fighters appeared from behind blue-white flashes to the left, streaking low over the square as they fired on the Dusahn fighters just ahead of them.

General Telles and his men rounded the corner and opened fire on the Dusahn soldiers, catching them in a three-way crossfire. It took less than ten seconds to finish off the enemy soldiers in the square, but there were more pouring out of the buildings on either side of the square.

Three flashes of blue-white light lit up the area. Combat Jumpers One and Three appeared in a hover directly over the dead bodies in the square, opening fire on the soldiers coming out of the buildings.

The third flash was Bulldog One, the Ghatazhak's last surviving cargo jump shuttle. It jumped in directly over the roof of the justice building. Within seconds, six Ghatazhak fast-roped down from either side of the cargo jumper's aft ramp, dropping to the rooftop. Four of them went to the four corners of the building, taking up sniper positions. The rest entered the rooftop door and headed down into the building.

"Two. You've got the square. One and Three are hitting ground level."

"*Two copies,*" Sergeant Anwar replied over comms.

"*Six has eyes up high,*" Master Sergeant Lazo announced over comms from the rooftop.

"*Four and Five on eight and descending,*" the leader of Team Four reported from inside the justice building. "*Picking up ten bads below us on six. We'll keep them busy while One and Three hit the prize.*"

"Understood," Telles replied. "One and Three, let's move."

"*Telles, Combat One!*" Lieutenant Latfee called. "*Surface vehicles moving in from the east. Two clicks! Two more from the west, three clicks! Fast movers jumping in north and south at five and seven clicks! We won't be able to hold position.*"

"Combat One and Three. Jump clear," the general ordered as his team hit the front door of the building, along with Commander Kellen's team.

Energy weapons fire erupted from inside the lobby of the building, catching General Telles by surprise. Two bolts of energy glanced off his armor, at his left shoulder and thigh. The second bolt struck Corporal Elken in the lower right leg, causing him to stumble and fall, but the corporal was focused enough to keep his weapon up and continued firing as he hit the floor.

"*They didn't show up on tactical!*" Commander Kellen realized.

"Telles to all Ghatazhak!" the general called as he dropped to one knee and continued firing into the lobby. "Beware of stealth bads!"

The general fired two rounds into the face of one Dusahn soldier, then dropped another who tried to help the one the general had just killed. Two more soldiers were well protected by a reception counter, firing through small windows cut into it to pass items through. But the weapons-proof, clear panels only went up about three meters, and the ceiling of the lobby was at least three times that height, and covered with dense, ornate stone panels.

"Are you injured?" the general asked the corporal, as he raised his weapon and started firing rapidly at the ceiling about halfway between his position and the counter on the other side of the lobby.

"Just my pride, sir!" the corporal replied, as he continued to fire.

The general's shots ricocheted off the stone ceiling, then bounced off the wall behind the reception counter hiding the four Dusahn soldiers who had them pinned down at the front doors. The general adjusted his firing angle, until his shots deflected high enough off the back wall to hit the inside of the weapons-proof, clear panels, and into the soldiers. He continued firing, lighting up the space behind the reception counter, causing it to glow a brilliant red-orange as the bolts of energy sliced through the Dusahn soldiers over and over. After nearly fifteen seconds, the general stopped firing, and the lobby went silent.

"Well, that's something you don't see every day," Commander Kellen said, a grin on his face.

"One and Three have taken the lobby. Headed for the package," the general announced as he reached down to help Corporal Elken to his feet.

As they ran across the lobby for the stairs on the far side, they could hear the screech of Dusahn fighters outside, and the sound of heavy energy weapons striking the ground.

"*We're not going to be able to hold if we don't get some close-air in here,*" Sergeant Anwar warned.

"*One! Six!*" Master Sergeant Lazo called from the

roof. *"Bulldog One reports the Aurora just jumped into orbit!"*

"It's about fucking time," the general said as he kicked the stair door open and fired down at four Dusahn soldiers who were running up to reinforce the guards in the lobby.

"Jump complete," Ensign Bickle reported.

"Dusahn cruiser, dead ahead," Lieutenant Commander Kono reported from the Aurora's sensor station.

"Target lock!" the tactical officer announced.

"Fire at will," Cameron ordered.

All four of the Aurora's forward plasma torpedo tubes under her bow erupted, spitting three shots in rapid succession. At the same time, her ventral rail guns began firing explosive slugs designed to overload the enemy's shields. As all twelve plasma torpedoes slammed into the forward shields of the Dusahn cruiser, the Aurora lowered her nose and altered course a few degrees to port, rolling slightly to starboard so that she could bring all four dorsal rail guns onto the target for the next sequence.

"Scootin'," Ensign Bickle reported as the Aurora jumped forward a few kilometers.

The Dusahn cruiser, which had been four kilometers ahead, was suddenly about to pass slightly high over starboard, only half a kilometer away.

"Proximity warning! Collision alert!" the automated warnings blared.

"Sorry, sir," Ensign Bickle said, silencing the alarms.

"Firing all plasma turrets! Firing all rail guns!" Lieutenant Commander Vidmar announced from the tactical station.

"Incoming message from the Ghatazhak!" Ensign deBanco announced from the comms station. "They're requesting air support for a rescue op at the city square in front of the justice building in Aitkenna!"

"Have flight ops vector Red Flight to help the Ghatazhak," Cameron ordered as a type of Dusahn cruiser that she had never seen before passed them on the right. "I hope you're getting good scans of this, Layla."

"I'm all over it, Captain," Lieutenant Commander Kono assured her.

"Shield busters aren't having any effect!" Lieutenant Commander Vidmar warned.

"Keep pounding them," Cameron ordered.

"Firing broadsides!"

As the Aurora slid past the Dusahn cruiser, eight mark two plasma cannons, located in her aft starboard utility bays, opened fire on the passing ship. All eight cannons continued firing single shots, one by one, maintaining a firing rate of one shot every two seconds per cannon, as they passed the length of the cruiser.

The cruiser returned fire, tracking the Aurora with her own energy weapons turrets, pounding the Alliance ship's starboard shields as she passed.

"Starboard shields are down thirty percent the length of the ship!" Lieutenant Commander Vidmar warned.

"Flight ops reports Blue Flight is ready to launch," Ensign deBanco reported.

"Mister Bickle, jump us out one light minute and come about. Mister deBanco, tell flight ops to launch all of Blue Flight as we turn. Have them engage the gunships trailing the cruiser."

"Jumping ahead one light minute, aye," the navigator replied.

"I'm picking up damage to the cruiser's starboard jump emitters, Captain," Lieutenant Commander Kono reported. "She may not be able to jump."

"How did we manage that?" Cameron wondered.

"I don't know," the lieutenant commander admitted. "An overload, maybe?"

"Flight Ops, Bridge! Launch Blue Flight as we turn," Ensign deBanco relayed.

"Jumping," Mister Bickle reported.

"Launch Blue ready-birds! Now, now, now!" Ensign deBanco continued.

"Tactical," Cameron called, "Ready four jump missiles, all nukes, high yields. I want that cruiser's shields down on the next pass."

"Yes, sir!" Lieutenant Vidmar replied.

———

Jessica stood nervously, watching as Tori operated the consciousness transfer equipment, and Michi monitored the unconscious bodies of both Connor Tuplo and Nathan Scott. "How much longer?" Jessica wondered.

"At least eight more minutes," Tori replied.

"How are they doing?"

"So far, so good," Michi assured her.

"*One! Six!*" Master Sergeant Lazo called over Jessica's helmet comms. "*Bulldog One reports the Aurora just jumped into orbit!*"

"Yes!" Jessica cheered, raising her clenched fists triumphantly in the air.

"What is it?" Michi asked.

"The Aurora is here!"

Michi looked at Tori, then back at Jessica. "That's good, right?"

"Hell, yes!" Jessica replied. "It means we might actually make it out of here alive!" Jessica stepped up to the clear tank, placing both hands on the walls, looking up at the unconscious body of Nathan, floating in the cloudy, viscous fluid within. "You hear that, Nathan?" she whispered. "We're getting the *band* back together."

General Telles and Commander Kellen stormed the basement door, opening fire into the guard post on the other side as they advanced. The general went right, and the commander went left, each of them followed in turn by four more men, two per side, while the last two remained in the bottom of the stairwell outside to hold the position.

Weapons fire bounced throughout the foyer, cutting into the furniture and the counter, and into the guards. Seconds after they had burst into the room, the battle was over.

General Telles stood, surveying the dead Dusahn soldiers, as two of his men placed charges on the heavy door that led to the detention wing.

"Fire in the hole!" one of the two men warned, stepping back from the door to the side.

General Telles simply turned around, bracing himself against the shock wave with the help of his assistive undergarment. Bits of debris bounced off his back armor as the door blew apart. A second later, the general turned around to see his men rushing inside the detention wing, weapons firing. So far, they had been lucky. Not a single man had been critically wounded, and only five had received injuries requiring them to withdraw from combat action.

From behind the settling dust, General Telles could make out the prisoners as they emerged from their cells. Coughing and choking, they filed out one by one, prompted by the shouts of his men. He scanned their faces as they passed, searching for the young woman's face he had seen in the holographic photo block on Captain Gullen's desk back on the Glendanon.

Finally, a young woman stumbled out, coughing as she tried to wave the dust away. General Telles put his hand out, stopping the young woman in her tracks. "Sori Gullen?" he asked her.

The young lady looked up at the general, frightened by his intense gaze. "Yes," she replied, her body trembling in fear.

General Telles took her arm, leading her to one side. "Stay with me," he told her.

"Why?" Sori asked. "What did I do?"

"It is all right," General Telles assured her. "I will take you to your father."

"Jump missiles away, delayed jumps," the Aurora's tactical officer reported.

"Turn complete," Lieutenant Dinev announced from the helm.

"Jump us back in," Cameron instructed. "One click out."

"One click, aye," the navigator replied.

"Target has launched something," Lieutenant

Commander Kono reported. "It just jumped away. It may have been a comm-drone, Captain."

"Stand by all forward tubes," Cameron ordered, realizing she could do nothing about the comm-drone.

"Forward tubes, charged and ready," Lieutenant Commander Vidmar reported.

"Blue Flight is away," Ensign deBanco informed the captain. "They're jumping to Aitkenna."

"Very well."

"Jumping in three......two......one......jumping."

The blue-white jump flash washed over the Aurora's bridge, translated through her main view screens, although greatly subdued. Again, the image of the Dusahn cruiser filled half the forward view screen, growing larger as the Aurora closed on the target from its aft port side.

"Fire all tubes," Cameron ordered calmly.

"Firing all tubes, aye," Lieutenant Commander Vidmar replied.

The bridge filled with repeated flashes of red-orange light as brilliant balls of plasma energy raced out from under the Aurora's bow toward their target a little over a kilometer ahead. More flashes filled the bridge as another wave of plasma torpedoes departed, followed by a third group.

"Pitch us up and jump past," Cameron instructed. "Ready on the stern tubes."

"Pitching up," Lieutenant Dinev replied as she raised the Aurora's nose slightly.

"Ready on the stern tubes," the tactical officer replied as the ship shook from the force of the cruiser's energy weapons impacting the Aurora's shields.

"Jump ready," Mister Bickle reported.

"Mister Vidmar?" Cameron queried.

The tactical officer looked at the countdown clock for the jump missiles they had left behind, the enemy ship continuing to pound their shields with energy weapons fire. As the clock neared zero, he gave the word. "Now."

"Jump," Cameron ordered.

Sixteen Super Eagle jump fighters appeared suddenly from behind blue-white jump flashes, streaking low over the buildings of downtown Aitkenna. They twisted and banked, chasing the Dusahn fighters that had threatened to cut off the Ghatazhak's escape, away from the square in front of the justice building.

General Telles emerged from the building's front doors amidst the line of prisoners scurrying to get outside. All around, his troops were ushering the prisoners into groups on either side, readying them for boarding.

The entire area lit up with two brilliant flashes of blue-white light, both accompanied by deafening claps of thunder and the sound of displaced air. Two massive pod haulers, known to those in the Pentaurus cluster as 'boxcars', appeared from behind the flashes, settling into a hover ten meters above the square. They descended to the ground, settling on four massive sets of landing gear, just as more Dusahn fighters jumped in to the north. As the fighters approached, Takaran fighters appeared from blue-white flashes to the east, immediately vectoring to intercept the incoming Dusahn fighters before they could attack the defenseless boxcars.

Massive ramps fell open from the class one cargo pods mounted underneath the gangly pod haulers, revealing their cavernous interiors. Under the direction of their Ghatazhak handlers, the prisoners ran toward the waiting boxcars, scurrying up their ramps to the relative safety of their interiors.

General Telles watched as nearly four hundred people, each of them an innocent relative of a captain or crew member who refused to bow down to the Dusahn, escaped certain death at the hands of their captors.

Lucius Telles, Commander of the last of the Ghatazhak, felt something he had not felt in some time. Pride. In his men and in his mission. For years now, they had been fighting the battles of others, protecting the interests of thugs and criminals, just to survive. But today was different. Today they had done what the Ghatazhak were *meant* to do. Fight for those who could not fight for themselves.

"General, I'll see to Miss Gullen," Master Sergeant Lazo promised.

General Telles nodded, looking down at the young woman who had dutifully followed him out of the justice building. "The master sergeant will see that you get back to your father safely," he assured her.

Sori Gullen looked into the general's eyes, finding them far less frightening than before. "Thank you."

———

The Aurora disappeared in a flash of blue-white light, reappearing a split second later only two kilometers away. A moment later, four jump missiles appeared from behind four small flashes of blue-white light, fewer than one hundred meters to the port side of the Dusahn cruiser.

As the missiles slammed into the target's shields, the Aurora pitched over, bringing her forward plasma torpedo tubes to bear on the cruiser as the ship continued to move away.

The nuclear warheads on the missiles flashed a blinding white, and when they cleared a few seconds later, the Dusahn cruiser's shield emitters were sparking and popping all over her port side. With no shields to protect her, she took the full brunt of the Aurora's last round of plasma torpedoes, and broke apart in a series of primary and secondary explosions.

———

Both boxcars began to rise slowly into the air, their ramps swinging upward. Again, Dusahn fighters appeared nearby and tried to turn toward the climbing boxcars to get a shot at them. But both the Super Eagles and Takaran fighters kept the enemy fighters otherwise occupied, and both pod haulers managed to jump away with their precious cargo, headed back to the Glendanon one hundred and fifty light years away.

Half a minute after the boxcars jumped away, Bulldog One jumped in over the middle of the square and touched down.

"Let's get everyone on board and get the hell out of here," General Telles ordered.

———

"*Telles to all Ghatazhak!*" the general called over Jessica's helmet comms. "*Phase two complete! Move to evac points!*"

Jessica noticed the fluid level in the cloning tank beginning to decrease. "What's going on?" she asked, turning to Michi.

"The transfer is almost complete. I'm draining the tank."

"Is that going to hurt him?"

"No," Michi replied. "Normally, we would have

removed the new host body from the tank and properly prepared it, but there was no time."

"What do you mean, 'properly prepared it?'" Jessica demanded, becoming more concerned.

"Disconnected it from life support, allowed it to become an autonomous system, without aid from artificial sources. Cleaned it up, dressed it, given it a haircut and a shave! It doesn't matter! We need to get it down!" Michi insisted as she grabbed a gurney and rolled it into position near the hatch at the back of the tank.

Jessica moved quickly around to help Michi as the fluid continued to drain from the tank.

"We're at ninety percent!" Tori yelled from the control console. "You've got two minutes, maybe three!"

"Shouldn't we have done this earlier?" Jessica wondered as she watched Michi override the hatch mechanism.

"We could not risk disrupting the transfer process until it was at least ninety percent complete," Michi explained.

"Then, why don't we just wait until it's done?"

"*Telles, Aurora!*" Ensign deBanco called over Jessica's helmet comms. "*Dusahn cruiser has been destroyed. Our fighters are engaging the gunships now!*"

Michi opened the hatch, allowing some of the viscous cloning fluid to spill out onto the lab floor. "Once the transfer is complete, Captain Scott will regain consciousness on his own, unless we heavily sedate him! That would require more monitoring, use of the medical bay on the next level... And do you want to carry his unconscious body out of here?"

"So, he regains consciousness. Isn't that what we want?"

"Not while all these tubes are connected to him!" Michi replied. "He could panic and rip them out! That could prove fatal!"

"I don't think we thought this through carefully enough," Jessica said, as she climbed into the tank with Michi.

"Ninety-three percent!" Tori reported.

"I'm disconnecting the monitors!" Michi announced, as she unplugged the cables that attached to the multitude of medical sensors strategically placed all over the clone's body.

"What do you want me to do?" Jessica asked, as she sloshed through the fluid still in the bottom of the tank.

"Bring that gurney in behind him!" Michi instructed.

"Ninety-four!" Tori reported.

Jessica turned around and grabbed the end of the gurney, lifting it up enough to get the front wheels over the hatch lip. Michi moved around to help her position the gurney in behind the clone body hanging from the top of the tank.

"Ninety-five!"

"I'm disconnecting life support!" Michi announced, moving around to the front of the body.

"Is that safe?"

"His autonomic functions are fully operational by now. He is alive!"

"Oh, my God," Jessica gasped, her eyes wide. She turned to look at Connor, lying motionless on the transfer table in the lab, the transfer apparatus on his head. *Thank you, Connor.*

Michi carefully disconnected the life support tubes

from their fittings on the upper left of Nathan's chest, letting them fall as she did so. Blood and fluids from the tubes spilled out into the cloning liquid that was still ankle deep in the bottom of the tank, turning the viscous fluid a pale red. Alarms began sounding on the control panel outside the tank.

"What is that?" Jessica asked, nervous.

"Disconnect alarms," Michi replied. "Ignore them." Michi looked at Jessica, noticing the distress in her eyes. "It's fine, Jessica. Trust me."

Jessica looked at Michi. The petite doctor was calm and confident, quite unlike she had been during the insertion. She was in her element. This was what she knew. Jessica could see it in both her eyes and her demeanor. Every movement had purpose, and she managed the tasks involved in the successful disconnect of the systems controlling the growth of this clone body for the last eleven months with practiced skill.

Michi disconnected the last tube and checked that all the ports on Nathan's chest were not leaking. Satisfied, she stepped back a moment, examining him. "His color is good, he is breathing normally." She turned toward Tori. "He is alive!"

Tori looked back at Michi, sharing a momentary smile. "Ninety-eight percent!"

"I will raise his legs, while you slide the gurney in under him," Michi instructed as she bent down to pick up Nathan's legs.

Jessica pulled at the gurney, pushed it down to get the back wheels over the hatch lip, then moved it under Nathan's naked backside.

"Ninety-nine!" Tori reported anxiously.

Michi moved around the gurney, making her way back to the hatch and climbing out of the tank. She quickly silenced the blaring disconnect alarms, then activated the harness winch and began lowering Nathan onto the gurney. "Guide him down!" she instructed Jessica. "Watch the transfer cables! Do not let them become tight or they might cause the transfer cap to pull free before the transfer is complete!"

Jessica put her arms around Nathan's slimy, wet torso, guiding him down onto the gurney, keeping an eye on the transfer apparatus cabling. She laid him gently onto the gurney, taking extra care with his head and arms.

"One hundred!" Tori announced. "Transfer complete!" he added, as he began shutting down the transfer process. "I'm copying the transfer logs to a data chip!"

Michi carefully removed the transfer cap apparatus from Nathan's head, letting it dangle to the side. "Let's get him out of this tank so we can clean him up."

Jessica took the foot of the gurney, pushing down on her end to help Michi lift the head up over the hatch lip, her eyes locked on Nathan's bearded face the entire time. Just like his entire body, his head and face were still covered with the slimy, viscous cloning fluid he had been submerged in for the last eleven months. His hair was long and matted by the fluid, as was his beard, but the face...the face was Nathan's, only younger.

They pulled the gurney over to one side, and Michi grabbed a bunch of towels from the counter nearby.

"Start cleaning him up," Michi instructed, tossing several towels at Jessica.

Both of them wiped the fluid off of Nathan's naked body as quickly as they could. Michi carefully patted the area around the fittings on Nathan's chest, taking care not to disturb them.

"What about those?" Jessica asked, nodding toward the fittings in his chest. "Is he going to have them forever?"

"We will remove them later," Michi assured her. "It's a minor procedure."

Tori came running toward them, data chip in hand. "I've got the transfer logs, and all the files from the last seven years," he reported, holding up the chip.

"This place is still wired, right?" Jessica asked.

"Wired?" Tori did not understand her meaning.

"To explode. To detonate. To self-destruct," she explained. "We can't leave any evidence behind. No one can know he's a clone."

"Oh, yes, of course. Since the beginning. You did the work yourself," Tori replied.

"Just checking," Jessica said.

"He's waking up," Michi said as she finished wiping his left arm.

Jessica stopped cleaning him and looked at his face, transfixed.

Nathan began to squint. His mouth twitched, then his throat, as if he were about to gag.

"I'm going to extubate," Michi announced as she disconnected the strap that held his mouthpiece in place. She twisted a small knob on the side of the mouth piece, and then pulled it out of his mouth, sliding the endotracheal tube out of him in one seamless movement.

Nathan gagged and then started coughing. Doctor Sato toweled his face and around his mouth as gently as possible while he continued to cough.

Jessica watched in trepidation as Nathan hacked

and coughed. "Is he all right?" she asked, becoming concerned.

"It was just the tube. It has been in there for months now, ever since he was weaned from the umbilical," Michi explained. "He will have some difficulty speaking, but that will pass."

Jessica watched as the coughing subsided, and Nathan finally opened his eyes. Slowly at first, squinting due to the bright lights. He coughed again, then tried to swallow, nearly choking.

Jessica stroked his wet hair, pushing it back from the sides of his face as Nathan looked at her. "Nathan?" she asked in a whisper. "Is it you?"

Nathan tried to speak, but only coughed again.

"How do we know if it worked?" Jessica asked Michi.

"Captain Scott," Michi said to Nathan.

Nathan turned his head slowly to look at Doctor Sato.

"It's me, Doctor Sato. Don't try to speak yet. Just blink once if you understand me."

Nathan closed his eyes slowly, as if testing them, then opened them again.

Jessica smiled, bursting with joy.

"Blink twice if you understand me," Michi instructed him.

Nathan closed his eyes again, then opened them, repeating the process a bit faster than before.

"Blink three times," Doctor Sato instructed.

"What?" Jessica asked.

"Just making sure."

Nathan blinked three times at a normal rate.

"Excellent," Michi said, smiling at him. "One blink for yes, two blinks for no. Do you understand?"

Nathan blinked once.

"Are you Nathan Scott?"

Nathan blinked once.

"Are you Connor Tuplo?"

Nathan blinked once again.

"What? What does that mean?" Jessica asked, confused.

"No, that's good," Michi assured Jessica, in an excited voice.

Nathan tried to speak, but was barely audible.

Jessica leaned down, putting her ear near his mouth. "What?"

"Cold," he said in a scratchy whisper.

Jessica looked up at Michi, smiling. "He's cold."

"Get a blanket!" Michi instructed Tori.

Nathan reached up with his right hand, pulling on Jessica's body armor to bring her closer.

Jessica leaned back down to listen.

"Miss me?" he asked, in a raspy whisper.

Jessica laughed, stroking his face as tears of joy ran down her cheeks. "A little. I've been kinda busy, though."

Nathan smiled.

Combat One jumped in low between the buildings, then slid forward into the square and set down a few meters from General Telles and his team.

"*Team One has the package!*" Jessica announced over comms. "*I repeat! Team One has the package!*"

General Telles watched as his men climbed aboard the combat jump shuttle. He paused to scan the square. No one was left. Everywhere he looked, all he saw was destruction, and death... But only for the Dusahn.

Four Dusahn fighters jumped in over the justice building and streaked overhead. The general looked up as the flight broke into two, two-ship elements, each element breaking in opposite directions to come around and attack his position.

"*We gotta go!*" Lieutenant Latfee called over the general's helmet comms.

General Telles stepped backward, a satisfied look on his face, then turned and climbed into the combat jump shuttle. A moment later, the jump shuttle began to climb, its side door sliding closed. As the Dusahn fighters began to fire, Combat One disappeared in a flash of blue-white light.

"*Team One has the package!*" Jessica announced over the Seiiki's comms. "*I repeat! Team One has the package!*"

"Hot damn!" Josh declared, a huge grin on his face. He looked at Loki, who had a smile just as wide. "The captain's back!"

"Get ready everyone, we're headed back to pick them up," Loki informed the Seiiki's crew. "Team One, Seiiki. Inbound. ETA three mikes."

"*Copy that!*" Jessica replied. "*Stand off until I call for you!*"

"Understood." Loki looked at Josh. "This is it. Do or die."

"I choose do," Josh declared confidently.

"*Team One has the package!*" Jessica announced over comms. "*I repeat! Team One has the package!*"

"What the hell is 'the package'?" Lieutenant Commander Vidmar wondered.

"I don't know," Cameron replied, "but that's Jessica Nash's voice, and she sounds awfully happy."

"*Team One, Seiiki. Inbound. ETA three mikes.*"

"The Seiiki?" Lieutenant Commander Vidmar wondered.

"Never heard of it," Cameron admitted. "But that sounds like Loki Sheehan."

"Jump flashes!" Lieutenant Commander Kono reported urgently. "Three of them! One hundred kilometers and closing! Dusahn warships! By the size, at least one of them is a battleship! They're firing!"

"Snap jump!" Cameron ordered. "One light minute!"

"Snap jump, one light minute, aye!" Ensign Bickle replied as he activated the jump drive.

The Aurora's bridge momentarily filled with subdued blue-white light.

"Comms! Warn everyone about the new arrivals! Tell flight ops to send all our fighters to recovery point Echo Two! We'll pick them up there!"

"We're not going to attack?" Lieutenant Commander Vidmar asked.

"We're here to support whatever it is Nathan and the Ghatazhak are up to," Cameron replied. "And I have a feeling it has something to do with that 'package'."

"*Team One has the package!*" Jessica announced over Commander Jarso's helmet comms. "*I repeat! Team One has the package!*"

"Alpha Leader to all leaders. Move to cover position one and the Seiiki," the commander instructed.

"*Beta Leader, moving to position one, with three,*" Lieutenant Commander Giortone replied.

"Who?" the commander inquired.

"*Red,*" Lieutenant Commander Giortone replied.

"*Gamma Leader, moving to one,*" Lieutenant

Commander Riordan replied. *"We're down to two. Dumdum is gone, Razz was too damaged to continue, and jumped back to the recovery point."*

"Alpha is three," the commander reported. "We lost Sanko."

"Alpha Leader, Delta Four! Panzrell and Kleri bought it! Sissy took a hit as well! I think he punched out, but I'm not sure!"

"Hux, Rubber," Commander Jarso replied. "Jump back to the recovery point and rendezvous with the Morsiko."

"I can still fight, sir!" Ensign Huxham insisted.

"It's not a debate, Hux," the commander instructed, noticing how shaken the young pilot sounded. "Get your ass to the recovery point."

"Yes, sir," Ensign Huxham replied. *"Good luck, guys."*

Commander Jarso sighed. "Daks joins me. Rio and Ziggy join up with Gio and Hedge. Let's get this done."

———

"Can you walk?" Jessica asked.

His hearing felt odd. It had a tinny quality to it, and everything sounded distant. He looked at Jessica and tried to reply, but it still hurt to talk. He nodded instead.

He was now sitting on a chair. They had pulled on the Ghatazhak assistive undergarment he had worn under his body armor when he came in as Connor.

As Connor. It was still a difficult concept to wrap his head around. It felt more like a dream. In fact, Nathan still wasn't sure that it was *not* a dream. *Do clones dream while they're being grown?*

He felt Jessica and Tori lifting him up. The Ghatazhak body armor he was wearing was lighter than it looked. But his legs were weak, as were his arms, and he felt very uncoordinated. It was his body. It was exactly as he remembered it, only it wasn't. So many contradictions that he could not reconcile. Confusion and comprehension. Confidence and doubt. Courage and fear.

He tried to walk, stumbling at first.

"Let the garment help you," Jessica told him. "Don't fight it."

Nathan's vision kept blurring. One moment, everything would be normal, the next it would be blurry...out of focus.

Everything about his body felt uncomfortable. He took another step, following Jessica's advice. He could feel the assistive undergarment tensing and flexing, helping to strengthen his legs and even out his stride, but it was still a struggle, and every step required concentration, as if it was talking his legs through the process of walking.

"*Seiiki is standing off, ready for pickup,*" Loki announced over comms.

"We're on our way out," Jessica replied. "ETA two!" Jessica looked at Michi, as she came running back over to help them. "Did you arm it?"

"Yes," Michi replied, picking up the helmet and energy rifle Connor had worn on the way in, and that Nathan would now wear on the way out.

"*Alpha Leader, Telles. Ground forces to the west of position one. Two clicks. Fast movers to the south, eighteen clicks. Fast movers to the west, eleven clicks.*"

"Understood," Commander Jarso replied as he prepared to jump back into the atmosphere of Corinair.

"All units, Aurora. New heavies in orbit. We are moving off to maintain safe distance as ops support. Heavies are launching fighters and troop shuttles."

"Alpha Leader, Combat One will take the surface forces approaching from the west," Lieutenant Latfee informed them.

"Copy that," Commander Jarso replied.

"Team One is coming out!" Jessica announced.

"Gio, you guys take the fast movers to the south. We'll take the ones to the east."

"Seiiki is jumping in!" Loki reported, in response to Jessica's call.

"What about the ones coming down from the new heavies in orbit?" Lieutenant Commander Giortone asked.

"We'll deal with them when they get there," the commander replied. "In about thirty seconds," he added to himself as he pressed his jump button.

———

Jessica and Tori helped Nathan to the front door of Ranni Enterprises. The sun had already broken through the horizon, and the landing pad outside was much better lit than when they had jumped in nearly thirty minutes ago.

Jessica paused a moment, letting Tori take most of Nathan's support as she looked out the windows. "Put that helmet on him," she told Michi. "And sling that weapon over his shoulder."

"He's not in any shape to use it," Michi argued, as she placed the helmet onto Nathan's head and secured the chin strap.

"Are you going to carry both?" Jessica asked. Although the doctor was as healthy as the next person, she was diminutive in stature to the point of barely being able to carry her own rifle.

"I'll take it," Tori, said, holding the weapon and slinging it over his free shoulder.

The lobby filled with a blue-white flash of light, followed immediately by the clap of thunder and a blast of displaced air that shattered the massive lobby windows.

"Our ride's here!" Jessica declared as the flying glass settled, taking Nathan's other arm to help Tori guide him out. She swung the door open and headed out, helping Nathan from his right, while Doctor Megel assisted on his left.

Nathan tried to keep his legs moving, but it was difficult, even with the assistive undergarment's help. His vision still slid in and out of focus, as if his brain couldn't quite decide on which objects to focus on, the near or the far.

They cleared the door and headed toward the Seiiki as it settled onto the landing pad fifty meters away, facing away from them. Jessica could see the cargo ramp coming down, and Marcus and Dalen come running out, both carrying energy rifles given to them by the Ghatazhak.

Two flashes of light came from either side of them, revealing the familiar cube-shaped troop landers used by the Dusahn during their attack on Burgess. Four soldiers leapt from each of the two hovering pods, dropping two meters to the ground with ease as the pods rose slightly and then disappeared behind jump flashes.

Marcus dropped to one knee, opening fire at the incoming enemy troops to his right, while Dalen did the same, firing to his left. With her free hand, Jessica grabbed her rifle and swung it around to her right, opening fire as well.

Tori followed suit, raising his rifle and firing to his left, although he didn't hit anything.

Two more landers appeared on the far side of the Seiiki, but a pair of Takaran fighters jumped in from behind and took them out before jumping away again.

Doctor Megel took two hits in his left side. The first one deflected off his torso armor, but the second found the gap between his front and back plates, ten centimeters below his armpit. The energy beam burnt through his ribs, then through his left lung, heart, and then his right lung, killing him instantly. He fell to the ground, pulling Nathan down with him, the grip of his right hand frozen on the back of Nathan's left shoulder armor.

Jessica and Nathan fell to the ground in a heap. Doctor Sato, who was following close behind, nearly tumbled over them.

Marcus and Dalen ran toward them, weapons firing, but the Dusahn soldiers on either side had found good cover, and had Jessica and the others pinned down at the edge of the landing pad, only ten meters from the Seiiki's cargo ramp.

Another flash of blue-white light appeared, followed by a flurry of red-orange weapons fire as a Takaran fighter swept the enemy position to Jessica's right. As the Takaran fighter pitched up to jump away, two more jump flashes appeared to the fighter's right, firing as their jump flashes faded. The Takaran fighter took the hits on its starboard side, at such a close range that its shields failed, and its starboard engine exploded, sending the fighter tumbling out of control, slamming into the elevated transit rails beyond the Seiiki.

More weapons fire poured over them as Jessica,

Nathan, and the others remained pinned to the ground at the edge of the landing pad. Jessica rolled over Nathan, moving into position to use Doctor Megel's body as a shield while she returned fire.

Two more landers appeared on the far side of the building, and soldiers jumped to the ground behind them.

Dalen spun around and opened fire, but was caught in the leg by return fire, toppling him over.

Weapons fire erupted from the top of the Seiiki's cargo ramp. Jessica glanced to her right, spotting Neli firing one of the plasma cannons that had been mounted on either side of the ramp, just inside the hatch collar. She stood out in the open, firing the mighty cannon constantly, sweeping back and forth in an attempt to keep the first group of Dusahn soldiers to the Seiiki's port side down long enough for Jessica and the others to sprint the last ten meters to the cargo ramp and up into the ship.

"GO!" Jessica shouted as she spun to her left and opened fire on the Dusahn soldiers advancing toward them from behind.

Another flash of light appeared, and a combat jump shuttle dropped in low, between Jessica and the enemy soldiers behind them. The combat shuttle opened fire, and Jessica heard the general's voice yelling through her helmet comms. "*Get out of there!*"

Marcus grabbed Nathan, practically carrying him to the ramp. Michi followed, helping Dalen to his feet, together heading for the Seiiki.

Neli stopped firing, reaching out to help Marcus with Nathan. It was a mistake.

The Dusahn soldiers that Neli had been keeping down rose up and opened fire again. Their shots slammed into the sides and back of the Seiiki.

Marcus stumbled as energy shots bounced off the ramp around him and Nathan. As he fell forward, an energy shot ricocheted off the port engine nacelle, and into the left side of Nathan's helmet, snapping his head to the right and taking his body with it.

Marcus struggled to pull Nathan's limp body up the ramp. Michi pushed Dalen past Nathan, sending him tumbling up the ramp and into the Seiiki's cargo bay.

"Lift off!" Jessica ordered, as she ran toward the Seiiki, still firing to her left.

Four more jump flashes appeared nearby as the Seiiki began to rise off the landing pad. Jessica ran the last few steps, jumping into the air and landing on the end of the cargo ramp as the Seiiki continued to climb, and the cargo ramp began to quickly rise.

All four of the jump flashes were Dusahn fighters which immediately opened fire on the Seiiki. Energy blasts slammed into the Seiiki's starboard side, sending sparks and pieces of her hull flying. But a moment later, the Seiiki jumped away.

———

"We're hit!" Loki exclaimed as the Seiiki's cockpit windows cleared, revealing the blackness of space and a myriad of stars. "Jesus! We've lost half our jump emitters on the starboard side! I don't know how the hell we managed to jump this far!"

"*The captain is on board!*" Neli exclaimed over their comm-sets.

"We didn't jump far enough, I'm afraid." Josh stared out the forward windows as their nose pitched down, revealing a large warship about four kilometers away, and headed directly toward them.

Loki looked up, his eyes widening. "Is that..."

"Yeah, I'm afraid so," Josh replied.

"What the hell are you doing?" Loki asked, noticing that their nose was dropping back down toward the planet.

"I've got no thrusters," Josh replied, frantically checking his controls.

"What about the mains?"

"Yeah, but I can't steer, and we're losing altitude fast."

"We need more speed to hold orbit!" Loki insisted.

"I know! I know!" Josh replied. "But if I fire the engines now, we're just going to spin out of control, and that sure as hell isn't going to help!"

"I'll try to reboot the flight computers," Loki decided, quickly shutting down the system. "Mayday! Mayday! Mayday!" Loki called over the comms. "The Seiiki is in orbit over Corinair, dead stick, with a warship bearing down on us. We're trying to restart, but our starboard jump array is fried!"

"Mayday from the Seiiki, Captain!" Ensign deBanco reported. "They're dead stick in orbit over Corinair and going down. They're attempting to restart, but they've got a warship bearing down on them!"

"I've got them, Captain!" Lieutenant Commander Kono reported from the Aurora's sensor station. "They don't have enough speed to hold orbit. Not even half of what they need. They're tumbling toward the planet. The Dusahn battleship is three kilometers and closing on them!"

"I can jump us in between them," Ensign Bickle suggested.

The equation flashed through Cameron's mind. The Aurora was the only warship in the region, and was the Karuzari's only real weapon against the

Dusahn. If she risked the ship to save the Seiiki, and lost, she could be losing the entire war in the first battle.

"The battleship is targeting the Seiiki!" Lieutenant Commander Kono warned.

"Comms!" Cameron called. "Give me the Ghatazhak channel."

"You got it," the comms officer replied.

"Jess! It's Cam! What's the package?"

"Cam! It's Nathan! Nathan is the package!"

"Mister Bickle. Do it!" Cameron ordered.

"Jumping," the navigator replied.

"Helm, keep us between the Seiiki and that battleship," she added as the Aurora's jump flash washed over her bridge.

"Tactical, fire everything you've got!" Cameron continued. "Comms! Tell flight to launch a tug!"

The Aurora shook violently as weapons fire meant for the Seiiki slammed into the forward starboard shields.

"Firing all cannons and rail guns!" Lieutenant Vidmar reported.

"The Seiiki is maneuvering!" Lieutenant Commander Kono reported with excitement.

"Belay that!" Cameron instructed Ensign deBanco.

"Slowly, but they're moving," the lieutenant commander added.

"Comms, get an update on the Seiiki's status. If they can, tell them to land on our port flight deck."

"Jump flash!" Lieutenant Commander Kono reported. "Just behind us! To the Seiiki's starboard side! A combat jumper!"

"Seiiki thinks she can make our deck, Captain!" Ensign deBanco reported.

"Good!" Cameron replied. "Keep firing!"

"Shields down to seventy percent!"

"Jesus, she's got a lot of guns," Lieutenant Commander Kono commented as the Aurora was shaken by another salvo.

"Combat One is requesting to land as well!" Ensign deBanco added.

"Send them to starboard," Cameron replied as incoming energy weapons fire continued to batter the Aurora.

"The battleship is turning, Captain!" Lieutenant Commander Kono reported.

"They're trying to get their tubes on us!" Lieutenant Commander Vidmar warned from the tactical station behind the captain.

"Shields down to fifty percent!"

"Tell both those ships to hurry the hell up," Cameron instructed her comms officer. "Dinev! Keep as much ship between the Dusahn and those two ships as you can, but keep a clear jump line at all times! Bickle, the moment both those ships are across our jump field boundaries, you jump us out of here, understood?"

"Shields down to forty percent!"

———————

"*Seiiki! Seiiki! You're cleared to land, port flight deck! Be aware, we may have to maneuver!*" the Aurora's comms officer called.

"Please don't," Josh mumbled. He glanced at Loki, a puzzled look on his face as he struggled to maintain control of his damaged ship. "Did he say *port* flight deck?"

"I think so."

"When did the Aurora get a port flight deck?" Josh wondered aloud.

"Combat One! Aurora! Cleared to land! Starboard flight deck!"

"Well, all right then," Josh said.

"Combat One copies!"

Josh glanced out the window as the Aurora loomed in front of them. The Seiiki continued to tumble as Josh twisted and turned his flight control stick, using the Seiiki's weak docking thrusters to try to get them into a stable flight attitude. "You couldn't get anything other than docking thrusters?" Josh grumbled as he continued to struggle.

"It's a miracle I got *those* working," Loki replied. He glanced out the window, as well. "Oh, God." He caught sight of the back side of the Aurora's forward section, just as they cleared the top of her main drive section. "There! Same level as the old flight deck! They've got two openings! One on either side! Steer to port!"

"Ya think?" Josh continued to manipulate his flight control stick, struggling to get the Seiiki's yawing roll to slow down.

"You're too high, Josh," Loki warned.

"I know."

"Josh."

"I know."

The Seiiki rolled back over, her nose coming down to point in the general direction of the port flight deck, but they were still yawing slowly to the left.

Loki stared out the front windows as the hull directly above the opening to the Aurora's port flight deck came rushing toward them. "Josh! We're going to hit!" Loki exclaimed.

Josh fired the downward translation thrusters at full power, and closed his eyes.

———

"Combat One is on the deck!" Ensign deBanco reported.

"Shields are down to twenty percent!" Lieutenant Commander Vidmar warned.

"I don't think they're going to make it," Lieutenant Commander Kono warned. "They're too high!"

The Aurora shook as more energy weapons fire slammed into their shields.

"Fifteen percent!"

"Roll us ten to starboard," Cameron instructed calmly.

"Ten to starboard, aye," Lieutenant Dinev replied as she applied a touch of roll thrust.

"Five percent!" the lieutenant commander warned, as another salvo slammed into them. "One more hit..."

"Seiiki is across the threshold..."

"Jump!" Cameron ordered as the jump flash was already lighting up the bridge.

"Jump complete!"

"Seiiki is on deck!"

Cameron jumped from her command chair, heading toward the exit. "Jump us to the recovery point! Have the XO come to the bridge and take the conn!" she ordered as she moved quickly toward the exit. "I'll be at the main hangar bay!"

The Seiiki pulled into the transfer airlock and stopped. Josh let out a big sigh of relief. "Not my best landing, that's for sure."

"I was positive we were going to slam into the side of the ship," Loki admitted.

"Remind me to kiss the Aurora's helmsman," Josh said.

"*Airlock secure,*" the deck controller called over comms. "*Pressurizing airlock. Stand by.*"

"You know, I'd never admit it to Lael," Loki began, "but I miss this. I really do."

"Even my crazy flying?" Josh wondered.

"Especially your crazy flying, my friend."

Cameron ran down the ramp from the command deck, then bolted down the corridor toward the main hangar bay. "Make way! Make way!" she shouted. She ran into the bay, slowing down as she ran across the deck toward the aft port transfer airlock, which was just starting to open. She continued to walk forward as the door slid open, and the battered Seiiki, or what she knew as the Mirai, rolled into the Aurora's main hangar bay.

Cameron heard someone yelling, and Vladimir ran into the bay from the starboard side, headed straight for her. He too slowed down as he saw the Seiiki roll in and come to a stop. Safety teams rushed toward the ship, as did rescue workers.

Vladimir came up to Cameron, standing beside her. "Is he..."

"I don't know," Cameron said softly, still staring at the back of the Seiiki.

"He's waking up," Michi said as she knelt over Nathan in the Seiiki's cargo bay, tending to his head wound.

"How is he?" Jessica asked. "I can give him a nanite boost."

"We need to examine him thoroughly first, all things considered," Doctor Sato explained. "But it's not bad. The helmet absorbed most of the heat. He may have a concussion, though. At the very least, he's going to be groggy for quite some time."

"If anyone has a right to be groggy, it's that man," Marcus declared.

"*We're shut down,*" Loki announced over the Seiiki's loudspeakers.

"Nathan?" Doctor Sato said, trying to get his attention.

Nathan opened his eyes slowly.

Jessica smiled. "We made it, Nathan. We're home."

"Home?" Nathan said, his voice still weak and scratchy.

"Help me get him up," Jessica said.

Marcus knelt down beside the man whom he had stuck to like glue for the last five years, while his true self had been locked up inside the head of Connor Tuplo, and helped him to his feet.

Josh and Loki came through the forward hatch, sliding down the ladder one by one, coming up to the captain.

"How is he?" Josh asked.

"He's going to be fine," Doctor Sato assured them.

"Is he?" Josh started.

"They're both in there," Michi replied.

Josh breathed a sigh of relief. By some miracle, he had his old captain back, without having to lose his new one.

"He looks younger," Loki realized.

Jessica laughed. "He is." She looked at Josh. "Open it."

Josh smiled and went to the cargo ramp controls at the back of the Seiiki's cargo bay.

The ramp began to lower slowly, revealing the interior of the Aurora's main hangar deck outside.

Gathered around the back of the Seiiki were at least twenty members of the Aurora's crew...

...And two familiar faces.

Jessica and Marcus flanked Nathan on either side, helping him keep his balance as he walked down the ramp, seemingly under his own power.

Cameron felt as if her heart would stop as she spotted Nathan coming down the ramp, flanked by her old friend Jessica, and that crusty old chief of the boat, Marcus Taggart. Her heart swelled as she watched her friends descend the ramp, with Josh and Loki behind them. She tapped her comm-set and spoke softly. "Now, Mister deBanco." Then she took a deep breath and barked. "Attention on deck!"

Ensign deBanco's voice echoed throughout the hangar bay, as well as the rest of the Aurora, as he made the announcement.

"Aurora... Arriving."

Thank you for reading this story.
(*A review would be greatly appreciated!*)

COMING SOON

"REBELLION"
Episode 4
of
The Frontiers Saga:
Rogue Castes

Visit us online at
frontierssaga.com
or on Facebook

Want to be notified when
new episodes are published?
Join our mailing list!
frontierssaga.com/mailinglist